DEGREES OF FEAR

C.J. HENDERSON

Introduction and Story Introductions by William Jones
With an Afterword by Joe Mauceri

Dark Regions Press, 2008

FIRST EDITION
Text © 2008 by C.J. Henderson
Cover Art and Interior Illustrations © 2008 by Ben Fogletto
Introduction and Story Introductions © 2008 by William Jones
Afterword © 2008 by Joe Mauceri

Desktop composition by Vincent Sneed/Die Monster Die! Books

"The Gardener," *Highway 19 & Others*, 2003; "Admission of Weakness," *New Mythos Legends*, 1999; "Hope," *Imeold*, 2002; "Misery and Pity," *Grimoire*, 1997; "Incident on Highway 19," *Highway 19 & Others*, 2003; "That's The One," *Questar*, 1980; "A Happy Mother Takes Away Pain," *Tales Of The Dreamwalker*, 2006; "Body and Soul," published in this volume for the first time, 2008; "The Horror," *Edge Of Evil*, 1998; "A Forty Share In Innsmouth," *Singer Of Strange Songs*, 1997; "Sacrifice," *100 Crooked Little Crime Stories*, 1994; "Pop Goes The Weasel," *Violent Tales*, 1997; "The Questioning of the Azathothian Priest," *Lost Worlds Of Time & Space*, 2006; "Pragmatic," published in this volume for the first time, 2008; "The Laughing Man," *War Fear*, 2002; "The Soul's Right Hand," *Cemetery Dance*, 1998; "So Free We Seem," *The Tales Of Inspector Legrasse*, 1996; "The Longest Pleasure," *100 Menacing Little Murder Stories*, 2003; "Juggernaut," *The Occult Detectives of C.J. Henderson*, 2002; "Degrees of Fear," *CthulhuSex*, 2004.

Trade Paperback
ISBN: 1-888993-57-X

Dark Regions Press
P.O. Box 1264
Colusa, CA 95932

CONTENTS

Author's Acknowledgement	7
Introduction by William Jones	9
The Gardener	13
Admission of Weakness	27
Hope	49
Misery and Pity	53
Incident on Highway 19	62
That's The One!	80
A Happy Mother Takes Away Pain	82
Body and Soul	101
The Horror	112
A Forty Share in Innsmouth	115
Sacrifice	126
Pop Goes The Weasel	130
The Questioning of the Azathothian Priest	145
Pragmatic	160
The Laughing Man	176
The Soul's Right Hand	186
So Free We Seem	206
The Longest Pleasure	217
Juggernaut	221
Degrees of Fear	247
Afterword by Joe Mauceri	264

LIST OF ILLUSTRATIONS

The Gardener	12
Misery and Pity	55
A Happy Mother Takes Away The Pain	83
Pop Goes The Weasel	131
The Laughing Man	177
The Soul's Right Hand	187
Juggernaut	223
Degrees of Fear	249

AUTHOR'S ACKNOWLEDGEMENT

It's always a pleasure to give thanks to those who have helped one create a work, giving credit where it's due, dedicating a work in their honor, thanking God for putting them here on this planet to help us along our way.

Caterers, police officers, tennis instructors, keyboard operators, *et cetera*, most occupations do not offer any such outlet to those who populate their ranks. Actors can make speeches when they are given awards. Writers get to do this.

Myself, there are plenty of people I've thanked on pages like this over the decades, and hopefully I'll get the chance to thank plenty more. Often times, when a book is just another book in a series, or just another collection, it's not all that hard to pick the person or persons to be praised. But *this*...

This is not that kind of book.

This is a big fancy production, one that covers my entire career. It's a showcase of stories from every period through which I've struggled. Who can I thank for that?

I have hundreds of fans I know by name, whom I communicate with regularly, whom I would love to honor in this fashion. There are publishers and editors that have been amazingly generous and trusting toward me, that have rolled the dice betting on my talent. I would not be where I am today without any of these loyal folks.

But... there is only one person who has been by my side for all of it. Who has supported and pushed and trusted and worked for me as long as I have myself. Indeed, there is no doubt in my mind that this book would not be in your hands, could not exist without her selfless loyalty and support.

Thus, it is with the greatest of joy that I dedicate this book to:

GRACE TIN LO

My wife, best friend, and the person who keeps me going each and every time I'm ready to call it quits.

INTRODUCTION
by William Jones

It needs to be said that the writings of C.J. Henderson are imaginative and are filled with pathos and with hope. His stories are both comforting and startling. And for these reasons, *Degrees of Fear & Other* is a wonderful collection. There are other reasons as well, but are to be found within the stories themselves—and they are legion.

Like many authors, C.J. Henderson writes in numerous genres. With each work he creates a world of beauty and horror—a place, sometimes, all too familiar. Yet, there is something uncanny about this familiarity. It can be unsettling, while also inspiring. This is motive enough to venture into the following pages of this book. But this collection is larger than that.

It is said that writers select a theme that they follow throughout their careers—an element that repeats and reappears in their works regardless of the characters and settings. I cannot say that C.J. Henderson is an exception to this specious rule, and for that I am thankful. What C.J. Henderson does is tell stories in the oldest of traditions. And from the first storyteller, there has existed a debate. What is the purpose of stories? Many have argued that it is to educate and illuminate. Others propose it is to entertain and feed the imagination. In fact, the variations are as numerous as the years of the craft of storytelling itself. But what is remarkable about C.J.

Henderson's writings is that somehow he manages to encompass nearly every one of these variations in his work. He defines that which refuses to be defined. This makes pinning him down to a solitary theme, or even a handful of them, very difficult. However, if I were to choose for this collection, I would have to say "Humanity" is the driving force—but not the solitary theme. This doesn't mean that a gathering of morality tales or didactic lessons are to follow. No, C.J. Henderson is too savvy a writer to fall into such a trap. "Humanity" in this book is good and kind and cruel and dark and yet hopeful. In short, it is all of a part of the human condition—and we as humans are such varied creatures.

It is this difference that C.J. Henderson seizes and grapples, and then transforms into a host of clever stories. Be forewarned, all is not pleasant within these pages because all is not pleasant in the world. There are all manner of monsters and heroes living in these pages. Sadness and happiness dwell here as do terror and hope. And it is this last thing, hope, in its many varied shades that is the most persistent. So while these tales might not capture the full magnitude of C.J. Henderson's ongoing theme, they most definitely refuse to let go of hope for humanity. If anything, it is that refusal to give up that best describes my dear friend C.J. Henderson. He is a man of talent, imagination, and most importantly, even when things are dark, he holds to hope with an unrelenting grip. Nothing more could be asked for from a collection of stories, written by an original, modern storyteller.

–William Jones
Metamora, MI 2008

DEGREES OF FEAR

There are many facets to "The Gardener." For all of its connection to H.P. Lovecraft's mythos, it is a very modern, or rather, postmodern tale. C.J. reveals a world bereft of a past—one were facsimiles replace what was once real. A city where history is the price of progress, and that progress is nothing but a mere façade devoid of true humanity.

THE GARDENER

THE RAKE'S WEATHERED BAMBOO tines scratched at the ground, assembling the brown and graying leaves scattered over the lawn into pile after pile. Ben Goodell pulled the ancient tool across the width of his parents' grounds, hour after hour, ignoring the increasing chill of the salty breeze twisting its way along Water Street.

There had been no wind earlier in the day when he had begun his yearly care-taking efforts. But, as the afternoon had waned, the dark zephyrs usually contained beyond the ragged ocean front cliffs of Kingsport had begun to billow, rattling the small, diamond panes in windows all across the town.

At first, Ben had cursed the growing inclemency, but he had quickly forsaken such futile pursuits for action instead. As the breeze began to threaten his colorless mounds he broke off raking, heading for the stack of regulation, city council-approved garbage bags he had picked up at the local hardware store before beginning his endeavor.

Unfolding one of the black, thick-plastic shrouds, he maneuvered it in front of the largest pile and began to sweep his gathered detritus inside, using his parents' rake with one hand. It was slow, sloppy, tedious work, but Ben did not mind. It gave him a chance to think.

Ben Goodell did not live with his parents, had not done so for ages. But, every fall the dutiful pilgrimage was made, from the luxury of his Manhattan penthouse to the steep, narrow crooked streets of his home town. Back to the tiny room of his childhood to tidy and clean and secure his meager birthright against the fierce New English ravishes to come.

Of course, his annual sojourn did not inconvenience anyone. Ben Goodell had no wife to desert, no children to abandon. Oh, there had been a girl, long ago, an engagement that had meant the world to him. But the girl had left one day without a word. It had been a heartbreak beyond reason and that had been the end of such things for Ben.

He had left Kingsport after that, turning his back on the ceaseless maze of colonial houses with their ancient vanes and antediluvian gables, setting his sights on an adventure that would relieve the sting of his Gloria's desertion. Ben Goodell had travelled then to New York City, turning his back on love for the more reliable venture of commerce. He conquered a dozen kingdoms over the decades, heaping up treasure that would have staggered Midas. Never resting, he threw his nets ever further, reaping airlines and banks and computer firms, restaurants, film studios, automobile manufacturers and all manner of properties until he became known as the man who could not fail.

Oddly, Ben drew little satisfaction from his prizes. At first there had been a tremendous thrill to it all—the power, the women, the heaps of gold and the army of desperate sycophants cringing in his shadow. Eventually, however, he realized that it was all too easy. And thus, pleased with his creations, but bored with them as well, every November he would take his Seventh Day to rest, heading back home to where he was once more beholden to a greater power.

Over the years, the chores had grown more numerous as his father fell further into disrepair. They changed as well, as even ancient Kingsport became enmeshed in the vulgar regulations of the modern era assaulting it on all sides. Ben struggled with his bag, grunting over the extra effort required, remembering how few years earlier it had been when all that would have been needed was a match and a watchful eye to eliminate his moldering burden.

But that was another time, he thought ruefully. Long, long ago.

Ben dragged his first bag across the lawn, dumping it at the designated spot on the curb for biodegradable trash. Not to be confused with the spot for plastics and glass, not to be bagged in their properly specified colors, not to be left at the spot assigned paper products and magazines, nor that where metals were to be deposited, nor household trash, nor...

God, Ben frowned at the notion of such regulations invading his sanctuary, you'd think with the checks I send Mayor Cooper every year they could preserve a little more of the charm around here.

Ben stared up and then down Water Street in bemused amazement. New York City with its lawyers and socialist politicians and its uncaring, mongrel teaming millions he could understand. But for Kingsport to be caught up in the same suburban progressivism, it made his head shake with sadly bitter frustration.

His hometown was a place that, for the most part, history had passed by—a forgotten pocket of musty, moss and ivy-covered houses where one structure in five still stood with one foot as firmly in the sixteenth century as in the twenty-first. Of course, if you included the seventeenth century, then half the town still belonged to the past, including every public building save for the concrete bunker of a post office the WPA had erected—the last time an outside influence had been permitted to scar the town's eternally somber beauty.

When had so much changed, he wondered. When had the outside world found its way into Kingsport?

"You look particular burdened, son." Ben turned to see his father approaching, a steaming mug in his outstretched hand. "Think it's time for a break?"

He answered the old man in the affirmative, gratefully reaching out for what he knew would be a stiff brace of bitter black coffee sweetened with a generous stirring of his father's homemade blackberry brandy. Ben downed a long pull of the steaming brew, smiling as much at its heady taste as at his ability to anticipate his father's actions.

Of course, he thought smugly, I ought to know the old man by now. He and Mother didn't have me until they were almost fifty—and since I'm almost there myself now...

Ben let the notion trail off within his brain. Yes, his parents were in their upper nineties. Yes, they would be dead soon. Yes, in many ways it really didn't make sense that they were still alive.

What did keep his parents going, he wondered sometimes. How did they survive, year after year, unaided, what was essentially an extremely hard life. He offered so much, so often, but it was always politely refused. His parents were so proud of him, but so unwilling to share in his success.

Staring at his father, he looked the elder Goodell up and down, trying to work the puzzle out in his mind. His musings in no way indicated a lusting after their fortune. They had none while his was massive. Nor did he resent their longevity, like so many of his contemporaries did that of their own parents. He saw them only the one time every year, and found himself missing them the rest of the time.

"So," said the elder Goodell. "What's new in that corporate kingdom of yours?"

Ben smiled. He had been waiting for this moment. Every year, sooner or later, his father quizzed his son on what he was doing, where his empire was going, what strategies he was unfolding. After more than twenty-five years, Ben never ceased to be amazed at the elder Goodell's knowledge of the financial world. For a man whose entire world was held within a three and a half mile circumference surrounding an antiquity of wharves and churches and overgrown graveyards, he always seemed to know so much.

Ben loved his father—both his parents. He tried often to get them to come to the city—to live, or even just to visit—but they would have none of it. They would not let him support them and they would not step a foot outside of Kingsport. And, although he loved them, he had not given their reluctance any real consideration over the years.

Benjamin Goodell was an important man outside his home town, one with numerous responsibilities and duties. Even one extra visit made over a long weekend would have been extremely taxing on his hectic schedule. So, every year he simply made his dutiful journey, travelling to New England in one of his expensive cars, leaving behind his corporate importance to clean gutters and scrape shingles, to rake and trim and mow and to perfunctorily ask his parents to come to see him, quietly awaiting their polite refusal in between bites of dinner.

Ben finished rattling off his list of upcoming battles—the Thornton merger, the Ridalex take-over, his desire to open casinos in both Nevada and New Jersey, the scheme to buy up formerly nationalized properties in former communist strongholds—all the rest. His father nodded after each description, staring out over the ocean down at the far end of Water Street as he listened to his son.

When Ben went silent, he continued to drink in the wizened, fragile form of his father when suddenly the enormity of his callousness swamped him. The sharpness of his father's mind could not belie the weakness of his frame. His parents were nearly a hundred years old. No matter what it was kept them going decade upon decade, they were not immortal. They were aged and frail and withered.

A strangled cry shattered within Ben's throat, threatening him with tears and worse. He washed it away with more coffee, struggling to hold onto his composure. He was a leader of men, in command of thousands of lives. He knew how to control his emotions. He did. Then, his father stretched out his back, his movements slow and methodical.

"Heh," he snorted with a dreamy pleasantness, "Guess I'm not as young as I used to be."

And Ben's eyes filled with tears as he watched the tiny shell of the only giant he had ever known amble back to their shrunken home in gently measured steps.

"WHAT DO YOU MEAN, you're going to spend another week there?" The voice in Ben's cellphone was more surprised than angry. Not surprised as in shocked, but as in flabbergasted. "They've got that many chores for you this year?"

The voice belonged to Brenda MacLoren, Ben's executive assistant. Calmly, he told her, "It's nothing like that. It's just…I don't know how to explain it except to say they're old. Old and alone."

"Alone…?"

"I mean that everyone they ever knew, everyone I grew up with, they're all gone. I don't know what keeps them from going crazy."

"They probably are," answered the woman. "You're just too soft when it comes to them to notice."

"I'll let that slide," responded Ben without amusement. "They're my parents, Bren. And they're old. Old enough that I don't think I'm ever going to see them again once I leave town this year."

"And that's so terrible?" snapped his assistant. "Maybe it's not my place but those two have you twisted around their little finger. We've got the Harper Conglomerate leverage in two—"

Ben cut the woman off with several coldly harsh words, reminding her of who actually worked for whom. Then, with instructions on what she was to do to ensure the continuing success of his empire, Ben told her in no uncertain terms of where he was going to be, for how long, and that the subject was closed to discussion. Snapping his phone shut, he turned to find the hard, frightened eyes of his mother locked upon him. Instantly he understood that the discussion was about to be reopened.

"What do you mean, you're staying on?"

"Mother—I just want to see you two a while longer."

"We're not spring chickens, Benny," she snapped at him. "And we're not made of money. We don't have the energy or the wherewithal to entertain you until you decide you've wasted enough of your precious time on us."

"Mother!"

"We welcome your help at this time of year, son—I wouldn't insult you with a lie to the otherwise. We're old and can't do like we used to. But that's no means for you to take advantage—"

"What are you talking about?" Without realizing it, Ben had slipped into his CEO voice. Defiant and somewhat threatening, he barked back at the old woman before him. "Take advantage, waste my time—where is this coming from?!"

The elder Mrs. Goodell pulled herself to her full height. With a dark sneer spread across her tight, dry face, she told her son, "You're done here. It's time you go home."

"But, Mother..."

"What?" the old woman snapped. "You've got nothing better to do? Lazy? Is that what ye've become? An idler? Ready to just move in and eat us out of house and home?"

"My God," thundered Ben. "What are you talking about?"

Mrs. Goodell staggered from her son's bark as if from a blow. Ben stared, not understanding anything that had happened. Why had his mother said what she had? Surely she could not have meant her words. But if she had not, then why say the things she had? And, he wondered, what was really wrong?

Ben reached out toward his mother, but she stepped away, gasping for air while swinging her aged hand at his. She struck his open palm a blow with her bony knuckles, her rough skin scraping at his soft flesh.

"Maybe the boy should stay, Elizabeth."

Mother and son both turned at the voice behind them. Ben looked on in surprise, hard pressed to believe his father could move so quietly. Mrs. Goodell stared in shock, wide-eyed and silent in her disbelief at her husband's words. It was, however, a short-lived silence.

"What did you say?"

The old woman's voice was a thing of angered pain, a viper blinded by disbelief, hissing for a moment to hold its tormentors at bay until it could clear its field of vision. Braving a storm his son could scarcely comprehend, the father dared the fates once more.

"I said maybe it's time the boy stayed. After all, the ship is coming in tomorrow night. Maybe it's time he saw it."

No words emitted from Mrs. Goodell. Instead, a scream erupted from the thin, old woman, a growling panic of hate and denial that tore through the two men, shaking the windows and scattering the cowering, witless starlings gathered in the barren, thorny bushes beyond.

BEN HAD NOT ARGUED further. His mother had left the room after her outburst. She had not cried, restated her case or said another word. She had simply headed up the narrow oak stairs for her room, the dry wood barely creaking beneath her withered feet. His father had given him the shrug known to all sons desperate to understand how a woman could hold so much power over a man.

"Well, perhaps ye'd better pack up, after all, Bennie," was all he said, however, leaving the younger Goodell lost in a painful confusion from which he could not disentangle himself no matter how hard he tried. And try he did mightily.

Through his packing and then all through the night, during his terse leave-taking, while getting into his car and pulling away from the house, he considered what happened. So lost in thought was he as he piloted his car up the slick cobblestones of Water Street that he drifted by the neglected house with the strange gathering of oddly grouped and painted stones in its front yard without even noticing it.

The place had been there since before Ben had been born and numerous stories were told of the old man who dwelled within it, spending his days speaking to his collection of peculiar bottles. The gnarled and dying trees of the musty, moldering abode had always bothered Ben as a boy, a nagging respectful fear that had never left him as a man. But, so agitated and confused was the younger Goodell with the actions of his parents that he sailed past it without a notice, his mind locked in swirling wonder at his mother's words.

He drove the serpentine alleys of Kingsport, connecting to Ship Street, passing the Congregational Hospital where he had been born without seeing it. Swinging off Green Lane past the Market House, he made the left onto Back Street with robotic precision, motoring its length until he reached the connection to State Route 1A that snapped him back to the modern world of asphalt and concrete roads. 1A lead to Interstate 95. That took him to 90, which took him to 395, which in the curious way of New English travel took him back to the Interstate, propelling him on through Rhode Island and onto Connecticut. He did not reach it, however.

Only miles from the border, he saw a sign for Mystic Seaport, a place of brightly painted wooden houses and wooden ships. It was home to a sterilely recreated past, erected as a haven for tourists desperate to believe they had touched what had gone before simply because they had snapshots of themselves standing in front of butter churns and spinning wheels all discreetly stamped PROPERTY OF MYSTIC CHAMBER OF COMMERCE. It was the idealized representation of a clipper ship on the sign that caught Ben's attention.

Again he heard his father's words within his head… "Maybe it's time the boy stayed. After all, the ship is coming in tomorrow night. Maybe it's time he saw it."

The ship? Ben wondered at the words. What ship? What ship could he be talking about? And why would it matter if he saw it or not?

Ben pulled off the road. He sat lost in thought, his engine running, his foot on the brake. What kind of ship came in at night? To Kingsport? And what made it so important?

Without hesitation, without thinking, Ben gunned his motor and shot back onto the Interstate. He toyed with the idea of simply cutting across the median strip but he could not take the chance of being stopped. He had to get back to Kingsport as quickly as he could.

Damn, he thought as he slid into the exit lane, this late in the year it'll be dark by five. Dad could have meant anytime after that.

Roaring up the small leg of road taking him back to the Interstate, he joined the traffic headed in the direction from which he had just come. Without further thought, Ben stared out through his windshield, watching the miles disappear between himself and the answer he found himself desiring desperately. He had realized even before he had left why the confrontation with his mother had become so important to him. For years he had never had to listen to another person. There simply was no one powerful enough in the world outside of Kingsport to command Benjamin Goodell to do anything.

He was in charge of his life. He had the money and power to make anything happen—easily. Take-overs and mergers impossible for anyone else were nothing to him. The resolve of corporate tigers evaporated into cold steam when they faced Benjamin Goodell. He was not a man used to being denied. He barely even understood the concept any more.

His mouth a grim line, hands locked on his steering wheel, Ben sped along the darkening fall roads back to Kingsport. Hour after hour he traveled, stopping only for the fuel necessary to take him home. Darkness came and still he drove, his car slicing through the crisp, leaf-dotted air. The miles disappeared, town after town falling behind him as the hours dwindled and his speed increased.

At slightly past eleven-thirty Ben left the asphalt highway, crossing that dividing marker between Kingsport and the outside world. His rear wheels slid dangerously as they connected with the slick cobblestones of Water Street. Ben shifted down through the gears at reckless speed, wrenching his steering wheel to the left, then the right. Without a thought he rushed along the quiet, darkened lanes of the somber town, determined to discover the answers to the questions he could not actually form within his brain.

He stopped his car in front of his parents' home with a horrible screaming of brakes. The shrunken house was still, all its lights extinguished. His engine still running, Ben left his car and ran across the lawn. Reaching the front door, he banged on it with fierce power, shouting powerfully for his parents. No matter how he raged, however, there was no answer.

And then, after another mighty slam, the door swung open. Ironically, Ben discovered that it had not been locked. A moment's thought reminded the CEO that his parents never locked the entrance to their home. Standing in the open front doorway, Ben threw his senses outward into the darkened home. No scent or feel of life returned to him, no sounds of movement, no hints of breathing, not the slightest stirring of life. Stepping backwards, down the slab granite front steps to the chipped slate walkway beyond, Ben studied the familiar yet somehow alien structure, trying to discern where his parents could be.

A ship coming in, the back of his brain reminded him. Where do you think they are?

Ben rushed back to his car. Throwing himself inside, he stepped clumsily back and forth from the brake to the gas, eliciting growls of protest from the powerful engine until he finally got control of himself and was able to pull away from the curb.

Get a grip, moron, he chastised himself. The docks are less than a mile from here. Let's try to get there in one piece.

As Ben cruised slowly through the streets leading to the ocean, he began to notice that all the homes in town seemed as empty as his parents'. A terrible notion came over him, an unsettling feeling that bore outward from his soul to tighten his skin, chilling the sweat leaking from his brow.

What if, he wondered. I mean...could...

The opening crumbs of the answers Ben wanted had finally begun to form within his brain, but he could not extend them, could not look at them long enough to see more than a few words before his attention would be wrenched off in some other direction. A horrible truth was growing in the back of his mind, a realization he had hidden from for longer than he could imagine.

As he slowed his car further, rolling quietly toward the centuries old dock area of town, bursts of memory began flashing through his head. Something about a ship—something he had refused to know—was stirring in his mind, bubbling past the locks he had strapped upon it decades earlier. Before he could gather all the myriad pieces, however, reality grabbed at him, forcing him to slam on his brakes.

The dock area was ablaze with spectral light. All the men and women of Kingsport were assembled on the wharves. In their hands they held candles and torches, gas lanterns and hurricane lamps. More than one gripped poles with buckets of flame hung from them. Ben noted that every person held their own light, and that all the illumination seemed to be coming from natural sources.

No flashlights, no battery lanterns, he mused as he automatically snapped off his headlights and silenced his engine. Why? Hell, why not just turn on the damn street lamps?

Ben exited his vehicle silently, moving down the short incline of Water Street toward the rest of the crowd. He did not fear anyone noticing him. Why would they care? They were the people of his parents' village—he knew most of them by name.

And, he noted, their attention did seem elsewhere.

Ben moved slowly, in some ways frightened, but still curious as to why everyone was so intently staring, not out to sea, but upward along the cliffs to the north of town. He knew where they were looking. The crags extending out of Kingsport at that point climbed steeply, terrace on terrace, until the northernmost of them hung in the sky like a grey, frozen wind cloud. It was not that far bluff that held their attention, however, but the solitary, ancient house which stood upon it.

It was a place of many rumors and wild stories, a thing the town whispered about—as it whispered about so much—but which it had always basically ignored. Ominous No Trespassing signs surrounded the property over which it towered, signs curiously erected not by the owner—whomever that might have been—but instead by the Kingsport town elders.

Of course, Ben should not have been able to see the unhallowed cottage, should not have been able at that time on such a starless night to see even the cliffs themselves. But somehow he could see it all. And, like the rest of the crowd, he saw the unintelligible door on the cliffward side of the house open. The crowd gasped, but the sound of them was overrun by the noise of a rushing billow that seemed to scream outward from the northern heights, a great shrieking hiss of approval that unfolded like a spray of clouds one could only hear.

The much ignored house faded from view then, the cliffs and trees and all fading from view even as the town's attention turned eastward out over the dark ink of the midnight waters.

Ben turned his head from person to person, looking for something in the eyes of anyone in the crowd that would give him the answers he sought. Where were his parents? What was everyone doing on the docks? With fire, no less? Why fire instead of sensible, modern electric power? And, for God's sake, where was this damnable ship?

Dread filled Ben's throat as the clouds suddenly parted and a laser-like stream of moonlight slammed downward to crash against the motionless water below. Fear sweat broke out across his brow. He smelled his body moistening as he realized there were no waves lapping against any of the pier's great wooden pillars. And then, as he felt the tension of the crowd all around him slip away, he saw it.

Out of the icy blackness slid a pale, translucent ship, a massive thing of fluttering sails and long decks that should not have been seen along that stretch of coast in over ten score years. Cold and forbiddening it was, a silent runner that cut the still frozen ocean with a bow that barely seemed to touch the water.

Ben noted creatures stuck to its hull, strange, tentacled barnacles with horrible staring eyes. How he could make them out at such a distance he could not comprehend, no moreso than he could explain a ship that could stay afloat with massive, pulsating worms eating their way through the planks and beams of its shining hull.

Its white sails fluttered with a noise that rippled time, shimmering—not with light reflecting from any source as mundane as the blazes surrounding Ben on all sides, but from cutting through the currents of space itself, from filtering the sounds of other dimensions into a fuel that gave it its own horrible life.

Ben shuddered, unable to look away, unable to comprehend how he could know the things he was realizing. He watched the undulating decks rise and fall to the beat of some terrible pulse. His eyes stared unblinking at the helm, his heart stopping as he realized the waxen vessel's wheel seemed to be steered by different hands every time he took note of it. The pilot always appeared roughly human, but there would be differences caught only by the corner of his eye—legs that would turn into the clawed lengths of a bird's underside, arms that would seem to be wrongly jointed, or suddenly serpentine.

But that was not the worst of it. The vague ashen vessel's captain could not hold the CEO's attention as he began to make out its passengers. One by one, the visages of those screaming, gibbering souls roped and spiked and sewn to the very fabric of the ship became clear to him.

"Mother," he screamed. "Father! Where are you?"

He recognized William Grangier, the head of Brendalno's Manufacturing, who had perished in that fire. Alice Harris, consumed by cancer. Murshlin and Tuttle, taken in the car wreck.

"What's going on? What is this?!"

People began to turn and stare. Neighbors of nearly half a century saw not the boy they watched grow, but an outsider as he stared at the sea and screamed.

More and more faces he saw, more and more men and women who had stood in the way of his success over the decades—MaCallan from Broklin Airways, Stevenson of the Linhurst Proxy, Sheldon Meyer...

"Father! Help me! What is all this? Why is this happening?!"

The crowd around Ben began to part, the hand-held flames lashing him with wicked shadows as his parents struggled to make their way to his side.

"Don't look at it, Bennie," his father's ancient voice begged. "Turn aside, boy—turn away!"

And then he saw the figure he had avoided for so long. Hands once beautiful were nailed to the phantom clipper's hull, the weight of a long suffering body dragging at them, creating a torturous agony that had spasmed the first of the sacrifices for decades. Golden hair hung ragged and clustered with burrowing sea life, obscuring the hollow, slime encrusted pits which once had contained blue eyes capable of possessing a young man's heart. One heart in particular.

"*Gloria!*"

The tattered, raggedly chewed head turned toward the sound of the familiar label. Its mouth opened, and laughing, screams burst forth from it condemningly.

"We did it for you, son," came the frightened sounds of an old woman. "We just wanted what was best for you."

Ben stared in reeling horror as the silent ship neared the dock. His brain spun madly, laying all the discordant facts of his life out plainly for him to see. His ritualistic visits, his father's curiosity into his affairs, looking for details, asking for names, needing to know—

"We never took anything for ourselves," a mother's desperate truth plead pitifully. "It was always for you."

Benjamin Goodell broke away from the crowd, racing to the end of the wharf. A many-voiced cry rose up from those behind him as he ran. He heard feet rushing after him, a thunder of panicking heels slapping against the dock. They were too late.

Ben was scant yards from the end of the pier. The ghost vessel slid across the water, closing with the shore with incredible, yet silent speed.

"Not for us," a parent's voice cried. "For you, it was all for you!"

And then Ben leaped, clawing the air as the world before him filled with shining nightmare.

"—AND, THE LEAD STORY on tonight's news is merely an echo of that from the last two weeks. The unstoppable worldwide collapse of hundreds of corporations continues as the unexplained disappearance of financier Benjamin Goodell sends even more tremors through the international marketplace. As you know, Goodell, forty-eight, vanished while driving alone on his way to New York City from..."

The sharks moved in eventually and gobbled up all the pieces. Goodell International disappeared much as it was created, one large bite after another. The event shook much of the outside world, but it did little within the small and ancient town of Kingsport save to set tongues to waging. And then, only for a few weeks.

It was understood that there would have to be some belt-tightening done by the community leaders now that certain generous donations would no longer be forthcoming. Still, Kingsport had been given much by its benefactor, and they would survive.

Clearing away the last of the fall debris from around the once proud cannon in the center of the town's only park, the old gardener pulled at the handkerchief in his back pocket. He rubbed his rheumy, addled eyes with it, giggling to himself as he sucked on the prizes he dug from their tired corners. No one paid him any mind. It was the least they could do.

Satisfied, the old ward of the town pulled his rake's weathered bamboo tines across the ground once more, assembling the brown and graying leaves scattered over the area into a tidy pile. He pulled the ancient tool with calm ease, his vacant eyes spinning happily as he did his job.

Noir, hardboiled, and the supernatural are three ingredients that make for a unique tale. They are three elements that readily blend together—for many readers, they almost beg to be combined, as though without one of them, something is missing. And, here these three elements also produce a uniquely contemporary mythos tale, even though the tradition goes back decades.

However, such stories using one or more of these elements are often outgrowths of a particular era—the voice of the times, so to speak. "Admission of Weakness" is that as well, a voice of the present. The story masterfully blends the aforementioned elements. Additionally, it brings into the mix one of Lin Carter's most memorable characters: Anton Zarnak. For those readers unfamiliar with Zarnak, this tale is a fine starting point. For the rest, it is a welcome return of an old friend.

ADMISSION OF WEAKNESS

"Pride is an admission of weakness; it secretly fears all competition and dreads all rivals."

–Bishop Fulton J. Sheen

Waterfront Terror

TREVLIN FLETCHER RAN, STUMBLING and gibbering, splashing through the puddled back streets of lower Manhattan. He did not waste time looking over his shoulder. He did not waste energy considering where he was going. He merely ran—straight and hard—his lungs heaving with arching pain, blood beating in his ears like a steel hammer pounding its way through mountains of ice.

Run, run...have to keep moving, tell people what I've seen...what's out there—what's coming! Run! Have to run, have to...run—

His legs ached from the torturous distance he had already covered. Just his escape from the merchant hauler alone would have tired most men—crawling up through the dark hold over the calamitous towers of crates and bales, hanging suspended above the frigid harbor waters, grappling his way down the anchor—let alone once he had reached the dock. The mad dash toward the cliffs of the city, fleeing into its canyons, block after block in the choking, fetid summer heat—

"Watch it, you idiot!"

Trevlin dodged madly around the slow cruising jitney. Not a native of New York, he was not accustomed to automobiles being in the streets at such a late hour. Then, as he staggered around the vehicle, suddenly the portion of his brain still dully cataloguing events for his memory—the one tiny wad of tissue in all his skull that had not given itself over to hysteria—realized what it had seen.

"You—stop!"

He screamed the word with a bellow not brought forth from his aching lungs alone, but from the depths of his tattered, ill-used soul. Staggering after the cab, he screeched painfully, his throat tearing from the strain. Blood flecked the phlegm-thick foam bubbling over his lips.

"For the love of God," he wailed pitifully. "*Come back!*"

Brakes squealed. Trevlin dragged his throbbing legs forward, inching his way to the hackney. His hands clawing at the door handle desperately, he threw himself into the backseat of the vehicle, telling the driver;

"Go! Go—move! *Go!*"

The driver released the clutch and hit the gas pedal harder than he would have normally, his passenger's all too apparent desperation coaxing him onward.

"Where to, pal?"

"Anywhere, anywhere—just get me out of here. Far out of here." Throwing money over the seat, the driver watched a rain of crumpled bills splatter against his windshield as his sweating passenger bleated, "As far as we can go."

The large block engine roared and the taxi burst forward into Chinatown. As the driver steered away from the main streets bustling with activity, favoring the clearer side alleyways, he took note of the man's costume in his mirror, rightly guessing him to be a seaman.

Maybe a shanghai jumping port, he thought. Or a stowaway bolting the watch crew.

Wondering what kind of trouble his fare was seeking to avoid, he asked, "None of my business if you say so, pal, but…you in the kinda trouble where you need the cops—or where you need ta avoid them?"

Gulping the city's thick, humid air into his burning lungs, Trevlin wondered, could the police help him? With what he had seen? He had to tell someone—but who?

"Who?" he wondered aloud.

Could he possibly be saved by men—mere men—armed with naught but clubs and knives and guns? Could anything save him?

Protect him? Was there any power on earth that could stop that which he had seen awakened?

no

The word was a darkened light that cut through Trevlin's brain with surgical precision. He felt his throat go dry and his bladder and bowels empty. And then, as the sailor's eyes flooded with tears, the shape appeared in the alleyway.

"What the hell is that?" muttered the driver. He hit his brakes even as the scarlet and black and gold form ahead raised its arms. Then, Trevlin screamed and fire filled the night.

The Master Arrives

SMUG SELF-SATISFACTION PERVADING his frame, the man stepped into the dark mouth of the alley. He was tall but slender, with a fine-boned, but sallow face dominated by dark, hound-aggressive eyes. More arresting than those features, however, was his hair—sleek and midnight black, as well groomed as that of a cinema star. The man's deep, thick mane was obviously a thing of rightful pride to its owner.

He walked unerringly, his nimble balance unaffected by the greasy cobbles beneath his feet. Moving almost gracefully down the unfamiliar passageway, the summer's terrible heat not seeming to cause any discomfort, he stopped abruptly before the single door of a small, narrow, two-story structure—one shoulder on either side by far larger tenements.

Ahhhhh, he thought with a delighted contentment as he stepped up to the building numbered thirteen, *this is where it starts.* Noting the face of his pocket watch, he commented aloud.

"And this moment is when it starts—with a stroke. Now."

The man's hand reached up, his index finger stabbing the bell to the side of the imposing slab of solid oak that served for the old structure's door. As he waited, his eyes ran over the walls of crumbling brick, black with generations of grime, their few windows dim and smudged with congealing soot.

Excellent, he thought. *Secluded, unimposing, dilapidated enough to put off all but the truly desperate...*

The door swung open noiselessly on well-oiled hinges. Cool air wafted into the alley from the building's interior, despite the horribly oppressive heat strangling the city. In the doorway stood a tall man, lean and rangy. A Hindu, he wore a tattered gray sweater and a pair of formless, baggy cotton pants. Indeed, he would have almost looked a beggar if not for the spotless white turban wrapped with careful precision about his head. His keen dark eyes locked with those of the man in the alley for only a moment.

"Sahib," he said with a slight bow. "You have arrived."

"You know me already, eh?" asked the man in the doorway.

"You are Dr. Anton Zarnak, sent to take over this post from your predecessor, Professor Guicet."

"And how can you be so certain I'm this Zarnak?" asked the man in the alley from behind a suppressed smirk.

"I am still packing the doctor's belongings to make space for your own. His demise was cruelly unfortunate. It left this city and thus by extension much of this world defenseless. You were sent to assume his duties. Neither of us has time to waste with games."

"But," chided the taciturn man, "you still haven't answered my question. How did…"

Without watching for a reaction the Hindu gave the massive oak door a subtle push, causing it to close abruptly in the man's face. When the bell rang again, the Hindu did not answer it, even though it chimed on endlessly. Finally, the door opened as the man from the alley let himself in.

"How *dare* you close that door in my face?" The man's normally waxen face was flush with anger. Dropping his bag in the middle of the foyer he stood with his arms folded across his chest, glaring at the Hindu as the man calmly continued packing a crate. "Did you hear me?"

"They have most likely heard you at Lo Fat's Duck House, I would imagine," answered the Hindu patiently. He threw the words over his shoulder, continuing his work, wasting as little time on the intruder as possible.

"This will not do!" growled the man. "I am Anton Zarnak! I've traveled halfway around the world to get here. I have studied for years for this moment—decades—and I will be treated with respect in my own home, by my own servant, no less!"

In the next chamber, the Hindu rose to his full height. His back to the angry man one moment, there was a blur that Zarnak could not actually follow, and then the Hindu was facing him, in the same room, separated by inches.

"I know who you are and where you have come from. Some time long ago, you made a trip to the far and cold East, seeking knowledge you did not deserve. You demanded it, loudly, foolishly, like a lout in a convent, seeking sex merely because you had discovered you had a penis."

Zarnak's face grew hot, his fine fingers clawing slowly at the seams of his trousers.

"With sad, head-shaking pity, and because they could see a use for you masked to most by your arrogance, those you accosted took you in and taught you. They gave you glimpses of other worlds and brought you slowly to the realization that the universe does not revolve around the human animal. Not even on occasion."

Zarnak found the part of his mind that had been trained to step past his reptilian cortex reaching out and hammering away at his hauteur. Suddenly realizing the man before him was no mere servant, the doctor replied slowly.

"You speak of my past as if well-informed."

"I was told only that you would arrive today," responded the Hindu. "But, I served Professor Guicet for fourteen years. The story I offer as yours, was his story as well. As it is mine. Seeing the same rude, self-important presumptuousness within your eyes which used to dominate both his—and my own—I could only surmise that you were another who thought the secrets of existence could be discovered in a manner akin to children at Christmas…tearing away ribbons, thinking they have found happiness rather than just another trinket."

Zarnak's manner collapsed inward, replaced by a more acceptable humility. Taken aback by his mistaken reading of the situation into which he had walked, he apologized.

"Please forgive me…"

"Singh," the Hindu answered. "Akbar Ram Singh. At your service—in payment for my sins—as you now stand in service to the world for yours."

"It is as you say, Singh," Zarnak admitted. "I was tasked to hold this place against the dark elements of existence. Serving all men is new to me, though, even after my decades in A'alshirie. But I'm here to begin repayment for what I've been taught."

"I believe you are sincere in your words," answered the Hindu. Wearing a sad expression, he added, "Which worries me all the more. As Coleridge said, 'And the Devil did grin, for his darling sin, is pride that apes humility.' I wish you were only but trying to deceive me with your words. Sadly, Dr. Zarnak, in my humble opinion, the one you seek to deceive is yourself."

Turning, Singh walked into the interior of the building, beckoning his new master to follow.

"And that is always a dangerous business. Perhaps if Professor Guicet had not left us so unreasonably early, the monks would have had time to prepare you better. But, that is the way of things. Mankind takes what it can get. Now it has you."

Standing before the door of the apartment's study, the Hindu rested his hand on the latch, saying, "an inspector of police has been waiting for you for several hours now. Your work begins, Sahib Zarnak. Please strive to survive long enough to have dinner."

The Scene of the Crime

LIEUTENANT THORNER LED ZARNAK into the sweltering closeness of the police warehouse. He was a big man, thick-shouldered and barrel-chested. A derby sat forward on his shaved head, its brim slightly discolored from the constant cloud of cigar smoke the officer used to screen himself from the world. Thorner spoke as they made their way toward the back of the building.

"Sorry to get you like this, your first day in town an' all, but…ah, what with Professor Guicet gone…I mean, what happened last night, he would've…"

"Please," Zarnak said with a wave of his hand. "This is to be my life. No sense taking a child's steps into the water. It will be just as cold no matter how long I take to acclimate myself."

Thorner wanted to turn, to run his eyes over the man behind him. He had gone to the oak door in China Alley a score of times in his career to enlist the aide of Dr. Zarnak's predecessor. The lieutenant had liked Guicet, admired him. They had dined together—in restaurants and each other's homes—on numerous occasions, closing many of the great island's taverns together as well.

But Thorner felt tall, hard walls growing between himself and the man behind him. Like most policemen successful in their work, the lieutenant was a shrewd judge of character. Sizing people up was no terribly difficult task for him. And so far, he did not like the size of Professor Guicet's replacement.

"But, well," said Zarnak in a soft but sharp voice, "luckily there's nothing saying that people who work together have to like each other."

"What?" Thorner let the one word escape, then went silent. Guicet had known what the big policeman had been thinking on occasion, but he had always made it seem as if the fact was only further proof the two were kindred spirits. Thorner knew that was not the case here.

Pulling in on himself as far as he could, the lieutenant hid his true self behind his badge and the character he had constructed over the years for presentation to the rabble in the streets. Suddenly he not only did not like Zarnak, he did not even feel comfortable around him.

"This is it."

The doctor moved forward toward the grotesquely misshapen arrangement of blackened steel resting in the back of the police warehouse. His hands gripped one the other behind his back as he approached the twisted blob. Zarnak had been told he would be inspecting a motor vehicle that had been subjected to some kind of great heat. As he stared at the unnaturally distorted tangle shimmering beneath a single light, the doctor was grateful for the clue Thorner had granted him as to what the thing before him had once been. Scrutinizing the contorted, melted frame, the globs of shapeless metal hanging in the air as if frozen, the doctor still found himself forced to ask the obvious.

"This really was an automobile?"

"Yes. A jitney cab." When his guest did not reply, the lieutenant added, "It's in such weird shape, it took us a while to even figure out what company it belonged to. Don't know what happened to the driver."

"Amazing…," Zarnak mused aloud. "Just amazing."

"You've found something?" asked the lieutenant.

"No, no—sorry. I was merely thinking aloud about automobiles in general. The concept of them. Mechanical transport…I've seen very few of them, actually."

"Seen very few?" repeated Thorner, absently pulling a cigar from an inside jacket pocket. "Good God, man—it's 1922. The streets are filled with them."

Zarnak did not turn from his inspection of the nightmarishly bent and boiled slag. Not yet daring to touch it, he responded absently to the policeman as he paced the ruin's circumference.

"I know. But I don't believe they had been invented when last I was here."

Thorner said nothing. The sallow-faced doctor appeared to him to be no more than thirty years old. Several questions ran through the policeman's brain, but he kept them to himself, staying behind his tall, hard wall. Answering them anyway, Zarnak said;

"No, I wasn't a child when I left the country. I'd just received my third degree. I'd had to wait for the war to end before I could graduate, of course."

"The World War disrupted things at a lot of the universities," the big policeman offered.

"World War?" Zarnak responded. "Oh yes, I heard someone on the boat mention..."

And then, the doctor went silent. Climbing a free-standing ladder which had been used earlier by a news photographer to obtain an aerial shot of the unexplainable slag, the doctor investigated its uppermost strands and spires. He was not surprised to find that unlike the rippled, bubbling surfaces below, that the tops of all the upward reaching columns were not only smooth, but concave as well. Descending the ladder, Zarnak finally rested his fingers on the fused remains before him. Drawn to one horribly twisted shaft of dissolved steel, he felt along its spiral ridges.

"Yes, lieutenant," he whispered, "you were right to come for me. Notice how these wiry strands of metal look to have been pulled aloft—how much of the total mass seems to have melted upward, sideways...and look here..."

The doctor pointed up along a thick, inverted pedestal of metal. As the detective drew closer, Zarnak grabbed his sleeve and pushed his hand up against the cool, burned black steel. Shoving Thorner's fingers up the curving wrinkle, the doctor kept the big man's hand moving over the smooth surface until suddenly it ran against a slight, almost unnoticeable jagged edge bursting through the polished skin. The lieutenant jerked his fingers away with surprise. As he looked at the scrape marks that had been drawn across his flesh, Thorner asked;

"And just what the hell was that?"

"The upper half of a femur, I believe."

"What?" asked the big policeman.

"You were complaining that you couldn't find the driver of the automobile, lieutenant." Turning, the doctor stared directly into Thorner's eyes. "Congratulations. You've found him."

A Discovery

"So," said Zarnak, staring at the dark circle in the middle of the lane, "this is where the wreckage was discovered."

Two uniformed officers stood at each end of the Chinatown alleyway, barring both automobile and pedestrian traffic. Thorner stood halfway between them, off to the side on the thin sidewalk, a new cigar clenched firmly in his teeth. Several storefronts down from Zarnak, the policeman leaned against the cleanest building he could find, staying in what shade was present to avoid the blistering sun. Blowing out a cloud of smoke, he watched as Zarnak bent down on all fours, making his way around the black, burned bricks like some sort of gigantic, spindly crab. The lieutenant could not imagine what the doctor hoped to discover.

Hundreds of people and vehicles had gone down the lane since the police had removed the ruined cab earlier in the day. The area had been thoroughly trampled, the black dust the lieutenant had initially noticed scattered across lower Manhattan. Still, that was why he had brought Zarnak in—why he stuck with the doctor despite his personal feelings toward him.

"Ah, lieutenant, I believe we have something."

Thorner did not move from his position. Did not respond.

"I'm certain you noted the fact that the street buckles inward concavely from the blackened perimeter here. The jitney was not the only thing consumed. The cobblestones here have been sheared away, like fruit scooped up by a spoon." Standing, Zarnak indicated the wall next to Thorner, then the one across the street from the same spot.

"Notice the line of soot on the walls—near the sidewalk? Keep that in mind. But first...look at this." Reaching into one of the inner pockets of his voluminous great coat, the doctor pulled forth a length of string with a metal sphere attached to one end. Centering the weight within the black circle, he extended the string to the edge of the darkness.

"You see, the street itself has been torn away in a curving line. Note how the string, extended from the midpoint of the disturbance does not come in contact with the roadway again until it gets beyond the burnt area. But now, observe this..."

Leaving the center of the street, the doctor continued to stretch the string until he came to the curb. Motioning with his hand, he waved Thorner forward to his side. Pointing down, he said;

"Where the string comes in contact with the edge of the sidewalk, there is a thin ridge of soot, extending both down the curb toward the gutter, and over it, onward toward the buildings beyond."

Moving out of the street, Zarnak then extended the string all the way to the nearest wall. Holding it tight against the building with his thumb, he added, "And, if we follow the trajectory here, we see that again, the fabric of the street has been hurled outward and splashed against the surrounding buildings."

"Yeah, okay," Thorner answered, rolling his cigar around in his mouth. "But, so what? What's it mean?"

"It means, my dear lieutenant," said Zarnak as he reeled in his weighted string, "that most likely I have arrived here just in time."

Explorations and Explanations

ZARNAK SAT AT THE desk in the study found on the first floor of the grimy little building at number thirteen, China Alley, sifting through the contents of a score of books. Some were texts he had brought with him. Others had been found among the volumes he had inherited from Professor Guicet.

Which, he thought, will all some day fall into the hands of whomever walks through the front door after I've been destroyed in my own unpleasant manner.

Sitting back in his chair for a moment, Zarnak closed his eyes. Reaching inside himself, he sighed audibly while shaking his head back and forth almost imperceptibly. After a moment Singh appeared in the doorway of the study. Carrying a tray, he entered the room and approached the desk.

"I have placed a call to the lieutenant. He will be here shortly. Now you must prepare yourself for the day ahead."

Zarnak opened his eyes. How long it had been since he closed them he had no idea. He had planned to work through the night until he found what he needed and then act. He had not planned to sleep—an intolerable delay—sloppy.

Dangerous.

Nor had the doctor asked for a meal, or for Singh to telephone for Thorner. Since he would have wished for both these things to have been accomplished, however, he merely nodded, turning his attention to the tray.

"First," said the Hindu, "you have steak and lima beans in curry. You have a great struggle ahead of you, one which promises some amount of physical exertion—beef and beans will provide you the energy you need. Then, red peppers and yeen choy—it's a great deal like spinach. The greens will keep your system flowing properly."

"And the curry, and the peppers?" asked the doctor.

"I like curry and peppers," answered Singh as he filled the empty cup on the tray with tea. Zarnak smiled thinly and picked up the pair of chop sticks near his main dish. Snatching up a strip of spice-dripping beef and several beans, he brought them to his mouth and popped them in, thinking as he chewed.

If I am wrong in my theory, then I am not the man the old masters should have sent to this place. Following the notion with a healthy mouthful of yeen choy and pepper pieces, he chewed with relish, adding, But, if I am right, then I'm not certain how exactly I am supposed to survive.

The doctor slid the greens and pepper bits around in his mouth, sucking at the thick, delicious twin tastes of the mushroom and oyster sauces coating them. As he grabbed another load of beef and beans, however, a sudden thought invaded his mind.

Then again, who says I'm *supposed* to survive?

Somewhat cheered by his sober rationale, Zarnak finished his meal rapidly as he finally began to piece together what he and Thorner would have to do.

Allies Bicker

"GUICET NEVER ASKED FOR anything like this." The lieutenant stared into Zarnak's eyes, searching for some clue as to what kind of game the sallow-faced doctor was playing.

"Guicet," answered Zarnak with impatience, "never faced anything of the magnitude that we will face this morning. If, mind you, we are lucky enough to be able to reach the arrival site in time to effect a reversal."

Thorner's teeth and tongue worked the cigar in his mouth. An uncomfortable tightness choking at him, the lieutenant removed his derby, mopping at the sweat pooling under it as he answered, "Funny how the first day you show up in town suddenly the whole world's hanging in the balance. Must make you feel important."

"You are a fool," Zarnak snapped with an irritation he could not bring himself to control. "If you are not here to help me, please have the good grace to stand out of my way while I try and finish what must be done by myself."

"Hey," boomed Thorner. "Just who the hell do you think you're talking to?" The policeman managed to throw a restraining arm around his anger for a moment, but then suddenly, the big man found himself unable to contain himself any longer. His face filling with blood, he bellowed;

"You know, I've had enough of your piss-ass bullshit. You arrogant bastard—I'm not your mother or anything else that wants to lick your face! I'm the one who's fucking in charge around here! This is my investigation—I call the shots here! Me—" Thorner's finger banged against Zarnak's chest, the iron force of it threatening to shatter the doctor's ribs— "do you get it? Do you understand?"

"Perfectly," answered Zarnak quietly. "You feel threatened by that which you can not understand, and so you rage at the messenger because you do not understand the message...much like a child ripping pages out of a Bible because they are unfamiliar with Latin."

Thorner's fingers curled, his arms throwing themselves skyward. Fists poised in the air, ready to piston down on Zarnak, the lieutenant bent himself forward through the horrific heat. But then, arms shaking, back frozen in position, head swinging from side to side, Thorner grappled his rage back into the dark corner wherein it usually lurked, throwing what chains over it he could.

Hating Zarnak, fearing the doctor's quiet assurance, the lieutenant spat, "You want my help—you want the city of New York to spend overtime money—you tell me what the hell is going on. I've got people to answer to."

"Hopefully people with fewer recent cave dwellers contributing to their racial memory's index," answered Zarnak calmly. "But, enough time has been wasted. The explanation you desire is simple. An ancient god is about to be brought to this island."

"What?"

"Do you remember the vacuum effect involved with the disturbance you asked me to investigate? The metal of the jitney automobile, raining upward and sideways? The soot-like residue of the cobblestones—ground down to powder, gouged from the material essence of the street and then exploded outward? Do you recall the curvature of the destruction, the circular scoop effect of the street, the smooth, limiting cuts across the metal of the jitney as it flowed upward—these confinements to the disturbance that destroyed the automobile and its passengers were caused by a globe in time, a doorway opening from some far beyond into our here and now."

Thorner half-closed one eye, working to concentrate his gaze even as he tried to consolidate his shattered thoughts.

"Someone opened a momentary gate to another dimension in this alleyway," Zarnak continued. "Most likely to eliminate the jitney's passenger. I have done extensive research since I saw you last—looking into what entities might possess the power to cause such destruction, which ones might be bound to this plane of existence at this time, what cycles are in communication...well, not to stray too far afield, what I have discovered is that the time is right for one of the more prominent Lemurian deities to establish a foothold in our world once more."

Thorner's mind reeled. He had seen many things with Professor Guicet—walls running with blood, plates floating in the air, spectral forms passing through objects...and the worm, the terrible, terrible worm deep in the subway—the officer shuddered at the memories, suddenly understanding on a conscious level why he and Guicet had really gone to so many taverns together. Stumbling over his words, passion and pride suddenly replaced with duty and control, Thorner pushed his derby back on his head.

"You're sayin'...some ancient god is tryin' to come set up shop here in Manhattan?"

"No, I'm saying that someone here is trying to bring something down on us all which I'm quite certain they do not understand and can not control."

"If they can bring it here," asked the lieutenant, "what makes you think they can't control it?"

"Any child can open a door," answered Zarnak, "allowing a tiger into its home. The simple truth is, Mr. Thorner, that none control Yama. They are controlled by him—as will be every man, woman and child scattered across the face of this world if we do not stop his arrival."

Thorner stared at the doctor once more. His eyes moved from Zarnak to the hole in the street to which they had returned, and then they fell to memory, seeing again the remains of an automobile so blasted and tortured it had taken nearly an hour's examination just to confirm that it had at one time been a vehicle at all. Finally, his teeth grinding into his cigar, the lieutenant asked;

"Awright, what'dya need us to do?"

The doctor did not hesitate to tell him.

Closing In

An hour later, Zarnak, Thorner, and the seven uniformed officers with them emerged from between the last buildings on the island's west side. Ahead of them lay the city's great shipping docks—hundreds of mighty merchant vessels berthed one after another, all unloading that which they had brought in, replacing it with new loads to take away.

With the police clearing the streets, the doctor had traced the path of the ruined cab back through the alleys of Chinatown to the spot where it had picked up its passenger. At that point, Zarnak had then begun the process of following the ethereal trail of Trevlin Fletcher back to its point of origin.

Every step made following the baking sun across the island filled the doctor with another sliver of fear. He could not avoid it. To trace Fletcher back to the point of his origin through his residual vibrations, Zarnak needed to feel what the man had felt. He had to collect the scant residue of the fleeing man's emotions, to allow each needle of terror to pierce his psychic skin and hang there, poisoning what courage or nerve he might possess with its craven stink.

Much in the manner of a bloodhound the doctor moved from point to point, gathering those scraps of scent still existent which Fletcher had left behind, propelling himself further and further until finally he was able to point toward the hundreds of ships moored along the island's coast.

"There!"

"'There' what?" asked Thorner.

"That ship, the merchant freighter, Congo Lady—that is our destiny." As Zarnak began to make his way across the street, the lieutenant stepped after him.

"So, what'da we do? What'da we need?"

"What we must do," answered the doctor, still walking forward, his speed increasing with each step, "is board that ship, find the high priest making the casting, and stop him."

"Huh, sounds easy enough," replied Thorner, suddenly—ludicrously—somehow feeling more at ease. The mood passed as Zarnak chuckled, shaking his head sadly. The big policeman inquired as to what the doctor found so humorous.

"My dear lieutenant," Zarnak answered, keeping up his brisk pace despite the weight of his bag, "you are, I suppose, a decent enough man, one struggling gamely to understand the circumstances into which you have been flung. I should make some attempt to take that into account, I suppose."

As Zarnak stopped in his tracks, uniformed policemen swarmed around him and Thorner in the unrelenting heat to divert the late morning traffic speeding around them both. As they did, their movements slowed by the staggering heat of the approaching midday sun, Zarnak continued.

"In the time of pre-history, a force named Yamath made itself known in an ancient kingdom we remember as Lemuria. He was called the Lord of Fire. To the Tibetans of our own time, he is known as Yama, the King of Devils." Pointing to the sun, Zarnak said, "Now think and tell me, has it ever been this hot here before, lieutenant?"

When the big policeman shook his head in response, the doctor told him, "No, I wouldn't have believed so. I'll tell you why it's so hot. Yama's presence is pushing its way through to this world. When the sun reaches its zenith, he shall be here. And at that point, all discussion will become superfluous."

"What?" questioned Thorner. "You mean *noon*? This thing you're talkin' about gets here at noon?"

"I could be wrong, lieutenant. I would dearly wish it so," admitted Zarnak. "But mistakes about such things are not normally a part of my repertory."

Not waiting for an answer, knowing from the sun's position in the sky that he had at most only a half an hour—most probably less—to stop what was coming, Anton Zarnak moved on, headed for the Congo Lady. To his credit, with only a moment's hesitation, the lieutenant moved into the doctor's wake, waving his men on behind him. The seven moved after their commander, mere inches of shadow trailing them.

Confrontation

THE GROTESQUE WOODEN FACE swung back and forth before the makeshift altar. The worship site had been formed out of packing crates and several old blankets now covered with heathen scribbling most men had never imagined, let alone witnessed. The dancing visage before it was a terrible thing containing three glaring eyes and wickedly fanged jaws, all of it painted in scarlet and black and gold. Stylized flames dripped from the face's twisted mouth.

Sub pat'kiaa, yef yef, gordic trum'el kuna. Yama hidie'ay, Yama gibgib'conna gibgib'conna...

"What the Hell are those monkeys doin'?" Thorner whispered through the handkerchief he was holding over his nose and mouth, pointing at the masked high priest in the hold before them and those who appeared to be his followers.

How had they taken the ship, he wondered. Had they been passengers? That statue on their altar? What was it?

What does it matter? snarled a different voice within the lieutenant's head. *Concentrate...*

The interior of the Congo Lady seemed forty or fifty degrees hotter than the outside world. The lieutenant and his men had already shed their ties. Several of the uniformed policemen felt themselves on the verge of collapse.

Yama hidie'ay, Yama gibgib'conna gibgib'conna...

On their way down into the vessel's hold, the investigators had found no living beings. The entire ship's company had somehow vanished. Reaching the ship's bowels, however, any questions as to the crew's whereabouts were answered. The bodies of sailors were found hanging from the deck beams of the storage hold's ceiling, their ankles roped in chains and docking cable. The flooring was thick with the sticky slime of their blood, the atmosphere of the massive room pungent with the odor of their disembowelments.

"That is the high priest," whispered Zarnak with urgency, pointing at the leaping figure wearing the wooden mask. "And he is but seconds away from completing his summoning. Order your men to fire."

"What?" asked Thorner. "What're you sayin'?"

"I'm saying kill him, and do it quickly! Before it's too late!"

Sub pat'kiaa, yef yef, gordic trum'el kuna. Sub pat'kiaa, yef yef...

Thorner listened to the heathen words spilling through the slits in the high priest's mask. His eyes took in the spinning, swinging bodies ornamenting the ceiling, his nostrils reminded him of his foe's determination, his feet moved uneasily in the binding scarlet carpet spread across the hold's flooring. It all seemed so foolish, no reason to order murder...then he thought of the eighty-nine dead, swaying above him.

Yama hidie'ay, Yama gibgib'conna gibgib'conna...

"Stop!" demanded Thorner. Rising up from behind the crate he had chosen for cover, the lieutenant aimed his service pistol at the high priest.

Yama gibgib'conna gibgib'conna bing shem!

"In the name of the law!"

The high priest focused on Thorner. Bringing his staff about, the capering butcher aimed his totem at the lieutenant and gave out a string of orders in his strange, clacking tongue. As one, the bloody collection of ritually painted, half-naked cultists turned and began moving on Thorner. Understanding the heathen's intent well enough, the big policeman gave orders of his own.

Instantly, his men revealed their positions and opened fire on the approaching cultists. Armed with only knives and bludgeons, the first line of the ragged band went down to a man, their murderous lives cut short by well-aimed lead. Behind them, however, the high priest unfurled the left sleeve of his robe with a snap. Instantly a wild spray of powder was released from within a careful fold of cloth, contact with the floor transforming it into a dense and putrid billow.

As the cultists retreated into the cloud, Zarnak and the officers poured forth toward the altar. The doctor sank to his knees, studying the scarlet runes crudely painted on the blanket draping the ever-so-carefully stacked crates. And then, Zarnak looked up as a distant rumbling began to echo throughout the hold.

"Oh, no."

The two words were all he could say. If only they had arrived even just two minutes earlier—just two insignificantly ever-lasting minutes—it might have been enough.

"What is it?" asked Thorner.

"We're too late," answered Zarnak, pointing at the altar. "Look!"

Rising out of the stone idol resting on the makeshift worship site, curling wisps of violet smoke billowed and sparked, plumes exploding outward in all directions.

"So, what'da we do now?" demanded the lieutenant.

"I don't know," answered Zarnak. Pulling a thick volume from his bag, the doctor began thumbing frantically through it, ripping many of its thin, worn pages. "It's possible there is a counter-spell, something that might redirect Yama's arrival—deflect it as it were...but I don't know any by heart. I have to find it...need time...just a few minutes..."

Always just a few minutes...

Thorner turned from the distracted Zarnak. Above the altar, a burning grin began to take distinct form. As the temperature in the boiling hold expanded exponentially, the lieutenant forgot everything he believed, falling through the thin crust of learning down into the deep and coldly dark pools of his instinct. Desperately, self-preservation reached into the well-memory of his soul—

Every evil thing, his captain had said once, no matter what—you treat 'em all the same because deep down they are all the same. They're all a bunch of cheap punks. Each and every one of them.

And then, his reality made simple for him, Thorner blew forth a deep cloud of smoke from his cigar and bellowed—

"Hold it right there, Yama!"

who are you

The words sliced through the lieutenant's brain like daggers, leaving his sensibilities fractured and bleeding. Ignoring the pain being inflicted on his rationality, Thorner stepped beyond mere humanity, retreating into the armor of his office.

"I'm the guy you need to listen to." The big policeman filled the air around his head with another stunning festoon of smoke. "Which makes everything easy if you know what's good for you."

His mind numbing with panic, Zarnak found he could not turn the pages of the book in his hand. Holding the volume with his right hand, he slammed the fingers of his left against the floor, splattering the thick blood there as he snarled;

"Work—damn you—work!"

At the same time, Thorner blew out yet another cloud of smoke, sneering at the ever solidifying Yama, "All you gotta do is take it on the lam, Yam. I'm givin' you just ten seconds to remove your sorry ass to some other jurisdiction, or I'm gonna slam you to a place so dark you'll think you were born blind with your head up your mother's ass. You buy me, dickwad?"

you amuse me, small one

All around Thorner, his men were going slowly mad. At his feet, Zarnak continued to thumb through his book frantically. The lieutenant saw his men staring, blubbering, losing control of their bodily functions one after another. Most of them had already fled the room, stumbling blindly back out of the hold.

They were good men, he thought, but they hadn't seen the things he had seen, weren't as prepared...

"That's it, Yama," barked the big officer. "It's time to put up or shut up."

Thorner crossed his arms across his chest defiantly. Smoke circling his derby, he could hear Zarnak muttering at his feet in some unknown tongue. Not daring to take his eyes from Yama's now-nearly solid form, the lieutenant demanded;

"What's it gonna be, asshole?"

In response, Yama's horrible laughter echoed through the hold, shaking the plates of the ceiling, sending the bodies of the mutilated sailors swinging wildly. The last of his men long gone, Thorner drew his weapon, aimed it at the center of the growing god-thing before him, and then threw back his head and screamed;

"In the goddamned name of the law!"

Zarnak leaped to his feet as the lieutenant suddenly spun around and fired three times, emptying half the chambers in his revolver not at Yama, but into the horrible deity's high priest as the man made a mad rush for the altar. Retaliating in the name of his fallen servant, the curling mass of ambrosian flesh and fire flashed black, a thousand strands of burning lightning blasting forth from its body.

The fierce bolts were drawn to the corpses hanging throughout the hold, to the slain cultists on the floor, to the officers staggering across the deck. To everywhere. Three passed through Thorner's body, knocking him to his knees. Next to him, Zarnak read the words he had finally discovered.

"Sub pat'kiaa sia, tel tel, gordic trum'el s'a. Yama kel'ay, Yama kel'ay, Yama gibgib' conna gibb'conna…"

silence!

The doctor turned his head at an angle, arching his body to resist the heated wind blasting forth from Yama's attention. As Thorner staggered back to his feet, Zarnak shouted, "The high priest must not have finished the last invocation. That's why he rushed the altar! I can *still* reverse the gateway."

"What can I do?"

"Get out of here—get your men off the ship—you, too—go, go now!"

Zarnak whirled back toward the solidifying god-thing behind him and shouted, "Sub pat'kiaa sia, tel gordic trum'el s'a. Yama kel'ay, Yama gibgib' conna, gibgib' conna…"

As the lieutenant hesitated, Zarnak snarled, "Go! And take the high priest's mask with you!"

Thorner ran toward the cultist's body while the doctor turned back toward Yama. He was a child, he knew, a babe with a gun at the end of an alley filled with wild dogs. Yes, he knew what to do—use the gun to shoot the dogs and clean the alley of his enemies. That was the theory.

You Will Cease!

The heat dried the sweat on Zarnak's brow. It boiled the tacky floor and walls, evaporating their coating of blood, eating at their paint. Once more Zarnak said the appointed words.

His mouth could not lubricate itself. He kept his eyes closed, with an arm thrown over them, to save his sense of sight. His once sweltering great coat, now dry and brittle, burst into flames. The doctor knew he could never have faced such a thing as the King of Devils if the god-thing had truly reached our world—but it had not. The last words, those that had to be spoken once Yama's presence was felt, those the great one-time master of Lemuria had been denied.

If I can just...a part of Zarnak's mind prayed. If I can just...

Yama erupted forth from his distant dimension once more, filling the hold with another savage burst of searing power. One of the violet shafts slammed against the doctor's right temple, knocking him down as it zig-zagged backward over his head, burning him across his skull to the nape of his neck.

"Sub pat'kiaa sia—"

silence!

Zarnak clawed weakly back to his knees. Then suddenly he flopped to his back, screaming as the inferno finally ate through his coat and peeled away several layers of flesh from his back.

"Tel tel—*ahhhhh, ahggghhh*—gordic trum'el s'a!"

you will Cease—NowCeaseNow!

"Yama kel'ay," screamed the doctor. Wailing in pain, his open tear ducts painfully dry, he sobbed, "Yama kel'ay, Yama gibgib' conna gibgib' conna..."

But, even as a part of his mind realized he might possibly succeed, another realization opened, reminding him of what had happened before—to the jitney...

A fleeing man had left the Congo Lady to spread the word of what was about to happen there. Zarnak had been able to read his intent from the pain he had bled into the streets. The sailor—his car and driver and himself—had been surrounded by a momentary gateway and consumed in a microscopic bit of the fire god's being. For a billionth of a second, the tiniest fraction of Yama had forced its way into our temporal stream and blasted everything within its reach.

At least, thought Zarnak with humble resignation, I'm the only passenger on the Congo Lady.

At the same time, he wondered abstractly if any of the vessel's twisted remains would be visible above the water line to mark his grave after the dimensional portal he was sharing with Yama snapped shut. Then, a sudden wild thought filled Zarnak's mind. Emboldened by hope, the doctor embraced mankind's most reckless insanity and spat;

"Yama kel'ay, Yama kel'ay—gibgib' conna gibb'conna gibgib!"

And then, he threw himself forward at the approaching god.

✠ ✠ ✠

Interlude

OUTSIDE, THE DAZED AND burned Thorner reeled in scrambling terror as the Congo Lady twisted in on itself, boiling in mid-air, falling into the harbor in an explosion of steam and screaming water. The terrible hiss of hot salt flooded the docks for a moment, then fell away against the breeze coming in off the ocean. As it did the lieutenant scanned the water with fearful diligence, but not a trace could he find of the merchant vessel he had just been aboard. Or half the dock next to it.

Still gripping the scarlet and gold and black mask of the high priest in his hands, Thorner stared at it dumbly for a second. Then, after a single wrenching moment, he laughed, loud and wildly, frightening the living and cursing the dead.

Epilogue

"I STILL CAN'T BELIEVE you survived."

The lieutenant looked down at Zarnak's hacking body. Spitting out another lungful of water, the doctor thought to try and explain, but wondered at how he could. In the last instance, when he knew Yama was departing, being pulled back to his own dimension, the doctor had done the only thing he could think of and attempted to step into the fire god's realm.

Being within the gateway—enough of his essence pulled into it by Yama's desire to reach him—he could grasp at its fabric as the King of Devils had grasped at his. Of course, he could no more hold onto it any longer than Yama could his own, but he had hoped, if for that fraction of a millisecond, if the contact with it could render him insubstantial enough...

"Just lucky, I suppose," he said, seeing no reason to burden the big man further. Thorner had carried on when Zarnak himself had frozen. Even if the doctor was never to succumb to such weakness again, he would always owe each new opportunity to confront it to the lieutenant. Sensing Ram Singh's approach from behind the gathering crowd, not questioning his servant's ability to know his business—grateful for it—he said;

"You know, detective, unless I were to die very shortly, and you to live far in excess of the normal human allotment of years, there's very little doubt that I will not outlive you. In fact, I probably already have." Zarnak hacked again suddenly, a last mouthful of water finding its way out of his system. Wiping his mouth, afterward he added a few more words quietly.

"But, all things considered, I'm not at all certain that is the most satisfactory arrangement the Fates could have made when they planned the destinies that would shape the world."

As Zarnak touched at the still smoldering line Yama's touch had zig-zagged across his head, Singh said to Thorner, "Congratulations, lieutenant. That is probably as close to an apology or a giving of thanks that anyone is ever likely to get out of the good Dr. Zarnak."

The officer blinked, his mind already smoothing over several of the things he had seen, readjusting his world enough so that he could remain king of it. Cars full of police poured into the area then, the new arrivals rushing to the aid of Thorner's uniformed officers. As they did, the lieutenant suddenly held up the mask in his hand.

"Bu-hey," he asked. "What'd you make me grab this thing for?"

Taking the heavy wooden piece from Thorner in both hands, the doctor stared at it and smiled.

"Quite simple, Lieutenant," answered the doctor with a lie as he laughed at his audacious good fortune. "I wanted a souvenir for my office."

And then, Thorner threw back his head and laughed once more. It was a clean and happy sound this time, however, and it stepped on the last traces of the King of Devils as a dog would an ant. Breaking off the joyful noise finally, though, the big man took Zarnak's hand and shook it, asking;

"Have you ever had a 'gin and sin?'" When the doctor admitted he had not, Thorner smiled. "A little orange juice, some lemon, a dash of grenadine...and a bathtub full of gin. You'll love 'em."

"Perhaps," said Zarnak, warmly humble at the feel of the sun on his grateful cheek, "I will. Perhaps I will."

Greek mythology speaks of Zeus and his two jars, one of "good" and one of "evil." From these jars he distributes to men blessings and ill, but to most he mingles both. Later, it is said that Pandora possesses one of these jars (today we refer to it as a "box"). And as the tale goes, once all of the evils had escaped the jar, all that remained was hope—and over the centuries, similar tales abound. Now C.J. brings us a story that engages this most ancient of subjects, but in a present day, head-on telling—he holds no punches.

Hope is eternal, and yet forever changing. Every culture has its own telling of hope. Here is one for our culture.

HOPE

"People will not readily bear pain unless there is hope."
–Michael Edwards

MOST PEOPLE DID NOT have the imagination to see anything other than flames. True, as time spun along endlessly they incorporated their own variations on the eternal theme—rivers of lava, belching pits that hurled smoke and magma and burning oils into the air, fiery rains, volcanic animals that vomited fire—human beings could be quite clever. But, the grand majority of the damned persisted in seeing their personal eternities in simplistic terms of licking red tongues that merely charred their flesh and consumed their vitals endlessly. For the keepers of the abyss, most of their charges did not offer much in the way of entertainment.

The man currently wandering the western heights of the Stygian depths was different, however. Throughout his centuries within the infernal regions, he had rarely suffered from any type of combustion whatsoever. His was usually a more interpretive picture of damnation, one that forced the punishment to fit the crime— over and over—an endless replaying of his sins with him on the receiving end of a trillion variations.

His name, by that point, he had forgotten. What he had done to deserve the torments of the pit had mostly faded from his memory as well. During his imprisonment, he had come to understand that he did belong where he was, that his lifetime of contemptible behavior had rewarded him with an eternity of constant pain in the name of celestial retribution. He had also—finally—come to the absolute end of his ability to care.

The man had suffered in every way possible that he had been able to imagine. His feet had rotted away so that he walked on leprous stumps, eating and drinking from slime-coated pools where he fought unidentifiable things for every crumb and droplet. He had been torn apart by beasts, dropped from galactic heights into rivers of spikes, lived with the shade of his mother constantly whispering into his ear, been eaten, digested and left in the sulfurous weeds as food for the insects.

Time and again he had been destroyed and reconstituted. Time and again he had made his humble apologizes to a God he had finally come to realize not only could not hear him, but was not interested in anything he might have to say. For years on end he had thought that perhaps he might have some chance at redemption. After he had realized that his sins and his sins alone had brought on his dire situation he had determined to make up for them.

Every torment had been suffered gladly. Every infliction visited upon him had been endured with a stoicism unseen in the annals of Hell for centuries. But apparently, it mattered not. He had known the rules—good behavior took you to Heaven. Wrong thinking was punished—forever.

Forever—

He hadn't realized, hadn't thought, hadn't bothered…had done as he pleased. And now, he was paying the price. For eternity. *Forever—*

Yes, he thought, he deserved punishment for what he'd done. He did. Even for the horribly terrible times in which he had lived—when human life didn't mean much to begin with—he had been a monster. Considered one in the past and considered one still in the present, his was a name unforgotten and unforgiven by humanity even if he himself could no longer recall it.

For the longest time, though, still he had believed there could be redemption. That somehow the past could be made up for, glossed over, ignored. That somehow the shame could end and what he once was could finally be undone by what he had become.

He no longer believed that.

There was no relief. He knew that now. He was damned. People had said the words—damn you—and it had been done. Bound to the pit by the righteous indignation of those who survived him. Doomed to forever watch the shadow of Great Satan rippling over the landscape, knowing that its terrible shape would mottle his back day after day, hour after hour—

Forever—

"Don't give up."

The words sounded tiny and thin, more a trick of the wind than any actual voice. The man had heard many great and pitiful noises since eternity had begun to stretch out before him, but this was something new. There was pity in the tone that swirled around his ear, encouragement...

"Don't give up."

Hope.

The man turned his head, searching for the source of the whispers he had heard. He had wandered onto a sparse and blasted plane, a thing of burnt stumps and crumbling dark rock. Sulfuric smoke rose like pollen from the mangy scraggle weed littering the landscape to the horizon. The man's eyes studied every twig and shadow, but he did not see anything that could have been speaking to him.

"Salvation is still possible."

The man's form froze in terrible hope. There was no madness in Hell—he knew this. The man had found eternal damnation to be a great equalizer that freed all minds. If they accomplished nothing else, the torments of the Stygian depths taught their students truth. The man knew that someone, something, was speaking to him. And that, maybe, just possibly, they might even be worth listening to.

"How can I believe that?" he asked. Closing his eyes, he raged to the smoke and heat, "I've been here so long..."

"You were condemned for eternity. Eternity knows no end. You just have to believe—"

"*Believe?!*" he snapped.

"Believe," the soft voice continued, "that God is forgiving, that redemption is possible. That you can be lifted up." There was a short pause, then the voice came to him one last time.

"You cannot give up. You can not."

The man looked about himself once more, the chains of despair cracking within him. Suddenly, he felt the resolve which had been ebbing from his heart for so long now springing full blown within his breast anew—once again a thing of weight and substance.

And then, off to his side, hidden in the shadowy trunk and branches of a broken tree, he saw the form of one of the demon spirits that plagued the captives of eternity. Smaller than those he knew, it was a soft beast, almost colorful. It was also—the shape of its stance declared—a cowardly thing. And yet, its words had rebuilt his confidence, reminding him of what he had always believed.

Redemption was possible. The God of miracles had sent a son that threw out the laws of old. Things were not set in stone. There were no absolutes. Each soul got to negotiate its own passage. He could wipe away the ancient marks on his soul's slate.

He could.

He just had to believe. He had to keep going. He had to persevere.

The man smiled. He would beat Hell. He would reach Heaven. God would hear his call, would see his mighty suffering. He would be redeemed.

And then, the shadow of Great Satan fell across the land once more. The small demon put a finger to its mouth and stole away quickly—fearfully. The man understood. He even smiled as the loathsome creature scurried off into the steaming darkness.

A demon that came to him in his hour of despair—that found him in his blackest moment of need and encouraged him on—surely that meant there was a God. Surely that proved he had to but try harder. Longer. For as long as it took.

From his mighty height, the Lord of Darkness and Lies noted something new stirring on the plane below. Focusing his vast attention, he saw his invisible hosts gathering around a particular soul. They were there to watch as it began a new series of torments. The foolish thing still believed in the escape clause.

That a deal wasn't a deal.

And then, to his delight, Satan noted that the soul in question was one of his favorites—an exquisite torturer that had spared itself nothing. Of recent, the Dark One had been almost saddened by that one's seeming final acceptance of its fate. But now, now it was like unto reborn. Satan thought for a brief sliver of time, and then sniffed the air. The odor was unmistakable. His favorite demon, Hope, had been there spreading its terrible misery.

His great mouth curling with delight, Satan stopped to watch the folly of optimism as it once more did its horrible work. His demons were laughing already. It was going to be another great show.

Sometimes the line dividing Good and Evil, misery and pity, is not readily clear. In this story, that comes to the forefront with the timeless conflict between two forces that perhaps require each other to exist.

But, as with many of C.J.'s stories, deciding which sides of that elusive line a character rests is difficult to discern—and often the answer is disturbing.

MISERY AND PITY

"When a man suffers himself, it is called misery; when he suffers in the suffering of another, it is called pity."

–St. Augustine

THE DIM SUM HOUSE was filled with cages. The patrons had brought their birds and hung them from the ceiling to show them off while they talked and ate with their friends. The restaurant itself was a dull and colorless place. This was a purposely constructed and carefully maintained motif, designed specifically to direct all attention, all glory, to the dazzling display of squawking feathers hanging overhead.

For several thousand years much of southern China had been alive with the ancient custom of taking one's bird with them to breakfast. The birds watched from above as the dim sum cooking carts were pushed from table to table, individual dishes prepared for each customer below the cages in turn. Modern, antiseptic health rules destroyed the delicate, feather-filled tradition, however. Now, there was but one dim sum house in all the Orient which still dared defy the new ways.

Of course, it defied the rules quietly. It was a hidden, private place, unknown to tourists, not admitted to by officials, a mysterious whisper that opened onto the world from the end of a black alley in the oldest section of Hong Kong. It was the last of its kind.

"I knew you were alive," said the man sitting under the silent, staring bird. "I just knew it." The man on the other side of the table remained silent, merely tilting his head and shifting his eyes to a degree that indicated he had nothing to add.

"But this story of yours," answered the man in sarcastic Cantonese, not his first language, but a dialect he was comfortable with, "let me see if I understand this all. The reason I haven't seen you in so long is not because you died—despite the funeral for you which I attended—but because you went off to prepare yourself for the cataclysm. And," the younger man tried not to giggle as he added, "you've been chasing around the world doing battle with werewolves and vampires ever since?"

As Jhong's eyes seemed to dart among the bird cages hanging from the restaurant's ceiling, he took in the amused expression on his old friend's face. His vision was limited by the darkness of the room, but he could see what he needed to clearly enough. With no discernable trace of emotion, he answered simply,

"Yes, Li."

Tilting back in his chair, Jhong placed his hands casually in his lap. He seemed at ease, relaxed. A careful glance told a different story, however. The corded veins running down his arms were tense. All the visible muscles of his body were taut, even those of his neck.

Although older than the other man at the table by almost two decades, his face remained practically unlined. His short, razor cut hair still shone a glossy black, reflecting all the light the secret room had to offer. Indeed, Li seemed to not be aging well in comparison.

"You must tell me of this," said the younger man, his smile growing larger—wider. Leaning forward, propping his elbows on the table, he rested his chin on his palms, saying, "this is a bit too much. Even for you."

"I met a man in America," answered Jhong, "who knew of the Guan Cee Qui."

"Vampires?" asked Li, his eyes twitching sharply as he voiced the word.

"Yes. It was his place to banish them—mine to stand at his side. We did this. Later, we did it again."

"You are this Qua'lo's dog?" asked the younger man, purposely taunting his friend. As if the news of the existence of vampires was nothing special, Li lifted the cup before him, but then set it back down without drinking, asking instead, "He gives commands and you listen and obey? Is that what you have become?" Jhong sighed softly. He knew what he had to do, what he had travelled so far to accomplish. His eyes closing halfway, he countered,

"It is his destiny to be drawn into conflicts with the unknown. Sometimes it is mine to be at his side. At one time I thought our fates to be unfairly juxtaposed. I have come to understand how truly fortunate I am in this manner. But," the older man looked at the cage above his friend's head. Admiring the colors he could make out of the bird within, he asked,

"If we are to speak of destinies, then tell me of yours. What is it you have become, Li Chon?"

The younger man lifted his head out of his palms. Stretching his arms out about him, he turned this way and that, staring at the many cages hanging about the restaurant. Drumming his longish nails on the table, he pointed toward the one he had brought, asking,

"Did you see my bird? Do you like him?"

Jhong's eyes flicked up, taking in the creature once more. It was smaller than many of the other birds in the restaurant that night, only nine inches in length at best. Its crest was a finely shaggy thing, wild blue feathers spurting up from a small head barely large enough to hold up its heavy, wickedly sharp-pointed bill. As Jhong's eyes met his friend's once more, Li continued, saying,

'They call it a Belted Kingfisher. It comes from North America. Just like your vampire-killer friend." The younger man's voice trailed off in quiet laughter once more. "It is fishing bird. Dives under water and spears fish with its wonderful bill. Brings them up, pecks them until they are dead, then it eats them."

The younger man's head rolled on his shoulders. He stared up at the bottom of the cage, his expression changing, going far away from the dining room, far away from the present. His eyes locked on the metal circle suspended above his head, his mood shifted greatly. In a softer, kinder voice than the one he had been using, he asked,

"In your wanderings with your American Kingfisher, have you ever come across the legend of the Ch'iang Shich?"

"One need not travel to the other side of the world to hear of the Ch'iang Shich."

"No, no," answered the younger man absently. "I suppose not."

"What brings such a subject to mind in this conversation?" asked Jhong, more prompting his old friend to continue than seriously asking a question. Still looking off toward the ceiling, Li said,

"The stories of these creatures are numerous. I shall tell one. Four journeymen came to an inn near Shantung one night. The innkeeper told them she had no room. But, they were too tired to go on, so the woman finally agreed to let them stay in an old shack off from the inn. She failed to tell them, however, that the unburied corpse of her daughter was laid out on a table just behind a curtain in the shack." Drumming his fingers faster, the younger man's tale took on a sense of urgency as his hard nails clattered against the table top.

"Three of the journeymen fell asleep at once. The fourth, though…he stayed awake. He felt an unexplainable dread within his heart and simply could not sleep." Finally moving his head so that his eyes could meet Jhong's, the younger man said with a smile, "He soon discovered the source of his fear."

"Which was…?"

"A withered hand pulled aside the curtain. As the traveller lay frozen in his bed, he watched as the body of the innkeeper's dead daughter moved toward him and his companions. Its movements were grotesque, its eyes glowing green. Of course, the girl was dead, her spirit long gone. By not burying her at once, the old woman had given who knew what kind of evil spirits a chance to take her body as their own."

"You tell this as if you believe it," Jhong said, watching for his friend's reaction. Li held down a laugh, answering instead, "I believe that you faked your own death so that you could roam the world looking for monsters to destroy—that's not so much more unbelievable than this." Li lifted the cup in front of him to his mouth, then set it aside and continued his story.

"The horror went to each man and breathed on them. Demon breath kills instantly, of course—in legends, anyway. One by one, it murdered the sleeping trio, poisoning them with its breath, sucking their souls into its own body as they slipped from their former homes. Then, it turned on the fourth man."

A dim sum girl came past their table then, pushing a cart of steamed spinach dumplings. Jhong asked her for an order. She set the small strainer with its four dumplings in front of him as well as a dish of soy sauce, added the price to the table's bill, and then moved on. While the older man wiped his chopsticks clean with his napkin, the storyteller continued.

"The horror of the thing's glowing eyes finally gave him the courage to overcome his fear. The last man bolted from the room and ran screaming into the night. The Ch'iang Shich followed. The man tried to hide behind a willow tree, but it saw him. Not capable of running further, the traveller backed up against the tree, watching as the dead thing came closer, using the energy it had stolen from his companions to come for his own soul. Giving out a hideous scream, the thing leaped for the man, ready to kill him with its horribly long fingernails. Unable to stand the terror invading his brain, the man fainted at that moment."

"And is that the end of the story?" asked Jhong as he lifted a second dumpling from the strainer in front of him.

"Oh, no. Fainting saved the traveler's life. The Ch'iang Shich's attack was so fierce that its nails drove deep into the willow. It was stuck—unable to continue its attack."

Wiping his mouth with his napkin, Jhong stopped another cart as it passed the table, asking for an order of curried squid. Another small container was placed on the table and another charge added to its bill. Tasting the squid, the older man asked,

"And the reason for this story?"

"To play with you." The long fingernails began drumming against the table once more. Tiny slivers flicking away as the hard points dug into the wood.

"Which is only fitting," he added as a phosphorescent green slowly began to creep into the back of his eyes, "Considering that you only came here to play with me." Jhong swallowed a second piece of squid, then asked,

"And is the game now finished?"

"That, of course, is up to you."

"Might I ask a few questions?" The glow hardened, brightened. Behind it, an answer formulated and was finally vocalized.

"Certainly."

"I heard about the accident that should have killed my old friend. I then heard that he had survived, but that many others were dying mysteriously around him. The car crash...he did not survive for days trapped in the wreckage. You," Jhong spat the last word, "You came to him, took his place, and have moved about in his stead since. killing his wife, his friends, neighbors."

"You have asked no question yet," the thing on the other side of the table whispered.

"When I called and asked to meet with you, it did not concern you that a dead man had telephoned."

"Dead people don't bother me," answered Li's body, a smile curling his lips. "But, those who cannot come to the point do. What are your questions?"

"Two in number," said Jhong casually. "First, it is my suspicion that you are the last of your kind. True?"

"Yes," answered the smiling demon without hesitation. "Modern ways have limited our access to the flesh. I am alone, as are you. But soon, we shall be joined together." The demon dug its claws into the table, peeling away curls of varnish.

"And your second question?" it demanded.

"Tell me," the old man asked, his chopsticks reaching toward the soy sauce dish. "Is it true demons abhor salt?" Before the thing across the table could react, Jhong slid his chopsticks under the small dish and flipped it into the monster's face.

Immediately it screamed, slamming its hands against the table, pushing itself back. At the same time, the older man scooped up the two food strainers on the table and brought them down on the thing's hands. Using the metal bowls for protection, he drove the creature's long, hard nails into the wood of the table, trapping its hands.

Instantly, wordlessly, Jhong pulled his knife from its sheath beneath his shirt. With one quick motion he slashed across the monster's throat, severing it to the spine.

Around the restaurant, people screamed. Birds flapped and cawed and whistled in desperate panic as their masters below grabbed for them and ran for the exit. People charged in all directions, overturning tables and chairs, food carts and each other. Hot oil splashed across the ancient floor. Flame followed.

"Kill you!"

The demon within the dead flesh of Jhong's old friend raged, straining against its imprisonment. With a sharp flex that tore muscle at a dozen spots beneath its skin, the monster snapped the table in two. Its opponent moved back quickly as the thing swung its arms wildly trying to both free its hands from the table halves and swat its foe.

"You have my friend's soul," said Jhong calmly, stepping backward carefully through the ruin all around him. "You shall not keep it."

The thing with the glowing eyes smashed its hands together, shattering the table halves and six of its fingers. Brushing away the wood still stuck to it, the monster laughed,

"And who will stop me? You? Humans do not stop Ch'iang Shich. Nothing stops Ch'iang Shich."

"False words," countered Jhong. As smoke continued to flood the now empty restaurant, he prepared himself, focusing his energy for whatever opening the creature might give him. "You are the only such demon left. If you are denied this body and mine, you will find no other."

"Then," it spat, heedless of the blood pouring from its throat, "I shall have yours!"

The monster lunged for Jhong, but the elder warrior easily dodged the awkward attack. The thing crashed into one of the few still standing tables, overturning it and following it to the floor. As it tried to stand, unable to grasp anything solidly with its broken hands, its foe told it,

"You were driving the car that killed Li. I assume you crashed on purpose. Use up one body, move onto the next. But this time, there will be no 'next.'"

As the monster made its way to its knees, Jhong brought his foot down sharply on its spine, snapping it precisely at its base. As the creature flopped back toward the floor, he moved on it with his knife in hand once more. Two strokes severed the muscles behind its knees. As the thing bellowed in pain, the older man grabbed the handle of one of the mobile cooking carts and flung it on top of his foe, diving for cover behind an overturned table at the same time.

The cart struck at an angle, its corner digging into the monster's hide. Then, suddenly its fuel tank ruptured, filling the air with burning metal. The explosion flooded the restaurant with flame, every wall host to several fiery spots. Stepping out from behind the now burning table that had protected him from the explosion, Jhong covered his mouth against the mounting smoke and fumes, reached upward, and then headed for an unblocked exit.

Arriving at the doorway to the kitchen, the elder warrior turned back to determine the fate of the thing he had just faced. The monster remained pinned beneath the exploded cart, crippled and helpless, screaming and cursing as its dead flesh charred down to the bone.

Satisfied, Jhong turned and entered the kitchen, leaving the restaurant by the rear door. Once outside, he circled the block and then joined those standing in the street far back from the blazing alleyway entrance. None had understood what transpired within as it had been happening. None remembered the older man's face. All such details had been lost in the mad scramble to remove themselves and their birds to safety.

Now, standing in the morning air behind the collection of mostly older men who had just fled the restaurant, Jhong watched as the ancient wooden building burned, watched as its ceiling and walls fell in on themselves before the fire trucks could arrive. The old men sighed at the sight, one of them saying,

"It is gone. The last of its kind. Gone."

"Yes," agreed Jhong, talking only to himself, "the last of its kind."

And then, the elder warrior walked away, giving the caged blue bird with the wild crest feathers and the long beak to the first person who would accept it.

No scholar, no academic, and no philosopher can provide a suitable theory as to why humans wandered from a life with Nature to create "civilization." There are countless proposals: trade, safety, religion, and perhaps the most convincing, fear of what lurks in the dark places of the world. But all of these reasons are nothing more than speculation.

In "Incident on Highway 19," civilization is still operating—and the reasons are still a mystery. Just as the ancients of Sumer kept records, so are they kept here. The world has progressed; it is sanitized, purified, and sometimes staged. But this doesn't remove those ancient terrors; it just hides them, and gives them new names. Over the millennia, they've remained the same. They are always there…waiting.

INCIDENT ON HIGHWAY 19
Excerpts from a Journal kept by Dennis Henry Cropton

January 1st

Well, a new year begins and so last year's work journal is put aside and a fresh one started. The wonderful thing about this year's journal, however, is the fact that it will be kept, transcribed and even spell checked on and by my new voice recognition palm computer—in service now, even as I speak. Ah, the marvels of this modern age.

And, more marvelous yet is the fact that I have drawn an assignment from our grand and glorious Department of Roads which—for once—pleases me to no end, although I'm certain that no one involved with making out the assignments meant it to do so.

In short, I've been stuck in "R&D," which in this case refers to the roadkill detail. An executive at last, manager of a department of one, given total charge of cleaning flattened, shattered and pulped mammals from the macadam of one ninety-eight mile stretch of turnpike and thirteen minor transportation ways running helter skelter across the vast northern tracks of our great state. Ah, but mother would be so proud.

This was, of course, another blatantly obvious move on the part of lovable district manager Beechum to get me to quit. Poor "Beach-ball," he just never will figure me out, will he? The fool thinks that anyone who's been to college is some sort of snob who won't rest until they have his job, as if anyone who wanted to grow a crop of ulcers and start having heart attacks in their forties by slash and burning their way to the top would go to work for the Department of Roads in the first place. Ahhhhh—oh my, yes—that's where the big money is. Insecure idiot.

The man hates me for so many reasons it's difficult to think where to begin. Oh, but you know, why bother? That's not the point of this journal, is it? No. This is my cover-your-ass, get-out-of-jail free card. For maximum pension-securing safety, every moment of every work day will be entered in great and minute detail so that there shall always be a record of how each millisecond was spent. As my sainted Dad always said, "if you keep the ground around your home clean, then your enemies won't be able to find any rocks to throw through your windows."

Besides, it's the glorious tradition of the department to keep such records. Ours was the first state in the union to clean its roads thusly, and my forbearers have kept such notes since early in this century. So, who am I to break with such a noble, employment-safe-guarding tradition?

And, with that all said, allow me to make my entry for today. I am, everyone will be pleased to hear, working hard. As for a description of those duties, I am at home, sitting in front of the fire, finishing this entry so that I can return to my morning coffee and my book (yes, Beach-Ball, college graduates still read real paper books). A wonderful way to start the workday, and legitimate as well, considering every road from here to the state borders in both directions is clogged with our usual over-poweringly deep holiday snowfall.

So, while some others of my fellow employees may have to struggle to reach work so they can begin plowing (some time two or three days from now, if they're lucky, I would think), I shall sit here enraptured by the joys of knowing it is my "punishment" assignment that has rewarded me so.

Ah, isn't it wonderful to have a moron for a supervisor?

January 19

And now, with the roads finally being cleared, it's time for me to go to work. Actually, of course, I've been at work for some hours now, and my new assignment is proving to be even more perfect than I'd previously imagined. Solitary driving's never been the chore for me it seems to be for everyone else in the motor pool. Eight hours of coasting mountain passes, drifting through uninterrupted forests with barely a house or barn to spoil the view for scores of miles, torture for some—true enough—but those are people I will never fully understand.

Even the actual work itself seems no big deal. Spot the flattened remains of a hedgehog or raccoon, pull over, shovel it up—bag it, tag it—move on to the next. The roadkill stew brews on in the back of the truck and the hours pass serenely.

There simply is nothing hard about this job. For deer or cows there is the winch and for anything larger there is the axe. And, it isn't as if I'm expected to get down on my hands and knees and scrounge around for every loose bit of skin and fur, or to scrub the highway clean of brains and bile and blood. Hell, if left for a few days, scavengers would pull the bodies apart to the point where the, oh so "civilized" gentry of our fair state would never know what it was they were driving over anyway. A few days past that and even the bones'd be scattered to the point where not one passerby in a hundred would make note of anything.

Really, wouldn't it be more sensible to just let the slain vermin fester where they fall, just leave them as reminders to an arrogant race of idiots that life is the briefest of flickers in a universe of wind? But, that wouldn't play in this day and age—not when everyone has their newly discovered constitutional right to ignorance—oh, no. No, now our world must be sanitized to a point unrecognizable as any place that might have spawned humanity so that the grandmothers who rule us all can breathe easy as they survey their domain from the safety of their air-conditioned bubbles.

What would they think, our governing matrons of conformity, if they were to have to view two, or even three, seconds worth of flattened fox or pancaked squirrel? Oh, the horror—bloody life thrust right in their faces—the trauma. Heavens.

Dolts. BoobsFoolsMorons—obsessed with making life perfect in a world so utterly pitching across a sea of chaos that one simply *has* to wonder what in the name of God powers their minds. Obnoxious, bored housewives and self-important little men, fighting in righteous defiance against all the obvious rules of nature, so as to protect themselves from ever having to entertain a rational thought.

Beach-Ball's one of these. So proud of his work securing women's rights to murder their unborn children, so puffed with self-importance over his efforts to keep guns out of the hands of citizens. His own mother killed by burglars, and still he blusters about how decent people can't be trusted with weapons. We know why you do such things, don't we, Beach-Ball? You fight for abortion rights because every child born is a reminder of your own mortality. As for disarming everyone around you, I'm certain I know why a pretentious, hateful person such as yourself would want to know that as many of the massing sea of humanity as possible were defenseless.

But, all neither here, nor there. A glance at my watch reveals that it is already 6:15. Well past the time I should be headed for home, yet here I am just finished scraping up the fragile remains of an unusually large raven. Ah, duty, never-ending duty.

Where were you at 6:15 today, Beach-Ball? Still hard at work like me? I doubt it.

February 8th

Well, this is a puzzlement. I'm on a not-much-used portion of Highway 19, maybe a third of the way past mile marker 53. I've found something that frankly has me beside myself with curiosity. Shortly put, I've discovered the remains of a creature which I cannot identify. I will admit at first I was going to just call it a raccoon and forget about it.

I mean, no one actually really cares what dead things I'm bagging out here. There's no one using our records to track population disruption or migration patterns or anything. Having spotted fur close enough to raccoon coloration to pass, there would have been no great disaster if I had simply written in "RACCOON" and let it go at that. But I spotted something in the mix of fur and fluid and sloppy, pulped organs that struck the word down so violently that my curiosity was forced to awaken.

To be brief, I'm not going to tag this removal because I can't. I can't write out a tag for it 'cause I don't know what it is. But, I am going to take it home with me and examine it.

I guarantee I'll know what it is by the end of the day.

February 9th

The thing on the ground had only two legs. It was no raccoon, no hedgehog, or weasel nor anything else I've ever seen. It isn't. It isn't a bear cub or a hairy baby or...

✠ ✠ ✠

It's about...what...ah, it's an hour later. I had to walk away from my examinations and get a hold of myself. I will confess to having made a rendezvous with Jack Daniels and his friend Löwenbrau. I am, as one might suspect, calmer now, but in no way has my fascination diminished. In fact, with the clutter of wild voices shoved from my head thanks to the smooth medication provided by Dr. Daniels, I'm finally able to think a bit more clearly.

Killing brain cells to be able to think. Huh—now *there's* a concept.

Anyway, wit aside, I must begin to record the truly amazing thing that's happened to me. From this moment forward, this record will be used to detail all my findings concerning this remarkable find I've stumbled across. I'm not claiming genius status—I realize it was just a chance discovery, but like penicillin, it was made and is now a fact of our age.

✠ ✠ ✠

Clearly my libations have effected me more than I thought. It's been around another two hours since my last entry. I haven't been sleeping—no, I've still been working, probing, examining the mass on my kitchen counter with an ever-growing sense of wonder. And, I'll say right now that I don't feel any shame for my previous entry. I'll wager doughnuts to dollars there's not a person on this planet who wouldn't have felt the need I did for, as the Victorians might have said, "a jolting stimulant." Hell—those who read these pages in the future may need a jolt of their own, and they'll just be reading about...

No—enough. If the proof really is in the pudding, perhaps I should shut up and get to the point.

I have discovered a new life form. While technically not alive, of course, the remains I have discovered are unlike anything ever known of in all of history. I've examined the carcass quite thoroughly now. Although the means I have at my disposal here at home are quite limited, still I've seen enough to know I've made the most important biological discovery of the modern age.

First off, the creature is bipedal in nature. If standing, it might come to roughly half a meter in height. Upon closer examination, its fur proved not to be hairs inserted singly into the body, but bunched gathers of hair extending from quills. *Quills!* Fantastic? Yes, but true. And, only but the surface.

These fur quills embed in the skin like a bird's feathers or a porcupine's spines, but in the center of each is a sharp barb, not so much like the porcupine's, but looking more like an insect's stinger. With the flesh practically falling apart, it was no great trick to extricate several of them completely with what seems their poison sacs intact.

I have no idea at this time what substance is inside these sacs, but I have experimented. It seems the barbs will catch onto almost anything. When they do, the slightest resistance will pull them free of the creature. When this happens, however, the sac is pulled free as well, but it is compressed by being squeezed through the smaller quill hole, a compression which forces the sac to empty through a vein in the barb. Whatever the substance is, it flows upward through the barb and is released into whatever the barb has fastened itself to. Although I can't say for certain that the liquid is an irritant of any kind, I am still quite glad I first handled the corpse before me with a shovel, and only with heavy leather work gloves since. At first I was merely afraid of infection. Haha—what an infection, eh?

I apologize for being so giddy, but there's so much more.

Once one begins to think of the thing as standing erect, the questions grow greater. Too much of its internal structure is completely ruined to make much of its torso. Indeed, its left side (where I assume it was struck) is so ruined that its upper limb is a complete paste. But, the right side shows possibilities.

I don't have the training to put down what I'm seeing in anything but the most rudimentary phrases. But, although I don't have a background in biology or animal husbandry, still have I eaten enough chickens to know the skeletal structure of a bird's wing when I see it. A furry-quilled bird's wing. A furry-quilled bird's wing that ends in a set of clawed fingers off-set by an opposable thumb.

And, yes—I know what I'm describing. Some sort of half-bird, half-chimp thing. It's large head (large enough to infer abnormal intelligence, perhaps) is crushed, but as best I can describe it, it is a furry bird's head, one with a beak half its size—a beak filled with teeth.

And before I go on I have to make something clear here and now. Don't think this is the alcohol talking. I'm a large man with quite a capacity. The two drinks I had, stiff as they were, were consumed hours earlier. I know what I'm seeing. There are teeth, sharp, needle-like teeth, rows of them, in this thing's beak. And by rows, I mean rows and rows. These teeth aren't arranged like ours, or like any mammal's or even a shark's. They cover the roof and base of the beak like lawns of grass.

And suddenly, I've just realized something. Clawed feet, clawed hands, large head, eyes set in the front—this thing is a predator. It *is* intelligent. It must be. Smart and dangerous. But, if that's the case, what is its prey? And…why has no one seen one before?

Hell—I think maybe two stiff drinks wasn't enough.

February 10

Damn. I don't know what else to say. There are stronger words, more violent, more shocking, but what would it matter to use them? In the dark of yesterday morning I was on top of the world. Then, in the light of dawn which followed I was hurled into the pit. Whatever I dreamed of doing with my discovery has evaporated.

Literally.

It has taken me a day to pull myself together and to be able to return to this journal to set down all that's happened. When I awoke yesterday morning, I found that I had passed out in the midst of my celebrating. Too much bourbon, too much excitement, too much adrenaline—all of it conspiring to render me useless before I finished my work.

Giddy foolishness—considering myself validated by my gift from God, sent to pull me out of the life I've earned for myself by squandering my talents and settling—always settling. College man, as if that shabby title meant anything anymore, as if I'd ever earned anything with it. And now, when blind and generous fate throws me a last bone, what do I do? I piss on it and flush it down the drain.

Self-pity. Always buy the giant economy size. Obviously I do.

I apologize to those who may read this, including myself. What is supposed to be a record of discovery is becoming a tear-sodden hysteric's grief rag. Perhaps a return to the facts will help.

My foolish drunken lark has resulted in tragedy. First off, I didn't wrap and freeze the remains as I'd planned. Too busy slapping myself on the back and refilling my victory mug. Second, and perhaps even more important, I made no visual records—no photos snapped, no video shot—even though both cameras had been laid out for such purpose.

I'm an idiot, and I've reaped a classic idiot's reward. Upon waking from my alcohol stupor, I returned to the kitchen to find my discovery had vanished—all of it, quills and claws and mashed innards—gone. Every sliver of bone and drop of bile. At first I suspected theft, some interloper come to steal away my great moment of fortune. The briefest reflection chased that notion away, however. Who would this thief be, since I hadn't told anyone about what I'd discovered? What intruder would see a smashed and dissected animal on the counter and gather it up? Last I heard, roving bands of delinquent bio-anthropologists are still rare in these parts.

Upon finally quieting my imagination and giving my more sober faculties (Ha—a play on words, that) a chance to observe the situation, I noted that the area of the counter on which I'd laid out my find had undergone a bit of a transformation. There was a blue-green stain to be found where I'd originally placed the body. The patch of discoloration was rectangular in shape, approximately the size of the newspapers I'd spread beneath the remains.

Bits of newspaper were to be found on the floor, all edges, all looking as if they'd been burned away from the main body of sheets I'd spread out. For lack of any better guess, all I can surmise from the meager facts at my disposal is that my find underwent some sort of...I don't know...spontaneous combustion? I discovered thin edges of char along the scraps of paper, but more, I found a pattern of smokey blue-green staining on the kitchen ceiling above the area where my find had been spread out.

I didn't go to work yesterday. Waking up late, spending hours searching the kitchen, my yard, everywhere for clues as to what might have happened—worse, trying to bestir myself from the funk that set in after I realized all I'd lost. Then the hours of sitting, staring, crying. What bourbon hadn't disappeared the night before was drained away then. Idiocy. Pathetic.

I'm at work today, however. Reporting that my "fever" has cleared, I've now cruised the vistas of our great state all morning, looking for the rotting flesh which is my calling.

My lunch hour is being spent in the rest stop off of mile 17 on Route 285. There were no reports sent in yesterday or so far today of any critter pies needing immediate attention, so even Beach-Ball was "understanding" in his treacly way over my absence. My drinking over two nights has left me with little appetite, however, so I'm using the time to make this entry—to try and determine what I can do next.

And, what is it I can do? I have memories of my discovery, and my notes, but nothing more. I have nothing I can show to anyone, nothing I can present anywhere that will gain me anything but ridicule and possibly suggestions to check into the benefits of therapy. But, Goddamnit, I know what I saw. I know what I held in my own two hands. I know the way it smelled, the odd plastic bristle touch of its fur, the orange and green globs wedged between its burst organs—

I know what I had. And I know what I have to do. If I could find one corpse, I can find another.

Even if I must create it myself.

April 13th

I've driven across Highway 19 every day since I lost hold of my discovery, but it's all been for nothing. I've covered thousands of extra miles over the past two months, tearing through the mountains to follow my appointed rounds, then heading immediately to that same spot to see if Providence has blessed me with another alien carcass. I've spent more hours than I can tell you driving these mountains, driving—especially at night—hoping to spot another of the beasts that I might run it down and reclaim my ticket to fame.

Slaughtering one's way to the top—not a new concept by any means, and not one that I find off-putting, either. But so far, nothing had given me any concrete hope that I shall ever be able to prove my great find was anything more than a drunken bit of make-believe.

Nothing, that is, until today.

Determined to put some sense to this all, I returned to the same spot where first I found the thing. This time, however, I thought to try a different approach. If mine were the only remains ever discovered in all of history of these creatures, then expecting another to show up with such speed suddenly seemed quite naïve. But, I thought, if I could find the exact spot where I had found the creature, I might be able to uncover a bit of proof that would at least help confirm for my own growing doubts if nothing else that what I experienced had all been real.

I did.

Sweeping away the leaves and other detritus along the roadway, I came across the exact location of the body I'd taken away. How could I be so certain, you ask? Because I found the same blue-green discoloration marks there on the macadam and the shoulder rocks and dirt as I had found in my kitchen—which remain there to this day on both the counter and the ceiling above. Experiments with mildew removers, abrasive cleansers and bleach haven't been able to diminish the soft colors in the slightest, the same as the elements of the mountains haven't been able to wear away the markings I've discovered here today.

I've gathered a number of large, flat stones to serve as a marker so that I might find this same spot instantly in the future. There's no way I could ever forget this stretch of road, but now the exact location is marked by more than just the tell-tale display of blue-green splotches.

I've also gathered up a number of loose stones colored by the creature's stain. Home with me they'll be going.

Finding and preserving these bits of evidence has convinced me that I did indeed experience everything as I imagined I had. Now, with this proof to spur me on, slight as it is, I've decided to change my tactics. I've assumed since the beginning that I'm the only person who's ever discovered such a beast.

Perhaps it's time to put that theory to the test.

June 23rd

I've searched the famed world wide web for any trace of any animal such as the one I found. None of the odd mutations I noted have appeared anywhere, in any other kind of beast—not even singly, let along in the combination I discovered. Even going to websites specifically designed for crypto-zoological interests, no one has ever even imagined such a thing.

Giving up on the Internet after roughly a week, I began to concentrate my search locally. Visiting all the major libraries in the state, I took out every book written on our local culture—histories, tour guides, farmer's memoirs, collections of myths and tall tales—anything at all that might've held even the barest hint of a lead.

I read them all, skimming obviously useless sections, but eyeing every page of every book. And still I found nothing—nothing that helped in any concrete way. Oh, there was a mention in Mildwin Zelanski's "Myths of the Mountain Regions" of a sort of migration of spectral lemmings that caught my interest. It concerned a legend of a wave of creatures that supposedly pours through the mountains every winter.

Following up, I discerned that indeed the mountain pass described in those pages was connected to the one where my marker still hugged the roadside. So, that area was known as a place inhabited by unusual beasts—things which visited the area but once a year. A migration from one hidden spot to another. Well, it would help explain why the things were rarely seen.

Finding this bit of confirmation has reaffirmed my resolve. Moreover, it has given me another idea.

Since this began I've been trying to prove what I know to be true by going to every outside source I can think of. It's now dawned on me while creating these pages that I got closer to the source by limiting my search—shrinking the boundaries of inquiry from the world to this single state. Now, I shall pull back again, moving from a statewide search to one of my own small department. After all, men have been performing this same task as mine for most of the last century. And, how blind we can be sometimes, they have been keeping records.

This is where I shall search next.

I have to admit I'm feeling very good about this idea.

June 30th

Haven't found anything in the old records, yet, but I have made a decision. Tonight I removed my kitchen counter top—not all of it, just the area containing the discolored rectangle—and have placed it under my bed along with the rocks I took away from the side of the road.

For some time I've been having the most nagging urge about my only bits of proof, that they weren't safe where they were. That I needed to make them more secure. Not all of the rocks have been placed under my bed, however. One of them, a mostly flat oval-shaped piece which, from the level of discoloration to be found on it, apparently took quite a heavy splashing, I keep with me at all times now.

Why?

What can I say? A good luck piece, a reminder of my true goal, a nag to keep me working—call it what you will, but I've found a great calm in making these changes.

It's all for the best.

September 5th

I am beginning to hate my job. There is a smugness to Beach-Ball that I now find intolerable. Thank God I don't have to look at his bloated face every day. Thank God that braying, puss-sac of a man never moves from behind his protective barrier of reports and safety awards.

He dared to question my mileage. Oh, he was clever enough about it. Commending me on my dedication, suggested a citation for the degree of efficiency. Claims he was wrong about me. Claims I'm the department's best employee.

What's he up to, I asked myself. At first I wondered if he knew about my discovery, if he wanted to know more about it, or even steal it. But even if he did know—even if that rodent, that flea, knew everything, what sense could he make of it?

God, how I hate him. If he bothers me again, I'm not sure what I might do.

September 13th

I was right! I'm not the first! Bless you Norbert Winston. God bless you for relenting at the end.

Since May I've worked at tracking down the records of every previous holder of my job. Most were simple men who kept brief, concise records. They weren't scholars, but neither were they ignorant. Even those who never saw the inside of a high school seemed remarkably more intelligent than many of today's college graduates. Still, none of them had anything in their records which held any real interest for me—except that one, wonderful predecessor of mine, Norbert Winston.

Norbert held the same illustrious position as myself during the late 1930s up through the 50s. He penned some forty-two journals for the Department of Roads and Transportation in that time. The first forty-one of them are quite readable studies of our mountains and valleys—his entries often wandering off into glorious studies of nature, both the flora and fauna and the God Norbert was certain had put them there in his solid, Protestant way of looking at things. It is toward the middle of the forty-second journal, however, where his positive, uplifting outlook on things took a sharp turn in another direction.

It starts after the entries for the second week of February, 1952. At that point there are some five pages torn out. There is no explanation given for the missing pages. They were simply removed. But, their absence is still a clue, bookmarking an interesting change in Norbert's overall attitude.

Suddenly his love affair with the wonders of the great outdoors and the forgiving God who created it all crashes to a distinct and irrefutable end. Although no explanation is offered within the remaining pages, Norbert's entries harden after the deletion. His outlook becomes that of the cynic, the doomsayer. The finding of a smashed deer becomes the excuse for a thirty-five paragraph rant on the futility of life. The onset of autumn is the cue for ten pages of dour rambling on the unfeeling, random nature of the universe.

It took no great degree of expertise in psychology while reading Norbert's forty-second journal to see that something had shaken him greatly. What, I had to wonder, had he seen? What had he found that'd terrorized his soul to such a depth? Of course, I thought I knew—was sure of it. But still, when one is trying to be scientific, jumping to conclusions is not a good practice.

Besides, what I had already was enough to inspire me. For forty-one and a half journals Norbert Winston wrote with the feeling and conviction of a deeply religious man. Indeed, some of his entries read like sonnets, odes to the glory of a great and kind Maker and His beautifully precise clockwork universe. But, after whatever Norbert experienced somewhere in the time covered in those cold, missing pages, that God existed for him no longer.

Beyond that point, Norbert referred to his Creator as "the fool," "the puppet," and many another derogatory label. "A blind and hopelessly lost idiot," he wrote at one point near the end of his last journal, "staring at an orange peel and proclaiming it proof of the sanctity of His glory, not aware that its fruit had been eaten by maggots."

What, I wondered in a fascinated rage, had Norbert witnessed that he'd found so distressing it shattered his entire world view? Reaching the final pages in his journal, I received my answer. In a manner of speaking, anyway.

Norbert's last entry implied he'd already confided in his younger sister the reasons for what he would be doing next. What he did next, oddly enough, was to commit suicide. By the end Norbert had found himself unable to work, to sleep, even to leave his own home. He ended his various phobias all at the same time with a double barrelled application of buckshot in his living room. A dramatic ending to his story, but not enough information to end mine. Which is why I tracked down the aforementioned sister. Eliena Winston—ancient, withered, but still alive, and close enough to the grave that she was finally willing to share her brother's story with someone else.

She had the missing five pages of his journal and with them she gave to me the peace of mind I've been searching for these past months. I'm not crazy. I did see what I thought I saw. I know so because Norbert Winston saw the same thing I did!

His description is not scientifically analytical, of course, but it matches. And really, it more than matches for he didn't find a corpse like I did—no! He saw the real thing. He saw Mildwin Zelanski's migration—hundreds of the creatures rolling through the mountain passes, running along erect, dancing, twirling, and more, Norbert not only saw them—he heard them! I quote him here as saying they sounded:

"Like hell things, like devils, monsters—worse—like machines. Living machines, obscene, piston-driven, steaming, hissing sacs of alien life, their jabber was a series of thin whistles that pierced the ear and condemned the soul."

I am reborn at this moment. I am a new man, a whole man. Reinvented, renewed, rejoicing. I know where to find my little things, and I know when. Excuse me while I find my friend, Mr. Daniels. We have much to celebrate, we two.

September 29th

Work has become a colossal pain.

First it means simply getting out of bed, something I am loath to do these days. And, why should I want to? What is there in the outside world for me until February? Blessed February, when my creatures will return. I've worked it all out, now.

They cross the mountains along the same route every year, at the same time. Going back to Zelanski's "Myths of the Mountain Regions," I found references that lead me to other authors. Surprisingly, our local legend has been investigated before. But no one has ever found its answer. They've found spore, tracks and scraped trees and tufts of fur no one could identify, but nothing else.

The reason is simple, of course. The things come through the mountains when the snow is far too deep for the casual observer to find them. Even Norbert Winston—he'd come across them while setting out traps. Had to reach the area on snow shoes. Had built himself a fortified windbreak where he planned to spend several days. That's where he was—sleeping—when they rolled through the pass he was in.

How can anyone expect me to care about anything else, when I know my creatures are coming?

✠ ✠ ✠

October 18th

Beach-Ball knows. He *knows*.

He called me into his office today. All nervous smiles and sweaty. Could see the fear in his eyes. Lot of people the same ever since I stopped wasting time on showers and soap and all. Told me people were complaining about the smell. And that wasn't all. He tried telling me my work was getting sloppy. I laughed at him. Called him a liar. Asked him which one of my roads wasn't spotless.

He hedged, saying it wasn't the roadwork, but my bagging. Said my tags weren't in order. Said more, but I didn't listen.

No, not that I didn't listen. It was more than I couldn't hear him. Him on one side of the desk, sitting, leering, me on the other, standing, judging. His words weren't important enough to hear. They faded, erased by the voice in my mind that just keeps whispering the magic word.

February.

November 5th

Don't know what kept me from thinking of this sooner. Today I begin the building of my stronghold. My vantage point. I have the plans all worked out in my head.

Fate has made this all too easy for me. I drive the mountains every day in a pick-up truck. How simple to take my supplies to my chosen site and drop them off, working a bit every day until the grand project is finished.

It'll have to be strong and it'll have to be warm. I have to be able to survive within it for two weeks. Of course, I might spend only a day or two in it before my diligence is rewarded, but I have to be prepared for the long haul. Whenever they show during those two magical weeks of February, I must be ready.

And ready means "dry." My stronghold will have to be watertight, as well. I'll need too much delicate equipment—video camera, tape recorders, a phone, a heater, some sort of generating system—can't risk the elements. It'll have to be high, above the snow line. And it'll have to be camouflaged.

And then, of course, the traps.

I'm going to be so busy.

✠ ✠ ✠

November 24th

Saw myself in the mirror today. One of those rare days when I returned home. Was hungry. Don't bother so much these days with food. No time. No need. Petty concern. Foolish.

Still, the pain tore my belly, so I tried to find something to placate it. Kitchen was bare. Remembered the last time I ate at home. Same thing—hungry. Only found some tea bags and dried beans. It was enough. Today, though, kitchen finally empty. That's what sent me to the bathroom.

My look has changed somewhat. Thinner. Eyes red, hollow, dark. Not sleeping enough, I guess. But, no surprise—there's no time. More foolishness. Beard getting longer. Bristly. Look like I should be selling cough drops. Notion makes me chuckle—then I remember.

Toothpaste.

Doesn't taste bad at all. I fill my pockets with extra tubes, plus bars of soap. Good for snacks.

December 15th

My hideaway is finished. Built strong. Dry. Warm. Would live there now but must not attract attention. Beach-Ball getting harder to deal with. Wants me to shave, bathe, explain my reports.

No longer sloppy about tagging. Took care of that immediately. Can not chance anyone finding out what I am doing. Tags have been perfect. No—now he claims discrepancies in my reports. Says I've written up tags for bundles that I never delivered to the incinerator.

Threatened my job. Can't risk that. Need my truck. Need my roads. Told him all the tags were legitimate. He said explain. Told him a man gets hungry.

Didn't take it well. Started shaking. I smiled at him to make him feel better. He started shaking worse. Told me to get out of his office. Idiot.

Eight more weeks. I can bear him for eight more weeks. Or I could just kill him.

Like I said—a man does get hungry.

December 27th

Awoke from sleeping in the middle of the night. The dreams were screaming at me. Do not bother with the bed anymore. Sleep on my proof. Need the feel of it. Smooth formica against my skin. Plastic smell so reassuring. My time coming.

January 8th

Beginning to think my proof is in danger. Afraid to leave any of it at home when I travel my roads. Took a hammer to the rocks. Made the pieces as small as I could. Ate them.

Scraped the stain from the counter with my plane. Big curls of happy formica. Ate them, too. Everything is safe now.

January 13th

Beach-Ball called me into his office today. Told me I had been given all the chances I was going to get. Said I was an embarrassment. Told me I was fired.

Caved his head in with his safety award. Dragged him to my truck. Just finished storing him in my stronghold. Fat bastard finally making himself useful. Have to admit—so far he tastes better than soap.

February 3rd

Fourth day within my stronghold. Snow still wonderfully high. Cold useful preserving Beach-Ball. Half of him?

Started with the feet so we could talk up until the end. He has actually proven to be quite funny away from the office. Glad now I killed him. He needed to get out.

Miss the office, my work—some, anyway. Curious, too. Wonder what they think—Beachy and I disappearing the same day. Left my truck miles away. No one on the road for over a week. Just snow.

No one can find us. Beachy says we are safe. Seems more anxious than me for arrival of the Yon'suna.

Know their names now. Ever since I made the proof of them a part of me, the dreams come clearer. I understand so much. Hard to explain. Angles of time flowing through the mountains. Planet has to reach certain harmony, bridges two realities for only a few moments each year.

Parade of the Yon'suna never ends. Continuous throughout time. Runs through all of space. Servitors, they are. Living in all realities…but not really. How to explain?

The proof told me, but what are the words I need to tell you? You?

Who are you?

February 8th

Have not slept for two days now. No need. Only need wait for the Yon'suna. Blessed Yon'suna. They who march the never-ending length of the Great One. They who search and clean and care for He who is All.

Existing in all places, dread opposite of the Lord of the Great Abyss, our fearsome Father who must be attended—the magnificent lengths of Him searched and cleaned and cared for—I have seen all I need to see, know all. Now, I but await their arrival so I might—

✠ ✠ ✠

That noise? The snow too high. Nothing can reach this area. What can it...the police? Here? Now?

They've heard me. Coming. Searched my computer at home. Found my truth as I found Norbert's. Begging me not to resist.

Not to resist? How can I not? Great Yog-Sothoth must be served, His stunning iridescence must be groomed! Our Father, who art the key to the gate, whereby the spheres meet, I am coming, my Lord, my Liege, my *God, SAVE ME...*

✠ ✠ ✠

Editor's note: At this point Mr. Cropton's entries ceased as officers Fred Sutton and Dolores Hanover caught up to him as he tried to flee across the snow. They report that Mr. Cropton was easily subdued. This abbreviated version of his journal has been submitted to the court as proof that no trial is needed, and so that his commitment to Brenwood Sanitarium can be facilitated as quickly as possible.

It is known by writers that sometimes characters take over a story, and in return, they bring the writer along for the ride. But sometimes readers have expectations of these literary creations, and when the characters don't do what readers expect, readers are occasionally disappointed. But what happens when the characters become rebellious, defiant? After all, there are literary precepts that must be obeyed. Characters can only go so far...

THAT'S THE ONE

"THAT'S THE ONE!"

The two officers continued to move in on the young blond girl as the tiny bottle kept screaming,

"That's her! She won't drink me. I keep flashing my tag at her, she picks me up, reads it, sniffs, and then she just puts me back down. Over and over and *over!*"

"We'll handle this," interrupted the senior officer. Turning toward the somewhat frightened girl, he asked, "All right, then, what's the story, Alice?"

"Please, sir," she answered, "I'm afraid."

"Afraid of what?"

"The fall down the rabbit hole was so awfully terrifying. I don't want to go on any further. I just want to go back home." The junior of the two enforcers had already positioned himself behind the girl. Holding the indignant bottle in his hand, the older of the pair said,

"Alice, you *have* to go on into Wonderland. You can't just go back home. That's not the way the story goes. You can't just go back the way you came—no one can. One must always struggle forward against the world no matter how absurd it seems." The senior officer sniffed absently at the air, then added,

"My dear, you have literary precepts to reinforce."

"I don't care," wailed the crying girl. "I want to go home!"

The older man with the bottle nodded. His partner grabbed Alice, holding her firmly. Quickly they pried her jaws apart and forced most of the bottle's contents down her throat.

Mike closed the magazine at that point. "Too bizarre," was his only comment on the story he had been reading as he put it aside.

Besides, he thought, I'm just stalling.

Mike picked up the gun again. He had bought it two days after she had left. It had gotten to the point where he could no longer remember how many times he had taken it from its box, cleaned it, loaded it, placed it in his mouth…and then backed down. The wastebasket was overflowing with crumpled suicide notes.

The newest one, fresh from his printer, lay on his desk looking up at him. Staring at the letter, he fumblingly picked up the revolver once more. Closing his eyes he slipped the barrel between his lips and began tightening his finger around the trigger—and then, once more, he set the heavy piece of metal back down on the table and walked away from it.

But, this time he did it for a different reason.

Suddenly he realized—he was being more than foolish—he was acting childishly and just plain stupid.

"I don't *have* to do this. I don't have to do *anything*. It's my life, Goddamnit! If I want to keep living it, then all I have to do is keep on living it!"

Mike smiled. No matter how definite his only course of action had seemed to be to take his own life, that had passed. He knew now he would not kill himself. When the door to his apartment started to open, he was feeling more content and at peace than he had in years. By the time his squeaking hinge caused him to look toward the door, the officers were already inside.

"That's the one!" screamed the revolver, huffing with indignation. "That's him!"

The path of least resistance is most commonly treaded. That is to say, people often take the easy way out. As with most tales in this collection, "A Happy Mother Takes Away Pain" does not follow that path. C.J. tackles social themes that are sometimes difficult to speak of directly. And that is the beauty of fiction. We as readers can turn away from the horror contained within fiction at any time, ignoring anything too painful. Still, for those who persist, catharsis can be found, both inside and outside of the story. This is a story of persistence.

A HAPPY MOTHER TAKES AWAY PAIN

THE WOMAN STOOD IN the shower, relaxing under the steaming splash of water cascading onto her from above. She had finished cleaning herself some time earlier. Now, she wished only to relax, to be herself, or more specifically, to be free of the voices and the pain of humanity.

The woman was a psychometrist, one who could tell the age of a stone by touching it, or know the lies within one's soul by staring into their eyes. Thus, she was not merely washing away perspiration, but also cleaning herself of both the filthy linger of humanity, the obnoxious stares and thoughts and miscellaneous dreams picked up from the riff raff as they stared at her, as well as the assorted bits of nightmare and horror adrift in the ether which constantly found their way to her despite her best efforts.

Turning up the heat, she treated herself to another few minutes of steaming luxury as she thought;

"I do not believe I could live in *any* other city in this country. Most people do not know it, but the water here in New York is the finest tap water in all the Americas." Eyes closed, she moved her neck back and forth against the roasting stream, telling herself;

"It is why the bagels taste so good here, better than those made *anywhere* else. The water…it is just so…*pure*."

Obviously such a consideration was more important to her than most others. After all, when *anything* that comes in contact with one's skin *immediately* releases images to their brain, flooding them with every aspect of that thing's history…purity in anything becomes a huge selling point. One of her acquaintances had gasped when they accidentally noted the total of her water bill. She tried to keep that fact in mind whenever she stepped into the tub to take a shower, but somehow she always ended up simply standing beneath the cascade, eyes closed, enjoying those few, free moments when the world was kept at bay.

finally removing herself from the shower, looking at the time readout on the small battery clock on the shelf above her sink, she smiled sadly as she thought;

"I may have to admit that perhaps I do spend too much time here."

The woman wanted to chastise herself, thinking of her ever-expanding water bill, if nothing else, but she could not. Because of her ability, it was almost the only place she found relaxing, that could put her at peace. Toweling herself, working the water out of her extremely long black hair, a voice from the back of her mind countered, asking;

"Where else can I be myself—*free* from prying eyes and random thoughts? *Free* from the noise and stink and nonsense of the crowds?"

She had no good answer. Beginning to dress, she sighed with each piece of clothing she pulled into place. Her underwear, surprisingly, was frilly. It was not exotic; it was not sexy. She had no need for sexy underwear, having no one close enough for whom she could wear it. But, it was pretty, charming, and at the end of the day when she would undress, could shed the armor she needed to protect herself from the world's vision, it allowed her to remember she was still a woman.

She stared at herself in the mirror for a moment, enjoying the idea that she was a female while she could. Then, she realized it was almost time for the world to come crashing in on her, and she bent to the task of covering her legs and arms, body and head, rapidly assembling the skirt and blouse, shawl and socks and gloves and boots and all the formless, drab camouflage she needed to hide herself from the staring, mindlessly gibbering planet all about her.

As she continued to ready herself for the day, her mind brought forth a snippet of memory—a chance moment, hearing a policeman speak about his kevlar vest. It had saved his life, stopping a bullet which otherwise would have killed him. One would think he would have been happy about such a thing, but he was not. The officer had grown to despise the vest. Not because it had saved his life—he was not a disturbed individual. He was merely a sad one.

What bothered him about the vest was his *need* for it, the fact that he could not go out in public without it. Or, more correctly...it was the fact that he actually *could* go out in public without it if he so desired...but that he was afraid to do so.

Having finished dressing, feeling the impulses focused on her from the outside, she walked straight for the front door of her building, her hand on the door's knob even as the doorbell rang for the first time. She was not expecting a client, but she had felt for some time the attention of the person who wanted her help. As she turned the knob—as the motion stretched fabric from her shoulder to her wrist—her mind spoke of the policeman to her.

She understood his fear all too well. After all, the slightest random touch from a stranger could overwhelm her, flooding her with all of their past in an instant. Failed romances, fist fights, screaming matches, all of it, all their pains and humiliations, all their failures and horrible, petty miseries—rammed inside her brain as if she were a child refusing medicine that needed to be forced down her throat. The way the officer felt about his vest, that was how she felt about all clothing.

Pulling the door open as the person outside was about to ring the bell once more, she discovered a woman of Middle Eastern descent. She was a modern woman, not festooned with a burka, but appearing more to be some kind of middle level corporate manager, or perhaps an administrative assistant of some sort.

"Hello," said the woman on the doorstep. "I beg your pardon, but—"

"Yes, I know. You've come in search of The Eyes of God. That is the name by which you know me."

"You are—"

The woman's voice dropped off as she who had answered the door turned and began to walk away, leaving the woman standing alone in the doorway. Caught off guard, the woman on the stoop stammered a few syllables, to which she was told;

"Yes, I am she whom you seek. If you would pursue your matter further, enter my home and close the door behind you."

The woman, only slightly put off, entered the brownstone, shutting the door and following her hostess to the living room. Even though the sun was high in a near cloudless sky, the windows were heavily draped. Several oil lamps were burning to light the room, a convenience the visitor suddenly thought might only have been lit for her. As she stared, her hostess poured tea into two cups, saying;

"I enjoy none of the titles by which I am known. My name is Lai Wan. Please, sit. Have some tea. Tell me your wish."

"My name is In'da Bin Goden. I..." the woman's voice trailed off for a moment, then she said, "two cups, as if you were expecting me. At the door, the same thing. I..." Holding her tea cup in her hands, waiting for it to cool just a tad so she might take her first sip, Lai Wan answered;

"I have felt you searching for me for several days. Once I knew you would arrive now, I prepared myself for the ordeal and had my home made ready. Now, please...tell me your wish."

"My mother is very ill," said In'da. "The doctors...they don't know what it is."

"I was under the impression they had told you she was suffering from a combination of Alzheimer's and Parkinson's."

"How?" In'da gasped slightly. Shock in her voice, she stammered, "H-H-How can you, do you...what? I didn't..."

"Listen to me, In'da Bin Goden; you are an open book to me. I know what you know. If I could not know such a simple thing, why would you have bothered to come here?" Controlling her frustration, trying to remind herself how unnerving a display of her abilities could be, Lai Wan finally allowed herself a sip of tea, then said quietly;

"Now, I will ask you for the last time...tell me...*what* do you wish?"

In'da unconsciously picked up her tea cup. Holding it close to her chest, clutching it, she said, "I know the doctors are wrong. I can feel it. There is something else going on, something that none of these, these..."

"Westerners."

And then, In'da began to cry. Lai Wan waited patiently, sipping at her tea, listening as the woman across from her forced her story out as best she could. The psychometrist could tell In'da was a typical modern woman, hating the mother she loved and killing herself for her perceived disloyalty. There was nothing new in it for Lai Wan, except the level of In'da's suffering and fear. Because of her abilities, she could see the daughter's entire life within her head. There was nothing about her relationship with her mother that should have been able to cause her such pain. There was also no doubt whatsoever in Lai Wan's mind that they loved each other.

Indeed, everything she could see and feel told her the pair were simply an ordinary mother and daughter, sometimes fighting, sometimes not. The psychometrist understood this. She knew that just as sons need to prove certain things to themselves by defying their fathers, so too do daughters need to become women in their own right by breaking with their mothers.

"My mother and I did the same dance," she thought quietly, "as she did with her mother, and she with hers."

But, even as Lai Wan knew that simple fact, she also knew if that was all she had felt when In'da Bin Goden had first started to search for her, her door would never have been opened to the woman. Somehow she knew there was more at work between the daughter and mother than simple guilt—knew that in the back recesses of her mind, that even In'da could feel it.

Once the woman finally made her plea, begging Lai Wan to come to her mother's hospital, to examine the old woman and make her own diagnosis, the psychometrist agreed. More than a little curious, she dared the outside world to discover what the unusual vibration was she was picking up from the frightened woman in her living room.

At the hospital, Lai Wan did the best she could to shield herself from the pain assaulting her from every room. When they finally reached In'da's mother's room, Lai Wan was slightly taken aback at the mother's condition. The old woman looked brittle to her—like ancient candy, so old its sugar had turned to dust. That was not what disturbed her, however.

Standing next to the mother's bed, she could feel pain radiating from the old woman. Not the physical pain one expects in a hospital. What she was sensing was something more—something dark and unpleasant.

"This," the back of her mind whispered, "is not going to be agreeable."

In'da, flustered, looking small and weak as she pointed politely to her mother, asked quietly;

"Can you tell anything...I mean...from there, here...er, ah..." In'da forced herself to stop talking, struggling to take control of herself—desperate to understand why she was so flustered. Facing Lai Wan, afraid she might displease the psychometrist and drive her away, she asked fearfully;

"I'm sorry. I'm just…tired, I suppose. Please, excuse me. Just tell me what to do."

"Stop apologizing, for one thing." Lai Wan said the words softly, her attention on the old woman before her. Not turning from the unmoving form in the bed, she added in a far away voice, "You were correct to bring me here. Even after these very few moments I am certain of it. Truthfully, I believed that to be so before we left my home." When In'da responded with confusion, Lai Wan explained;

"You have been here with your mother enough that much of what is afoot here has left its scent on you. You have sensed these things yourself, which is why you sought me out. I tell you now, you were not incorrect." Moving a step forward, the psychometrist added;

"But, to tell anything more, I must be in contact with your mother. Please move to one side that I might touch her."

So saying, Lai Wan approached the bed. As her hands moved toward the old woman, she could feel her daughter in the background, taste the panic written across her face. Handing In'da a handkerchief for the tears she could smell rolling down her cheeks, the psychometrist thought;

"Those who call me Mother Voodoo and Second-Sight Sarah, how I wish they had no reason for such labels. There is no doubt this reading will prove disturbing. Misery hangs in the air about this woman like soot around a chimney."

Her hands but millimeters away from the old woman's face, Lai Wan reached for the woman's head, the only exposed skin. Regarding the old woman with suspicious eyes, her hands still not quite touching her, she thought;

"Something is wrong here—something in the air, something that burns with a corruption I have encountered before."

As Lai Wan's hands finally came in contact with the old woman's face, she went stock still, all her concentration thrown forth into her probing.

"Something…"

And then, Lai Wan broke contact with the old woman, pulling her hands away from the wrinkled head—quickly—like a child finally learning what it felt like to play with fire.

"Oh, no…"

She stepped back looking shaken—frightened. Staring down at the unconscious old woman in disbelief, her eyes unblinking, her mouth dried on her suddenly, turning her voice to a near silent croaking as she whispered;

"Not *again*."

LAI WAN AND IN'DA sat in the visitor's room at the end of the hall. They had left the old woman's room because, despite her coma, the psychometrist did not want her to hear what she had to tell the daughter. Avoiding looking into the daughter's eyes, Lai Wan was just about to finally say something when In'da spoke first.

"Please," she said. "You're beginning to frighten me. What is it? What did you see, or ah, feel, or..." Finally able to meet the other woman's gaze, Lai Wan told her:

"When I lay on hands I do not merely gather impressions. I enter that which is another person's mind and soul combined. I merge within the reality which they create for themselves."

The psychometrist spoke slowly. Cautiously. In'da Bin Goden was by that point nothing more than a gaggle of wounded nerves. Straining to tell what she must without causing a panic or a scene, Lai Wan continued, saying;

"From this vantage, nothing can be hidden. Not the physical or the mental. Which does allow me to give you some small comfort...Your mother has neither Parkinson's or Alzheimer's."

Only as she said the words did the psychometrist realize her mistake. Before any warning could be given, In'da sprang forward unexpectedly, catching Lai Wan up in a strangle hold hug. Horrified, she attempted to pull back, but it was too late to escape the daughter's clutches, too late to prevent what had to happen next.

Even as In'da sputtered random phrases of thanks and relief, a thing which could only be described as a demon appeared within the room. In truth it was not really there, was actually merely an image the daughter was picking up from Lai Wan. But that was enough to pull comprehensionless screams from the woman.

Horrid as it was, the monstrosity could have been worse. The thing which appeared for only a flashing instant was no soldier demon, not a fighter or a great worker of magicks. It was the most minor of such things—a slob, really—a sneak thief, a generator of boils. A nobody.

Not a thing all muscles and horns and power, it was instead a small creature—some four feet high. It was disgusting, however, all snot and boils and drooping moustache, sharp but crooked teeth, scraggly hair, wild tufts growing out of every part of its body, thick, cracked nails, running sores, drool dripping from its mouth, and so forth.

Its legs and arms were horribly spindly, its abdomen bloated, its rear sloppy with fat. None of that made In'da scream, however. Not its pointed ears or its wild, bushy eyebrows, not its pocked skin or the thick fluids which oozed out of various breaks in its skin. No, what had made In'da Bin Goden scream had been its wildly evil, pathetic eyes, and the misery they promised.

The thing disappeared nearly as quickly as it had appeared. Pushing herself away from Lai Wan as she screamed, curling into a tight sack of tired flesh against the wall, she demanded;

"What was *that*?! What the hell was that?"

Staring coldly, Lai Wan snapped;

"Never touch me without my *invitation—never*!"

"I'm sorry," the woman apologized. "I'm so sorry, but that thing—that thing! What *was* that?"

"That was an image you picked up from my mind; it is the demon tormenting your mother." In'da made to protest, but Lai Wan cautioned her to silence, explaining;

"Listen to me carefully. Many of those giving the appearance of Alzheimer's, Down Syndrome, Tourette, and so forth, are really victims of demonic possession. These diseases really exist, of course, and in the vast majority of cases they are what their victims are suffering from."

In her most comforting, yet authoritative voice, Lai Wan continued to talk, explaining to In'da that over the centuries various beyond things, for lack of a better term, had learned to torment their victims in manners which allow them to remain undetected. In far earlier times these creatures would have been called demons. But that was back when their antics were obvious—and easily spotted.

"Now, they have refined their aggression," the psychometrist explained. "No suspicion of possession means no exorcism."

"You're saying my mother needs an exorcist?"

"No," answered Lai Wan. Entirely calm and self-possessed once more, she answered, "She needs no outsider.

"She needs you."

"But how," asked In'da. The woman wanted to help her mother, and although frightened, was ready. "How? I mean, what can I do?"

In control of the situation this time, Lai Wan said simply, "Give me your hand."

In'da did as instructed and, before she could even blink, let alone question why she should do such, suddenly she found herself along with Lai Wan, the two of them somehow transported to what had once been a fabulous Oriental garden. In truth, if one looked closely, one could still see traces of its one-time glory, but now most of that lay in shambles—overgrown, befouled, tangled. Grey—ruined.

Everywhere the pair looked, they saw intricate fountains festooned with orchids, flower beds surrounding weeping willows, dainty waterfalls and all manner of beauty, now overgrown and made ugly and twisted by some invading force. After a moment, it became evident that there was a central plaza to the garden which had been completely overgrown with thorns and weeds, with thickets bearing poisonous fruit and steam-spewing, pus-covered vines.

Oddly enough, if one looked closely, they could note that the grass and flowers and the such of the garden have not disappeared; they had simply been overgrown. Underneath the alien invasion they still appeared to be perfect. As they wandered slowly through the near silent landscape, In'da asked;

"Wh-where are we?"

"We have not left the hospital," answered the psychometrist. "You are still sitting in your chair. But we are also on the dream plane. More specifically, we are on that section of the dream plane where it intersects with your mother's mind. We are, essentially, walking through her self-image." Looking around wildly, In'da blurted;

"I don't...don't understand."

"In'da, you understand that every individual creates their own reality, do you not? As John Milton said: 'The mind is its own place, and in itself can make a Heav'n of Hell, a Hell of Heav'n.'"

Lai Wan paused for a moment, giving the other woman a chance to soak in what she had said, then added;

"In other words, whatever we see within our head colors our perception of what we see in the world around us."

"You mean..."

"Yes—we are walking within your mother's soul."

In'da waved her hands all about, practically spinning about as she shrieked;

"*This?* This is my mother's *soul?*"

Lai Wan reached out, taking In'da's arm gently as she told her;

"It is, but it is being poisoned by a demon which has made its way into your mother's heart. If I recognize the signs, this is the work of a creature known as *Shaitan*—one of the *Djinn*."

"What can we do?"

"*We* can do nothing. What must be done can only be done by you." Staring into In'da's eyes, the psychometrist told her, "You must engage the djinn in combat and destroy it."

"Me—fight a demon? Are you insane?" The daughter touched her chest absently, reacting with a frightened jump as if the sensation had come from another. Her head trembling madly, she whimpered;

"I can't—it's *impossible*...I, what would, this is madness, I, I...I..."

With the speed of thought Lai Wan made a swirling motion with her arms. Immediately In'da found the psychometrist in front of her, holding her arms at her sides, her eyes blazing as she stared into In'da's, hissing;

"Your mother is in the grips of this creature. It can, and most certainly does on a routine basis, cause her unending, unbearable pain."

"But..." Shaking the woman, her voice inching up into a snarl, Lai Wan snapped;

"You listen to me, In'da Bin Goden, your mother's intellect and emotions and thoughts will be consumed by this thing—bit by bit, morsel by morsel—until there is not enough of her mind left to generate a steady stream of drool over her gibbering lips."

"No."

"You know that I am telling you the truth. You can feel it in the air here. You came to me because you wanted your mother released from her pain. There is only one way she can be released, and that is if you take action. But then..."

And at that point, the psychometrist released her hold on the other woman, stepping back from her as she said;

"You do not really like your mother all that much, do you?"

Shocked, partly at what had been said, partly that she who said the words could suspect their power, In'da snapped;

"How dare you?!"

"You forget," Lai Wan gently reminded the daughter, "once you open yourself to me, all is revealed. You might love your mother out of instinct, mouthing the words out of habit, but the two of you have never gotten along."

Spinning away from the psychometrist, shutting her eyes as she did so, In'da screamed;

"Be *quiet!*"

But it was too late for any kind of tactical retreat for In'da Bin Goden, either from Lai Wan's words, or from the situation into which she had willingly placed herself. Their invasion of the mother's mind had gone on too long. They had walked the corridors of her soul defiantly, without guile or whispers, and as one must expect, they had finally been observed.

"My, my—my-my-my—what have we here?"

A monstrous form, humanoid roughly, but shattered, with bones sticking through its skin, with features mounted in the wrong place, appeared before the pair, its floppingly long tongue wagging in the air before them. Sitting on a large rock in the middle of a great stand of cattail reeds, the thing somehow stuck out its hand and stroked In'da's chin with its clawlike nail as it chuckled;

"It's the beloved daughter, come a'calling." Even as In'da pulled back, the oddly-jointed thing was somehow still at her side. Running another hand over her back, up toward her skull, it cooed;

"What a lovely, long neck you have—my—my-my-my—uummmmmm, so tasty looking. Tell me, are you tasty?"

From the side, Lai Wan caught In'da's attention, letting her know that if she wished, they could abandon the garden at the speed of thought.

"Merely tell me you would leave your mother to this odious thing," she assured In'da, "and we shall depart immediately."

Before the daughter could react, the demon caught her in a powerful handhold, wheeling about to confront Lai Wan at the same time. While In'da trembled in fear in the thing's grasp, it spat at the psychometrist;

"The Dreamwalker—that explains much. Keep your advice to yourself, bitch. This ungrateful tramp and I are just getting to know each other."

"You have no say in this matter, eater of offal. If In'da wishes you dispelled, you shall be flung to the desert winds without a thought."

"You think me dismissed so easily?" The demon ran its hands relentlessly over In'da's body, almost singing its words as it answered, "You wound me, deathwhore. Oh wait, no—you can't. No one can dislodge me from *this* soul!"

To this, Lai Wan could only sneer. Pointing a finger forward toward both In'da and the demon, she cried out;

"Whose ears are your lies aimed at? Mine? You know I am not so easily fooled? Hers? But she is already here, ready to destroy you—and so your lies could not trick her." Advancing on the demon, her finger still stabbing the air, the psychometrist added;

"Maybe you hope to fool *yourself*. Could you, *djinn*? Could you lie yourself brave?"

Enraged, the oddly shaped sack of life released its hold on In'da, shoving her to the ground so it could move forward on Lai Wan. Its clawed toes drawing irregular circles in the dust, it growled;

"Defy me all you will, dreamwalker. You have no power here."

"'Tis true, beast," Lai Wan admitted. "In this instance I can not order you from this place. But…" With a slowly forming, deadly smile spreading across her lips, the psychometrist pointed to In'da and said;

"She can."

Without hesitation, the demon wheeled about and moved on In'da once more. Embracing her, it licked her body with its long, sore-covered tongue, answering;

"My darling In'da, stop what she, herself, has set in motion? You can't be serious, dreamwalker. You forget…she's the one that invited me in here."

And then, the demon's voice became a wicked, chastising laugh as it detailed how every rejection of her mother's advice, every turning of a deaf ear to what her mother had to tell her, every time she had tossed her head and sadly pitied her mother's feeble little mind…because, after all…She knew so much better than she who had given her birth, had thrown open the doors to its arrival. Its arms multiplying into dozens, it grabbed and pinched and teased its newest victim, reminding her;

"After all, with your mother always criticizing, always picking-pickingpicking, always so annoying, so demanding, giving you so much interference…why, what else could you do but invite me in to shut the old bitch up?"

With those words, the demonic presence seemed to have pushed the woman trembling within its rude grasp too far. With an impossible strength, something which could only have been found on the dreamplane, In'da rebelled, pushing her way loose of the demon's smothering grasp. Stumbling backwards, she screamed that she could not have called the thing, that the idea was absurd. After all, who knew how to summon demons?

To her protestations, however, the demon merely smiled, rows of broken teeth with leaves and bugs and a Slim Jim wrapper stuck within them exposed as it did so. Licking its lips, it assured her;

"But you did, every time you groaned when your mother asked for a favor, every time you dragged your feet when she needed your help…every time you cursed the sound of her voice, you were naught but a lighthouse, guiding me to her shore."

In'da screamed her defiance. It was an agonizing sound, mere tone and fury on the one hand, but the throat-tearing noise captured all attention and threw the focus to her. Drawing herself to her full height, the woman commanded;

"No! I cast you out. Begone from this place!"

It was a superb performance, one for which the demon took the time to show its appreciation. While it applauded, it smiled, criticizing her delivery.

"Yes, nicely done," it admitted. "Good, round tones. But really, you pathetic bundle of knucklemeat…You really didn't think it was going to be that easy, did you?"

Leaping forward, the demon grabbed In'da. Wrapping its various appendages around her once more, it sneered as it reminded her how she had spent years defying her mother, ignoring her every word, putting her off, hating her. Its grip grew tighter at the daughter's inability to refute its claims.

"Did you actually believe a measly few words, no matter how heartfelt for the moment, were going to send me running for the door?" Spinning In'da around, its fingers wrapped within her hair, the thing mocked her as it revealed;

"Foolish cow—you don't even truly believe that you're here. You reek of the fear that this could all be true, that your mother's pain could be your fault."

Laughing, the demon sent In'da spinning, splashing down into the mud, a great clump of her hair remaining in the thing's scaly fist. Oddly enough, in the ethereal reality, she could see the trail of blood this left flying through the air. As she sobbed on the ground, the demon whispered yet more truth to her;

"Such weakness merely makes me stronger, foolish bitch."

And with that, the demon flipped In'da over in the mud. Before she had even landed, face in the thick sludge, it straddled her, rubbing itself over her body, its bizarre form rolling this way and that across her spine, through her fingers, against the backs of her knees, much of it opening into one giant mouth which drooled monstrously over her, spewing;

"Your mother is *mine*! *You* gave her to me!"

In'da struggled beneath the horrid thing's cruel weight, but she could not free herself. The demon laughed at what it considered her last gram of defiance. Sneering, it chided the daughter for her ingratitude, reminded her of how it had listened to her pleas, her throbbing entreaties for someone—anyone—to spare her of the burden of her mother.

"Indeed, I rush to your aid," it added in a wounded tone, "pull your mother as neatly from your back as you might pick up a pin, and what 'thanks' do I get? None at all."

Then, somehow suddenly on its feet once more, the demon presence lifted and threw In'da across the garden. She screamed as long as she was airborne, then went abruptly silent as she hit something which sounded both solid and heavy back in the overgrown brush. Tearing hair from its body, the thing danced in the mud, screaming to the heavens;

"*None!*"

While the horror cavorted, Lai Wan appeared at In'da's side. Gently, she cradled the woman's head in her hands, telling her;

"Do remember, all of this is only as real as you wish it to be. You are not here. You are not hurt." Gasping through broken, bleeding lips, In'da murmured;

"But the pain…"

As a storm broke overhead, darkening most of the garden, even as its lightning illuminated selected flashes of it, Lai Wan held a finger before In'da's face, telling her that the pain of which she spoke was;

"Born of your guilt." She gave the thought only an instant to sink in, then added, "Do not give in to the djinn or your mother will be lost."

Dancing under the ever increasing lightning, the demon, its rubbery skin slick with rain, screeched to the shattered sky;

"Foolish bitch! You've changed nothing by bringing this ungrateful baggage here. She gave me this soul years ago. The thoughts and memories I've stolen, given to me, freely they were, on a platter fashioned from the finest hate—"

And then, the demon halted its gyrations, turning to stare with laughing eyes at In'da as it added;

"And inlaid with the purest selfishness I have ever seen."

Pulling herself up, In'da rebelled against the horror's words, reborn in fury. Savagely, she grabbed up a thick branch from the ruined garden, hefting in both hands with menace as she screamed;

"NNNNOOOOOOOOOOOOOOO!! I didn't do this to my mother.

I didn't give her to you!" Swinging her weapon wildly, sometimes connecting with the shifting form, sometimes not, she swore to it;

"Not on purpose!"

Another swing slammed her weapon against the demon.

"Yes, we disagreed. We fought over stupid things. But I never wanted you in her life…"

Another swing missed, turning the daughter completely around. As the demon stopped jumping to laugh, his closed eyes brought him a smashing blow to the head as In'da cried;

"Never!"

Beginning to feel the sting of the daughter's strikes, the demon reformed itself, flinging three of its appendages into In'da's midsection, knocking her away. A second salvo sent them flying forth once more, this assault leaving her face torn and gashed. Spitting into her wounds, the demon shouted;

"Liar!"

As the bleeding woman wavered on the edge of collapse, Lai Wan appeared at her side once more. Whispering into her ear, she said;

"Shaitan has not the brains to lie about this. If you are to win through you must strip away all falsehood." And then, fixing the woman with her gaze, the psychometrist told her;

"You can not speak the truth if you can not bear to know it."

And, at those words In'da gasp in horror.

"Oh my God…" Struggling to rise, stiff, bleeding and broken, In'da cried, "It's true. There were those moments…when, when I just couldn't take it any more. When I would think to myself, if only she'd shut up, if she would just leave me alone…"

Looking around her, staring into the design of the garden, seeing her mother in every leaf, in every stone, she sobbed;

"I just wanted to get away from you—but for *just* a minute—just one miserable little *minute!*"

Turning on the horrid thing cackling against the roar of the store, In'da attacked once more, shouting;

"I did think those things. I did wish for them—I did. But not so something like this could happen."

Laughing at the woman's attack, the demon threw itself upon her, tearing her skin, shattering her bones. Drinking her blood. Ignoring it all, or moreover, embracing it, In'da told the monster;

"I never meant to turn something like you loose in my mother's soul." Kicking her repeatedly, clawing digging away flesh, shredding organs, the demon shouted;

"But you did…'she wants to run my life,' 'She won't leave me alone,' 'Oh, why can't she just curl up and *die?!*"

Helpless, curled up pitifully, bleeding and broken, In'da wailed through blistered lips;

"How? How can this be possible? Yes, I was tired—wanted some time to myself. So I, I exaggerated…to make myself feel better. Like so many do—I admit that. But it was no invitation…"

As she spoke, the demon returned to her and stepped on In'da's back, grinding her down into the muck. Gasping in the mud, however, the daughter ignored the pain, saying;

"I never wanted anything like this. Nothing like you. I swear. I swear it. I swear…"

And then In'da, totally beaten, as near death as one could reach on the dreamplane without actually terminating, looked upward with her one good eye and told the demon quietly, plainly—

"I love my mother…"

And in that moment, everything changed. The demon, large and monumental one moment, suddenly took on a shriven and, in some ways, nearly comical aspect. The tiniest of noises escaping its rough lips, the thing looked one way, then another, and before it could do much more, time ran out and space folded on the demon, leaving it somewhere other than the garden. With the passing of the creature, the storm also dissipated, the returning sun showing a garden rapidly healing itself. Everywhere, weeds withered and fell away, replaced by thick vines heavy with melons, fields of brilliant daffodils, trees budding with flowers and fruit at the same time.

In the center of all the returning beauty, Lai Wan helped the bleeding, broken In'da into a sitting position. The woman was one eye from night, and in terrible shape, but through her pain she asked weakly;

"Is it…did we…?"

"Save your strength," the psychometrist told her. "The demon is gone. As your complaints and pettiness drew it here, your honest declaration of your true love for your mother drove it away."

"I meant what I said. I…"

"I know," Lai Wan assured her. "If you had not meant what you said, you could not have driven off the djinn."

All about the pair, the garden shone with a green glisten nearly as bright as the sun overhead. Worried that she would not long survive, In'da asked quietly;

"What happens to me, it doesn't matter. But...my mother...will she—"

"Yes—" answered, Lai Wan calmly. Pointing to a spot in the distance, In'da could see her mother, vital and fresh, with all her faculties obviously clear. The old woman was smiling and her outstretched arms were filled with love and the longing to hold her daughter.

"Thanks to you."

As mother and daughter hugged near the center of the garden, Lai Wan stood off to the side, in its very center. There, while dam and offspring shared their century-long instant, the psychometrist gazed upon that which was the center of the mother's soul, that which she had placed in the most treasured spot of her heart. All about her, wherever Lai Wan looked, stood a never-ending stone shrine, its hundred of statues of In'da—as a baby, a toddler, learning to cook, to tie her shoes—more. They were everywhere, in all sizes and shapes, In'da dressed for the dance, for church, for the first day of kindergarten, middle school, high school, college, dressed for her first day of work, her first date, her first sleep over, her first Halloween, in a costume her mother had made her—more. Thousands more. All carved in stone to be captured perfectly forever—all the images a mother would keep in her heart of hearts of her darling daughter.

"You are a good daughter, In'da bin Goden," said Lai Wan quietly. "Or, at least...you remembered how to be one in the end." Staring out from her spot in the center of the garden, Lai Wan watched as all of In'da's wounds miraculously healed at her mother's touch. Holding back a tear, the psychometrist thought;

Indeed, it is as the old ones say—a happy mother takes away pain.

And suddenly, both women were back in the patient visitors room. In'da blinked, surprised to find herself covered in sweat, her clothing crumpled, dirty and ripped, but her body healthy and unbruised. Looking down, seeing that she and Lai Wan were still holding hands as they were earlier, she said;

"We're back."

"We were never gone."

"It was true. It was all true."

"No, actually," answered Lai Wan. "It was not. I lied to you." As the two women stared at each other, the psychometrist explained;

"I told you that the demon drew it's strength from your mother. That it was slowly killing her. This was not true. The Shaitan draw their power not from their seeming victims, but from their *loved* ones." When In'da stared blankly, Lai Wan took pity on her considering all she had just endured, and explained;

"It is the caregivers they victimize, those who hold the hands, who stroke the brows, change the bedpans, clean the colostomy bags..." Gripping In'da's hand with both of hers, she told the woman;

"You could never have beaten such a creature fighting for yourself. If you had known it was feeding upon your suffering—yours—not your mother's, you would have given up. It would have been easier." In'da smiles at Lai Wan, admitting;

"And wanting to do things the easy way is what started all of this in the first place, isn't it?"

Silence reigned in the room between the two women. It was not an awkward quiet, but one filled with the knowing relief only the most fortunate ever experience. Then, in response to something she picked out of the ether, Lai Wan said quietly;

"I sense the nurses are quite excited. It seems one of the patients nearby has come out of her coma." Looking for but a moment into the psychometrist's eyes, In'da found her answer and stood immediately, running down the hall to her mother's room. Her work done, Lai Wan stood and headed for the door, thinking as she walked;

"Yes, a happy mother takes away pain. But then, so do happy children."

Perhaps this sounds like the setup for a joke: What happens when two of H.P. Lovecraft's characters meet in a speakeasy? Well, if one is tormented by evil and the other is evil, the result might be surprising.

That is the case with "Body and Soul," when a blond haired, blue-eyed man with cold knowledge and a vacuum of imagination returns. At the same time, we learn what has always been the missing part of the man's nightmarish experiments.

BODY AND SOUL

"Leave the flesh to the fate it was fit for! The spirit be thine!"
—Robert Browning

The man at the bar sat with a stillness generally reserved for the dead. In some ways, the idea was morbidly appropriate. Malone had not passed on, of course, but there was an aching part of him which found comfort in the idea, and another part of him steeling himself toward making the idea concrete—for himself or someone else.

"C'mon now, Bennie," called the bartender. "Let me slide another mug in your hand. You're acting like a wake should be a somber occasion."

The solid mass of hard-wound steel that was detective sergeant Benton Malone would have thrashed any other living being for such a speech. The cold wooden box stretching down the bar held his darling Kathleen and if any man had ever loved a woman more, the news had not reached that particular Boston tavern on that cold November evening. But, the man behind the bar was Malone's own uncle Kevin Peter Malone, and if the man who had bucked him on his knee when a babe could not cajole him now, then none could.

Quietly, Malone accepted the offered flagon and drained it below the halfway measure with a single gulp. As he did, his uncle gave a hand signal to the four musicians sitting in the corner. They knew him well enough, knew the situation, and so decided to play something simple, and to play it softly. They chose "My Wild Irish Rose," and the strategy of their performance was a tribute to their art. The men came in one at a time, Flynn starting them quietly on his accordion. MacDonald came in after a while on his tambour, followed quickly by Boyle who brought his penny whistle to play so sweetly that he was barely noticed. Mullen, however, could affect no such entry. When his deft hand set bow to fiddle, all ears heard, and all hearts were made the way he wanted them.

The quartet, at that moment, wanted to encourage melancholy. Usually it was their duty at such functions to keep things lively, to take the old back to younger days, and to remind all of something other than the occasion at hand. That worked for families, and for helping to comfort the grief of the city's fire fighters or constables when one of their own had fallen in the line of duty. But such tactics were not appropriate that eve, and all knew it.

Sergeant Malone was a powder keg that night, an unstable force, like an approaching typhoon or a building volcanic eruption. There was no doubt he would reach critical mass sometime during the evening. The only question the assembly had was "when." Sitting far back from the solitary figure at the bar, at a table situated near the rear door, a favored spot for those not keen on notoriety, two figures obviously not part of the regular scene at the Green Harp watched the proceedings with varying degrees of interest.

One, a tired, frightened looking young man sat squeezed into the corner, his arms wrapped about his knees, feet pulled up onto his chair. He was a mousy specimen, used up and closed to finished though only in his early twenties. By contrast, the tall, slender man with the pale blue eyes and the straw-like hair next to him leaned forward, elbows on their table, sipping at his drink as if the gathering were one thrown in his honor. He sat his simple wooden seat with an easy pride that befitted a king in exile. Leaning over to one of the Green Harp regulars, the stranger asked in a smooth voice;

"What has happened out of the ordinary here?"

"I don't take your meaning, sir."

"The fellow at the bar, the one everyone is working so hard to keep mollified. Some connection to the deceased, I imagine. But what's their story? Why's the mood in here so positively foreboding?" The speaker was obviously used to giving orders, but he somehow found it within him to add the courtesy, "if you don't mind my asking?"

"Auck, not at all," answered the man at the next table. As the blond-haired man signaled that a new round should be brought for both himself and his neighbor, the regular introduced himself then said;

"It's a sad and terrible story, theirs is. The man, that's big Ben Malone. Police detective he is. Good one, too. His main detail is keeping the heathens down Chinatown way in their place. Whenever the tongs start spillin' over the boundaries, upsettin' the ways of decent folk, that's when they send Ben in."

"And the woman...?"

"Oh, and now ain't that the saddest bit of all. That there laid out in the pine and silk, for all to see and remember as she was, is sweet Kathleen O'Conner. A beautiful girl if ever there was one. They were betrothed, they were. And Sunday next, he would have been waitin' at the front of St. Pat's, he would, for her to come walkin' down in her great-grandmother's lace—but, well...not now. Not now that Toung Wu has thrown us all inta the fire."

Several more rounds of drinks and a number of carefully crafted questions brought the blond gentleman the entire story. Toung Wu was the head of the most notorious of all the tong clans that sprang up in Boston after the end of the Great War. More than just a gang chieftain, he seemed to serve as a religious leader as well to the worst elements of the Oriental underworld. Stories abounded about the man which made him sound a combination of Methuselah, Edison and the Devil, himself.

Wu controlled smuggling and prostitution rings, counterfeiting operations, opium dens and every other unsavory type of enterprise from slavery to the theft of sacred relics. There were rumors he had actually tried to assassinate the President of the United States, and that the only thing he had found standing in his way, stopping him from plunging much of the Western world into unimaginable chaos, sending him instead to crawl off into the darkness to lick his wounds, had been Ben Malone.

The detective had apparently had numerous run-ins with Wu's operations—most thought far more than he told anyone about, including his superiors. Indeed, it was generally believed that the sergeant, along with a handful of fellow officers known unofficially as the Gentlemen of the Shillelagh, had practically bottled up the mastermind and his minions at one point. That was when Wu had sent Kathleen the letter.

A device employed to cripple his enemy, the devious ganglord had sent the girl a missive, letting her know that Ben Malone would not stop him again. Having learned of her existence, and of her importance to the detective, Wu had informed her that the next time he needed to keep Malone away from one of his operations, he would simply kidnap Kathleen and hold her hostage against the sergeant's interference.

He apologized for such necessity quite pleasantly, letting the girl know that she would not be harmed as long as the man who claimed to love her did as he was instructed. Indeed, Wu insisted, the two of them could not only be guaranteed of no ill will coming from his direction if Malone would but cooperate with him, but that they could be assured wedding gifts of diamond and gold, of silk and jade and pearl and all manner of treasures.

Wu let her know, however, that if Malone did not stop interfering with his machinations, that he would be forced to treat her as less than an honored guest when his operatives delivered her unto him. For her sake, he suggested, if she thought her fiancé unreliable in such matters, she might think seriously of leaving him before the inevitable came to pass.

"Ah, me ah me ah, me," said the regular. "It was a terrible cleverness with which that letter was written. And it would have gotten Wu everything he wanted, if, that is, it had been sent to anyone but Kathleen."

"Why's that?" The bespectacled man asked his question with a lively curiosity, one the man at the next table did not think to question. More interested in telling his story, he answered;

"Because she was a real woman, and in love with her man, not with the idea of being in love. She did what Wu wanted her to, all right, she showed Ben the letter. But when he read it, and she saw the thoughts it brewed up in his mind stormin' about behind his eyes, she cut him off right proper.

"She told him if he dared to stop bein' a man for her sake, that was the only thing that could drive her from his side. She was as wild a rose as ever grew, and you never in your life saw a man as proud and happy and as in love as Ben Malone that night, I'm tellin' you true."

The man went on at some length describing the party that followed the incident of the letter. The Green Harp had filled with Malones and O'Conners and the best friends of each, and if ever two people had been married one to the other by the presence of their loved ones alone, it was them.

"But then, as you can guess, the party ended. Wu got up to somethin', to this moment Ben ain't said word one on what it was, but it was big and it was a final blow between the two of them. And even though he surrounded his darlin' with a squad of Boston's Best, the yellow devil got to her somehow and...well, that was that."

The blond-haired man nodded absently, his mind hearing all he was being told, but still working on some other matter within his head at the same time. The man at the next table did not notice, his attention firmly affixed to Malone.

"So," asked the outsider, his tone not betraying his intention, "when did all this happen?"

"Why, only this mornin'...the poor lass. She hasn't been gone from us even half a day, and yet look at the two of them. I'm tellin' you as true as if the words were straight from the Lord, Himself, that lad's goin' to do somethin' improprietious—sure an' Jesus fed the masses."

The blond man looked at his pocket watch, pursed his lips while he did some slight mental calculation, then responded;

"Maybe he won't have to."

And, so saying, the outsider rose and walked to the bar, specifically to the open casket. Those who bothered to watch him do so noted the stranger had a medical bag in his left hand. As he peered into the coffin, the bartender stepped immediately toward him, questioning;

"And what exactly do you think you're doin'?"

"Examining the body; why do you ask?"

"Because," answered the elder Malone in a whisper, "there's some here that might not like it."

"Even when it could mean that your precious Kathleen might walk and breathe and be whole once more?"

Time stopped. As completely as the world of the living can freeze, can be rendered inanimate with a stroke, the inside of the Green Harp and all within it entered a state of self-imposed suspended animation. It was an immobility made from equal parts fear, disbelief and hope, and after several long moments the silence of it was finally shattered by a deep voice that growled;

"And just what in hell do you mean by that?"

"What I said, sir. Would you hold your precious Kathleen once more? Touch her hair, feel her cheek, kiss her lips, and suddenly have her whole and filled with breath and life? Would something like that interest you?"

Malone looked at the blond man as if he were a cabbage which had somehow stood itself erect and barked like a dog. Rather than continue on toward anger, however, the detective felt a weight somehow lift from his shoulders. Not knowing if it were gone for good, or simply one of those temporary moments of relief even the worst of men were granted on occasion, he smiled—briefly, but sincerely—and asked;

"I won't even bother trying to discover why you're in here this evening. It's a free enough country, I guess. But I will inquire—what's your name?"

"Dr. Herbert West."

Malone smiled again, less briefly, knowing what would follow would lighten his mood in one way or another. Nodding his head several times in a knowing manner, he said;

"Yeah, I thought there might be a title in there somewhere. Well, go ahead—doctor. You've got my attention, and most likely all the friends and family of my darlin' Kat'leen here as well. So, tell us…give us your best medicine show pitch—bang your tambourine for us, Dr. West."

"So," answered the bespectacled man, softly, "your suspicion of me is that I am a con man. The only reason then, if I can judge by your manner, you want to hear what I have to say, is for your amusement."

"And what if it was?"

Dr. West rested his medical bag on the stool between himself and the detective. His face was tight—nostrils shut, mouth pinched. He allowed a single short puff of air to escape his lips, the sound of it echoing in the stillness of the pub. The sense of his anger flashed across the open room along with it, holding the moment frozen until West spoke.

"I admired much of what I was told of your exploits cleaning up the waterfront trash around here. I made the offer I did because, and only because, hearing those stories, while watching your grief, I decided you might be a decent man. I haven't met too many of those."

"I ain't—" Malone moved his hand through the air dismissively, while changing his view toward the floor. He only got out the two words before the doctor cut him off.

"Don't stun me with your modesty; if nothing else it just wastes time. I'll be brief so your fiancés' friends and family can go back to their drinking." Much of West's anger was returned to him in that moment, but he continued with no detectable change in emotion;

"I've seen many men in pain, sir, but few so intense as your own. I'm not a man much given to pity, but that may be understandable to you, because you see, I am a man who has died and been reborn."

A dark and steady mummer crept into the Green Harp and made certain to sweep past every table. All present at the wake struggled to make sense of the man with the medical bag—the blond man near Kathleen's casket, the one who said something about her breathing once more.

The man who claimed to have been murdered and restored.

"I am making you a proposal, detective Malone. I was torn into pieces, and yet regenerated. Restored. Intact. Made whole." West raised his hand and held it aloft as if the sight of it proved something as he insisted;

"Whole."

"And you can do the same for Kat'leen? And you would do so why? And how?"

"I would do it because I would like to test the process. I was not an active witness of the first completely successful use of my own discovery, you see." West said the words as if they were amusing. More—obviously amusing. Then, his eyes delightfully sinister, he called to the forgotten man at his table;

"Isn't that right, Dr. Cain?"

As attention from around the Green Harp focused on the cowering person at the far table, he instantly became more agitated. His head moved up and down in response to West's question, but most could not decide whether he were shaking it in agreement, or merely shaking uncontrollably. Striding back toward the table, taking a position in the center of the room, West raised his hands, turning one way, then the other as he proclaimed;

"Yes, I am raised from the dead—reanimated, resurrected—whatever term you wish to apply, it fits me well. I was utterly destroyed, and yet Dr. Cain here was able to rebuild me, recreate the full and whole me from but random scraps." The doctor took several steps toward his companion, then asked;

"Didn't you, old friend?" Cain winced at the words, but managed to finally croak out a response.

"Yes. It's all true; just as he said."

Various of those around the pub turned from the man, unable to meet his wild eyes. Even his uneasy, constantly shifting pose was difficult to watch. West rested his hand on Cain's shoulder for a moment, a gesture of comfort which actually made the other doctor shrink back further against the wall. Turning once more toward the crowd, West strode back toward the bar, calling;

"So, Mr. Malone, or any of you, for that matter—shall I proceed? One simple injection at the base of the neck is all that is needed. No blood, no carving, no indecency, I assure you. A single needle, an ounce of fluid. If nothing happens, if I'm a fraud, I'm certain you high thinkers will be able to effect some sort of violence which will leave you happy."

West moved closer to the bar, thrusting his thin, bespectacled face to within inches of Malone's. Staring into the detective's eyes, he added;

"But if I am no fraud, well then, would you not be the luckiest man since they wrote down the last miracles of the Bible?"

Many throats gasped; the parish priest moved forward, fire in his eyes, but Malone held up his hand, calling for all to hold themselves still. In a voice quieter than most imagined him capable of finding, the detective said;

"I'll not have blasphemy in her presence."

Uncowed, West retorted angrily;

"Blasphemy? To claim that man can match God miracle for miracle? I think not, sir. The dark ages are gone. In this century man strides across his puny planet in ten league boots. He crosses oceans, competes with the birds for the clouds. He can cook his food without fire now, talk to his fellows on the other side of the world if he desires. When evening comes, he no longer cowers in his cave, he throws a switch and cries *let there be light!*"

A dozen sets of hands made the sign of the cross, others balled into fists. All looked to Malone for their cue. Whatever his decision, they would follow his lead. Feeling the weight of their eyes slamming against him from all angles, the detective let go a weary sigh. Finally, he focused his eyes for the first time on those of the doctor, searching the man's inner being as he said;

"I'll not debate the right or wrong of what you're saying. I'm not qualified, and frankly, I don't care. For just one minute with my Kat'leen, I'd walk naked into Hell and wrestle down all of Satan's horde one by one, and if it took a million years, and it lost me my soul in the process, I wouldn't care, as long as I could hold her and kiss her one last time."

West smiled, his frame going rigid with anticipation. His hands ready to plunge into his bag, he stopped as Malone continued, asking him;

"But you tell me, Dr. West, can you promise me that when you're done, I'll truly have my darlin' back? As she was? Her soul shining out from her eyes like always? Are you telling me that you can call her being back from Heaven?"

West was silent for a moment, and then, just as he was about to answer, his companion slammed his feet against the floor and awkwardly propelled himself upward out of his chair. Falling backward against the wall, he half-rose, half-leaned, as he shouted;

"Now, there…there, Dr. West, is a question. Flesh you can make dance. I've seen it. God help me, you're proof that I've done it as well. But, tell us, please…"

Cain began shaking again, barely able to hold himself erect even using the wall for stability. His voice going quiet, pleading, he begged;

"*Please*—no matter what you've accomplished with the bodies of man, can you do it…can you reanimate *souls*?"

The silence previously imposed upon those within the Green Harp deepened to a point where people became self-conscious over the thundering of their heartbeats echoing throughout the tavern. Again Dr. West made to answer, but before he could Malone put up his hand in a friendly enough, but halting gesture. Grabbing up a shot glass near his other hand, the detective tossed back the bit of rye within it, then set the glass down, saying;

"Don't bother to answer; it doesn't matter. I wouldn't have you throw such cruelty at the woman I love." As West peered at Malone, the big man came off his stool and began to check things about his person. He felt under his jacket, making certain his twin revolvers were snug in their shoulder holsters, checking the knife he held ready on his belt, et cetera. As he did so, he told the doctor;

"We don't go to heaven or hell, doc. This is hell, right here. Kat'leen's made it somewhere else. I wouldn't drag her back just so I can feel better. That's not love—that's fear."

Malone turned and fixed his uncle with a glance which shook the older man for a moment. The bartender drew himself back, his lips going tight, his neck stiff. Then, just as suddenly he relaxed, nodding slightly, closing his eyes for a moment. As all watched in silence, he grabbed up a bottle and a shot glass, setting the glass next to the one Malone had just emptied. Filling the new one, he then refilled the one next to it.

"To Katie," he said, picking up one of the shots. "Wherever she is." Malone nodded. Picking up the other, he turned his head sideways, then said;

"Aye," and downed his drink. After that, the detective headed straight for the exit, with no man saying a word. As the door closed behind Malone, West turned back toward the bar for an instant, giving the coffin stretched out there a last, longing glance. He wondered for a moment at the detective's words, and his companion's questions. He had never really given the idea of the soul much consideration.

As a doctor, he knew there was a consistent loss of weight at the time of death, a fact many had used to argue for the existence of the soul. His mind whirled with thoughts for a moment. Was there a soul? Did they exist? And, if they did, did he actually have the power to reinstall them within their human hosts?

West sighed, and made to collect his companion. A man with a keenly developed sense of knowing when he had overstayed his welcome, he was just about to steer Dr. Cain toward the front door when the bartender called out;

"I thank you, Dr. West."

"Yes? For what, if I might ask?"

"You helped the lad set his course clear. Whatever he's to do now, he'll do it without hesitation. It's for the best."

West wondered for a moment at the bartender's statement. Surely they both knew where Malone was headed. Certainly they both knew how the evening would end.

Chinatown would run red with blood that night—of that there was no doubting. There was also little doubt that another coffin would grace the bar of the Green Harp the next evening, or that the laments of that next evening would be even more pitiful than the ones surrounding them.

The doctor thought to make comment, but before he could, suddenly Flynn started in with his accordion once more, squeezing out the opening of some tune West did not recognize. Boyle and MacDonald followed him quickly enough, and in seconds the velvet strains of Mullen's fiddle joined them. All about him, the doctor watched the crowd grow openly emotional, tears dribbling down cheeks, men closing their eyes against the pain of memory.

With a sigh, West got his companion to his feet and headed for the door. Medical bag in hand, he hustled Cain out into the night air. They needed to move on, before some within the Green Harp actually began to think on his words and started to make connections to himself and recent events in the area.

Once outside, he hailed the first livery driver he saw, instructing the man to take them north, up into the main part of Boston. As they pulled away from the curb, West leaned over toward Cain, and asked him in a whisper;

"So, what do you think? Now that we know we can resurrect the flesh, shall we go after the soul as well?"

Cain stared at West, searching frantically in every corner of the cold, crystal lake blue of his eyes for any indication that the doctor might be joking. Finding nothing of the comical, or the sacred there, the cringing man merely whimpered. West shook his head sadly, then turned to stare out the window of the cab.

The night sky was filled with the wonder of galaxies, but he saw naught but tiny lights.

"The Horror" not only hits at the heart of H.P. Lovecraft's writings, it also touches upon a reanimated, modern fear. Purity of blood, heritage and race were themes that Lovecraft dwelled upon—knowingly or unknowingly. In the classic, "The Lurking Fear," this is readily evident. And here C.J. has penned a story in the tradition of "The Lurking Fear," rekindling old American fears, but with a modern twist: an unknown condition. Just as Lovecraft worked with the cultural horrors of his day, so does C.J.—except here, a new light is cast on those fears.

THE HORROR

"ANOTHER ONE," HE WHISPERED, half in shock, half in doomed resignation.

John looked at himself in the mirror. Specifically, he stared at his abdomen. A few days earlier he had found a pimple inches from his navel. A pimple—at his age. But, it had not been like the pimples he could remember from thirty years earlier. This one's head had been hard and brittle—blackish. Disgusting.

Now, to his horror, he had found another. Also near his navel. In fact, almost an equal distance to the left of it that the first one had been to the right. What did such symmetry mean?

And the spots, he thought, running his fingers over his arms—feeling each one of them. The damned, damn spots. Red, purple...some large, some small, all of them unsightly and horrible. Horrible.

It was bad enough when they had only been on his back, his shoulders and upper arms. But then they'd started to spread. He'd found them in his hairline one day, still mostly out of sight, but threatening to expose themselves to all who saw him—to expose *him*.

How long would it be before they started appearing on his hands? His face? How long?

I can't stand this, he thought. Although still staring at the mirror, John no longer saw himself. His eyes had glazed. Instead he saw the way he had looked when he had just graduated from college—twenty and a few years earlier—the distant past.

He had been perfect then. Not model perfect, but perfect like a human being was supposed to be. With smooth skin and a full head of hair. With arms and legs that could work all day, eyes that could read a street sign two blocks away. Not a half dead carcass covered with...with whatever they were.

John had gone to his doctor. After he'd found the first few spots, he'd showed them to the physician during a routine examination. The doctor dismissed them as nothing, "just merely the first signs of old age, that's all," he had said. But John had been suspicious the man was merely putting him off—that he actually didn't know what the spots were. He wished he had the nerve to question the physician's authority—drawn from years of practice and a wallful of black-framed degrees—but he could not. Besides, it was only a few spots.

Then.

Now, it was not a few spots. It was scores of them. *Scores*. So many he could not see them all, but he could feel them when he ran his hands over his back. Scores of spots, and pimples. *Pimples*.

Over the last year he had found pimples everywhere he found the spots. He would break them open, drain them, then scrub them with cleanser and hope. But they came back—over and over—rough, scaly skin filled with blood and pus. Damning him.

What were they, he wondered fearfully. What was happening to him?

At first he had ignored the growing infestations. But now it seemed like there were more every day. More spots, more pimples...more waggles. That was his name for the strange, minute excess pieces of skin that had started to grow out of him. He had no idea what they could be. They were not like the spots—hard and dark. They were still pink flesh, still moved like skin. But they simply were not...*right*.

They were just growths. They were small, easily hidden, but they were not anything John could explain. They looked like tiny fingers growing out of his body. Tiny, boneless, nailless fingers poking out of him.

He had seen so many things on the news and in the papers over the years—viruses that ate a person's skin away; diseases that blotched the flesh, then killed the host; flies that burrowed under the skin to lay their eggs, leaving their young behind to eat their way to freedom. A hundred countries had poisons that killed and mutilated humans. And the rumors you always heard that the CIA was experimenting with germs and bacteria on the public at large. John did not want to be paranoid...but if there was a normal explanation for what was happening to him, he did not know what it was.

And his wife...she was no help.

She was older than he was by several months, but she could not grasp what he was worried about. She had tried to understand, to be supportive, but finally, she had snapped, yelling at him,

"For Heaven's sake, John...it's just old age. You're just getting old!"

Just she had said. *Just* getting old?

How could she not understand? She was older than *him*. Couldn't she feel it? It had to be more important than simple old age. It *had* to. He was...he was...

John could not think of the right word. Everything he tried—special, important, worthy—they sounded so empty, so vain, as if he were...as if he were not any of them. As if he was just some ordinary mortal.

Turning away from the mirror, from his wife and her shallow understanding, John hugged himself, rocking back and forth, trying not to touch *those* spots on his arms.

How could his doctor not understand? How could his wife be so blind? How could she *not* know what it was like for him? Old age? Just *old age*? Why was he the only one that felt the horror?

The horror.

Sometimes all one needs is to believe. For fans of the band, Fried Spiders, this is a popular mantra. For the rest, perhaps not. It is with a humorous twist this story explores the dark recesses of mankind. It is a lesson on why we should not under estimate the terror humanity strikes across the universe.

A FORTY SHARE IN INNSMOUTH

"For those of you just joining us here in Boston's venerable Fenway Park, tonight promises to be our most spectacular voyages ever into the realm of the beyond." Marvin Richards, host of the wildly popular show *Challenge of the Unknown*, had to choke back the smile threatening to ruin his carefully manufactured impartiality. It was difficult for him. Not because he was anything but the consummate professional, but because *this* time, he had *really* done it.

"For now as promised earlier, we shall conclude our investigation of the disappearance of Thomas Millwright, Alan Bart and Ray Nuttall—the three men who vanished from the streets of London nearly thirty years ago. As our regular viewers know, all three men were involved in the supernatural disciplines…"

"How can he ooze that crap with such a straight face?" asked Marc Thorner, the show's new chief animated effects engineer.

"That's why they pay him the big bucks and we have to pray for overtime," answered his assistant, Larry Spezzi. The pair were content to leave things at that, but another voice joined in, offering;

"No—he can do it because he *believes*."

Thorner rolled his eyes. Spezzi covered a chuckle with his free hand. The speaker, an attractive young woman named Lora Dean, had been with the show throughout its first season. Their last show in the spring had coincided with a massive nightmare that had blanketed the globe. And certainly, one could indeed blame that live presentation for the hundreds of thousands of unexplained deaths which occurred that night. All one had to do was believe in witchcraft and malevolent dwarf races.

"Nuttall's diary revealed a tale of demonic summoning," said Richards, his calm tones echoing through the stadium, reverberating through homes throughout the city, the country, the world. "If notations made within his diary are true, then an ancient god was summoned by Nuttall, Bugg-Shash, the Black One, the Filler of Space—He Who Comes in the Dark—a creature or power of the outer dimensions which only the purity of light might disperse."

"Jeez, Dean," scoffed Thorner, ignoring the voice filtering through the speaker above their heads. His attention focused on his guide board, he begged, "Gimme a break, will you?"

"You weren't here," answered the correct young woman. Watching through the observation booth's thick, darkened plate glass, she reminded him, "The man you replaced was, though. He died that night. Along with twenty-seven more of the crew."

"Hey," interrupted Spezzi, "if you're so worried about what's goin' ta happen tonight, then what're ya doin' here? Why aren't ya stashed away safe somewheres?"

Lora admitted in her mind that it was a good question. She tried to say so, fighting to push the words out of her mouth. But she found she could not. Her lips had sealed one against the other, forcing themselves together all the harder the more she tried to speak. The young woman *had* been there—she *knew* what had happened. Convincing others, though, had become impossible. The more proof people gathered proving *Challenge* was responsible, the more the doubters shouted them down, terrified their opponents might be right. Happy to answer his own question, however, Spezzi told her;

"What do people say when they pass an overturned schoolbus—that they was lookin' because they was so concerned about da little kiddies? Nah. That'd be a lie. Alla us—we look because we wanta see blood. Small twisted-up broken bodies."

The technician turned from his work for a moment. Staring at Lora, he smirked cruelly as he told her, "You're just human, Dean. An' human beings crave da bizarre an' da horrible." Snorting at his analysis, Spezzi then turned back to his work, adding, "Which is good 'cause dats why we all got jobs tonight."

"Bart and Nuttall had originally summoned the beast," Richards told the audience—the tens of thousands in the arena and the hundreds of millions at home. "Chanting under the influence of mild hallucinogens, listening to the music of then popular rock group, Fried Spiders, the pair somehow stumbled on the exact mood and tone necessary to summon the elder beast from its otherly dimensional lair."

Lora had to admit that Spezzi was correct. After last season's closing episode, the world had become greatly interested in Marvin Richards' weekly productions. No one could actually prove the producer's blind stumbling had unleased the horrors it had. No one in authority would even give such a notion the slightest credence—that was left to the masses, reading their horoscopes, calling their psychic hotlines, throwing salt over their shoulders. Throughout the summer they had bought every article and watched any newscast dedicated to the season closer of *Challenge*, and they were tuned in that night, by the hundreds of millions, hanging on Richards' every word—waiting.

"Nuttall and Bart managed to make their way to the light—which as we noted earlier was the only way to repel the shambler—and stay there long enough to involve Millwright, apparently against his will. But, again according to the diary, once thus entangled in the younger men's nightmare, the older, more knowledgeable Millwright was actually able to reverse the spell and repulse the demon now waiting for the three of them…but only for a time."

Lora shifted uncomfortably from foot to foot. Her job used to be *so* easy. It had been so simple to ignore the legion of guests come to talk about being vampires and witches—about living in haunted houses or having seen a lake monster—about being abducted by aliens, probed by aliens, forced to have sex with aliens—come to show their amulets and monkey's paws and Mothman photographs, to tell their tales of Roswell and aliens corpses hidden in freezers by the government…

Oh yes, she thought, the government.

They had come to the show, had taken Richards away for "discussions" and "debriefing." The producer/star had never spoken of what had gone on after the FBI had come to see him, or the FCC, the Secret Service, the CIA, or any of the dozen others. He had bluffed or made deals or pleaded or defied them with the searing ridicule that they might actually be labeled "believers." A hundred such theories had been put forth, none of which Richards had either confirmed or denied. Conjecture meant publicity, and after having gotten through the bureaucrats, he was not about to throw away a free summer's ride on the Speculation Express.

And now, she thought, here we are...at it again. *Again.*

Lora bit at her lower lip, right hand grabbing her left wrist. Her legs tight, one against the other, she tried to get a grip on her nerves, to stop the dread boiling upward from the lower regions of her brain. She could not, however, for the harder she tried to dismiss what their show was investigating that week, the more her legs ached to bolt for the door.

"Millwright was killed only a week after the events described in Nuttall's diary," Richards continued. "Not by some fantastic, otherworldly thing from afar, however, but in a simple automobile accident. His death was duly recorded by the local coroner, his body removed to the town mortuary. But...that was not the end of things."

No, thought Lora, her body shaking. Not by a long shot. His body disappeared from the morgue, the same day Nuttall and Bart disappeared as well. Without a trace.

Not true, objected a voice from the back of her brain. Shuddering, swallowing against the bile creeping upward in her throat, Lora agreed. The young woman tried desperately to reject the details forcing their way to the center stage of her brain, but she failed—Richards' voice filling in those blanks she had been able to create.

"A gelatinous mass had been found on the street halfway between the Windsor Tavern—the last place Nuttall and Bart had been seen—and Bart's own flat." While Lora cringed, rich color coroner's photos flashed on all the screens in the booth, showing those in Fenway and those at home what the young woman was so desperate to forget.

"The bloody slime you see coating the sidewalk proved to have been human in origin. After an extensive examination, both teeth and bridgework matching portions of all three men's dental records were discovered in the blackening pink slop."

Lora's eyes fixed on the decades old photos. How could everyone remain so calm, she wondered. How? *How?*

She had held Nuttall's diary in her hands. The feel of the battered old thing alone should have been enough to convince anyone that they were dealing with something beyond their comprehension. The cheap plastic binding, the yellowing pages—the thing reeked of human terror. You could feel it in the paper, see it in the garbled, panicked scrawl of the later entries.

Even when the man had been describing his relief that the trio had managed to save themselves, gone was the steady hand found earlier in the book. Compared to the entries made before the fatal seance, the shattered penmanship of the volume's last few pages looked like the work of a lunatic. Thinking to herself of what Nuttall and Bart were supposed to have survived—if even for a time—Lora decided that lunatic might be too kind a word.

How about *damned*, she asked herself. How's that for a word for people who go mucking around with things they don't understand? Looking about at the others calmly going about their jobs, she thought, this isn't some kind of game—for Christ's sake—what are we doing? We're getting ready to demonstrate how the suicide died by putting the same gun to our heads.

"So now," asked Richards, "the question remains, were these three men liquified unto death by a horror they called down upon themselves? That, ladies and gentlemen, is what we will now try to prove, once and for all."

And then, Lora Dean shuddered. Involuntarily she moved toward the rear of the room in jerks and starts, one trembling backward step after another. Her shoulders hit the wall, the cold of its tile cutting through her. No one noticed her retreat, however, nor heard the small whimper that passed her lips as her escape was thus cut off. Despite their mocking tones, Thorner, Spezzi, and everyone else in the booth was riveted at that moment, all their attention pouring forth toward the stage below.

"We cannot, of course, supply our audience with narcotics," announced Richards, "but we can duplicate all other aspects of the ritual as described in Mr. Nuttall's diary."

Even at a distance, Lora stared at the stage in the center of the vast arena below her. Trembling, she watched as a somber young man approached Richards. One of the production company's gaffers had been outfitted by the costuming staff with black horn-rimmed glasses and a patch-elbowed tweed suit, television's subtle way of conferring scholarly dignity on the tome he was carrying.

"Tell the audience what you have there, Robert."

"This volume, commonly referred to throughout the supernatural underworld as *Mad Berkley's Book*, is believed to be the only single source for the worst elements of such esoteric volumes as the *Unaussprechlichen Kulten*, the *Cthaat Aquadingen*, and even the long-lost *Necronomicon*."

"And this book was found amongst Ray Nuttall's effects—correct, Robert?"

"Yes, sir…along with his diary. Both of which were loaned to us tonight by his estate."

Lora went tense, her fingernails digging futilely against the hard tiles behind her. She could feel the thin, pricking fingers of panic tearing at her, jabbing her spine, scratching the sensitive skin along the line of her shoulders. Sweat beaded across her skull, the first stale lines of it oozing down the back of her neck. Her eyes stared unblinking as Richards waved forward the Satanic priest he had hired to read the correct passage. She tried to remind herself that the man was a fool. She had met the so-called Reverend Ralaratri during the taping of their show on cults. He had only been interested in being paid and chasing every warm body in the studio, whether in pants or a skirt.

He's a phony, a clown. He's not a priest; he's just a performer. Just like Richards.

Yes, Marvin Richards, the voice from the back of her mind whispered, *the man who summoned the last nightmare that almost destroyed the world—*

"God…"

Lora choked on the word, its power somehow seeming small and distant, and in the face of what they were doing, perhaps even insignificant. She thought about the word "God." Was that not what they were attempting to contact? Some kind of god? And apparently just one of dozens, all held back from humanity by some veil she could not understand.

She had looked through *Mad Berkley's Book,* tried to read it, to comprehend what it held, but if Nuttall's diary had felt disturbing to the young woman, Berkley's volume had terrified her. Although its binding had been dry—practically desiccated—still the book had somehow left her hands feeling clammy, greasy. She had left off the reading of it cursing her curiosity under her breath. Now Lora wished she had the strength to curse.

A tear formed in her left eye, growing slowly in size, but refusing to break loose. The weight of it dragged at the woman, stabbing at her paralyzed eyes until they finally surrendered and blinked, knocking the repellent moisture free. The tear crashed against her blouse, soaking through to her breast.

Drips, thought Lora, *falling from the sky—even indoors. That was what the diary said. That's how it comes. That's how you know it's here!*

Lora fought her unreasoning panic, shouting within her mind

that it had only been a tear. Doing so, she found the strength to move forward, her eyes searching the clear night sky for any dark shapes that might be forming over the stadium. She knew it was not possible—even if the invocation were to work, it had not yet been voiced. But it would be—soon.

On the stage below, Marvin Richards had just finished introducing the members of Fried Spiders—all still alive, gathered together by money and flattery from their lives as accountants, bartenders and clerks to once more pick up their dusty instruments and prove that entertainment knows no honor—only desperate need and the pitiful ability to delude itself with momentary self-importance. Somehow, a collection of balding, overweight and somewhat confused men in their fifties dressed in fashions three decades out of date was reckoned as showmanship. Lora might have laughed if the terror did not have her so firmly in its grip. Nor was that the limit of it.

Lined against the inner wall of the arena, an entire battalion of marines stood to the ready. Richards had staged a show consisting of two average comedians and seven even more average dancers for the local army base. That and a check covering their transportation expenses had gotten him hundreds of armed men ready to defend the world against the kiss of Bugg-Shash.

Lora noted their weapons, tightly clutched, all of it for form only—death-dealers posed by the stage manager like puppets. Part of her mind wondered, could their bullets be of any use against the horror to come?

Can Gods die of lead poisoning?

Lora giggled at her joke. Below her the stadium lights were being dramatically shut down one by one. As the cameras switched over to infra-red, half of Lora's mind wanted to expand her tiny noises outward into full-blown laughter, to simply collapse into a heap on the floor and to laugh and laugh until whatever was going to happen was over. The rest of her clamped a hand over her mouth and screamed in her ear, clinging desperately to sanity by giving in to the one insane notion in the air—

It's real! she told herself. It's real and it's *coming!*

And then Lora Dean gave in to the helplessness assailing her. What else could she do, she wondered. She knew it was coming—*knew* it. In the depths of her soul, even as the clownish Satanist on the stage stepped between the prop candles into his neon pentagram and began to intone the words on the prompter before him, there was no doubt that somewhere beyond the limits of her imagination's ability to dream, that a black, fetid shape was sputtering free of its slumber and staggering onward toward her world.

She wanted to run, to stash herself "away safe somewheres" as Spezzi had put it. But where was that safe haven? An idiot god that existed only to bring death was on its way, a slobbering vileness that slid through the darkness, a thing that could be turned by the light, but never stopped. There were lights behind the booth's darkened glass, but how long could she stay within their wretchedly small reach?

And then, all thought fell from Lora's mind as the first dark drops began to splash against the glass plates.

"It seems something is happening," said Richards, the producer cutting to the host's mike, overriding the satanic priest's. Too busy calculating his overnight ratings, the producer failed to gauge the changes around him, either the slimy grayness of the drops striking him, or the immeasurable cold and blackness following them. In the near-distance, a dark but delighted chittering began to trill, and across the stadium, the spectators awoke to the horror that they were about to get their money's worth.

Wet, noxious fingers of invisible blackness stroked heads and bodies, slurping and tasting, coming to those who had called for their touch. Instantly the crowd rose like a mad animal, panic leaping through the pitch black from body to body like electricity. Fright pushed and smote and struggled, jamming doorways and stairwells with flesh, pulling Bugg-Shash free of its dimensional restraints all the faster. And then, the shooting started.

All around the stadium, marines lifted their weapons skyward, firing into the approaching darkness that blocked the stars and smothered the moon. Their bullets had little effect, only the red glow of each third round's tracer trail casting a moment of pink-orange light in the way of the hungry god's wanton path.

In the past, the tiniest fires had repelled the chilling slitherer, but not then. When called by groups of one or two, only the tiniest vestige of the elder thing had ever come forth onto the earthly plane. But this time it had not been summoned by a handful of creatures, but by an entire world! Tied together by cables and satellites, all looking for Spezzi's blood and small twisted up broken bodies, their desire to be entertained by the forces of Hell had finally been satisfied.

All across the Earth, in homes and taverns, in television stores and communal rec rooms, clinging uliginous liquid dribbled down out of the above, followed by the almost never-ending length of Bugg-Shash. Across every time zone, in both light and darkness, the rapturous horror sent forth a billion tongues, unable to check its desire to respond to the overwhelming call.

And thus was its undoing.

In tiny bites, answering the isolated summons of this or that magician over the millennium, the Ebony One had always been the relentless lurker, patiently waiting in the darkness until it could escape the hated light and come for its victims in a gelid splash of nauseous blackness. But this time, this time the call was overwhelming, pulling the bloated horror in a billion directions at once, stretching it across the face of a world.

Desperate to flee the repulsive light, Bugg-Shash strained to find only those voices in darkness, but there were too many lights and lamps webbing their way to the half world of sunlight. Too much of the shambler's essence pulled forward, the ancient vileness tried to kill enough of the summoning vermin to give it the energy to retreat, but there were too many calls, all of them protected by the glow of their televisions.

Too many...simply too many...

✠ ✠ ✠

"Are you listening to me, Richards? Have you heard anything I've said?!"

"Yeah, yeah," answered the producer, still trying to talk to both his contacts in Hong Kong and Germany at the same time. "Streets full of rotting gook. Dead people all over the world. Car wrecks, plane crashes, people trampled and crushed. Yatida, yatida...I heard you."

"But it's our fault," whined the network contact. "*Our* fault!"

Assuring his people he would get back to them, the producer/star of Challenge of the Unknown hung up all his phones, shut down his mobile switchboard for the moment, and then turned to the nervous man behind him.

"We didn't do anything," he said with calm assurance. "We didn't trample anyone. We didn't kill anybody. Okay? They didn't put away Orson Welles for the Martian invasion stunt, did they? And that was a phoney. This was real—we told everyone it was real. It's not our fault if they didn't believe us."

The network man vacillated between tears and rage, unable to find any chinks in Richards' armor. Frustrated, he pointed to the producer's assistant, Lora Dean. The young woman was still cowering in the corner, hugging herself, murmuring low with her eyes shut tight. His finger shaking, the network man snarled;

"*They* didn't believe us? *Us* didn't believe us. Look at your own damn people, for Christ's sake." Crossing the room, Richards put his arm around Lora.

"Hey, kid," he said softly with a gentleness that practically approached concern. "You going to be all right?"

Slowly, Lora opened her eyes and looked up at her smiling boss. Sucking down his callous strength in greedy amounts, she managed a bit of a grin, then stammered, "You know, you know...I don't know if this is the time to, to bring it up, but...you don't pay us enough."

And then, Marvin Richards' marvelous inner control snapped. Laughing, he bent down and kissed the terrified woman on the cheek. He hugged her with open passion, not as man to woman, but with the joy of an athlete embracing a teammate at the moment of a championship win. Tousling her hair the way he would a dog's, the man cackled;

"You're absolutely right. Your salary is now doubled—starting yesterday." Still laughing, Richards spun around wildly newly energized. Pushing the network man toward the door, he levered the annoying worrier out into the hall, promising to be right behind him. Then, in a moment of amazing tenderness, he somehow managed to break off calculating profits long enough to ask Lora;

"Look, I've gotta go jump on this thing—you know—deal while the wheel's in motion. But, are you going to be all right?"

"I, I think so," answered Lora, shutting off her memories of the recent past like doors to a winter day—slamming them to save what heat she still possessed. "But, could...could I ask you a question?"

"Sure. What is it, kid?"

"Did we really kill...a god...just for higher ratings?"

"Yeah," answered Richards with the shock of newly acquired awareness. "Sure looks that way, don't it? Ain't it cool?"

Grabbing a cigar from his desk, a reward Richards allowed himself on only the most exalted of occasions, he bit off one end and spit it across the room. Firing the other end, he tilted his head to the side and added, "You know, they're absolutely right. There is no business like show business." And then, the producer/star disappeared through his smoke, off to battle the kind of leeching horrors he was used to—the reporters and lawyers and government officials waiting in the hall.

Lora watched the door shut, cutting her off from the pandemonium beyond. She had read enough of *Mad Berkley's Book* to know that they might have repulsed or confused the Filler of Space, but killed it? That she was not as certain about. Clutching at herself, the young woman found she was quite content to stay in her chair, legs pulled up, arms wrapped around them. Humming softly. Not closing her eyes.

Not daring to close her eyes.

The next day, when a passing janitor reached in to shut off the office's still burning light, Lora started screaming—a plaintive wail all the raises in the world could not silence.

Sometimes horror is found in a bleak view of the world. Imagine a place where the horrors never cease, where they are endless. To fix such a broken world would take great sacrifices. It just so happens, this short but poignant story begs the questions: who makes such sacrifices?

SACRIFICE

HERBERT SAT AT THE kitchen table, unable to eat. The television before him blared on and on, its icy glow ruining his digestion, stealing appetite from his empty stomach. He had turned it on, hoping the scheduled comedy might take his mind away from the world around him. Herbert had forgotten the news briefs which started off every hour. He pulled at a hangnail while the screen assailed him.

—*TWINKIES INJECTED WITH CYANIDE...TEN DEAD IN JERSEY NURSERY SCHOOL...*

The television sat at the end of the metal table, its cord trailing off somewhere into the books on the shelf behind it. Beaming out at Herbert, it offended him daily, taunting him with ever increasing numbers of blandly different unthinkables, daring him to turn it off, to even turn away.

"I won't," he thought. "No matter what it makes up. I won't give in."

Herbert unfolded his arms and pushed his rapidly cooling *Kraft Macaroni & Cheese Deluxe Dinner* away from himself, down the table, out of reach.

—*NO CLUES IN THE WILMERDING REST HOME ARSON CASE...*

Somehow, he just did not feel like eating.

"There's no avoiding it," he admitted. "I just haven't done enough."

Herbert shuddered at the thought. He wondered if enough could be done, if *anyone* could do enough. He had tried. God, how he had tried. At least, he thought he had. Each time the world had escalated its attempts to cave in on itself, so had his efforts to put things aright. More sacrifices, a greater effort...

—MORE AT ELEVEN ON THE...

Stretching out, straining to reach to the end of the table, he clicked the set off in midtragedy, chewing at his nails as he wondered at it all.

✠ ✠ ✠

MARY HAD DECIDED TO cut her hair again, shorter than the last time. She snipped at it randomly, without any thought set aside for style or appearance. Although she had not left much the last time, she did manage to find some loose bits to clip, shears pressed into the sides of her head, angling after this fast growing follicle or that one. Looking at herself in the mirror, staring at her handiwork, she wished she had not thrown out every last cigarette was glad that she did.

In the end, it had been such a little thing to give up. Anything to get back at the radio.

—FOUR MORE WINTER WAR CASUALTIES WERE DISCOVERED TODAY, FROZEN TO DEATH IN THEIR HOMES, VICTIMS NOT ONLY OF THE COLD, BUT OF THE CITY'S MERCILESS UTILITY BARONS...

Anything to keep her mind off the world locked outside her door. She had passed on going to the play with Frank, even though she did like him and he had seemed very secure about the whole thing. Something had warned her, however. Something had let her know that the streets just were not the place for her to be. Something made with Japanese technology and German plastic bought on Canal Street for ten dollars which nightly turned the key in the lock of her warm, secure cell.

—TAKING HIS OWN LIFE AFTER KILLING HIS WIFE AND THREE GIRLS...

She had not noticed over the last months—not really—how her hair had started getting shorter, and then shorter, and her nails, shorter, and her meals, smaller, and well, who really needs cigarettes, anyway I mean, the way the world is?

✠ ✠ ✠

JOE HAD HEARD ENOUGH. The nightly news had only been a rehash of the slop that had poured out over him from his paper on the way home, more details dripping off the pages and out of the set like broiling fat falling into a fire. It was bad enough that everyone in the office had been talking about it. *Talking*. There was a euphemism for it.

"You mean those people in El Paso?"

"Yeah. They stuffed the drugs inside ketchup bottles."

"Four dead, right?"

"Yeah. Pretty spicy stuff, huh?"

And then the laughter. Four dead in the morning. By the train ride home, and the evening paper, two more had died, making all the jokes funnier by fifty percent.

Turning the TV off with the fingers remaining on his right hand, Joe left the den, heading for his bedroom. No wife waited anymore. Even his dog had deserted him, frightened by the morose, continually cynical atmosphere which had settled around his master and then spread outward through his home and all the things in and around it.

"Maybe Lucky didn't run away. Maybe he was only stolen," Joe whispered to himself. "Or killed."

Forsaking his bed, Joe pulled a blanket from it and then curled on the floor in the black, shivering in his chilly darkness. Duty now for the future, he thought, smiling weakly, trying to fit the edges of his blanket around and under both his rear end and his feet.

✠ ✠ ✠

HERBERT SAT IN THE kitchen, still at the table. Tears ran down his face, slow but unstoppable. Nothing he ever did was enough. Maybe the axe would help—maybe. But, if he was wrong, said the little voice in the back of his head, there would be no second chance.

"No second chance?" he asked the air in a small, confused voice. What could he be thinking? There was always a second chance. Clicking his set back on, he watched the small white dot in the center grow in size.

—MORE BOMBINGS IN THE CENTRAL LOWLANDS FORCE U.N. TROOPS TO...

The picture faded away as he clicked the screen back to blackness.

There's no reason for all of this, he thought. I've just got to make a bigger sacrifice. Something they'll all notice. Something worth the effort.

Lifting himself from his chair, he went to the drawer in his desk where the tools were. He considered the chisel and several of the planes for a long moment before shutting the drawer again. Then, turning to the umbrella stand next to him, Herbert pulled free the saw standing in it, bracing his leg against the chair next to his dresser.

After the eye-crushing pain of the first few strokes, he suddenly found he could not move the saw. Forcing his eyes open, he spotted the problem immediately. Pulling the blade upward, he untangled the pant threads caught in its teeth. Then, with a path cleared, he set back to work, grimly clamping his jaws and bubbling lips together, gamely sawing stroke after stroke, ignoring the swooshing sound and the bone powder and the blood until he had finished his work and had toppled to the floor.

"Maybe that," he thought. "Maybe they'll notice that."

But, even as he fell off into unconsciousness, Mary's radio kept reporting its grim fascinations, and Herbert just kept wondering—as did Joe and the army of their fellows, all sawing away, just how much grist the mill demanded.

"All the world's a stage," said the great poet. But what happens when the audience realizes it is part of the play, part of the comedy, part of the tragedy? They then must question: who is the director, and why must they follow the script.

Of course, all of this is a part of "Pop Goes the Weasel." It is a tale that transforms a playful song into a terrifying chant, and reveals that all the world is a stage, and everyone is acting a role, but not living life.

POP GOES THE WEASEL

For a spot so few could actually find—especially on a regular basis—it was amazing how many people had heard about it. Uproar was the hottest name on the edge circuit, a common well for the city's mutants, where all manner of fashionable lepers went to see who they could come crashing down upon.

It was not a place to merely be seen—personalities avoided it, even the tough poseurs who thought throwing tantrums in front of people with cameras somehow made them individuals. Uproar was a place for the daring and the reckless, the cunning and the dangerously brave—a stage for the truest of exhibitionists. The club was a test—like the fun house or a roller coaster. What made the evening memorable was surviving it.

One did not find Uproar easily. It was not always open. And when it was, it was not always open at the same times. And…those times it was open…it was not always in the same place. There were reasons. It would be hard to put an order of importance to them, but they existed nonetheless—each one gaining or losing rank as they were rated on an individual basis.

Some of the loose collection who nominally ran Uproar did not always want to see the same people. Some of the others found that view amusing. To them the lack of policy was a great way to ensure

seeing nothing but the same old faces. Some were willing to put up with such an inconvenient gathering place because it was hidden and obscure and thus a secret pleasure—others, because it was so well known. People created their own realities in Uproar, programming their way of thinking about the place to allow their own personalities to find being there desirable.

In other words, in the manner of so many of the world's great salons, going there was often times an experience worth making a few excuses for.

Or at least, that was what John had been hoping.

He had heard about Uproar at the office. That girl, Cindy—the one he wanted so much…the one he simply could not think straight around—had mentioned it. When he had asked what she was talking about, she said,

"Keats."

"John Keats…?"

"Yes," she answered. She gave the acknowledgement with a spark of her personality, an unconscious reward for his having shown some intelligence beyond the typical tekno-babble of the day. Her neutral face—not yet having gone over into terrified-city-girl-putting-up-a-bitch-front-because-I'm-just-not-sure-any-of-you-*are*-worth-it-anymore—emboldened him. Taking a wild leap, he offered,

"There is nothing stable in the world; uproar's your only music."

And, hearing Keats quoted so correctly, she had smiled. It was a thin lipped, bravo-of-appreciation smile…an invitation to try and continue to entertain. John, heady with victory, propelled by the thick euphoria of his own thoughts about the woman before him, confirmed her suspicions by admitting,

"I overheard you mention 'uproar'…if the subject was Keats, I thought…"

"So, you listen to my conversations, do you?" she purred, luring him onward.

"Sure," said the low-level supervisor, pulling at his tie. "Look at what I do for a living. Look at how long I've been doing it. A janitor walking by can distract me. A beautiful woman who discusses Keats…are you kidding?"

Her friend, another woman from the editorial department, bristled at the word 'beautiful.' As she started to make her quite strong feelings on the subject known, John cut her off.

"Pardon me," he said sarcastically. "I said the woman is beautiful. I also said she discusses Keats, but I don't think that's what's got you so upset."

For once in his life—John was willing to defy the norm. He had wanted to talk to a woman who was worth talking to for so long, he just didn't care anymore. Notching up the sneer in his voice, he snarled,

"I didn't touch her, make a pass at her, ask for her phone number, leer, whistle, hiss, bark, thump, pound, bray, click my fingers, clap my hands, smack my lips or touch myself in any way. I just said she was beautiful."

Turning away from the friend, John turned back to Cindy. Studying her face, he said in an analytical tone,

"And look at her, would you? The shape and contour of her neck, the perfect, sharpline thinness of her lips. The depth of her eye sockets, and well, of course, the pulling chocolate brown of her eyes. Look at the blue-black of her hair, how it teases the curves of her face." And then, he spun back, daring,

"Are you saying she *isn't* beautiful?"

"Well, I..."

The friend stammered. Not so much because of John's speech—although it had put her back a step. No—her true difficulty was with her friend. She had looked into Cindy's eyes, and had seen the spark that let her know her friend had actually been reached by the man between them.

And, in that moment of calm where suddenly everyone in the room knew what was happening—in the one instant where if one of them seized the reins of reality they could rule it and change all of their futures, John said,

"Would you like to go to Uproar tonight?"

And that was what, on a Friday night in old New York, had taken John and Cindy to a second row table in the city's most talked about spot. It had been an impulsive thing on both their parts. Neither of them had ever been to the club. But John did know one of the mailroom guys who had been there.

Brian had been there—it sometimes seemed that he had been everywhere. For John, meeting Brian had been like finding a wild kid brother. If there was something you wanted, Brian could find it. And, for his new big brother, Brian had moved heaven and earth to find the spot Uproar had slid to that night.

That night it was underground. Brian had met John and Cindy after dinner and led them to the hole in the sidewalk doubling as the club's entrance de jour. Cindy had stared at it with a moment of trepidation. It was just a rectangle in the sidewalk, a molded concrete stairway leading down into the darkness.

There were no handrails, there was no light. Only occasional short bursts of steam filtering upward to catch the eye and inveigle or put off, depending on one's feelings about damp, hot air. The trio had gone in, Cindy and John taking a table, Brian scouting the bar for, as he put it,

"Hey, if I knew, it wouldn't be scoutin'."

A waiter who obviously worked on his resemblance to Anthony Perkins took their order and brought their drinks. His attitude caught John's attention. When the man was gone, Cindy asked,

"You seemed interested in something about the waiter."

"Oh," answered John. "It was nothing. I just found him a little… unique." Cindy flashed her eyes to indicate she wanted to know what kind of unique the waiter was. John told her.

"Well, he didn't tell us his name. he didn't try to be our pal. He didn't condescend to us—try to make us feel like two bits because we aren't as cool as him. He just came, did his job, left us alone."

"You're right," she agreed. "That's pretty unique for a New York waiter. Especially a gay one."

"He was gay?"

Cindy just smiled again, and John felt his ability to function skip out of sync with the rest of the world for a heart-punching moment. His tongue moved about uselessly, waiting for orders. It knew John wanted to form words, but too many conflicting messages were crowding the circuits for his tongue to make any sense of them. All he could do was smile back and stare.

He prided himself on being clever enough to pick up his drink and take a long sip. It was only a momentary cover but it was at least one moment where he did not have to look like a jerk. It was a wonderful moment, too.

Cindy had dressed in black, a color that showed off her rich skin nicely. She had picked a lace evening dress, one that dipped to a dramatic low décolleté. John's eyes ran over the beautifully sheer sleeves, wondering what they felt like. And, as he did so, without thinking, she extended her hand toward him.

John was almost surprised at what he did next. He did not bother to debate what he should do—to list the reasons she had done what she had done and then calculate the proper response. He reached out and took her wrist, letting his fingers touch the sheer fabric.

"Does it feel the way you thought it would?"

"It feels cool," he told her.

John was amazed with himself. He was amazed he could stay so at ease—amazed his hand was not shaking. He had begun to wonder if people could still do simple things—make the smallest of human gestures without being fined or imprisoned. One of the voices in his head which had ruled his adolescence—which still held more power than it deserved—leered from the background.

She *knew*, it whispered. She knew you wanted to touch her sleeve, and she just let you. She *let* you. Do you understand? *Do you? Do you* know what this means?

No, he admitted. I'll let her tell me.

And then, Brian returned to the table.

"Hey—show's gonna start any minute."

"Any idea what they're going to do tonight?"

"Hey—who knows?" he answered. Spreading his hands and shrugging his shoulders, he said. "It's the Uproar. Anything goes, man."

The trio sat back wondering what would happen next. Just like everyone else in the room. Brian had told John and Cindy about the kind of entertainment the club provided. Or, to be more specific, the kinds of settings they provided so their patrons could amuse themselves.

The Uproar's function was to serve as backdrop for the ultimate amateur hour. Clever guests were often invited, to be sure, just to make certain no one evening was ever totally forgettable. But, for the most, management merely set the stage and then allowed the inmates to run the asylum. It was a plan that had yet to fail.

Their most familiar opening was merely to set a podium out in a stark spotlight. This was an invitation to the poets, the lecturers, comedians, singers…anyone with the nerve to stand naked and brave the hordes shielded only by their talent. Many had found such courage, with varying results.

People had stepped up to the spotlight and done card tricks, told tales of their grandmother's spice bread, built card houses, read the tarot, explained the fine points of heavy diesel mechanics and led the assembled in a rousing chorus of "99 Bottles Of Beer On The Wall," a version that reached such levels of riotous gaiety that tales of the evening were close to reaching mythic proportions.

One sad looking little fat man had told jokes to which he could not remember any of the punchlines. To cover, he would scream the word "Saltines" or point in the air and shout "Big and scary cow," or do something else equally inane. Perhaps the crowd had merely been in a kindly mood that night, or mayhap his trembling need had reached out and convinced them that there was more fun to be had in joining along with his madness than there would be in seeing him dissected by the kind of cruel rejection of which they were indeed capable.

Whichever, he had been crowned Festival King and been given free tankards of flavored brandy until he had broken into a song he claimed chronicled the day of his firing entitled, "Fuck You, Terry." He sang eighteen choruses of it in the Uproar, eventually leading a conga line out of the club and onto the West Side Highway. The resultant traffic tie-up was reported on all the news shows the next day. No arrests were made, but the incident was the beginning of the Uproar's wide-ranging public notoriety.

Of course, not everyone that stepped into the spotlight had a good time. It took just the right combination of talent, luck, and gall to get away with standing up in front of the most jaded audience in one of the world's more morally corrupt cities. Many of the Uproar's regular spectators came only to shame and sneer those with the courage to rise to the stage, not caring if the talent displayed was of a caliber to bring kings to their feet. Uproar audiences prided themselves on being hard to please. Beer bottles bouncing off performers was not uncommon. People having to step around pools of blood as they took the stage was almost boring in its regularity.

But, in its mercy, management did not always provide such a stark setting. For those with nerve but no particular talent, sometimes props were provided. These were always hidden beneath a layer of camouflaging silk—a hint that one would have something with which to play.

One woman had pulled back the silk to find a bottle of volatilly high proof rum. She had requested the lights be brought low. Then she had lit the potent alcohol and told the ghost stories her great grandfather had spun for her as a child. The bottle had burned for several hours and she had held everyone spellbound with eerie tales of the Louisiana back bayou country.

One old man had found a pair of swords. With a gleam in his eye, he challenged an impertinent lout in the front row to a duel. The lout accepted, walked up on stage, chose a weapon, and immediately ran the old man through. Just one of the many show stoppers that brought down the house at the Uproar.

People had found all manner of things under the billowing silk sheet which they had used to varying degrees of success—a can of sardines, an ostrich feather, a box of Pop Tarts, a plastic bag filled with still buzzing flies, two bottles of barbecue sauce, a small statuette of Mickey Mouse, a broom and dustpan, a length of clothesline, a bottle of Drāno, these and a thousand more items—most getting one use and then being consigned to history, but some repeating over and over.

Like Willie.

Willie the Weasel was a slightly oversized jack-in-the-box toy. Simply told, one turned the crank on the side of the box, heard the tinny notes of "Pop Goes The Weasel," and waited for the moment when the spring catch finally slipped, releasing Willie. The small weasel puppet would then, of course, pop up as such toys always did. The difference was, Willie would always have something grasped in his paws.

The Willie toys were always the most interesting. Oftentimes they were quite valuable, as well. Several times he had come out holding pairs of tickets to top Broadway shows. Once he had been clutching a small but still sizeable sack of uncut diamonds to his plastic-haired chest—once a check for a thousand dollars made out to cash. Another time, simply a thick wad of cash, itself.

In an audience participation setting like the Uproar, oftentimes various members had been inspired to join the troop quickly when such profit raised its head. Not sharing could bring ugly results. Even sharing could bring ugly results. But then that was part of the Uproar's charm.

Of course, Willie did not always hold riches, or even things desirable. Once he had opened and popped into sight with a tarantula crawling over his head. One time he had been clutching a straight razor—another, a bottle of poison. Neither of those performances had been particularly attractive, although they had indeed both been memorable. And, more than once, Willie had appeared holding a gun.

That prop, like so many others, had not always brought out the best in family entertainment from the Uproar's participants.

One man had been quite clever. He had emptied the weapon and then juggled the bullets. Every so often he had allowed one to fall, caught it in his mouth, and then spit it at the audience, shouting "BANG!" while continuing to juggle the remaining cartridges. He proved to be amazingly accurate, hitting someone with each expectoration. His closing line, when he was down to juggling only two bullets, brought the house down. Just as he let the second to last one fall, he shouted,

"You know, each time I do this…"

And then, he caught the bullet in his mouth and spit it out, hitting a woman off to the far side who had thought distance had made her safe. As she shrieked in surprise, he finished in a sinister tone,

"It just gets easier."

But his use of the .38 had by far been the most clever. Many people just stood helplessly with it, confounded by its deadly weight. As confident as they had been when turning Willie's crank, actually holding a real gun in their hands turned out to be quite a different thing. Several were reduced to tears. Some had shot into the ceiling, the floor, or the wall behind them. One had fired into the audience. One had found a more personal target. And he, possibly, was the saddest spectacle the Uproar had ever seen.

Big and bearded, a raucous, fast spending glad-hander, he had taken the stage and found Willie beneath the brilliant red silk. Instantly the crowd had screamed:

"Turn the crank. Turn the crank."

The large man had obliged, singing Pop Goes The Weasel in a loud, booming voice until Willie had appeared, pointing the .38 at the spot directly between his eyes. The image set the spectators to all sides of him to laughing. Not gentle, we're-with-you laughter, but the type whose tone is laced with this-is-what-you-deserve. It was the chilling nasty braying of an audience who has been waiting for the bad guy to get the pie with his name on it.

Sadly, the large man did not understand that feeding vultures does not encourage them to go away.

With a tragic deliberation, he took the pistol and—aiming it toward the stage beneath him—shot himself through the foot. Although the action sent some Uproar patrons rushing for the door, most just laughed all the harder, shouting,

"More, more! *More!*"

And he had given it to them. Shell after shell, he fired then into different spots on his body, crippling and ruining himself further and further until the .38 was empty. And, finally at the end, the Uproar had cheered his insane performance. Of course, having fired off six rounds within an enclosed space, he had made everyone in the club temporarily deaf, including himself. The only applauds his sad life had ever received, and he could not hear it.

People, of course, wondered what could prompt others to act in such a manner. What they did not understand—as they condescendingly assured their fellows that *they* could never get caught up in such a frenzy—was the true nature of the Uproar and its camp followers.

The club generated an atmosphere all its own. Beyond the liquor and the heavy air of nicotine and hash and other, more exotic combustibles...the Uproar was a mood. Not a building but a frozen minute outside of the regular down time known as the real world. It was its own little universe, one which left behind the regulations of society, making up its own rules as it went along.

People wore all manner of costume there, from the most outrageous exhibitionistic strip and bind and piercing, to the most overblown Edwardian flourishes possible. On some nights the kitchen and bar held every food and drink imaginable. On others, they served only bread and glasses filled from vats of Kool-Aid heavy with rum and bourbon and floating fruit. Whatever they did, they did not often do the same thing two nights in a row.

The Uproar was a state of mind. It could be moved to laughter, good fellowship or generosity just as easily as it could be prodded off to sneers and violence or the cold vacuum of thrust-aside loneliness. The important point to those buying their way onto its nightly ride was not so much where the train was bound, just that it kept moving.

That evening's first performer got the train rolling without any trouble. He took the stark podium and began to talk about the government. He mentioned farmer's wives killed by the FBI, men shot down in their homes over three grams of marijuana, women and children burned alive because they thought America had something to do with the phrase, "land of the free."

He was a wild-eyed, fiery middle-aged man, one who had not come to convince or pander. He cared not who listened, who believed—who in the audience might fear him, or whom he might sway. He was there to bellow, to list the crimes of a slaughter house-minded occupational army—a centralized sack-and-burn bureau who considered no one outside their reach.

He told of farms and homes being seized by a government that merely wanted to expand parks—killing the property owners who would not voluntarily vacate. His eyes filled with tears as he wailed against the countless acts of vicious, hateful theft and brutality, and the seemingly never-ending insanity of it all.

He read from magazine clippings and scraps of newspaper. He quoted from memory, retelling the humbling details of one atrocity after another—all legal, all sanctioned, each more horribly numbing than the one before it.

He explained how morality and personal responsibility had been targeted as enemies of government, of how a conscious decision had been made to bring them down, to turn the world over to the halt and blind and frightened. He might have been mad—a great number of the audience was convinced he must be—but few thought he was mistaken.

The Uproar was known for many moods, but silence was not one of them. Oh, it might hush in a moment of expectation, but for the sad man with the grey hair, it went stone still, as if interrupting his speech with something as mundane as breathing might be some crime whose punishment was too servere to bear.

And then, when he had the audience in the palm of his hand, the man's voice dropped to its lowest point as he whispered,

"But, what does it matter? What do any of you care? Our king swims in a pool of blood, and he feeds his family and vassals your neighbor's souls. But, as long as they're still harvesting from the other side of the street…let the festival continue."

And then, he left the stage and disappeared into the darkness beyond the arena. No one clapped, no one spoke. The silence that followed went on for one agonizing second after another as everyone searched for the ability to breathe once more. While they did, one of the managers approached the flat-topped podium the grey-haired man had spoken from and set something atop it masked in silken scarlet.

"Oh, Christ," said Brian softly. "It's Willie."

The shape of the jack-in-the-box was too well known to be disguised from the regulars. The manager made a brief speech, complimenting their last performer on his unique outlook. As he did, John stared at the ominous block under the shimmering red sheet.

He had been as caught up in the mood of Uproar as any other first timer. The stories of Willie poured over his mind, the ones that guaranteed riches bubbling to the surface to overshadow the ones filled with horror—enticing him forward with promises of wealth like a state lottery ad.

Could I? he wondered, gauging his ability to be an individual. Could I really go up there?

Next to him, Cindy asked,

"Why not?"

And, before he knew it, John...quiet middle-management John from the tax department...was walking toward the stage. The man making the speech looked down at him and said,

"Can I help you?"

"No," answered John, not actually certain at all what he meant. "I can do this myself."

The manager stared at John for a moment. He had never seen the person before him. He was certain John was a newcomer. In the split instant their eyes met, the manager searched for what had sent such an inexperienced piece of meat up to the dog altar. Thinking he knew the answer, he said to everyone,

"I thought it might be difficult to coax someone up on stage after our last act...but, as you can see...they're crawling out of the woodwork." Then, the man stepped back, made a flourishing bow, and moved away from the podium, saying,

"Ladies and gentlemen, I give you our next performer."

John's hand grabbed at a corner of the silk. Even before he uncovered the metal box beneath, people began to chant softly,

"Willie, Willie, Willie, Willie..."

And finally, the jack-in-the-box was revealed. A small anticipatory gasp went through the crowd, and then, all eyes shifted to the metal crank sticking out of the box's side as the chant shifted to the familiar,

"Turn it, turn it, turn it..."

John stared at the box. A dozen voices raged within his head, different levels all speaking up at the same time. Caution screamed for him to go slowly—to think, be careful...while fear urged him away entirely.

Run, it told him, clawing at his knees and teeth, trying to set them shaking. Run—get out before anything can happen. You know the stories about this place—what it does to people—you don't need this.

As the chanting grew louder, precious seconds dissolved around John as he sifted through the voices in his mind.

What have you got to lose?

What does it matter?

You can't make a fool of yourself now—not in front of her. *Not her!*

Right—better to leave. Leave now.

No, turn it. See what it is. Impress her.

Forget her. Run.
Run.
You can do it. You *can* do it.
RUN!

John's fingers touched the crank just as the audience's chanting began to tinge with impatience. The toy responded with its familiar clanging brass notes.

ALL .. AROUND .. THE .. MULBERRY .. BUSH…

John's nerves screeched at him. He had never done anything like what he was doing. No grade school plays, no debate club. No fling with stand-up comedy. He had never even proposed a toast at a family function—never.

THE .. MONKEY .. CHASED .. THE .. WEASEL…

It just was not him. Heat and sweat were pouring out of him. He could feel his face going flush, his heart beating faster, the blood in his forehead banging against his skin–tighter, tighter, faster…

THE .. MONKEY .. THOUGHT .. 'TWAS .. ALL .. IN .. FUN…

Why, he asked himself. Why did you come up here? What in the name of God did you think you were doing?

POP! .. GOES .. THE .. WEASEL

This stupid damn thing—why doesn't it open already? How many times is the damn thing going to go around? Shit. Why did I do this? Why did I do this?

ALL . AROUND . THE . MULBERRY . BUSH…

Who cares what comes out? What could you do? You're going to mess this up. You're going to screw up. You got on stage…to perform for her…

THE . MONKEY . CHASED . THE . WEASEL…

Her?

THE . MONKEY . THOUGHT . 'TWAS . ALL . IN . FUN…

Your first date? This girl? What do you have to say to her? What kind of performance do *you* have up your sleeve that's going to win her over?

POP! . GOES . THE . WEASEL

This is just like you to blow something like this—

ALL AROUND THE MULBERRY BUSH…

Pulling some dickheaded stunt—

THE MONKEY CHASED THE WEASEL…

Idiot—

THE MONKEY THOUGHT 'TWAS ALL IN FUN…

You deserve to get the fucking gun.

POP!

And suddenly...Willie opened.

Oh. Well.

John stared at the dark cast .38.

Isn't it wonderful to always be right?

The audience hushed, the chanting and laughing and the giving of odds and collecting wagers all dying away as everyone concentrated their collective focus. The steaming, two hundred and thirty eight eyeballed stare made John's flesh itch. Shaking his head to knock the crawling sensation away from his skin, he reached down and grabbed up the gun.

I'm not losing her, he thought, staring at the weapon as if it could understand him. I'm not lousing this night up because of you.

Well, another voice whispered in his head, if you're going to do something, you'd better get started doing it.

What, he asked himself. And just what am I supposed to do?

John looked at the gun, the first he had ever touched in his life. He could see that it had bullets in it. Six of them. Six. A handful of death. A whole handful.

"What now, suit boy?" called out someone.

"Time to play, Soupy," said another.

Hate poured through John. Red anger over the hopelessness of his life. That he would take a woman to a place like this. That places like this even existed.

This? he cursed. *This?*

His anger went cold, then steamy. He felt his hands shaking, the muscles in his feet bunching and knotting. He felt his arm lifting the gun. Up away from Willie.

This is how you impress someone? This is how we slay dragons now?

John eyes panned the crowd, the leering, bug-eyed faces. He felt the pulsing ether all around him, filled with the desires of the animal force pouring outward from the audience. The crowd mind was deciding what it wanted to see, sending him messages, trying to batter his will into giving them the show their whims were dictating.

Playing puppet for these assholes?

The gun rose past waist level, to chin level, eye level...

This is all it comes down to now?

Over his head...

"NOOOOOOOOOOO!"

John screamed loud and long, dragging out the word, bringing the gun down club-like on the jack-in-the-box at the same time. His cry continued as he smashed the pistol's butt down against Willie. The plastic weasel snapped in two, then three, then four.

"NOOOOOOOOOOO!"

The weapon crashed against the box, denting it, dinging it, pulverizing it.

"No! No! No! No! No—Goddamnit all. NO!"

I'm sick of this, he told himself. I'm sick of dancing to someone else's tune.

Hurling the gun away, John slammed the now lop-sided box with his fists. Metal bent, sometimes ripped. His fingers caught and tore and bled.

"I'm sick of existing..." he bellowed, picking up the half-flattened toy. "*I want to live!*"

And then, he hurled the jumbled ruin at the back wall with all the force he could muster. The awkward hunk slammed against the black bricks, chipping their paint, leaving a set of three red stone gashes before it bounced off into the darkness.

And with that, his performance ended. Some of the crowd might have applauded. Some might have cheered. At least a few assuredly wanted to buy John a drink, just to share a moment in his presence after such a clearing rage—just for the smell of him. He did not notice.

He did not care.

Walking down off the stage, John extended his hand to Cindy, even as hers came up to meet him. The two hundred and thirty eight-eyed beast stared, watching with hungry fascination as she got up and moved close to him...as their eyes met, and their lips formed lines that meant they understood...watching with dreaming envy as the pair moved to the door...

And left to go home.

Some horrors are beyond the mind's ability to comprehend, and some horrors the mind simply refuses to accept. When this happens, that which is terrifying does not vanish from existence; instead, it just goes unseen, always lurking in the margins. Such a horror is uncovered in "The Questioning of the Azathothian Priest," and it requires a singular person to carry the burden of the world. And he does it with his usual aplomb.

THE QUESTIONING OF THE AZATHOTHIAN PRIEST

Recorded by Dr. Anton Zarnak

The judge's pupils rolled, slamming against the upper lids of his eyes with a martyr's force. He groaned loudly, not with sound, but with the twisting of his body, hissing his pain throughout his chambers. Already knowing the dread answer, still he asked;

"You can't be serious."

"I've never come before you, your honor, when I wasn't serious."

The speaker was a middle-aged man, tall and rough-shaven, regulation length dark wet curls slopping across his head. It was August in New York City, and the weather was draining the life from the planet. Captain Thorner did not like the city when it reached this stage of unmoving heat. He had only felt it once before. He did not care for it then, either.

"A man's been *shot*, Captain," the judge moaned. "Murdered. And you want me to dismiss it."

"It's been known to happen."

"And that *man* was known to be in the hands of the city's police department at the time," the judge said, his words set at a distinct tone, as if anyone needed any reminding. "The man was being questioned by police while his lawyer waited in the next room."

The judge closed his eyes for a moment, his left hand to his face. Rubbing at his eyes, more for distraction than anything else, he mused, "It's not bad enough the city fathers look like fools, not ready in any way—Canal Street just buckles—an earthquake, an earthquake in New York City...and now you saddle us with this, this..."

"I'm aware of what it looks like—"

"Oh, you are? Then tell me, Captain," demanded the judge, his voice trembling with a rage bordering on the religious, "what am I supposed to tell that boy's mother?"

"Your honor," interrupted the only other person present. "Before you tell anyone anything, I propose you set aside your biases and read the report."

Silence fell across the room in ripples, fat rolling ones, like layers of caramel folding into a pan. It emanated from the judge, the strength of it sniffing for lies or half truths, deception of any kind.

"And why would I believe *anything* you have to say, Dr. Zarnak?"

The other man stared at the judge. His visage made him seem a youth, but though his face was unlined, his eyes whispered of uncounted years. He was tall, slender and saturnine, with a fine-boned visage as sallow as antique ivory. His hair was thick and black as night, save for a dramatic silver streak that began at his right temple and zigzagged backward to the base of his skull.

"Because I am a man of honor and I know of things that you cannot imagine."

The sallow mouth moved precisely, spitting words cold and crisp, "You pray that what they say about me isn't true. But, in your locked away heart of hearts, you know it is, and you fear that all your power is just some worthless speck, a puff of nonsense in a mad world."

"Anton," said the captain softly, his fingers brushing the doctor's arm, auras joining for the moment of contact needed for true conversation...

The single word worked. Zarnak reeled in his anger—resumed his mask. He could always count on Thorner to remind him not to dwell on any single stupidity in the world around him. It was always those kinds of moments that killed Zarnak's kind, those ridiculous instances of emotion where logical and calm reason were sacrificed in an insane attempt to beat another at his own game. Ego. Mages could not afford such luxuries. Going where he should have in the first place, he set a vibration in his voice that would make the judge more...open to suggestion.

"Your honor," a pause was added to allow the moment of

THE QUESTIONING OF THE AZATHOTHIAN PRIEST

respect, given to balance the weight of the coming request, "for everyone's sake, just read the report."

Judge Tyler Reis's head snapped back a quarter of an inch, the sides of it tightening visibly at the ears. His emotions jumbled, his subconscious pushed him along the path of least resistance while his momentarily scrambled consciousness pulled itself together.

Reis looked down at the document that was suddenly in his hand with shock. It was political suicide to touch a case like this. An honest man, but a careful one, he wanted no part of the nightmare he could see headed for whichever member of the judiciary signed off on this one. Why had he accepted it? He had told himself he would stay out...

It did not matter. Reis shrugged with resignation. He had allowed them to make contact, to force his hand. His breath filled with the chill of long dreaded fear, the defeat in it so palpable that it pained him to listen to it. Sitting back in his chair, he decided to just get it over with. Folding back the cover sheet, just a title page containing certain city-significant numbers, he started with the first paragraph.

> My name is Dr. Anton Zarnak. In my capacity as a trained psychiatrist, I was brought in by Capt. Mark Thorner to assist in the interrogation of one Tidril Belbin. The following is a transcription of that account, with commentary by myself at the appropriate junctures.
>
> To begin: I arrived at the station shortly before 9:00 PM, the time scheduled for interrogation. I studied the prisoner beforehand through the standard two-way glass. It served no purpose. Despite the relative newness of these stations, subject knew he was being observed. Moreover, he assumed a stance designed to indicate that he could see through the glass as well, and that he was studying those on the other side.
>
> I note this here since I would expect others to as well, and I wish to strongly point out certain aspects of this interrogation as uniformly disturbing to those in attendance. On more than one occasion during the preliminary observation, Belbin made references which made no sense unless taken in context with what was happening on the other side of the wall, down to and including the rejoinder "Gods bless you" when patrolman Daniels sneezed, and then said "Thank you" to Belbin as he wiped his nose.
>
> Seeing the futility of continuing the "unsuspected observa-

tion" we moved inside to confront the suspect. While he was questioned by Captain Thorner I put together the following portfolio on the man.

Belbin could best be described as benevolently arrogant. I see him as a potentially dangerous individual simply because he absolutely believes that existence is futile. If he were to choose to retire from the folly of said futility, he would end his life in a millisecond. I believe if the idea were to come into his head on its own, he might possibly die then and there.

If he were to decide to feel pity toward others, though, he could become the most dangerous of random killers the world has ever seen. There are no simple terms to label such an individual. He is powerful—within his own mind—to the point of invincibility.

Further: On the question of Rationality: Belbin is the most rational of creatures. He is highly intelligent, ruthlessly logical and exactingly precise.

On the question of Sanity: Belbin would be insane if his belief in himself were misplaced. Since it is not, he must be thought of as—

"Sane?"

Reis slammed the document against his desk.

"I won't stand for this, Zarnak. Who do you…oh, I won't go there again. But, damn you. How am I supposed to explain this to anyone else?"

"You're not, Tyler," said the Captain softly. "You're supposed to understand what actually happened, and then figure out how to explain it all. Any way you can."

"But, what are you asking me to accept here? For God's sake, Thorner, I mean…yes…what you've brought me in the past—" images flashed through Reis' mind—dozens of sailors, slaughtered for their blood, tornadoes caused by "things," as the Captain had called them, "personalities, angels—well, demons really. But, incredibly powerful, Godlike,"—The winged bodies that had been brought in, burned and slashed—that ape thing…

"This is…"

Reis went silent. He knew someone had to read the report. Someone official had to sign off on one of the most terrible murders in the city's colorful history. During the war, people were easier to distract when the insanity hit and Zarnak prowled the streets. But now, with the monster Hitler and the miserable reptile Tojo off the front pages, the newspapers were always looking for some new creature to bleat about to the rest of the sheep.

Tidril Belbin could be that monster.

Judge Tyler Reis turned back to the report. He skimmed over the rest of Zarnak's opening remarks. They mostly concerned things with which the judge was already all too familiar—the circumstances of Belbin's arrest, the young women's bodies found, the mindless carving, blood paintings, the charnel pits. Indeed, what was in the report was old news—there was still information coming in, new discoveries, new terrors to hide being unearthed in Belbin's mansion...

Freak palace is more like it, Reis thought, remembering the horrible, horrible photos. Monster—goddamned monster...

"It's not a good enough word, anymore," the judge muttered under his breath.

"What isn't?" asked Thorner.

"Monster."

Thorner moved his eyes in a noncommittal gesture. He added his shoulders to the motion. Zarnak sat impassively. Waiting. The judge skimmed the rest of the regular formula of the report, finally getting to page 8, the statement. Its statement. Belbin's words. His justification, his attempt at self-exoneration, absolution, legitimacy...

Reis shut down his indignation and his horror and got down to business by reading;

Explanatory Excerpt 1:
Here within Belbin explains himself in relationship to his deity.

Bel: You must understand, I am a priest of Azathoth. I do what is expected."

Tho: Meaning you're thinking of yourself as a member of the clergy? You're thinking this gives you some kind of special rights?

Bel: [amused] Meaning, Captain Thorner, friend of Anton Zarnak, that as a priest of Azathoth, I need not really worry about such as you.

Tho: Really. When you want to leave, you'll what? Snap your fingers? Snap. Like that? And this Assholethoth, he'll just come and save you?

Bel: Hardly. Azathoth pays his followers no mind. Nor does he need to. After all, I am powerful enough to destroy you all with but a moment's concentration. In other words, I have only accompanied you here because it pleases me to do so.

Tho: You're a tough guy, is that what you're saying?

Bel: I am all-powerful, Captain.

Tho: You? You're the one who's all-powerful. Not this god you shill for?

Tho: Azathoth simply is what is. At the center of all time and space, all existence and dreams, all that can be and will be, there exists Azathoth.
    Greatest of them all.
    What you must realize, of course, is that we do not exist as he exists—we but exist somewhere within the deep and violent crevices of his mind. All of us, Captain Thorner, friend to Anton Zarnak, you and all you know and all you do not know. Azathoth creates fate and destiny, love and chaos. His dreams are our substance. His nightmares, our calamities. He is the absolute, true, pure and only lord of existence.

Tho: Well, if you won't mind the asking, why would it please such a powerful nabob as yourself to consort with us lowly types?

Bel: Please, Captain, what more could I ask for? I plan on placing the city under my control. I've decided mastery of one small planet is something Azathoth can be directed toward. Please understand, his unconscious whims are our reality. There are those of us who have begun to unlock his secrets. Once I've finished my work here, it will be safe for me to proceed with my overall plan.

Tho: Your work here? And what business do you think you have here outside of answering for your crimes?

THE QUESTIONING OF THE AZATHOTHIAN PRIEST 151

Bel: [smiling] Captain Thorner, friend of Anton Zarnak, you two individuals are really the only people who could stop me, if, of course, you knew to what extent my powers reach. But by coming here quietly, I am able to have you both together in one place, not yet prepared to think of me as a menace worthy of your full powers. You consider me nothing more than a simple madman, a psychopath. Your thoughts at present are to do no more than evaluate me.

Tho: And what are you here for?

Bel: I've come to eliminate the two of you.

REIS FANNED HIMSELF WITH the report. Though the horrible heat had begun to subside, still it sent the sweat running down his face—neck, chest, everywhere. The fanning turned the rivulets into icy fingers, chilling his body. As he closed his eyes for a moment, a shudder ran through him. His voice a whisper, he asked;
"Why does he say he came to eliminate you? You two? Why would he want to?"
"It's all in the re—"
"Just *tell* me," snapped the judge.
"Belbin thought it was within his reach to take over the world," answered Thorner matter-of-factly. "He felt Anton was the only mystic close at hand who could counteract his abilities. He also claimed to be somewhat worried about me because I was the one member of the force who had consistently been able to deal with things beyond the normal mortal ken. Working as a team, he saw us as, at the least, a formidable nuisance. His plan, therefore, was to get us both in the same place and destroy us."
"And why didn't his plan work?"
"We destroyed him first." Zarnak's cool words brought a rising bile into the judge's throat.
"Yes, that's why we're here in the first place—because you allowed this pathetic lunatic to be..."
"Your honor," Zarnak said the title drily, flirting with the idea of finding it humorous, "every minute you spend arguing with us allows this affair to drag on longer—the main thing I believe you wish to avoid. Again I recommend that you...read the report."
Once more the doctor set that particular vibration in his voice

that bent the judge toward cooperation. Once more the judge turned back to the report. He picked up where he had left off, amazed at the self-assurance of Belbin. Wondering if it came from his faith, Reis skipped to:

Explanatory Excerpt 14:
Here within Belbin explains Azathoth itself.

Tho: So when you offered these sacrifices to this...Azathoth...

Bel: Offer sacrifices...[amused, distant]...I do not offer sacrifices to anyone or anything, Captain.

Tho: But the women you...murdered...why did you do it? Weren't they...don't you offer sacrifices to this thing of yours?

Bel: You are so hopelessly mundane, Captain Thorner, friend of Anton Zarnak, so wonderfully low.
   Azathoth does not accept sacrifice. He does not bestow gifts. A priest of Azathoth is an explorer. A miner. Those who flock to the mindless one do so to gain insights, notions on how best to manipulate the universe.

Tho: You want to explain yourself?

Bel: Through drugs and dreams, I have found my way through the layers of reality and deception on down through to the center of existence. There lies Azathoth, steaming and whirling, mad beyond reason, not maybe even living—not actually alive in the sense that we understand it.
   He is perhaps more of a, a reaction, a contradiction. There is no way to know if awake Azathoth would actually be conscious. If he ever does awaken, of course, we will all blink out of existence. Instantly. If he ever remembers us, the planets we stride, the voids in between, we will snap back into existence. And if he remembers us as fiddler crabs, then we will snap back into existence and fiddle our lives out on the bottom of the sea.
   Dr. Zarnak knows this. I have seen him, skulking the high planes, gazing on great Azathoth, watching from afar, afraid to approach closer. I am not afraid.

> I have learned the dreams Azathoth enjoys. I live them to give myself a scent he finds pleasing. I curl within the folds of his immenseness, each time bringing away knowledge and more. Azathoth is power. He is power that I mine for myself.

Reis set the report down as his phone clanged on his desk. He took the call, not caring what it might be about. Anything that turned his attention away if for even a moment from the Belbin insanity was welcome. The questions on what to do with the new quake victims that were being found proved all too easy to handle. Before he knew it, the judge was finished with the caller. His mouth dry, neck sweating, he cradled the receiver back on its perch.

I'M GETTING TOO OLD for this, Reis thought sadly. He was, consciously, thinking on his appointment to manage the disaster relief coordination. Subconsciously, however, he was thinking of Belbin. Just too goddamned old.

He breezed over part of the suspect's statement where he confessed to the murders. "Confessed," of course, was not exactly the right word. That implied resistance on Belbin's part, a certain amount of coercion to gain the admission. The priest had needed no prompting to list his dark crimes. He laid out what he had done, to whom he had done it, how often, to what degree, with the thoroughness of a surgeon and the dull precision of a certified public accountant.

The lists of atrocities went on for pages. Kidnapping the victims, drugging them, incarceration, mutilation. All of it was there on the page, Belbin's words recorded in court approved detail, how he had skinned the girls alive, taken tongs to their fingernails, burned out their eyes, used razors on their tongues, on their fingers, their underarms, their ears and breasts and abdomens...

Reis read Belbin's descriptions of the things he had already read about in police reports: the bathtub filled with blood, the bloody fingerprints everywhere, the walls and ceiling of the old main room, painted with blood, festooned with organs, the four poster bed in the center of it all, draped with intestines utilized as curtains...

Reis looked up from the report for a long moment. His mind whirled, desperate to find an escape route. He found nothing. He knew Zarnak had somehow tricked him into picking up the report, into accepting the resolving of the Belbin mess.

If only the madman hadn't been appointed an attorney, thought the judge. Hell, he hadn't even wanted one. But, oh no, procedure is all, and so now we have this gadfly buzzing, and the police asking for a cover-up, and this, this...he shook the report in his hand with violence...and we have *this* to explain it all away.

With a dry and weary sigh, Judge Reis returned to the report, turning to:

Explanatory Excerpt 23:
Here within Belbin explains his power.

Tho: So you think of yourself as what, exactly? Some kind of demon? Or God? What?

Bel: I am but a man, like yourself, Captain. I have simply armed myself, as you have armed yourself. My weapons are merely more powerful than yours. As mankind has learned to plunge daggers into the hearts of atoms to split them open, so too have I absorbed the knowledge of this power from great Azathoth. Indeed, to wipe this city from the face of the planet would be simplicity itself.

Tho: Then why don't you?

Bel: As I told you, Captain Thorner, friend of Anton Zarnak, I like this city. It will serve well as my capitol. [highly amused] But I will obliterate some other municipality if you so desire.

Tho: Yeah, well, maybe later. Right now, why don't you tell me exactly how you're going to eliminate Dr. Zarnak and myself.

Bel: I have no specific preference. Is there some way you wished to die, Captain? I might be able to oblige you.

Tho: Oh, well, that's swell of you. But perhaps you could just outline any way that comes to mind, strictly for illumination, you see. After all, to us, the way we see it, you're a prisoner. You have no weapons, your hands are cuffed, your legs are shackled...it seems like eliminating people should be a bit out of your reach right now.

THE QUESTIONING OF THE AZATHOTHIAN PRIEST

Bel: You view the world through such a narrow window, Captain Thorner, friend of Anton Zarnak. But why not? The simplest way to dispose of you both will simply be to think you out of existence. First, though not necessary, I would most likely seek to remove your restraints.

[at this point Belbin stared at his handcuffs. One by one the links began to disappear. There was a sound akin to escaping steam accompanied by small flashes of light as each one slipped out of existence]

Bel: At this point, it is all a matter of whim, really. I might collapse the building on you, combust you down to ashes, reinvent you as...as maybe fiddler crabs...the possibilities are endless.

Tho: And we're helpless to stop you. You're saying there's simply nothing we could do to stop you?

Bel: Quite. Allow me to demonstrate. Captain, please pull your service revolver and shoot me.

[Belbin's cajoling at this point went on for some time. Eventually, not so much to humor him, but more to frighten him into silence, the captain did attempt to bring forth his weapon. He could not. His limbs were frozen in place, as were my own. I am certain Officer Daniels will report the same sensation]

Bel: You see, Captain Thorner, friend of Anton Zarnak, I am completely safe. If you try to rise, looking to defend yourself with physical violence, you will find you can not. My power is infinite at this point, and you are well within the boundaries of my infinity. Your aide, poor Officer Daniels, so less experienced in these matters, I have reduced to a puppet.
    Dr. Zarnak's mind I have entered as well. No spells can he utter. No hand gestures can he make. I set these precautions into motion before you even entered the room.

"You're telling me you actually watched his handcuffs disappear—link by link—right there in front of you?"
"Yes, your honor."
"No sleight of hand, no stage trickery?"

"No, sir."

"And you really did try to pull your weapon?"

"If I could have gotten it out of its holster," said Thorner, "I would have shot him then and there."

The judge stared, unblinking. He could not have imagined such a response coming from the seasoned commander. Thorner was the most highly decorated officer in the city. Reis knew him to be extremely capable and cool under pressure. Without questioning him further, the judge turned back to the report, picking up where he had left off.

Tho: So, when exactly will all this eliminating take place?

Bel: As soon as I have ascertained what exactly your friend, Dr. Zarnak, is up to.

Tho: What do you mean, Tidril?

Bel: Captain, you play the game well, but there is little you can do against one who can read minds. Do not look surprised. Surely you must understand that one who can pierce the veils between dimensions can peer into the thoughts of mortals. Or should I say, most mortals.

Dr. Zarnak is clever enough to shield his thoughts from me. Even immobilized as he is, it is certain he is trying to find some way past your shared predicament. Aren't you, Anton?

Zar: There is no need to.

Bel: Really?

Zar: Yes. I've already taken precautions against you, Tidril. How could I not? I have observed you, obscenely licking at Azathoth's teat, suckling power. When I was called here to observe you, I knew things would come to a moment like this. You are too careful a being to expose yourself by accident. Any creature that can whisper in Azathoth's ear without bringing about its own end is certainly capable of tip-toeing around the police.

No, I assumed you wished to be captured. And, considering that you are a creature without remorse, such meant you had something in mind.

Bel: How amusing. The good doctor lives up to his reputation. And how will you accomplish this?

Zar: I will wait until you are distracted with some moment of foolishness, and then I will cause you to cease to exist.

Bel: I believe you might. And wouldn't that be foolish on my part, to allow you to use my own flamboyance of the moment against me. Very well, Dr. Zarnak, friend of Captain Thorner, perhaps I should put things to an end here and now.

[So saying, Belbin smiled and raised his hands. At this point the building began to shake.]

Zar: Officer Daniels—fetch Mr. Belbin some tea.

[At this point Officer Daniels pulled his service revolver and fired, shooting Tidril Belbin between the eyes. The priest died instantly. The earthquake his summoning began faded as quickly as it had begun]

REIS RUBBED AT HIS burning eyes. Looking absently toward the window of his chambers, not focusing on anything, not looking at the others in the room, he asked;

"What did you do, Zarnak?"

"Belbin was correct. I had observed him on Azathoth's plane. It is my duty to watch for such creatures. When I was summoned here, I suspected the possibility Belbin was ready to make some sort of move. Before going into the first observation room, I spoke to Officer Daniels, giving him what you might call a post-hypnotic suggestion. I told him that if I ordered him to get some tea for anyone, he was to pull his weapon and shoot to kill."

Reis closed his eyes. It was all far beyond him. He was a good judge, a good weigher of evidence with a sound talent for gauging the truth in a man's voice. Thorner, Zarnak, Daniels, none of them were lying. As much as he wanted to believe they were, he knew they were not.

"How long will it take for you two to produce an alternate report?"

"Already done, your honor," responded Thorner, his tone level.

"Pretty much reads the same. Says at the end that Belbin broke his cuffs, strength of a madman, that kind of thing. Says he turned over the table, got his hands around my throat. Officer Daniels was only doing his duty."

Tears formed in the judge's tired eyes. Such a simple deception. And, it was not as if he had not protected the police in the past. The court appointed lawyer would buy it—surely. The papers, the radio stations, of course they would accept it. It made the perfect end to the story—mad killer forces police to kill him. All neatly tied up.

Reis rubbed at his eyes once more. The horrible heat had dropped considerably. It had been building for weeks, every day a few degrees hotter than the one before, less than the day to come. Ever climbing, until, that was, the earthquake.

Earthquake.

The judge's body sagged. Perhaps with the happy ending, with the madman and all his terrible secrets to chatter about, with the earthquake and the still mounting property damage and loss of life, perhaps no one would notice his signature on the case. Perhaps no one would question his ruling, perhaps—

"Zarnak," Reis asked, eyes still closed, ears carefully listening for the answer to come. "Was he really as powerful as he thought he was? I mean, he claimed to...to be like a human atom bomb. Was he? Could he? I mean—"

As the judge's voice quavered, Zarnak answered quietly, soothingly;

"He was just a madman, your honor. One the good police of New York City dispatched with their usual aplomb. Really, nothing more should be made of it."

Softly, the report on Tyler Reis' desk was replaced with another. That done, the two men withdrew from the judge's chambers, exiting out into the hall. As they made their way down the hall, Thorner asked;

"Is that what he was going to do, when he started the earthquake runnin'? Was he goin' to Hiroshima the city?"

Zarnak thought for a moment. His friend had seen so much over the years, dealt with so many sinister nightmares. It was true that Thorner was a strong man, and a good one. But Zarnak knew all too well the kind of fear atomic devastation brought to the mind once it was actually understood. Deciding his friend needed distraction more than truth, he offered;

"Perhaps we should just go and get ourselves a little drink."

With a shudder, the captain nodded, adding;

"Perhaps we should go and get ourselves a *lot* of little drinks."

Dr. Zarnak did not argue. Reaching the front door of the courthouse, the two stepped out into the waning daylight, the smell of smoke and the howl of sirens still thick in the air.

Here is a tale filled with a little bit of everything. For those familiar with H.P. Lovecraft's works, and particularly his short story, "From Beyond," there are several gems. Fans of supernatural detective fiction will also spot some familiar elements. And yet, we need not know any of these things to see what lurks hidden in this story: Life is unique, and when so much as one life is lost to evil, the entire world pays a price.

PRAGMATIC

Professor Piers Knight was more than happy to hand his bags to the young man offering to carry them. His flight from New York City's JFK airport to its counterpart in Munich had been exhausting for him. Despite the inordinate amount of air travel the fates had forced upon him over the years, the professor had never been able to accustom himself to surrendering that much control over his life to outside forces. His distrust of airplanes was so intense he found it impossible to sleep on them, no matter how long the journey.

"So, Herr Knight, how was your flight?"

"Not very restful."

His phobia over water travel was not quite as intense. As he explained it, he preferred to drive places over any other form of transportation simply because when driving he was in command of the vehicle. And, while the professor was readily willing to admit he knew little to nothing about piloting boats, the back of his mind was somehow comfortable with the thought that if the captain of some ship he might be traveling upon were to suddenly become incapacitated, he might be able to pinch hit for them. But, if such were to happen to an airline pilot, he knew that if everyone was counting on him to come to the rescue, the craft would be going down.

"So," asked Knight as he settled into the back of the vehicle to which the young man escorted him, "do we have time to go to my hotel first before you take me to see Herr Strassen?"

"I'm afraid not, sir. Things have actually gotten a bit complicated." When the professor inquired as to what degree of complication had been reached, he was told, "Actually, sir, we're heading straight for the hospital."

"What? What are you talking about? Why would we do that—that doesn't make any sense." Forcing himself to stop chattering, Knight took a deep breath, then asked sensibly, "What's happened?"

"Frau Hoffman suffered a fall late last night," the chauffeur explained. Pulling out into traffic, he proceeded to weave in between the other cars on the road. Notching his speed higher by the second, he added, "She's been stabilized, but it's forced everyone to step up the timetable. She's going to have to deliver the baby as soon as possible."

The professor said nothing to his driver, but his brain began pelting him with non-stop worries. The news he had just been delivered was in no way anything he had been prepared to receive.

"What in Hell do I do now," he wondered, rivulets of panic searching for cracks in the granite of his calm exterior, splashing forward to erode his confidence. His eyes unblinking, staring off at the passing scenery, catching none of it, his mind hissed at him;

"This means no prep time, no way to study the situation, to prepare the room...there's no time to interview the mother—does she know what she's getting into? There's no time to talk to the doctors...do they understand what's being attempted? Will they listen to me, do they really understand what we're attempting? Do they believe—do they?"

"*Can* they?"

Professor Piers Knight suddenly began to cough violently, as if somehow having a physical reaction to the thought. So unexpected was his brief seizure, his driver called back to him.

"Herr Professor, are you all right?"

"Well now that, my dear young man," answered Knight in a voice cracking with strain, "will remain to be seen."

"Piers, ach du lieber, it's good to see you again."

"Herr Strassen, do we still have time?" Knight took the extended hand of the beefy German, barely noticing exactly how sweaty its palm was, or the slight tremble running through it and the rest of the large man.

"You Americans, always right to das point." Dr. Otto Strassen was large in the academic manner, a swelled balloon of a man, the type whose back and front were so similar when seen in silhouette as to be indistinguishable from one another if not for the fact of his massive nose.

"That doesn't answer the question, though, does it?" Knight, half a foot taller than Strassen, looked practically emaciated next to the beef-ball of a man.

"No, you are correct, as always." Taking the American by the arm, Strassen led his fellow academic to a quiet corner of the maternity ward. Once out of earshot of anyone else, the rotund doctor whispered;

"Frau Hoffman has been stabilized for the moment, but both she und die baby are in danger if die baby isn't delivered soon."

"What's the problem?"

"The fall has wrapped the umbilical cord around die baby's neck as well as shifting it into some other sort of bad position. Along with die mother's injuries, they are both at risk if die baby is not delivered quickly."

Knight found himself sweating despite the plentiful air conditioning. He was not prepared, had not readied his equipment. It was why he had flown to Germany when he did, giving himself what all had assumed would be a minimum of two weeks to make certain everything would go flawlessly.

"Damn," he thought bitterly. "The things I do in the name of the Brooklyn Museum."

With Strassen waiting for his reply, the professor allowed himself a moment's reflection. It had been over four months previous when the entire affair began, when he had received the call from his old colleague, asking him if he had ever heard of the resonant frequency. When Knight had confessed he had not, Strassen had explained;

"It is das perfect pitch of der human voice, das note, which when struck, can shatter glass. You are familiar, yes?" When Knight assured Strassen he was, the rotund man had continued, asking him how many people he thought were capable of achieving such a sound. When the professor guessed that it must be relatively few, he had received a surprising answer.

"Nein. Believe it or not, many people are born with such capability. But, most of them do not live very long."

"Are you saying," Knight had asked, "that something in being born with the ability causes early fatality?"

"Ya, but not any something most people would be capable of imagining." Strassen then paused dramatically enough for the professor to hear the deep intake of breath being swallowed on the other end of the line. After a few more dramatic seconds of silence, the doctor said;

"You are one of der only men I would even dare mention this to. Most in our field are not so, ah…'liberal of mind,' shall we say, as you and I."

"Otto," asked Knight, genuinely intrigued, "just what is this all about?"

"The resonant frequency, it does not just shatter glass. It is also mankind's perfect weapon against das supernatural. That particular pitch, when focused correctly, can repulse, and even destroy…demons."

The professor, of course, had been stunned by the information. Piers Knight did not instantly judge his colleague mad, however. Strassen had been correct; the professor was one of the few academics in the world he could trust to hear him out after making such a statement. And the doctor knew why. Like himself, Knight was a student of the occult, a studier of the unbelievable, of those things beyond. Together, ten years earlier the two had ridded Strassen's beloved Munich Opera House of a particularly obnoxious poltergeist infestation which, if left unchecked, would have guaranteed the ruination of the fall season that year, as well as threatening the closure of the magnificent music palace altogether.

To Strassen, such was completely unacceptable. It was a horror beyond thought, and thus he had risked his career to prevent its occurrence. Now, another such situation had arisen, and he had once more turned to the only other academic whom, once he had told him his tale, would assist him rather than seek his ruin. He had not, of course, asked for Knight's cooperation in the matter on the blind chance the professor would possibly be willing to help him. Strassen might be blindly loyal to the Opera House whose board he had sat upon for nine years, but he was by no means a foolish man. When he had first called Knight to enlist his assistance, it was not only because of his beliefs, but also because of his position.

"Piers, mein old friend," he had begun when first he had called, "still sitting atop der most under-used collection of artifacts the world has ever seen?"

Professor Knight was one of the directors of the prestigious Brooklyn Museum. Originally the site had been planned to be massive, one of the greatest repositories of art and culture, as Strassen had said, the world had ever seen. But, while its collection was gathered, one which could easily fill to over-flowing the designed series of galleries, its actual construction was cut short. In the end, the museum ended up being only a fourth of the size initially planned, with its massive, and ever-growing, collection forced into storage in its basement as well as in buildings all around it.

The professor took the budget cuts, political manipulations and societal apathy which had reduced the museum so in size as a personal affront. Thus Strassen had begun their conversation by appealing to that chink in Knight's otherwise fairly solid armor. Realizing that he was being maneuvered, but still curious as to the particular destination to which he was being guided, the professor had insisted Strassen get to the point. Comfortable with being blunt, the doctor had said;

"I want you to go through your over-crowded storage bins and find something, something I want you to bring to Germany. In other words, old friend…I have a deal I want to propose."

The bargain in question turned out to be a thing so fantastical that even Piers Knight had to raise an eyebrow. After informing the professor about the resonant frequency, as well as those horrors which seek to destroy any whom might grow to be able to utilize it against them, Strassen had then sent Knight to his keyboard. Checking through the museum's data records, it only took a matter of a few moments to find what his colleague was after.

"How did you know it was here?" The professor had asked the question in a tone of complete and quiet amazement. He had always been certain he knew more about the Brooklyn Museum, its exhibits and stores and its ten thousand treasures not seen in decades, than anyone. He would have been surprised if one of his fellow directors had known of an artifact he did not. To have such come from an outsider struck him as defying logic.

"Piers, you are such der controller. You have heard of die Shield of Tol'kaimi previously, ya?"

"Of course I have," answered Knight, still somewhat amazed. "Who in our business hasn't?"

"Exactly," answered Strassen. "You are merely upset by der fact I knew it was hidden away und forgotten within your treasure trove und you did not. Relax your grip a bit. I have been hunting for the past three months, combing old records, calling in favors—finding the shield has practically become my life's work recently…"

"Why?" The professor thought he might know where the heavy-set doctor was going, but preferred to hear it spelled out. Strassen was more than willing to oblige him. The Shield of Tol'kaimi had been created by the Incas, their greatest shamans called together to forge a weapon to help them hold off the hordes of demonkind. Those ancients had knowledge of the resonant frequency, and had determined to protect those who would be born to survive and then in turn protect their people. Much was sacrificed to bring the desired safeguard into being, but the shield proved worth the effort.

Indeed, so powerful were its protections, its reliability against those supernatural predators that attempted to make prey of the Incas for the next several hundred years were all repulsed without effort. Sadly, however, it was that very effectiveness which lead to the great race's downfall.

When the Spanish had arrived, they were, as most schoolchildren have been taught for centuries, misbelieved to be magical beings. What was not taught said youngsters over the centuries was the additional information that when the Conquistadors began raping and slaughtering their way across the Central Americas, the Incas had unleashed those of their race whom the shield had protected on the day of their birth. Songs, no matter how perfectly pitched, however, had no effect on the invaders. The Inca fled, their faith in Tol'kaimi's Shield shattered beyond repair.

"You ask 'why?'" Strassen had sounded monumentally disappointed. "I would have thought it an easy enough intellectual exercise for one such as you, my friend. You know my position with the Munich Opera House, ya?" When Knight admitted as much, the doctor had continued, saying;

"The simple truth is, demons are not der only beings in this universe that can locate those about to be born with the ability to hit the frequency."

And then, finally, Strassen had revealed to the professor a most unusual proposal. He had found a family of music lovers who were expecting the birth of their second child five months hence. That baby, the doctor's people were certain, would be born with the resonant ability. Greatly desiring to protect the child, desperately wanting to be the board member who secured a pitch perfect soprano for the opera company, the doctor had searched relentlessly until he had found the whereabouts of the Shield of Tol'kaimi. Overjoyed to learn it was in the Brooklyn Museum, under the control of one of the few men in all the world he could approach with such a scheme, he had made his proposal.

"I know this is greatly in the order of 'duty now for der future,'" Strassen had admitted, "but I plan on being a board member of the Munich Opera House for a long time."

He wished for Knight to bring the shield to Germany at the proper time, and to assist him in protecting the baby in question during its birth. At first the professor had been a bit stunned at the scheme suggested to him, but Strassen knew how to appeal to his former "ghostbusting partner," and after not much discussion at all Knight had agreed. Digging the shield out of storage proved to be not much of a problem, either. A carved granite circle some six inches in diameter, the piece weighed roughly eight pounds. Not a terribly great weight, thought the professor at the time, but the legends made note of the shield needing to be raised to the heavens while being used.

"Eight pounds can get more than a trifle heavy after a while," he told himself as he carefully lowered the piece into his valise. Then, hefting the black leather shoulder bag into place, he concentrated on the additional pull on his shoulder, calculating what it would be like to hold Tol'kaimi's defense above his head for any extended period of time.

"And just what will it be," he wondered. "Five minutes? An hour? A day and a half?"

Knight had stared forward into a mirror resting against a back wall of the storage area at that point. He recognized the piece after a moment—it had come from the *petits appartements* of Marie Antoinette at Versailles. The decorator had been her architect, Richard Mique. The paneling surrounding the still bright glass had been carved and gilded by the Rousseau brothers. Beautiful in its simplicity, it deserved to be seen by the world, and yet due to the pedestrian minds of those who ran the world, the money for such things went elsewhere.

Hypodermic needles were purchased to give away to drug addicts, condoms needed to be bought to distribute throughout the city's high schools. The state needed to pay women to have children, as long as they kept those children's fathers out of the picture. It also needed to pay for the sandblasting of buildings to remove the names of monsters from the past such as Washington, Franklin, Jefferson—others.

Knight stared at the reflection of his bag in the mirror, thinking on what it contained, on what he meant to do with it. For a moment he had been feeling guilty over his actions. He was, after all, considering removing a registered antiquity from the museum without permission, preparing to take it into what might be a hazardous environment. Did he have such a right?

As the question floated naggingly within his mind, his gaze suddenly moved outward from his reflection to the body of the mirror itself. As he focused on the compelling simplicity of the frame's uniquely delicate work, he found a streak of anger sizzling within him.

"No," he told himself finally, "I don't have any such right. But then again, what about the rights of the Rousseau brothers, to be remembered down through the ages, to have their artistry admired?" Hefting his bag once more, he had then turned and headed for the exit, muttering;

"Somebody should get some use out of the things stored away here. I'll hold the damn thing over my head if it takes a month to deliver the damn baby."

And, so saying, the professor had relocked the storage area and headed for home. He had several months to study the history of the Shield of Tol'kaimi, to learn its proper use, and to prepare himself for holding it aloft for who knew how long.

That had been months earlier. Now, in the present, standing in the hallway of the hospital whispering with Strassen, suddenly Knight had been presented with an entire new set of problems. He had come to Germany two weeks early to rehearse with his support team, to meet with the doctors who would be performing the delivery. Yes, his colleague would have made certain the medical professionals present would be sympathetic to their cause, but to go in cold, with no sounding out of each other, learning the necessary procedures, where to stand, what to expect—he, after all, knew as little about delivering babies as they did the theory behind rejecting demonic presences from the tangible world. What a recipe for disaster if—

"Dr. Strassen, Professor," it was Knight's chauffeur from earlier. "The doctors are calling for you. They say they have to deliver the baby now!"

"Ready, Piers?"

"Oh, I'm ready all right," agreed the professor sourly. "Just don't ask me exactly what it is I'm ready for."

✠ ✠ ✠

IN LESS THAN TEN minutes Knight was inside the delivery room, scrubbed sterile and dressed in a paper gown. The Shield of Tol'kaimi had been sterilized as well, making it much too hot for the professor to handle for the moment. While waiting for the eight pounds of stone to cool, the professor called for the chauffeur to bring him his bag. Having the younger man open it so that he might remain sterile, Knight directed him to remove a somewhat bizarrely shaped mechanical item, calling out at the same time;

"Where can this be plugged in?" When both Strassen and the attending physician asked what the device was, Knight replied;

"It's basically nothing more than an illuminator, but one that goes through all the various spectrums at a high rate of speed. For the most part its effects will be invisible to our eyes, but if there are things here lurking in between those spectrums, they will be revealed to us." Turning more to his colleague, he added;

"Handy little gizmo, invented by Nikola Tesla. Others since his time outfitted it to run on AC or DC, as long as the proper adaptor is used."

"Enough!"

The single word came from the doctor in charge. Turning away from the academics, no longer caring what purpose they hoped to suit twenty years in the future, he began snapping orders to his nurses. The doctor was concerned only with the lives of his patients, and knew there was no more time to spare concerning what had to be done in the then and now. Frau Hoffman and her baby were both in mortal danger. Far more time had been spent waiting for Knight's arrival than he would have preferred. Now that the professor was there, his contraptions and devices ready, the doctor's duty was clear.

As the physician turned to those on the table, consulting with the nurses in attendance, the chauffeur found an out-of-the-way spot for Tesla's light. Setting it atop a cabinet in the corner furthest from the operating theater, he uncoiled its power cord. Making certain he could plug it in without straining the cord, the young man did not hesitate to do so and, with that action, the doorway to Hell was opened.

"Mein Gott in Heimel!"

Even in the first few seconds of light cast from Tesla's lamp, shapes began to appear all about the room. Humanoid in the most casual sense of the word, they were strange and twisted forms, clawed and winged, gangly, leathery and possessed of nothing to indicate they were anything but monstrous in all manners and intentions.

"Keep the light safe," Knight snapped at the chauffeur. The younger man nodded, closing his eyes at the terrors all about him, holding onto the light as tightly as he could. Not having the luxury of closing their eyes, however, both the nurses in attendance recoiled in horror, only to turn around and find that more of the hideous things were behind them. Frau Hoffman's husband, present to act as her coach, screamed along with the women. The doctor, an older man made of tightly wound fibers, barked orders to his nurses as well as Herr Hoffman in German, cursing the lot of them for their weakness, reminding them of the job they were there to perform.

At the same moment, Knight grabbed up a towel and hoisted the still burning hot Shield of Tol'kaimi aloft, holding it above his head. Turning slowly, he presented the face of the Incan artifact to each demon in turn, forcing them if not backward, to at least halt their advancement. As the medical team began their work with the expectant mother on their table, the professor attempted to circle them, using the stone disc to turn back those things straining to break through the protective circle.

Of course, the demonic shapes those assembled could see were not physically present. They could not simply grab up a chair and bash in the baby's skull. Restrained by whatever barrier it was which had held them at arm's distance from the human race over the millennia, the demons had been forced to find other ways to wreak havoc across the earthly plane of existence. As Knight continued to circle the delivery table, several of the creatures began their traditional assault.

Wretched flesh bag, one of the terrors sneered at the professor, *take your foul stone and begone, or pain and suffering will follow you all your days!*

"Pain and suffering have followed me longer than you can imagine, Helldweller. You'll have to do better than that."

Despite the air conditioning, the presence of so many demonic forms within the room had begun to drive the temperature upward. In less than a minute the mercury had climbed ten degrees, with no evidence it would stop any time soon. Sweat pouring down his face, Knight could feel the heat of the shield oozing its way through the towel. His fingers were warming quickly—burning—his palms growing moist.

This thing shall not be born, came the snarling voice within the professor's head once more, *shall* not *be born*/notnotnot *be born*/not *be* not *be* not *be* not *be born!*

Knight blinked his eyes hard, staring from one demon to another, trying to ascertain which one was actually barking within his mind. Continuing to circle the table, trying not to step in too close where he might interfere with the operation in progress, trying also not to give the trio too much room where he might leave them open for demonic invasion, his eyes kept darting, straining against the odd flicker of Tesla light, searching out the thing he needed to silence.

"Which one are you," he asked the voice within his mind. Then, inspiration striking, he directed more questions at the chattering annoyance. "I mean, which of you is the one so puny, so useless, so utterly worthless that you were given the task of whispering in my ear, I imagine, as a means to keep you out of the others' way?"

As Knight continued firing off his own mental barrage at his unknown adversary, he wondered how the others were holding up. The professor was certain both the doctor and his nurses were being urged on toward mayhem in the same manner as himself. It was the way demons had been destroying those capable of reaching the resonant frequency for ages—slither inside the mind of the attending midwife, or of a mother wondering if she was capable of all that was required of her, a father uncertain if he could support another mouth—searching for the doubting, the weak-willed, the confused, whomever they might find shallow and frightened enough to be manipulated into doing their bidding.

Death to the meat/death to the meat/deathdeathdeath—

In the maternity ward in Munich, however, the demons were at a disadvantage in that they could not maneuver anyone into thinking the murderous thoughts crossing their minds were their own. Tesla's light had revealed the truth. As long as Tol'kaimi's Shield kept the foul creatures from actually making contact with any of the medical personnel's auras they could not be fooled. Despite its weight, Knight managed to keep the eight pound disc above his head, but he felt his strength fading.

Death to the meat/death to the meat/deathdeathdeath—

The professor had just gotten done with a long flight—a journey during which he was unable to sleep. The heavy stone was putting a strain on his fingers, his wrists, shoulders and spine—even his knees. Sweat was gathering across his body. The dribbling of it, soaking into his clothing, running down his arms, inching over his forehead into his eyes, collecting at the base of his nose, across his upper lip, moving down his chest, trickling into his groin—

"How can it be so hot in here," he wondered, even as the demon choruses continued to echo within his mind—

not be born/notnotnot be born/notnotnot be not be not be born!

"How the hell long is this going to take?" Not looking at the professor, the doctor shouted back at him.

"I'm delivering a baby. These things are done when they're done—now shut up and stop trying to make it take longer!"

Death to the meat/death to the meat/deathdeathdeath—

At first, no one noticed the chauffeur leaving his post. The demons made no attempt to interfere with the now unguarded light. Strassen, busy reading from the Von Juntz text on expulsion, was concentrating on reinforcing his colleague's magical barrier. Everyone else's attention was rightly focused on the mother to be. Thus, as the young man crossed the room, he was able to pick up a scalpel, but as he drew within two yards of the table Knight stopped chanting long enough to ask;

"Why have you left your post?"

not be/notnotnot be born/notnotnot be not be notnotnot be born!

One look into the chauffeur's eyes told the professor all he needed to know. Racing around the table, desperate to keep the stone shield aloft, Knight tripped over one of the nurses' legs, stumbling as he shouted;

"Strassen—your man!"

The chauffeur raised the scalpel, chuckling as he moved forward on those surrounding the mother, his head hanging awkwardly to one side. Catching a glimpse of his approach, the second nurse let out a cry. Her shriek distracted the thing possessing the young man, the terror of it delighting the creature. It sucked the juicy fragrance from the air, then turned back to the table, snarling;

"Death to the meat!"

Strassen hurled his heavy, leather-bound copy of Von Juntz at the chauffeur, catching him in between his shoulder blades. As the younger man went down, the heavy-set academic threw himself atop him, crushing him to the floor. Knight managed to untangle himself from the nurse and reach the pair at that point. He attempted to kick the scalpel from the chauffeur's hand, but off-balance as he was still holding the shield over his head, he missed, allowing the younger man to drive the blade into Strassen's thigh.

Death to the meat/deathdeathdeath—

As Strassen shrieked, rolling off the possessed chauffeur, Knight moved in, kicking at the man's head.

Death to the meat/deathdeathdeath—

The chauffeur dodged the blow, swinging wildly, managing to slash open the professor's leg below the knee.

Deathdeathdeath—

Feeling blood exploding free, Knight knew some vital artery had been opened. Knowing he had but seconds, even as the younger man began to rise, the professor used the only weapon he had—

Deathdeathdeath—

And swung the Shield of Tol'kaimi full force, catching the possessed chauffeur in the chest. The stunning blow sent the off-balance man stumbling across the room and into a gurney covered with medical equipment. Even as he turned back toward the operating theater, however, Knight knew the damage had been done.

Deathdeathdeathdeathdeath!

In the eerie illumination of Tesla's lamp, he could see the demons pouring forward, thrusting their insubstantial tongues into the ears of the doctor, the nurses, the Hoffmans—could hear their lies and threats and vile, luring insinuations.

Deathdeathdeathdeath!

Turning back toward the table, Knight tried desperately to return to his post. Staggering, he limped along, blood sluicing down his leg, drenching the floor—

Deathdeathdeath!

Losing his grip on the shield because of the cumbersome towel, he pulled it away, clenching the still burning stone circle in his bare hands. Doing his best to ignore the burning pain, he shoved the shield skyward, ordering—

"Begone, Hellspawn!"

But he was too late. Although the doctor had delivered the child, safely removed it from its mother, the damage had been done. The demons were everywhere, spreading their poisonous suggestions. Already the nurse's eyes were glazing over, taking on the same disturbingly blank look the chauffeur's had held. Herr Hoffman seemed to be swaying as well.

Deathdeath!

Finding Tol'kaimi's defense no longer effective, Knight struggled, his own mind filling with the hissing of demonic tongues. Their voices were so insistent, their assurances so soothing, the professor found himself teetering for a moment. Then, summoning what strength he had remaining, he shouted;

"For God's sake, Doctor—"

Death!

"Slap the baby!"

Somehow hearing Knight's voice over the cacophony within his head, the doctor lifted the child aloft, then forced himself to smack its backside soundly. The action, as it has for tens of thousands of years, forced air into the small girl's lungs, air she exhaled as babies have since time immemorial, in a startling acceptance of individual life.

And, with that scream, the worlds in between light and darkness exploded, the air fried, and those scores of demons unable to escape the child's first sound consumed like dry leaves in a fire.

"So, MY OLD FRIEND, was that what you had in mind?"

"Mein Gott," Strassen replied to Knight, "it most certainly was not. Can't you Americans do anything without bringing down the ceiling?"

The two academics sat quietly in an observation room, waiting to be discharged from the hospital. Both had received treatment for their injuries, but their blood loss had been such that neither was going to be allowed to leave until their doctor was satisfied with their recovery. The two laughed for a moment over how out of all those involved in that afternoon's excitement, only they had suffered any injury beyond the momentary. Even Frau Hoffman had been able to visit them, albeit in a wheelchair, to thank them for all they had done. Once they were certain they would not be interrupted further, Strassen said quietly;

"It was a good thing you did today."

"It was a damn foolhardy and dangerous thing I did today," Knight responded. "And before we forget, you know the reason I did it, so…"

"Ya, ya," answered the rotund academic. Reaching to the floor for the brown leather bag at his side, Strassen hoisted the valise and then handed it to his colleague. Opening the bag, Knight reached inside and then pulled out its contents. The core of what he held in his hand was a nautilus shell, one fashioned into what seemed a semblance of a goblet. A reptilian leg crafted from a metal which reflected like silver, but took none of its tarnish, served as the vessel's stem, a broad, three-toed foot forming its stand along with a balancing spur. The metal work continued up and over the sides of the Nautilus, dipping down and into its mouth and surrounding the circumference of its lip with a ring of wildly pointed, needle-like fangs.

"Und there you have it," said Strassen. "I get my singing star, one to train to perfection from birth, und you get that silly looking thing which has gathered dust in the basement of der opera house for no one knows now long."

Knight turned the prize over in his hands, studying it from all angles. Staring into the mouth of it, not knowing what exactly he might find there, the professor asked about the necessary papers for removing the artifact from the country. Strassen assured him everything he needed was within a side pocket of the piece's carrying case. As Knight repacked the bizarre goblet, his colleague said;

"Und so you have your prize for your museum; I have mine for my opera house. But tomorrow, another such baby will be born somewhere, und who will be there to save it?"

"There will be more than a single baby in danger tomorrow," answered Knight, refusing to follow Strassen down the road he was looking to travel. "There have been people of all ages in danger every day since there were people, and there always will be. Some will perish and some will survive."

"You," answered the rotund academic, "are a very pragmatic fellow, Piers Knight."

"'The Arab who builds himself a hut of the marble fragments of a temple in Palmyra,'" answered the professor, obviously quoting, "'is more philosophical than all the curators of the museums in London, Munich or Paris.'"

"Jacques Anatole Francois Thibault," replied Strassen, "The Crime of Sylvestre Bonnard. Very well, your point is taken. We do what we can in this life…"

"Because we can do no more," responded Knight, finishing his old friend's thought. The two chatted while they waited for their doctor to return and officially release them. After a bit of inconsequential chatter, Strassen said, almost sheepishly;

"You know, that thing I just gave you…I would hate to let you go without telling you, der rumors are that…well, that it is haunted. Cursed. Some such thing. You don't feel cheated, do you?"

"Cheated?" Knight laughed, smiling as he added, "Are you kidding? When the board hears it's supposedly haunted, they'll be even happier. Nothing packs in Americans like a chance to hobnob with evil—at a safe distance, of course."

"Ach, that explains your choices in presidents."

Before Knight could respond, the doctor who had treated the two academics' injuries returned, announcing that they were discharged. Gathering up their various bags, the pair thanked their physician, then headed for the exit, both content with what they felt had been a good day's work.

Nearly everyone enjoys a good Viking yarn. The difficultly with such stories is capturing the essence, the spirit of the fabled Norsemen. In the tradition of "Beowulf," C.J.'s "The Laughing Man" brings to life a rugged, harsh world where men struggled to live, and lived for the struggle.

To those historic warriors who faced in battle the "The Men of the North," fear not only came in the form of combat, but in rumor. And for any warrior, fear is a powerful weapon. But for a Viking, it is deadly.

THE LAUGHING MAN

"A thing derided is a thing dead; a laughing man is stronger than a suffering man."

–Gustave Flaubert

EDINGTON: 878 A.D.

Across a landscape all gray and green, darkened by a never-ending drizzle and more blood than most could contemplate, moved eight tired and frightened men, all sharply aware that their time was running out. Keen was the group's growing despair, despite the promise with which their battle had begun. Part of a great Norse raiding force were they, two hundred strong, come to the English shore in the morning darkness to loot a castle and break the back of their enemy's forces. Homeric had been its beginning—tragic was its end.

The eight were the last of the Northmen still drawing breath, and one of them was faltering, wickedly close to leaving his fellows to share what scarce luck they had remaining amongst themselves. Cut off from their fellows by impish fate, they had stumbled across the English lord's store of treasures. Accepting providence, the eight had laden themselves with gold and jewels and headed back to their waiting ship, expecting their fellows to follow in hearty triumph. It did not happen.

Wretched coincidence had turned the battle, as suddenly and sharply as if on the toss of a god's coin. The Norse forces were obliterated cruelly, all save the octet struggling their way back to the

beach. And struggle they did, and massively, for two king's ransoms did they have between them. But, no joy did its weight bring for each step taken through the dreary, bogging countryside sank deeper into the grasping English soil. Slower and slower became their progress, weighed down as is was by sacks and chests of bloody plunder. While at the same time the sounds of pursuit—the clatter of armor, the strike of hooves and the bay of hounds—scrambled along behind, warning them their end was drawing fast near.

Reaching a poor but serviceable road, the refugees fell upon it greedily, giving thanks to Odin to have discovered more solid ground upon which to rest their weary legs. Dirt was it as well, but the very lord they had robbed so cleanly had seen to the trail's being hard-packed and strewn with shale and cinders so that passage of his wagons might be more easily obtained. The eight staggered onward under their mighty load, grim and silent save for their labored breathing—steaming air snorted harshly from bellowed lungs.

After but covering a third of a league, the fugitives reached a gentle but speeding river. Stopping at the timbered bridge leading over its narrowest stretch, the one of them highest in rank dropped the chest he was carrying, cursing the skies and fates and any others who would listen.

"Calm, Birstin," answered another. "Why rage ye here?"

"Fool, see ye not the sign of our folly?" When his fellows answered not, he pointed to the water before them. "Did we make a crossing to reach our English host? No! Then, if we are to return to our boats, to our homes and loves and sons and stock, would this be the direction in which we should travel? Think any of ye that 'aye' be the answer?"

"Perhaps," answered one of the others. Eager for something more concrete to wrestle with than the eminent slaughter snapping at their heels, Birstin turned with a rapid speed to face his fellow.

"What say ye, Olgenson, that I be wrong?"

"No, you are surely right that lost we have become. But besides acting as signpost, this river may also be our salvation from English doom."

"Speak plain," demanded one of the others.

"We be not far from the sea, that we know," answered the man. "Well, follow the river, come to the shore."

The others nodded. Some smiled. Birstin moved his head as well, agreeing in principle. "Aye," he admitted, "your brain be clearer than mine as far as direction lies, but little good it does us."

When the others questioned their leader's words, Olgenson provided the answer for them.

"The English are too close. They'll find we took to the road. When they come to this spot, they'll chase us down to the sea long before we can reach the boats. Unless..."

"Unless what?" snapped Birstin, desperate for a miracle, even one not of his own making.

Staring down into the thick waters below the bridge, Olgenson followed the river on its way to the sea with his eyes, his brain weighing a decision balancing narrow options. Straight he forced himself to stand, despite the oozing wound throbbing in his side. Grinding his teeth for a moment, he leaned against one of the bridge's support columns.

"Unless," he said, desperate to not betray his rapidly waning strength, "we convince them we have not gone along the river."

The others broke out in a babble of questions, but Birstin quieted them with a wave of his hand. When he asked what Olgenson proposed, the dying man told him.

"If all but one were to drop into the waters and wade downstream for a length, their trail would be much more difficult to discover. With luck, the English would miss the movement and proceed on down the road."

"Why all but one?" asked Firdal, Olgenson's boyhood mate.

"Because if one were to stay behind and defend this spot, it would appear he were attempting to keep the English from crossing after his fellows. Once he be killed, the fools will proceed without thinking, convinced the others have gone down the road that one appeared to be protecting."

It was obvious to all in the desperately small party that Olgenson spoke the truth. Hope surging against the banks of their gloom-cast resignation, the men began to prepare themselves for one last dash for freedom. Not overlooking the obvious as were his fellows, however, Birstin turned to Olgenson.

"And who be this hero who dies for the rest?"

"I name myself," answered Olgenson. "On one condition."

As the others listened, grim and silent, the dying man said, "To be deprived of husband and father will be hard enough for my family. They'll not be deprived of my share of the booty we've won this day. I'll die for us—here, gladly—but only because I'll know that when you reach home, a full half of all taken by our hand will go to my family."

Growls of complaint were heard, but at the same time, the faint sounds of the coming army behind them crackled through the trees, whispering their way through the fog and rain. Birstin, gulping a huge wet breath down into his burning lungs, pulled off his glove and spat on his palm. Then, extending his hand to Olgenson, he waited for the other man to do the same.

"'Tis a thieving bargain," he said with a grin, "but then, 'tis thieves we are this day, and dead men spend no gold."

"Aye," answered the dying man. As the others followed suit, spitting on their hands and joining their grasp to the one before them, the dying man said, "And I would know."

As the others stepped away, Olgenson opened his fur vest enough for the others to see the savage piercing English steel had inflicted on his side. Pulling the garment fast again to help contain his leaking fluids, he said, "Perhaps if Father Odin's voice were not so loud within my ears, my nobility might not be so fast to surface. But, what man wouldn't die, to see his son a king, eh?"

Harsh laughter broke out from the others. As the sound of the English slithered through the fog to their ears once more, however, Birstin ordered them all over the side of the bridge. Splitting up the plunder Olgenson had somehow managed to carry between those who would survive him, the seven made signs of good fortune for their comrade and then disappeared into the waters below, slogging along under their golden burdens. In but a handful of seconds they were gone, no sight or sound of them remaining. Moving to the middle of the bridge, Olgenson positioned himself as best he could and then began his wait.

Time passed slowly in the fog. The dying man flexed his fingers, looking to see if he could still make them work to his will. They closed, the ten of them, but only after a fashion, and stiffly at that. Leaning against the side of the bridge once more, Olgenson pulled his vest tighter about his weary body. The man could feel his life slipping away, dripping down his leggings, slathering across his boots to mingle with the English mud. His vision was blurring and the images before him constantly doubled no matter how often or how forcefully he blinked his eyes.

"Damn," he whispered to himself as a terrible fang of pain bit through him. "Damn."

You will not die, he told himself. You will not fail your fellows, or your family. You want Friwulf to be a king, don't you? Then stand up and be a man who deserves a king for a son.

spasm emptied his stomach and dragged tears from his eyes. Finally in control of his rapidly failing body once more, he muttered to the woman before him.

"You cannot be here for me. Odin's handmaidens take only heroes from the field of battle."

Heroes only do we take to Valhalla, she corrected. *But all the slain do we designate*.

Olgenson nodded sadly, hope drying within him. The approaching noise of the English put them but a minute or two down the road. The width and breadth of the extensive clamor surprised even him. He had expected tens of men, perhaps even scores. But the nearing din bespoke the arrival of hundreds.

Fool, he thought to himself bitterly. His grip on his spear hardening, he asked himself, and how did you think you would ever hold this spot against such a force?

With a warrior's soul, came his answer.

The female form slipped the fallen sword back between the man's fingers, and then she was gone, the light of her no longer forcing aside the dismal gray shroud of morning. Wisps of fog sliding over his frozen body, Olgenson gasped down a final breath and then waited for the inevitable.

DOWN THE ROAD, THE English came on in strong pursuit. Although the main body of them marched along the rock-dried lane, dozens more moved along to both sides of it as well. It had taken some time to slaughter all the Norse within the castle and its walls, longer still to extinguish the multitude of fires they had set. Eventually, however, the storerooms had been checked, and the theft of the king's treasure had been discovered. Instantly every man who could still draw air through his lungs was pressed into the search for the rogues who had penetrated so far and made off with so much. Exhaustion or wounds did not matter—there was no choice. The raiders had to be found. Finally, at the bridge leading to Devron, it appeared that they were.

There at the mouth of the crossing, his one hand holding a sword in defiance, the other keeping a spear to the ready, stood one of the Norse bastards in question. Holding his hand up to indicate a momentary halt, the captain serving as the column's commander reined in his mount, then leaned down and asked his second, "And what do you make of this?"

"Left behind to slow our progress. Thinks some heathen Charlemagne dubbed him Roland, I suspect."

Eying the silent figure standing before them in the mist, the commander thought for a second.

"Maybe. Quite possibly, even," admitted the leader of the pursuing forces. "But then, bait comes in many flavors. With the fog so heavy about us, who knows what may be hidden in the shadows behind him. And around us. Before we lose more ground this morning, let us see what this quiet fellow has to say."

Understanding, the second-in-command called out in the Norseman's tongue.

"Stand down, brigand. Tell us where the others have gone and you shall be dispatched swiftly and spared the tortures you deserve."

No answer came from the rigid form. As the English looked on, the warrior at the bridge remained motionless, only bits of his fur and cloak moved by the surrounding winds. Again, the Englishman called out.

"Speak, man. If you value your dignity, tell us where the others have gone."

When grim silence remained their only answer, the commander snapped, "Enough of this. If left to hold us at this spot he was, salute his effort, for already has he squandered too much of our most precious time."

With a wave of his hand, the English captain called forth a line of archers. Indicating their target, he ordered the group to fire. Ten arrows were notched, ten strings drawn back and touched to cheek, ten missiles then sent to knock away the single flea blocking the road before them. Eight shafts found their mark, five driving into the dark figure's chest, one its neck, another its thigh and the last its face. Strong enough to knock down a runaway horse was the force of the barrage, but the pierced form did not topple. Unaffected, it stood on, still holding its ground in fierce silence.

"He makes no sound?" whispered more than one voice.

"He does not fall?" questioned others. "Perhaps he cannot. Perhaps it be only we who may die this day."

Scoffing at the ignorance of those behind him, the captain snarled at their superstitious fears, insisting, "'Tis no man before us, 'tis but a scarecrow from which we cower."

As his nervous troops relaxed somewhat, the commander ordered, "Enough time have we wasted with this heathen trick. Resume the march."

As one men and horses began their forward movement once more. Despite their bolstered spirits and their leader's assurances, however, all English eyes remained fastened on the figure still holding the bridge. Stiff and quiet it might be, but still it did not seem a construct to them. None doubted what they saw was a man. Of course, many thought, a man's remains might be used thus, by desperate comrades at the end of their road. Heartened by such notions, the English soldiers continued to move onward against the bridge. And then, the laughter began.

It was a curious noise, a gravelly chortle that dug deeply into the bowels, a thick curtain of angry amusement that slapped at the advancing force with vicious disdain. Those few on horseback found it impossible to force their steeds forward. The mastiffs which had been leading them up until that point shied back as well, their tails low and motionless.

"Attack, I say," bellowed the captain. "Attack!"

His sword drawn from its sheath, the commander tried to force his men forward, but hesitation shattered their lines. Too many wild, discordant thoughts were flooding their minds.

Their foe should have died. He did not. Perhaps he never lived, but then, if that were so, how came he to laugh? Were they doomed? Cursed?

Terror struck down man after man, the dark specter of the unknown making lead of flesh, riveting them to the ground, their tunics soaking with sweat despite the chill. Knowing that he could not allow the situation to continue unchanged, the captain dug his heels into his horse's sides viciously.

The shocked animal overcame its fear and bolted forward in much the same manner it might have charged back inside a burning stable. His sword to the ready, the commander charged the stolid figure, screaming;

"And now you die!"

All eyes stared forward unblinking. Terrible laughter echoed through the trees, swallowing the fog, licking at the men's ears. Horse and rider drew closer, the laughing man moved not. The commander drew back his blade, an army held its breath. The captain reached the upgrade, drawing nearer, his arm swinging, and then, the figure moved.

Suddenly, the arm holding the spear seemed to jerk forward. In an unstoppable flash, the long pike came down before horse and rider, piercing the commander's body, knocking it from his mount.

The captain flew away from his steed which then reared up in terror, turning on its heel and running back toward the English lines. None waited to greet it.

With one heart the English turned and fled into the surrounding forest. Reason deserted them as mad screams flew from their lips, mingling with the terrible laughter every man swore he heard all the way back to the castle.

On the beach, the escaping seven heard nothing of laughter, merely the beating of wings and the sound of the heavens welcoming to their great hall and hearth and well-stocked table one of their own with whom they were well pleased.

C. J. has many vivid characters in his fiction. But perhaps the one to have the most words penned is Theodore London. In "The Soul's Right Hand," Teddy London is in his element—and that is in the middle of "Good and Evil."

Accompanying London is his loyal cast, who attempt to set the world right, no matter who or what struggles against them. This is "classic" London.

THE SOUL'S RIGHT HAND

"Pride is an admission of weakness; it secretly fears all competition and dreads all rivals."

—Bishop Fulton J. Sheen

BUT THAT, OF COURSE, is only the legends," the reporter told the audience she believed would exist several days in the future. "And we, as always, are after the truth. That's why this is where tonight's show *really* begins..." Walking the fifteen paces from the elevator to the door she sought, the woman continued, filling in her theoretical viewers.

"At the one detective agency greedy enough to reopen the Dorson case."

Her statement, of course, was not true. Greed had nothing to do with the agency's interest in reopening the case. But, the woman was a reporter—not a judge—and thus her interpretation of the facts was all she deemed important. Helping to further her indictment, the camera panned over the frosted glass of the door indicated, framing the black, serifed words painted in its center:

Theodore London
Private Investigations

As it did, Barri Mezeltin pushed a handful of the red hair WDEL prized so highly back off her face, waiting for the lens to frame her once more. Once it had, the woman assumed the most serious of

the seventeen expressions she knew how to project and, ignoring the irony of her statement, spoke once more to the empty air as if her audience of millions was already hearing her, as if anything she had to say held any true value.

"There is always someone ready to profit from the misery of others. Tonight, we shall watch the London Agency work to help another millionaire murderer escape the reach of justice."

And, so saying, Mezeltin made a gesture with her off-camera hand indicating she wanted the door opened. The site assistant handled the task, giving the reporter and her cameraman access to the agency's reception area. On the other side of the door, the first thing the camera found to focus on was a slightly heavyset, balding man with a near foot-long ponytail snapping off orders.

"Boss, shake a leg—the ol' clock on the wall sez we gotta get movin'. Doc, don't forget my demo bag. Cat, grab yer gear. Are ya sure ya got everything ya need?"

"How would I know?" answered the short, strawberry blonde in the bib overalls. "You tell me what we're going to run into and I'll tell you if I've got it covered."

The balding man was about to reply when the door to the hall finished opening. Sensing strangers, he turned toward the intrusion marching straight for the trio of TV people.

"Hey, hey—no further!" he barked. His hands pushing the air before him, he snarled, "Whoever ya three are, we ain't interested. Take it out of here. Now!"

"No, Mr. Morcey," interceded a much younger man sitting in the overstuffed chair in the reception area's back corner, "I invited her."

Morcey skidded to a halt. Whirling around to face the speaker, he pulled in his first impulse—as well as his second—asking instead through gritted teeth, "Unnnn-huh. And what made ya do that jolly thing, kid?"

"Mr. Morcey, last year on this day I went through a nightmare. But, as bad as it was, since then the press has made my life a never-ending hell with their assumptions and innuendo."

Leveling an accusatory finger in the reporter's direction, the young man added, "They tried to have me jailed, and when that didn't work they made a laughing stock out of me. Her in particular. So, yes—I want them there tonight when we go into that building. I want their cameras there. I want my goddamned reputation cleared once and for all."

"Sweet bride of the night," muttered the balding man. "Dis ain't no luau we're goin' to. We're gonna spend the night pokin' around in da place where you lost your fiancé and your hand. Ya really want a bunch'a…"

"Now, now, Paul," a voice called from beyond the doorway behind Morcey. "If our client wants to invite a few more people along, who are we to complain? It is his party, after all."

"But, Jezz-it, boss…from da sound of dis, we're gonna have enough trouble just puttin' a cork in ol' Father Halloween without having to nursemaid a buncha…"

Theodore London came out from his back office, followed by an older man clutching a small black bag. His hand up to cut off his partner, the detective focused on the intruders, telling them quietly, "Good evening. We're on our way out, so I will make myself clear. Ms. Mezeltin, one of my associates, a clairvoyant, predicted your arrival and recommended we take you along, as well as Mr. Prentiss."

The cameraman was startled to hear his name given by a complete stranger. Before he could say anything, however, London turned to the site assistant and told her, "I'm sorry. You weren't mentioned. You'll have to leave." The young woman looked to Mezeltin for instructions. Ignoring the flunky's need for official approval, the detective added;

"Now."

Having dealt with the unknown on several extreme occasions had brought to life certain abilities within London which he had no ethical dilemmas over using. The younger woman found herself backing toward the door, despite her desire to ignore the mere male demanding her exit. Sensing the advantage in cooperation, Mezeltin told the girl, "Do it. We can carry on."

The reporter turned to London before the younger woman could reach the door, however, and asked, "We can join you? No scam?"

"Ms. Mezeltin," answered the detective, "my associate told me in no uncertain terms that there is great danger ahead for all of us tonight. Now, we as a group are somewhat prepared for what we may see or…experience. You, however, are filled with the cynical arrogance typical of the self-important and the vainly ignorant."

London stared at the woman for a moment with an appraising eye, then added, "Yes—you should attract whatever's ahead of us nicely—the glow of your stupidity is certain to scream out to whatever it is we find. Should give us a good handful of seconds to react while it goes for you."

Mezeltin's nostrils flared as her face flushed with blood. Everyone had *something* to hide. Enduring the curiosity of the various arms of the electronic press was something one simply did in the same manner they endured the IRS. Despite all the chatter about people's hostility toward the media, however, no one had ever actually dared talk to the network anchor that way—not Academy Award winners, not Mafia godfathers, not senators. No one.

Finally catching hold of herself enough to respond, the reporter hissed, "Who the hell do you think you are—the Ghostbusters? Just what was all that crap supposed to mean?"

"Oh—I'm sorry," answered London, his tone so honestly sincere the woman was shocked into accepting it. "I thought I'd been clear. All I meant to say is that you'll make excellent bait."

Mezeltin stared—frozen more by her inability to respond to the detective's statement, but frozen nonetheless. She repeated London's last word under her breath with contempt, but if the detective heard her, he did not respond. Instead, he turned to those assembled and snapped his fingers, saying;

"Well, people—as Paul said—we've got our invitation to the dance. Let's get on our waltzing shoes, shall we?"

Morcey rubbed his hands together with anticipation. Fourteen months earlier, he had been a janitor. Destiny had thrust him into the role of London's right-hand man. So far it was a part he had not tired of playing. During his time at the detective's side he had seen monsters aplenty—towering horrors that filled the sky, winged lizard men and demons claiming Hell as their mailing address. He had dispatched a vampire and dealt with the horror the Bible labeled as Lilith. There had been moments of doubt for him, of course, flashes of inadequacy when measuring himself against the terrors he and his companions found themselves making a trade of opposing.

Indeed, even as he headed for the hallway the balding man was wondering if that night he might not finally stumble and join all the others who had fallen during their crusade. But, even as doubt wormed its way out of the evening shadows to gnaw at his fragile confidence, excited anticipation steeled the walls of his soul, giving him enough balance to carry on.

So, thought Morcey, feeling his emotions balancing within him, it's 'here we go again,' is it? Well, good.

The last one out, the balding man killed the lights, locked the door, and then joined those gathered in the hall as the elevator opened. Patting the oversized bulge under his jacket, the former maintenance man thought—

I've said it before, and I'll say it again. Just because you're up against things from Hell, doesn't mean you can't kick their ass.

The ex-maintenance man smiled to himself. In all his adventures with the London Agency, he had not met a horror that could not be taught some excellent manners by a few rounds of flying lead. Sadly, Mr. Morcey was not the clairvoyant London had spoken of earlier, or he might have known what his blind faith was about to cost him.

"Now LET ME GET this straight," said Mezeltin slowly. "You're saying that..."

Doctor Goward turned to the reporter, his black bag resting on his knees. While Morcey had driven London, Cat and the agency's client to the job site, the professor had volunteered to ride with the newswoman and her cameraman. An intense man with blazing blue eyes, he was a doctor of philosophy and theology who divided his time between teaching at Columbia University and travelling the world to investigate paranormal activity. For some time, like a number of select others, he had stayed in close contact with the London Agency making time for them whenever they called. He had not been disappointed so far.

"What I'm saying is that you, madame, can not have the slightest idea what to expect tonight because we ourselves do not know what to expect. I shall explain." Goward settled into the somewhat comfortable backseat of the television crew's rental car. Pulling his pipe from his jacket pocket, he used it as a prop as he began his impromptu lecture.

"One year ago tonight, young Mr. Dorson and a group of his companions decided to contact the spirit known as Saman. That's S-A-M-A-N...I'm certain you've noted the similarity to another dark creature of popular legend, eh? Anyway, Saman is the Druidic God of Death. He assembled the souls of evil men condemned to inhabit the bodies of animals, annually, on the first day of Samhaine—otherwise known as La Samhna, Samhuinn, Nos Galengaeof, All Hallow's Eve, or in the language of the provinces—Halloween. The time of death, the blood festival."

"You wouldn't be trying to scare me, would you, doctor?"

"Scare? No. Educate? Yes." Goward stuck his pipe in his mouth and bit down on the stem just for the momentary taste of it. Then, he removed it once more and continued.

"Samhaine," he said, "was originally an entire season—the dead zone between years when the world renewed itself. To the Druids, it was the time when the door to the other world was opened. Over the centuries, the season of Samhaine has shrunk repeatedly until it reached its present three days…"

"Halloween is three days long?" asked the reporter.

"Why, yes. Halloween, All Saint's and All Soul's."

"Oh, right," agreed Mezeltin. "I've heard of those. But before, that stuff about evil men's souls being put in animals…?"

"Just one of the legends. There are those who say Samhaine was the night the Druid shamans entered the realm of the dead to guide the souls of those that had died over the preceding year to their final resting place. They were also to bring back knowledge and enlightenment. Others say it was a time to bribe the spirit world so as to avert malefics in the coming year."

"But…"

Goward raised his hand, holding the woman's words at bay. He had heard all the questions people could ask repeatedly throughout his career and knew there was nothing she could ask which he could not answer quicker without her help.

"The problem with these kinds of things is that you just can't trust the legends. I've seen some things come round that…let's just say…if I'd stuck to their Biblical and textbook descriptions, we wouldn't be having this conversation right now."

"Then," asked the reporter with the slightest touch of involuntary hesitation, "you're saying you believe Dorson's story."

"That his hand was bitten off by a Jack o'Lantern? Oh, it could be, my dear lady. It could be."

"Really, Dr. Goward. I mean…"

"Ms. Mezeltin, put aside the finely tuned skepticism they taught you in journalism school for a moment and for once—try to look at this thing from your victim's point of view."

"My victim?" The reporter feigned ignorance, asking the professor, "What are you talking about?"

"Oh, please," growled Goward, perturbed at the woman's ploy. "You're too long out of high school, and if you were ever an innocent it was at such a time in the past that even the basic look of it is lost to you now. Your victim is James Dorson. The man lost the woman he loved and his own right hand in one evening. Yes, there is no denying that he made what, on the surface, indeed seemed to be outrageous claims. But, you and yours made no effort to investigate those claims at all."

Goward bit on his pipe once more, pausing not so much for the taste that time but to irritate the reporter. Sensationalists always galled him, but he held a special contempt for those as ruthlessly exploitative as Mezeltin. Optimistically, however, he went back to instruction, a tool far the more natural to him than condemnation.

"You announced that he was found in a state of alcoholic and drug-induced inebriation. That proved to be false. You did not retract the statements. You claimed he murdered his fiancé. She was missing—still is missing, in fact—but the point is there is no proof the woman was murdered by young Dorson for there is no proof that anyone was murdered at all."

"We did not say he murdered…"

"Don't split hairs, young woman. You judged him in the court of innuendo and you hounded him as long as their was a dollar to be made by doing so. When he claimed that a monster stole his fiancé, you demanded psychiatric tests. When he passed them and proved he wasn't insane, you demanded a trial since he clearly had to be lying. When he said his hand was bitten off by a Jack o'Lantern, you scoffed. When vegetable matter was discovered in his wounds you accused him of putting it there."

"Doctor Goward—really! What else could it have been?"

"I'll tell you, madame. It could have been exactly what he said it was. The Jack o'Lantern is the emblem of a spirit who has been refused entrance to both Heaven and Hell. It is supposedly the form Saman chooses often. If a group of foolish children meddled in something beyond their understanding and managed to interest a thing from beyond in their nonsense…who's to say that it didn't come down amongst them—on the one day out of the year that it is free to walk the Earth? There are numerous stories of gods and demons carrying off nubile young women—as many as there are tales of them killing or mutilating those who might oppose them."

Mezeltin looked forward at the back of her cameraman's head. Joking when they had first pulled away from London's building, Prentiss had remained quiet ever since the reporter and the professor had started arguing. He knew the redheaded woman would be angry at being abandoned, but he honestly did not know what he could say back to Goward. Mezeltin, however, could think of plenty.

"I don't believe this. You're supposed to be educated? You're supposed to be…'a man of science'…and you sit there and spew this kind of malarkey? You're trying to tell me that I'm the villain because I wasn't sucked in by this nonsense?"

"What I'm trying to tell you," responded Goward in an even, but grim tone, "for your own good, believe me, is that there are things that even a great and powerful anchorwoman might not know. And if you go into this unprepared, it is possible you might not like the outcome."

"Really? Do you expect me to believe that…"

"No," interrupted the professor. His face dark and serious, he pointed with his pipe, telling Mezeltin, "I don't *expect* you to believe anything. In fact, going into something like this with a firm set of beliefs is about the most dangerous thing you can do."" The reporter merely stared, cuing Goward that he had finally trained her to wait for him to continue. He obliged her immediately.

"You must understand, when the mind goes up against something that contradicts everything it believes, it freezes. The person you love tells you they hate you—you freeze for a moment. Unprepared for such a statement, it takes time for the brain to recover. Now, if you believe there's no such thing as, oh say, werewolves, and then you see one…in the moment it takes your brain to adjust to the new information your senses have just fed it—you're dead."

"So you're saying that the best way to go into this is to not believe in anything?"

"Not quite. We all must believe in something. You simply must be prepared to alter those beliefs when they are challenged by unquestionable evidence. We drop beliefs all the time. You've been doing it your whole life. No Santa Claus—fine. The president isn't the smartest man in the world—fine. Your parents aren't perfect, the policeman is not your friend, socialism doesn't work—oops, sorry, as a journalist you might not have figured that one out yet, but whatever, you get my point, I'm sure. We are rational beings, we adjust. Survival simply depends on the speed with which we make those adjustments."

"So," answered Mezeltin, pulling a cigarette from her bag, "I just need to have faith in 'Bloody Jimmy Dorson' and everything will be swell—eh, professor?"

"Faith in Dorson?" responded Goward. "I would hope your faith would be in something higher than that. As Donne said, 'Reason is our soul's left hand, Faith her right. By these we reach divinity.' Whatever you put your *faith* in, madame, be certain you chose something not easily shaken. Losing a belief is one thing, losing one's faith is the end of all things."

"I've got faith," sneered the reporter as she pulled in the first deep drag from her cigarette. "Ratings. That's what I have faith in. That's all I need to have faith in."

And then, before either of the people in the backseat could speak again, Prentiss slowed the car, pulling up next to the one he had been following for the last two and a half hours. Killing the engine, he informed his passengers;

"Looks like we're here."

All three of them sat looking out at the dingy, boarded up black and gray building. At one time it had been a slaughterhouse, a clearing facility that could move over fourteen tons of meat in one day. Now it was merely another crumbling, rusting reminder of the impermanence of everything.

The one-time Ferguson's Finest Cuts sat in a refuse strewn clearing that had served years earlier as its combination loading area and parking lot. Weeds and thick grasses leached upward through myriad cracks in the crumbling asphalt. At its edges the lot had already begun to give way to the surrounding forest. Runner vines, wild brush and various trees had all begun the quiet work of reclamation. Staring out the window at the rusty walls of the abandoned building, Goward commented;

"Funny how so many of the places I go to find the things I search for end up looking like cheap movie sets." Throwing open his door the professor exited the renter with his oversized travel case, circling around the car to join the others. Then suddenly, he stopped as if reconsidering. Turning back again, he returned to the open door of the news people's car.

"Ms. Mezeltin, Mr. Prentiss," he told them, "in all good conscience I cannot allow you to follow us without giving you a final warning. When Theodore called you 'bait' earlier, I do not think you realize how serious he was."

"Please, doctor," answered the reporter. Exiting by her own door, she said, "You're a paid employee of Dorson's. I understand you want to protect your client. But the news goes where it wants."

"My dear young woman," Goward responded, smiling sadly. "Young Mr. Dorson is not my client. I accompany Theodore and his people whenever they call because this is my line of endeavor. No one is paying me to be here, or to tell you the following."

The professor shifted his bag from one hand to the other, then

"With Cat and all her marvelous devices along, my preparations fall to little more than making certain my pen works." Quickly doodling a happy face with a Jack o'Lantern smile, he turned his notebook around and showed it off, saying, "Ready."

"Oh yeah," answered Morcey. "Comedy—phi beta kappa comedy. Dat'll keep us safe from monsters. James—you ready?"

James Dorson stood in the center of an elaborate pentacle chalked across the center of the floor. The young man had traced it over the lines still visible from when he and his friends had done the same the year before. Thick red candles stood waiting around the outside perimeter, their black wicks pointed upward, ready to be lit. Around each of them sat globs of dusty wax, all of it where it had been left by the police after they had finished their investigation months earlier.

"Yes," answered James, cradling the same tattered book he had the year before against the hard steel of his prosthetic hand. "I've been ready for this moment for a while now."

His mind flashed back to the last time he had stood in the center of the old butchering room, his fingers moving the pages of the antique book he and his roommate had found. What a way to spend Halloween—drinking, passing joints and snorting cocaine, summoning the master of the dead—what could be better?

He heard again the creaking in the far corner, smelled once more the thick run of bovine blood, felt the cold wind against his cheek, saw the...the...

"Dorson."

London's voice cracked like gunfire off the concrete walls. All eyes turned toward the detective as he walked out to the center of the room. Taking James by the elbow, he asked the young man;

"Are you going to make it through this? You know what'll happen if you're not ready." The boy stared blankly for just a moment, and then, he laughed. It was not a warm or friendly sound, but instead a high-pitched, trilling giggle that set everyone's nerves one notch higher.

"Do I know what will happen?" he whispered, spit blowing from his lips as he spoke. Tears rolling down over his cheeks, salt mixed with the hanging strands swinging from the end of his chin as he answered.

"Oh, yes—I know what happens if I'm not ready. I motherfucking know all about it! Okay?!"

A wipe of his hand cleaned his chin, but did nothing for the fractured look in his eyes. Stepping back a pace to give the young man enough room to breath, London reached into his jacket and pulled forth a flask. Unscrewing the top, he handed it to Dorson.

"No problem, son," said the detective. "Join me in a belt?"

"I thought you didn't drink," responded the young man, taking the flask.

"Not as a habit—but special occasions call for special ceremonies. Bottoms up, James."

Metal fingers clenched the flask, jerking it out of the detective's hand. Dorson took a healthy slug then passed the flask back to London who did the same. The detective then handed the bottle off to Morcey who drank and passed the rapidly emptying flask to Cat. Drinking and then passing the flask to Goward, the short strawberry blonde asked;

"Any more bullshit to get out of the way, or can we get on with it?"

"You heard the lady," said London with a grin. "Too much male bonding going on for her. Let's get things in motion."

Before the detective could step away from the pentacle, however, Dorson grabbed his arm, hissing, "Quit joking! This isn't a fucking party!"

Somehow slipping out of the crushing steel grip without any real effort, London simply smiled and said, "Everything in this life is what you make it, son. Whatever it is you want out of tonight—now's the time to do it."

Nodding his head, the young man bent to light his candles while the detective rejoined the others. Outside the circle of investigators, Mezeltin slapped her cameraman on the shoulder.

"This is it," she snapped in his ear, disregarding the fact that he had been poised and ready to shoot since Dorson first moved into the pentacle. Used to the reporter's ways by that time, however, Prentiss said nothing. He simply recentered his stance and continued to wait for something worth taping.

Next to him, Mezeltin clicked on her mic's battery pack, did a quick sound level check, and then turned back toward the center of the room. Dorson was reading from his moldering book, barking out the same passage he had the year before. As he did, Goward pulled closer to London.

"That chant he's using," the professor whispered. "It doesn't really relate to Saman, Samhaine...not even the Druids. And his circle...a scorpion laid down over two sets of parallel lines. It's a combination of the fifth pentacle of Mars and the second of Mercury. He's trying to bind a demon to his will while attempting to gain the impossible—having a wish granted that contradicts the natural order—but still..."

"He says he made something happen once," London reminded the professor in a low voice. "Let's just wait and see what happens this time, shall we?"

No one had long to wait.

"I've got a reading," whispered Cat. As London crossed to the monitors, she told him, "temperature's dropped ten degrees in the west corner of this room in less than a minute. Five more in the time it took me to tell you that. Eight more, twelve—twenty degrees total, twenty-two, twenty-four..."

And then, the squat woman turned her head a moment to consult another section of her jury-rigged assembly. As Dorson continued his chanting, Cat turned back and pointed toward the center of the room, announcing;

"We've got movement."

As everyone watched, a bluish mist began to spin upward out of the dusty concrete. The vapor swirled rapidly counter-clockwise, moving faster and faster with each rotation completed. Solid eddies appeared in the twirling wash, gelling before everyone's eyes. Then, as oranges and greens began to blend with the mix, London snapped;

"Incoming! Brace yourselves, people."

His hand had already pulled out his .38. Morcey's Auto-Mag followed. The balding man held the over-sized hand cannon skyward with both hands, his eyes glued on the center of the room. As he watched, the swirl of colors suddenly rushed inward on themselves and then exploded upward, shattering against the low ceiling.

Burning sparks streaked throughout the room, setting fire to anything combustible they struck, melting or scoring what they could not burn. Everyone else beat at or at least checked their clothing while Cat shouted;

"The cold spot's expanding!"

Instantly the temperature in the ancient slaughterhouse dropped dramatically. Everyone's breath solidified in the air, joining the acrid smoke hanging throughout the room. Then, the cold and steam and smoke all rolled back into the west corner of the abandoned slaughter room, hanging there for a moment before blowing forth across the floor.

Dorson and his candles were blown out of the center of the chamber. The candles all smashed against the far wall. The young man did not make it as far, coming to an abrupt stop against Cat's machinery. Goward made to move forward to help the two untangle themselves, but London caught the professor's arm, stopping him. As Goward looked up, he followed the direction of the detective's hand pointing toward the center of the room. The cold air had formed a small cyclonic funnel there, the force of it pulling the chalk design up off the concrete—fleck by fleck—until both the old and new pentacles were gone. And then, it appeared.

It was a mostly humanoid form, some nine feet in height. It seemed part scarecrow, part skeleton, both held together by sack cloth and creepers. The specifics of it seemed to change second to second, no one's eyes able to focus on either its body or limbs for long. Its head, however, was another matter.

Atop the shifting figure sat a blazing Jack o'Lantern. Its eye slits were filled with an intense fire, as were the slices representing its nostrils and mouth. Hundreds of vines curled out of the top of it, hanging down around it to the floor—green vestments filled with tiny figures that crawled and slithered in and out of sight. Its mouth—like its eyes and nose—was not carved, but rather appeared to be a putrefying opening created by age. Double rows of long, shining seeds lined the oozing crack top and bottom. Grating the black and white striped teeth against each other, the thing growled—

Who calls?

Dorson, finally managing to get himself up off the floor, pulled himself erect and snapped back;

"I do, you miserable son of a bitch!"

The young man had seen the monstrosity before—knew it from the three-hundred and sixty four nightmares where he had summoned its memory, awaiting the moment when he would face it once more. Around the room, the rest of the crowd struggled to match his familiarity.

A part of Goward's brain kept his hands scribbling furious notes even as another part of it stood paralyzed by its inability to make sense of the apparition before him. Cat, her monitoring equipment smashed, was digging through her bag for her white sound generator, purposely ignoring the thing in the center of the room. She knew the amount of time that would be lost if she stared at it. And, also knowing what happened to the last woman the thing had supposedly seen, she wanted a weapon in her hand before it came for her.

While London and Morcey waited with their own weapons poised, Mezeltin and Prentiss dealt with the horror in their own ways. Prentiss had shifted over into professional mode, the only segment of his brain still functioning. It was the part of him that allowed his hands and eye to close-focus on a child burning to death, preserving the image of it for others to view rather than moving to rescue the child itself. As for the reporter, she was already calculating what Prentiss's film would be worth on the open market.

On one level, the part of her that was still female shuddered at the musky death smell filling the chamber, at the crawling vermin falling from the thing in the center of the room. The greasy feel of violence stabbed at the sliver of soul she still possessed, but she ignored the ancestral warnings stirring within her, commercial concerns overriding anything as mundane as self-preservation.

Unlike any of the others, however, Dorson was not waiting, watching or making decisions. Implementing the plan he had devised over the months, he spat back at the thing.

"Don't tell me you don't remember me?"

I remember you—you brought me the Companion

"I didn't bring you anything, you bastard," screamed Dorson. "You took her. You stole her! She was the only thing I cared about, and you took her from me!"

Spoke the words, you did—called me forth and brought me the Companion—pleasant the year she has given me

"No!" bellowed Dorson. Holding himself from attacking the thing before him, the two pounds of steel hanging from his right arm reminding him of the folly in such action, he said;

"She wasn't for you. It was a mistake. You—whatever you are—I know you. You're cursed to walk the inner void. No rest. No Heaven, not even Hell. You can't bind her to you."

Already done—grateful to the one who brought the Companion...happy she is, too

And then, the glowing eyes went blue and cold as the thing's gelid voice added, *see for yourself*

All eyes went wide as the creature's body suddenly erupted open. Before anyone knew what was happening, a vaguely female form fell out of the gooey split, dropping to the floor with a squishing thud. Dorson whimpered;

"Andrea."

He wanted to pull her up, stroke her, tell her everything would be all right. He did not. That was the infantile ending television would give the story—the kind of sugary slop that would simply ignore what a year in limbo as a demon's consort would do to a person. Desperate to escape the plea of his emotions, Dorson forced himself to stare at his former lover.

Her head had been washed clean of hair. One of her eyes was pused over, the other hidden in swollen ridges of cracked and oozing skin. All of her limbs were now gangly and distorted, each of them a different length. Insects crawled in and out of various passageways they had dug through her body, following the path of the creeper vines which had bored through her before them.

It was a drooling thing that lay on the cold concrete before James Dorson, a mucous-covered abomination for which death would be the highest blessing—except that it was possessed by a creature which would not let it die, that held onto it for its soul the way someone lost in the forest clutches their flashlight.

"You can not have her."

can not lose her

"I've come back to barter for her release."

And then, the pumpkin thing laughed. Scores of seeds blew out from its mouth, splattering against Dorson, sticking to his clothes, his face, his claw.

Barter, shrieked the terror. *with what would you barter? your self? what need have I of you? nothing is completed by you—soul is not completed by you...need her to grow...need Companion to open otherside gate*

Across the room, Morcey pressed up against his partner, whispering into London's ear without taking his eyes off the tableau before them.

"Jezz-it, boss...what's the kid doin'?"

"He's pulling a switch on us," answered the detective. "And I'm not sure where he's going with it. Start backing people out of here. Cat first. I'll cover us."

Even as the balding man holstered his weapon and headed off toward the others, in the center of the room Dorson continued to wrangle with the towering horror he had summoned.

"I've studied the old books," he told it. "I know. There's no way you can open the barred gate with Andrea. You stole her. She wasn't yours. You can't achieve a soul through theft and you know it!"

still better than nothing—still better than sit the lonely dark with no sound, no life, no Companion

"But you could get what you wanted if you had an offering."

And then, the oozing thing cocked its head, focusing on Dorson.

Something in the young man's tone caught the creature's attention, a something that held out a blinding crumb of hope. Its breath frozen in its chest, the monstrosity waited a four second eternity until Dorson pointed toward Mezeltin.

"Take her," he said, "in exchange for the release of Andrea's soul. I offer her to you."

Instantly the room exploded in bedlam. Morcey pushed Cat and Goward toward the door at the same time against both their wishes. Prentiss stopped filming, the shock of what he had just heard causing him to drop his camera. London stepped forward toward the center of the room, uncertain what to do next. As for Mezeltin, she stood her ground, unable to bring words to her lips, but holding herself far from panic.

"Yes!" cried Dorson, his eyes wild and dancing. "Her—take her! You deserve each other!"

London began to move forward, protest framing his stance. Instantly the towering thing directed an arm in the detective's direction, calling forth the freezing wind that had borne it to the room from the other side. London was knocked backwards and sideways, whipped around at least three times before he hit the far wall. His .38 spun away from him, clattering off into some unseen dark corner as he flopped to the floor dazed from the unexpected blow.

Near the door, Morcey put all his effort into one tremendous shove that sent Cat and Goward stumbling backward into the next room. Then, twisting the lock, he spun around, pulled his Auto-Mag once more.

"Jeez-it, lady," he shouted toward Mezeltin, "can't you figure out the skinny here? You wanta be that thing on the floor? Get your ass out of here!"

And then, seeing no other option, the ex-maintenance man leveled his weapon and fired. Twice. The heavy shells, both of which would have knocked over any man alive, tore through the horror's pulpy, undefined body with ease, burying themselves in the back wall without affecting the creature in the least. As everyone in the room covered their ears against the thundering reverberations, the thing hissed;

you would seek to give harm? to me? madness and folly have not left the human race—But I shall...

"No! Forget him," shouted Dorson. "He can't harm you. But time is running out. Do you accept my offer or not?"

The monstrous shambler cocked its head at an angle for a moment, and then grinned. Raising the mass of branches and vines acting as its left leg, it stamped the floor, shattering it. A massive crack spread outward directly toward Morcey, dropping the balding man a score of feet into the basement below. Then, the oozing thing finally answered Dorson, telling him;

I accept

With a snap of its branching fingers, the sobbing heap that had once been Dorson's fiancé—had once been human—disappeared in a green flash of smoke and sparks.

she is gone...beyond the veil...beyond the barred gate—she is on the otherside where I cannot walk...not yet

Then, the creature stuck its hand out toward Mezeltin, whispering;

but soon

The reporter looked at the thing beckoning to her, and then, in a voice more powerful than she realized she had within her, she sneered at it.

"Stuff it, pumpkin brain." As shock spread across the monster's face, he reached out to her again, but his power did not affect her. Laughing, the reporter told it, "I've covered wars where both sides ate their prisoners. I've seen the charnel houses of three different serial killers. I've even covered two Democratic conventions. You're just one more sideshow freak to me—asshole."

It was a bravery wrung from nerves pushed to the limit, but Mezeltin held her ground, telling the thing, "You got his little girlfriend because she was a scared, drugged up little jerk who didn't have the sense to resist you. Dorson's learned what it takes to beat you back, though—and so have I."

her faith is strong

"*Her* faith? Her *faith*? Faith in what?!"

"Like I told the professor, jagoff," sneered Mezeltin, enjoying the rush of power coursing through her, "Ratings. That's all I believe in, and that's what you two have handed me. I loved every minute I spent raking you over the coals this last year, keeping your name on the front page of every paper from coast to coast, jerking you in and out of court just because I could. Now, I'm going to get to do it all over again, as well as get rich in the bargain."

The reporter walked up to Dorson, her hands making fists. Nervous but spiteful laughter broke from her lips as she smacked him across the face, yelling at the same time;

"What do you think the world will pay for the video we've shot here tonight, you idiot? You've handed me the spirit world on a silver platter. The London Agency, the final resolution of the James Dorson case, pumpkin brain here. You puke—with what we have on tape already..."

And then, Mezeltin stopped. Memory clawing at the back of her brain, her face blanching in terror, she spun around, staring at the pieces of Prentiss' shattered camera scattered across the floor. The cameraman, still hunkered in shock, did not even raise his head as the thing in the center of the room sneered in triumph.

ahhhhhhhhhhhhhhh, no 'tape,' no faith

And then, the twig fingers beckoned once more. The wind howled and the ceiling shattered. As abruptly as the reeking thing had arrived, it departed—sucking the helpless reporter along in its wake.

BY THE TIME GOWARD and Cat managed to re-enter the old slaughter room, London had found his feet and Morcey had managed to hobble up from the basement. Both men were badly bruised—the detective with two fractured bones, his partner with three broken. Prentiss they found huddled in a corner. Looking up, the cameraman said a single word, "Gone," and then went mute. He afforded the team no trouble.

Dorson lay in the center of the room—his life extinguished, his body unmarked. Although his cold mouth was neutral, betraying no easily identifiable emotion, there was no doubting the look in his eyes. Without comment, the London Agency packed its things and went home. By the time any of them reached their beds it was November. None of them were upset by that fact.

Not in the least.

It is not unusual for C.J. to revivify dead characters, breathing fresh life into them. In this collection, there are several wonderful reunions with long adored and sometimes dreaded fictional figures. Such undertakings require a deep understanding of the characters, settings, and awareness of the present moment. To resurrect a creation from the past requires that the writer understand how the character fits into the world then and today; otherwise, the result is a pastiche, with nothing new added. In "So Free We Seem," something new is defiantly added. Here, in every respect, is something new made of something old.

SO FREE WE SEEM

"So free we seem, so fettered fast we are!"

–Robert Browning

IT WAS THE STRANGEST thing the inspector had ever seen. The first thing he noticed, as had those few others who had peered into the old house out near the swamp, were the traps in the doorway. Immediately, there in the front foyer, surrounding the mail slot in the door, spread in a semi-circle, he had come across two lines of traps. Mouse traps. Rat traps.

"In here, el Grande…"

Their positioning made them appear to be set for something their owner must have felt was going to come through the mail slot. A quick inspection showed the opening to be only one inch by three, covered by a springed hinge that had to be opened with a bit of effort.

"Come in and meet the former Hector Claro, and…" the officer's voice shifted to a supercilious tone, "let me tell you right now, Inspector…"

What, wondered former Inspector-of-Police John Raymond Legrasse, could the man have been expecting to come through such a tiny and hard to open aperture other than his mail?

"You're not going to believe this."

Legrasse hated to admit it, but his one-time lieutenant was correct. Even after all he had seen in his time, he did not believe what he found in the next room. It was too odd. Too *despairing*.

"This isn't one of your pranks, is it?"

Too perplexed by the oddity of the inside of Hector Claro's home to make one of his usual wisecracks, Lieutenant Joseph D. Galvez shook his head gravely, admitting;

"I could but wish my sense of humor were this magnifico."

Legrasse nodded, understanding the smaller man without need for further explanation. The scene in the humble home's main room was one snatched from nightmare. The one-time inspector of police fell into old habits at once. In less than a minute his virgin notepad was bleeding its first page and a half—

Victim found sitting in a corner diagonally positioned as far from the front door as possible.

Victim appears to have been facing front door at time of death.

Found, foyer: on arrival: various spring traps set within the doorway. Immediately, three large traps—set but not baited—spread in triangle formation before the mail slot in the door.

Further on, spread in semi-circle, two additional lines of traps. Mouse traps. Rat traps. Just in the foyer.

Inside: traps everywhere—scores? Hundreds? Set out...

Patterns?

"Can you believe this guy," asked Galvez. The man's voice was indecisive, unable to pick a tone, to slide into either humor or concern. Or worse. "He surrounds himself with traps. He's scared of what? What? I dunno."

"You want to know why he did it?" asked Legrasse, half in humor, half seriously. "I'm still working on *how* he did it."

Galvez snorted, then sprang another trap with the cane in his hand, a handsome thing covered with graceful carvings which he had acquired from the umbrella stand in the foyer.

"Crazy," the Spaniard muttered, "set all these traps, but don't bait them. How you supposed to catch anything that way?"

It had been decided that, although they would, of course, need to leave as much of the insane landscape intact as possible to see if there was any clue as to what had happened in the old Backtown house out near the swampfronts, some would have to be sacrificed for both basic mobility as well as general safety.

"Smells wonderful," snapped the lieutenant, rubbing another wipe of preventive gel under his nose. "Don't he?"

Legrasse merely flashed his eyes in response. Galvez went silent. Though his one time commander was now merely consulting, only a citizen, still he was Legrasse, who had lived through it all, and won against the devil himself. They had been through much together, and Galvez knew his old boss well. Already he could see the old instincts taking over, could sense his boss was closing in on what had happened within his mind. He watched Legrasse's hand moving across the page, knowing that somehow he would unravel the bizarre scenario before them.

Victim seems to have bolted all other doors behind him. All other rooms are cut off from the front room. Cracks around doors are stuffed with rags, old newspaper, slivers of cardboard cut to fit. Boards appear to have been nailed over all of this wherever possible.

Victim seems to have been afraid of something approaching him, something small enough to fit under a door, or through a mail slot, any small crack.

Victim does not seem to have been restrained in any manner. If this is the case, then the only conclusion one can have is that he remained in his corner, surrounded by his traps, until he starved to death, by choice. Dying of thirst was preferable to him rather than...

Than what?

And then, Legrasse's eye caught a detail he had previously missed. Indeed, one that everyone had missed so far. Staring at the desiccated corpse in the corner, he asked Galvez;

"Do you see that bulge in Mr. Claro's breast pocket?"

The lieutenant indicated that he did. Legrasse asked him to fetch it if he could. Galvez stepped into the opening already made near the corpse and slid his hand gently inside the pungent cloth. His hand came out with its prize, a thin, leather-bound volume with a stub of pencil attached to it by a short length of string. The lieutenant paged through it quickly, then announced;

"It's a diary."

Legrasse accepted the black book and opened it to its first page. In a simple style made up of competent, but uncomplicated sentences of mostly one and two syllable words, Hector Claro introduced himself and his dilemma to the inspector.

Claro told his tale from the beginning. The first date showed that it had been some four weeks back, after a particularly violent storm which had rained lightning down on the swamps for an entire night and half the next day. Legrasse remembered the storm vividly. He had been caught outside in it and had been drenched in moments. The noise and electrical power of it had sent much of the city into a panic. Normally calm, well-mannered horses had gone wild in the streets, crashing carriages and trampling citizens. It had been one of those times Legrasse was glad he was no longer a public servant, and the memory of the violent night connected him to Claro in a personal way.

The man told of finding scores of dead fish and other swamp creatures the next day, floating on their sides in the muddy, boiled water behind his home. Great trees had fallen during the night, and the swamp had gone through such convulsions that Claro even noted a fresh spring bubbling up through the crayfish encrusted mud.

At first he had been pleased by the events. The shocked fish had provided him with a much needed windfall. He had quickly set to gathering and preserving as many of the still living, but insensate fish as he considered safe for the salting. The new spring was fresh, and looked as if it would be a constant rather than a fluke. All in all, the storm seemed to have been a blessing for Claro, unlike what it had proved to be for the rest of New Orleans. But then, the next night came, and his opinion of things took a different turn.

Claro's next episode told of a noise in the night, that of a rat trap being sprung. Due to his proximity to the swamp, the man had many such devices set about in the corners of his home and was not overly concerned by hearing one go off in the middle of the night. But, instead of the squeals such a sound usually brought, if they brought any noise at all, he heard instead a series of strange, unfathomable sounds the curiousness of which forced him to leave his bed. Lighting his table lamp, he went out to examine his small home's main room where he found the most curious scene.

Claro described finding the trap dragged across the room from where it had been set all the way to the front door. He could tell this had happened easily enough because of the wet, sticky trail left from the trap's original position to where Claro discovered it, smashed and ruined beneath his mail slot. He could only think that he had snared quite a large rodent, one of sufficient size and strength to move the trap, although wounded unto the point where it was bleeding profusely. This line of thinking was diminished, however, when he realized that the smearing crossing his floor was not made up of blood.

Legrasse absently noted a faded line of coloration on the door, one leading from deep inside the large room into the foyer, indeed, directly up to the mail slot, which supported Claro's story. The dead man's words described the trail as a bluish-green, one with neither the smell nor taste of blood. He was confused by this, but with the simplicity of most swamp dwellers, soon forgot the incident, tired as he had been from the ordeal of collecting and salting down his windfall.

The next night, however, he was again visited after dark, and the night after that, and the one after that. He lay in his bed on all three occasions, the covers pulled up and over his head, frightened to the point where he questioned even the need to breathe. Every day he set out more traps, but each morning he found fewer of them sprung. On all three nights he listened intently as something, or some things, crawled and slithered throughout his simple home. Whether they were searching for something, or simply madly dancing, he had no idea, nor much inclination to find out.

Legrasse read on, fascinated. Galvez waited, balancing himself in various poses, using the cane from the umbrella stand to keep from toppling into the myriad traps. On the one hand he was impatient to find the answer to the riddle of the dead man and to close out the case. On the other, he was more than willing to wait to see what his former commander could determine. Together, the two had seen some horrific and terrible things in the bayou land outside their city. Indeed, in Galvez's mind, the mystery of Hector Claro could scarce compare to some of their previous exploits.

"Better safe than sorry," the lieutenant cautioned himself, and continued to play with the cane, twirling it in one hand, studying its odd carvings, amusing himself in any way he could think of while he waited for Legrasse's verdict.

The inspector had almost forgotten Galvez, however, his full attention falling to each successive page of Claro's diary. Legrasse had become engrossed with the man's description of the fourth night of his home's invasion and reread it simply to hear its words again within his head. That night, whatever had been searching about in the other rooms of his home, even under his own bed, found its way to what was on top of his bed.

Claro wrote of a weight passing over the blanket he kept tight across his face. Anything with eyes would have seen his form beneath the covers, he reckoned, but whatever this was, this probing, he had just eluded found him again, and Claro beat at it with his chair until the seat had become splinters.

Racing about madly, the man had smashed the tentacles, beat them with his fists, even bitten into one of them. Although the tendrils retreated in seconds in the face of his attack, still Claro was left drenched in sweat from his encounter.

He spent the next day closing down the side of his home facing the swamp. It did no good. The next night the lengths returned, and again he was forced to do battle with the sucking, grasping coils. They came over the next two nights as well, and Claro began to take note of certain things. Each night the tentacles came earlier and stayed longer. They were beginning to be able to predict where he would be, what he would do. They were beginning to not fear him. Which is when he had decided to start setting the traps.

Legrasse gave the book over to Galvez, telling him to read some of it while he thought about things for a moment. The Spaniard nodded, handing the inspector the cane he had been toying with so that he could hold the book in two hands. While Galvez started, Legrasse thought on what he had read.

The book told of tentacles coming through the windows, slots, cracks, even his sink drain. Why the man stayed in his home, he did not explain. Nor did he explain why he did not at least leave at night, did not call the police, did not ask his neighbors for shelter, or assistance.

What could it have been, wondered Legrasse. *Why* was it? What did it want? Why did it come? Why?

Maybe Claro was just too stubborn to admit defeat. Maybe he simply went insane, bought the traps and spread them out, relying on the only thing that had truly worked for him. The last entry he had made, sitting in his corner, disturbed Legrasse the most.

free, free at last

The inspector studied the cane in his hand as he tried to piece the sad occurrence into a whole. Certainly the storm had unleashed whatever had found Claro. Perhaps it was some long lost horror, sealed away within the fresh spring so recently uncovered.

Legrasse stared at the corpse in the corner and wondered, did the dead man know something that some outre thing wanted to know, something it did not want anyone else to know? Or was Claro just the poor unfortunate bastard who happened to be the only thing nearby when the storm somehow opened a random portal that some bug just happened to accidentally poke its way through?

The inspector quietly checked Galvez's progress. He could see the man was barely halfway through the notebook. Looking about, Legrasse then took note of a section of the dead man's leg, where the pants were up far enough to reveal flesh above the sock line. Round red welts like sucker wounds appeared to circle the victim's leg.

Legrasse wondered at it all, at what the searchers could have been after. What was the point, he mused, of coming night after night, but never taking anything, never actually doing anything—*anything*. Why?

Absently smacking his hand with the butt-end of the cane, the inspector took a closer note of the carvings etched into its length. There was nothing remarkable about them, although he did notice they seemed somewhat fresh. Still, they seemed of no great importance. Indeed, his mind left them instantly as he noticed Galvez coming to the end of the notebook. Tossing the cane back to the Spaniard, Legrasse turned in his small clear space in the traps, studying.

Wondering.

"Hey, John," called Galvez, "anything you want me to do while you stare off into space at the tax payer's expense?"

"It's your investigation," replied Legrasse absently. "Be creative."

The lieutenant nodded, looking for a direction in which to head. Legrasse looked down at the traps, wondering about them again.

He had been puzzled about them since he had arrived. So far all he had learned had only added to his puzzlement. He still could not believe Claro had set out all the traps. Their placement was so finely meshed, so intricate. And the patterns he had noticed, swirls and star-shapes, intersecting each other over and over throughout the main room—

Why, wondered Legrasse. Why would he do it?

The traps had not been working, the inspector remembered. Yet Claro had gotten more and more of them, ultimately painting himself into the corner, so to speak, with them.

Across the room, Galvez picked the next spot where he would knock a new hole in the traps so that he could move toward the back rooms. Sealed off as they were, none of them had been investigated yet. To the lieutenant's way of thinking, it was high time they were opened.

Ignoring Galvez's actions, Legrasse concentrated on the traps. There was something he was not seeing, something that was passing him by. He stared down at the floor again, trying to look at everything once more from the beginning, struggling to gain a new perspective.

The traps were everywhere. In tight, sophisticated patterns. Why? How could Claro have managed it, with only two hands? It did not seem possible. And, even if it were, why had he done so?

Galvez spotted the point where he could place his next footfall without disturbing too many of the traps.

Of course, he thought, the traps aren't so tight everywhere. Fairly sparse back by the door when you first come in. And where the patterns run up against one another. Indeed, that was where Galvez had been making his strikes, in the freer areas between the patterns.

Convenient, whispered a voice from the back of Legrasse's mind. He caught the tone, realizing instantly his subconscious was trying to tell him something.

The footfalls had been conveniently made, slivers of space left between each of the patterns, just right for a human of average height, spaced just so, placed directly where the average human eye would see them, would pride itself on being able to take advantage of them.

Galvez's arm stretched out, positioning the cane for its next strike. And, as it did so, the inspector's memory superimposed another image on the scene. He thought back to voodoo rituals he had witnessed, to the foul priest he and his men had stopped only months earlier, all of them, scratching patterns in the sand or the mud, making their magic gestures with their totem sticks—

"I'm going to take a look in the back rooms."

The lieutenant pulled his hand back, even as Legrasse's mind raced. What if Claro had not set the traps, or even if he had, if after his death, something else had moved them? Changed their positions, moved them into patterns...

Galvez's hand began to descend—

Into the same patterns it carved into Claro's cane, the cane left at the front door, where the traps were not so thickly spread, so that one could enter, and pick up the cane!

"No!"

Legrasse screamed at Galvez, even as he threw himself at the lieutenant. The lieutenant shouted as well, raising his free hand in response, trying to bring up the one wielding the cane, but it was too late. Both men went down painfully, rolling over and over in the flesh-tearing maze.

MOST OF THEIR PAINS had long subsided, but Galvez was still not certain of Legrasse's reasons. Yes, he understood about the traps being laid out in the same patterns as those on the cane. He understood about the interconnected manner of most magics, and how, yes, perhaps he had been maneuvered into striking each of the patterns in turn with what could very well be thought of as a wand. And, yes again, considering the detail in which Claro had written in his journal, the fact he did not mention patterning the traps was an odd omission. Still...

"You could have just told me not to hit the traps again," he muttered, his dignity still as sore as his flesh.

Legrasse sighed. His hands and legs and arms and face had been snapped and gouged in just as many places as had Galvez. He had lost as much blood, had pulled one of the crushing things off his nose and one off an ear. He did not answer the lieutenant, however. There was no point.

As they stood on the edge of the swamp, watching the old house burn, he did not see where it mattered. When the conflagration was finished, the officers waiting nearby would dynamite the spring Claro had written of, the one they had found with so many sinister gouges roping up through the mud surrounding it. Afterward the entire area would be salted, then forgotten.

Holding the cane for a moment longer, Legrasse wondered if what he had seen in his mind were even possible. Could the blind lengths have carved the patterns, planted the wand, arranged the room to be discovered just so, waiting for some unsuspecting wretches to trigger the ritual?

And to what end?

"Just to take advantage of the fact that a storm somehow opened a random portal that some bug just happened to accidentally poke its way through?"

At that point, Legrasse did not care if he were right or not. Better sore ribs and a swollen ear than some foul horror flopping about loose. One poor dead bastard was enough.

But, maybe Claro was not the only one that had gotten too near the edge. The inspector wondered if, perhaps, he too might not have seen more than he could bear at this point. Maybe he was growing overly paranoid over the unspeakables he had encountered. Perhaps he was weakening, assigning them too much credit, too much ability. But then, how could one ascribe such beings with too much ability?

He might've been wrong, he snorted, but that didn't mean it wasn't possible.

Muttering a curse in Hector Claro's honor, Legrasse threw the cane as hard as he could into the blazing cremation before him. Then, he turned and walked back toward the police wagon parked well back from the swamp and the burning house. Like the snorting horses waiting there, he had grown tired of the smell.

Fiction is about plots, characters, complications, and emotions. And "The Longest Pleasure" plays with the most overlooked of these aspects: emotion. Clever tales such as this not only tell a story, but they allow the reader to join in the process. Yes, this is true of most every work of fiction. But in this case, the doors of imagination are left wide open, allowing the reader to share in the experience. The tale's setting makes this all the more engaging. All in all, this is a metaphor that inspires emotion, and it draws them from the reader like water from a well.

THE LONGEST PLEASURE

"Now hatred is by far the longest pleasure,
Men love in haste, but they detest at leisure."

–Lord Byron

THE SUN BEAT DOWN on me without mercy—blazing, tearing the world apart—the hottest sun the world had ever known. I was in the desert, a middle eastern one, the kind with no plant life—just rolling dunes and vast, unbelievable stretches of dusty grey sand. Survival did not really seem like an option.

The post I had found to lean on was still digging into my back. It hurt no matter how I moved, but I didn't care. It didn't matter. Nothing mattered. Except waiting for Tom.

HOW WE HAD GOTTEN stranded in the desert alone, without supplies and left to die, none of that was important any more. The heat, the baking, frying dryness that had burned my skin and cracked my tongue…that was all that mattered. That and waiting for Tom.

When I had first started to make my way forward out of the dunes, I'd stopped sweating in less than half an hour. It had only taken my body that long to adjust to the situation…to understand that we were lost in a hell of burning glare and blinding pain, and that it was going to take everything we had to get ourselves out alive.

Where Tom was at that point, I didn't know. Or care. For the first time in years I had actually forgotten about him. I'd had more important things to worry about. Every step across the drily blowing sand had been a nightmare. Caring about my own neck had shoved the memory of Tom from my mind for the moment.

For the moment.

It took me two days to find my waiting place. Two days struggling across the fires. Across the suffocating forge ever blasting at me—draining me, reducing me, searing and boiling and charring me—stripping me to the most basic components...those that kept one foot moving after the other.

Step after step...step after step...step after step...after...step ...after step...

Until somehow blind instinct finally dragged me to the dirty wallow and the sickly tangle it supported. What I had found wasn't much. The *oasis*, for lack of a better word, was a hellishly small thing. It had no trees, no lush patch of veld surrounding it. It was a mud hole, no more than two by three, with a scattering of some scrub cactus and tangled weeds and bits of grass and the such around it. So small, in truth, and yet the lie of it as wide as an ocean. That was where I found the rifle.

The pole driven into the ground near it by some unknown traveller gave me something to lean against. The rifle I found at the base of the post gave me something to hold. Something to hold as I leaned in pain and waited for Tom.

I had to wait because I knew he would come. I *knew* he would find the oasis. Say what you wanted about Tom, no matter what you had to admit that he was a survivor. He would survive the desert. He had to, I thought, as I leaned against the uncomfortable post.

He just had to.

And, he did. I don't know how long it took, but eventually I saw him, on hands and knees, dragging his way across the sand. Coming toward me and the water at my feet. My burnt fingers twitched. Skin cracked as they tightened around the stock of the rifle. Just for fun, I lined Tom up in the sight's cross hairs.

Just for fun.

"Come on," I whispered, throat scratching, head reeling. "Crawl. Crawl, you bastard. Like you made so many *others* crawl."

How many lives did you ruin? I wondered. How much pain did you cause? Ruthlessly. *Needlessly?*

I gripped the rifle tighter—more determined.

You're still in my sights, Tom, I thought grimly. But, suddenly it's not so much fun any more.

I kept my bead on him. I wanted to fire so badly I was shaking. Suddenly I didn't care to let him reach the water. Somehow, seeing him crawl toward me—head gleaming in the sunlight...such a tempting...*perfect* target...

One bullet—such an easy shot—a simple pull...and it would all...*finally* be over.

I could move away from this painful post...and make my own thirsty way out of this inferno. Just one...easy...shot.

But, as I watched Tom drag himself across the broiling dunes, imagining the scraping heat of the sand scrubbing away his skin, as I remembered all he had done, I finally decided against the bullet. With each passing second, I simply watched him strain to pull himself closer. Foot by foot. Until finally, he was before me, inches from the mud hole.

As I lowered the rifle Tom thrust his head under the water. He sputtered and retched, but kept himself submerged in the wallow, gulping it in as deeply as he could. I let him drink undisturbed. Then, after a long moment, he pulled his head up out of the water. Dripping wet, refreshed and arrogant, he smiled at me, his blazing Irish eyes twinkling as he sneered,

"HaaHaaaaaaaaa. You're still a fool, Harrison. Just like all the others. Weak and stupid—all of you." Shoving his left hand into the water, he splashed it across his head and back and neck.

"That's why I always won," he added. "That's why I always—"

And then, Tom's body froze as sudden, incredible pain exploded within him. Red claws of agony tore through his guts. His eyes went wide, distorting grotesquely. His hands slapped at his neck, blistered fingers digging and rubbing in futile desperation.

Finally, I thought, as Tom rolled across the sand, dying in pain that seemed all I could have hoped for. Finally, I could step away from the gouging pain of the pole.

I sighed with relief as I pulled my back free from the puncturing horns. The animal skull that had been placed atop the pole to warn desert travellers about the poisonous waters at my feet was an ominous, nasty looking thing. I waited for Tom to see it, waited for recognition of what I had done to him to show in his eyes. The glimmer of realization coincided with a bleating scream that tore itself loose from the center of his tattered soul.

Earlier, when I'd had Tom in the sights of the rifle...oh how I'd wanted to pull the trigger. Now...now I was so glad I didn't. A bullet would have been too clean.

Too easy.

As I struck out once more across the desert, I whispered,

"Remember me over the next few hours, Tom. As your guts boil and your stomach bleeds. Remember the stupid weakness I showed in letting you gobble down your death."

I hadn't had a drink in three days. But it was worth it. Worth waiting for him to catch up with me. Worth it to see the look on his face...

I knew it was quite possible that I wouldn't survive. That perhaps my hate had killed the both of us. At that point, however, it didn't matter. I'd reaped all the pleasure I needed from life at that point. All I could want.

The longest pleasure of all.

There are some creations in the vast world of Lovecraftian mythos that cannot be stopped. These are perhaps the most frightening of things—as there is no hope in standing against them. However, where Teddy London walks, hope follows—for he is a juggernaut as well.

JUGGERNAUT

It's a gruesome thing, from what I'm told. An unstoppable monster—all legs and claws and molten muscle that fangs down on a man like water cascading across pavement. Everywhere at once, always coming, always from every direction, relentlessly. As endless as the sea, as patient as the mountains. They say it can't be killed, can't be turned, can't be avoided. Inevitable as tomorrow, final as judgment. That's what they whisper, anyway.

Circles confuse them. Spheres, the very thought of bending frightens them like a shadow that isn't cast by anything in sight, and yet's still there crawling across the ground toward you. Curves are their unknown, and they fear them. But it's never been quite understood that curves cannot block them forever—nothing is so fearful of anything that it can be held in check forever. Creatures of sufficient intelligence can figure *anything* out sooner or later. And despite what most people believe, the Hounds of Tindalos *can* think. Trust me, I know.

My name's Teddy London. I used to be just a simple New York City private detective. Then I died. It wasn't long after that initial revelation, the first time I walked the dream plane—just removed my physical form from out of time and space for a moment to avoid dying, or more to the point, dying by being dragged off to some nether dimension by something or other that would torture me for my arrogance from now unto eternity—that I decided that perhaps it was time to change my line of work. Or at least, how I went about it. Since then I've spent a lot of time learning new tricks. A bit of on-the-job training, so to speak.

"So, boss—what'dya think these things look like anyway?" The question was from my partner, Paul Morcey. Balding, a bit overweight, but as loyal and sharp as you could want in the person watching your back. He's seen most everything I have, and he's still around, which says a lot. People don't tend to last long in this business.

"Well, some reports," I told him, indicating the papers on my desk, "say they're greenish, hairless dogs with blue tongues. Some describe them as black, formless shadows. Then there's a layer of the dream plane where they're seen as mercury-like creatures whose bases glide smoothly over anything at lightning speeds, but the surface, due to contact with the air, is a constant boil of unbreakable spines…"

"So, in other woids, they're tough to get a positive I.D. on before it's too late."

"No I.D.," I admitted, "but we've got their M.O.. Why don't you explain a little about them, Doc."

Professor Zachary Goward took center stage. The Doc's always been good for background on this or that beyond-the-edge nasty that I've run into. I've gotten help from all manner of people along the way. Just trying to stay alive, which is really all I've been doing since I got my first peek behind the curtain and learned there really are things out there going bump in the night. You see, the problem with stumbling into something like this is…well, basically, just what do you do once you know about these things?

Most of the world thinks beings like vampires and dimensional shamblers and the walking dead and all are just stories. Oh, a part of their mind believes, but ultimately they're too intelligent for all that—don't you know. And so, when they finally do stumble across something—something all teeth and tentacles—they freeze. It's the slightest of moments, that infinitesimal split second they need to adjust to what's being seen, to run through the files in their brains to find some kind of label for the horror for which they have no immediate designation. Of course, by the time they do find a name for it, they're usually dead.

"These things, the hounds of Tindalos," said the professor, "aren't really dogs of any kind, of course. They're creatures of

immense power possessed of the ability to travel through time, itself. Millions of years ago, the reports say, they dwelled in a city of corkscrew towers somewhere here on Earth. Where this was, what has happened to the city, where the hounds are now, what's become of them, et cetera, all unknown. Not even any guesses worth mentioning, although I do have a theory."

"Spill them beans, Doc," said Paul. My partner has a way of cutting through the red tape that has to be admired. He's the only person I've ever come across who wears his enthusiasm for this work openly. Most of the rest of us could leave it behind, permanently, without a second thought. I know I could. Not Paul, though. Smiling, he added, "It's been a while since I've wrestled with something beyond me comprehension."

The problem with getting mixed up with this "from beyond" stuff is that there's just too much of it. The concepts are all big and overwhelming. Little is known for sure, and what is known is wrong half the time, or insufficient. For instance, there really are vampires, but they aren't afraid of religious icons. Or sunlight. And they don't drink blood, either. They simply pull the energy out of you. There's no sexual thirst, no entrancing kiss—that's romantic bullshit cobbled together by a century of hacks to trick money out of the gullible. Real vampires just break your legs or your back and then strip away your remaining years while you claw the ground in pain.

"If the hounds are anything we know of already," Goward told those assembled, "it would be the fallen angels of the Christian Bible, actually, the rebels who followed Lucifer when he attempted to overthrow the Heavens."

"Angels?" asked Cat, an electronics expert still willing to gamble her life now and again on one of my stunts.

"Sometime in prehistory," answered the professor, "there was a great upheaval between two powers. If you like 'God and his angels,' fine. If you want other labels, I'm not opposed. These Tind'losi appear to be the basis for the legend of the fallen angels. Whatever they and their masters were, are, whathaveyou, they seem to have rebelled and then been sealed away in their city outside of normal time as a punishment. You see—the hounds cannot navigate curves—"

"Oh, but excuse me, doctor," asked Pa'sha, a weapon's maker from the Caribbean whom I've known longer than anyone else in the room, "but if you could explain that concept even just a tiny bit more thoroughly."

Goward sighed. I didn't blame him. That's what this game is like—you're just constantly shattering people's notions of what is and isn't real or permanent or whatever. And worse yet, once someone who's just gotten a taste of the beyond finds out you've stopped something—some thing that's weird, supernatural, paranormal, ultradimensional—whatever, suddenly you're supposed to be able to do anything, stop *anything*. Hey, Marge, ain't that the guy who killed a rat with a shotgun? Let's give him a Bowie knife and point him at Godzilla.

"As briefly as possible," Goward answered Pa'sha, "Tind'losi occupy the angles of time, while mankind, as well as every other living thing, I imagine, live within the curves of time. I know this is a difficult concept to grasp, I'm not really comfortable with it myself, but it does make a certain mathematical sense. You see, if the hounds were pulled outside of normal time as a punishment, they would have to be bound away from humanity by some sort of cosmic geometry. This notion of them being Lucifer's troops—why not? The hounds of Tindalos are the only creatures in all arcana which are described as existing under such conditions. Perhaps Tindalos *is* Hell. It would explain a great deal—why there is no trace of their city on Earth today, why they hate humanity so…"

"How's it explain that?" asked Paul.

"Tind'losi can only come after human beings whom they have seen. Which, because of their unique situation in the universe, means that humans have to make the first contact."

"But how could a person contact these things if they exist outside normal time and space?" asked Cat.

"There are ways," said the professor. "For instance, a man by the name of Harvey Walters once found a gemstone which, when meditated upon, allowed him to look into the far past. When he did so, he was seen by a Tind'losi which apparently, once it had made visual contact with him, was able to track him through the millennia, traveling through the angles of time until it…" Goward paused for a moment, then composed himself, finishing with, "Anyway, it's from Mr. Walters we have so many of the descriptions of Tindalos and the hounds, et cetera."

"Okay, okay," said Morcey. "So, dese things is tough to kill and they come after ya worse than the IRS. So what's all this got to do with us?"

A while back I'd thought that maybe we might've finally seen it all. I mean, as a group, we'd tangled with vampires and succubi,

Renewing his grips upon the spear and sword he had chosen for his task, he dug the butt end of the spear into the ground so as to use it as a crutch, holding the sword as high as he could with his other hand. He could feel thick bubbles of blood foaming in his throat, but still he hung on, refusing to die, keeping his feet despite the cold and hungry agony tearing through his insides.

Finally the Northman came to a point where his pain was so intense he simply could not feel it any longer. He thanked the gods for that, even though a terrible, heavy weariness began settling upon him in its place. Shoving that aside, he growled fiercely, bloody spittle flecking his lips.

"I will not fail," he vowed. "I will not die. I shall not, I cannot."

Of course you will not fail

Surprise pried Olgenson's eyes wide. The wind that whispered in the dying man's ear was a thing of steel and red hot courage. It was a female breeze, but one that knew not children or hearth or the moon-brought blood. It was a warrior's sound—an echo of iron that somehow calmed his fears and bolstered his waning spirit. Turning his head in the direction of the words, the Northman smiled in a giddy awe as he beheld a singular shape form in the midst of his double vision.

Tall she was, with hair that flashed from sunlight to hellfire as she walked toward him. Her legs were long and powerful, booted in metal, as were her equally strong hands and torso. The fur of a bear hung as a cloak down her back, placed there as more a thing of decoration that for warmth. Her head was sheathed in a winged helmet, a glorious affair of strange feathers and tiny horns which so held Olgenson's attention that he could scarce drop his vision to the woman's eyes.

What do you see, Kaarl Olgenson?

"I see a woman...I, I..." and then, thoughts flashed together within the dying man's mind, giving him understanding. Focusing on her silver tipped spear, almost seeing the winged horse pawing the ground behind her, he knew beyond doubt what was happening to him. Still, with all the strength he could muster, he spat, "No—stay back from me. I cannot join you."

Her grim lips parting, the Valkyrie asked softly;

Cannot join me?

"I must stay here. I must defend this spot. I—" A great hacking tore through Olgenson. Thick strings of bloody mucus slobbered free from his nose, splattering against his heaving chest. Dropping his sword, he hung onto his spear with both hands as the terrible said, "Please listen to me, for I will say this only once—I have witnessed horrors easily beyond your comprehension. If you enter that building thinking this to all be some kind of game, you will be nothing more than cannonfodder for whatever we find—or should I say, whatever finds us."

Mezeltin blew smoke in the professor's direction, telling him, "Ohhh, you're worried about me. That's so sweet. I'm touched. Now, can we get on with this?"

Goward turned and walked away, not able to concern himself with the reporter any longer. Catching up to the others already pouring into the building, he shook his head as he walked up to the front door. The mood around the old structure was, contrary to its dreary condition, calm and peaceful. Despite the look of the place, he neither saw nor heard anything that appeared dangerous or even out of the ordinary. The air felt clear and crisp, with no scent of rain or fog to be found. In truth, it could not have seemed more harmless.

But, knowing how little faith one could place in mundane senses like sight and hearing, or smell and touch, Goward crossed himself in the traditional Roman Catholic manner, whispering, "God in heaven, I pray Thee, have mercy on us."

Looking back to see Mezeltin and her cameraman standing next to their car, laughing and smoking, without breaking stride, he added;

"All of us."

And then he went ahead through the door, not at all surprised that the atmosphere inside the building was even more depressingly dreary than that outside.

"Alright, people," Morcey called out, one eye on his watch. "We got a schedule to keep. After all, dis ain't government work. Let's run it down, shall we? Cat?"

"All ready, mein Fuhrer," answered the woman. "We've got motion sensors in place throughout the building and as long as everyone wears their differentiators I'll be able to tell if and when we have guests. We've got temperature monitors at each site as well, Geiger counters, video and audio recorders—all of it tied in to my monitor here. Keep me in one piece and I'll keep you up to date on who or what's crawling around in the basement."

"Doc?"

single length, it merely poked and prodded and rolled, intent in its search, but making no discovery. At first.

Claro's words dropped icicles down the back of Legrasse's shirt collar, making each vertebrae ache in turn as they uncomfortably made their way down his spine.

> It were a horrible feeling, not being able to see, not being able to breathe, just scared and waiting for the damn thing to go away. Just holding my breath and waiting and praying and none of it doing no good. No good at all.
>
> It just kept digging and scratching and tugging, like a big finger, but a stupid one. Like something that had never seen a bed or a blanket. I think how dumb it were was more frightening than anything else. Even a bear, or fox, or anything, anything that ever crawled up out of the swamp should have known what it had found. But this thing couldn't tell it had found a man under a blanket. So it just kept poking and digging at me.
>
> And then, it found me. The crawling bastard thing finally found its way under the blanket and it slid under my leg and up over the other in a motion so fast I couldn't react. But, as it started to circle under my leg, like to grab it, or squeeze it, my fear left me, or it filled me, whatever, I don't know. I only know that was all I could stand.
>
> It was a madness that took me then. I rolled out of my bed screaming. In the darkness, I grabbed at the thing coiling around my legs and I pulled it from me and smashed at it, beating it with my fists, beating it against the floor.
>
> With a lightning speed it jerked free of my hold and retreated out of the room. I followed it, my hands grabbing for something to use as a weapon. They found a chair. I wasn't thinking, didn't care. I grabbed up the chair and ran to follow the thing, whatever it was, to break it, to kill it. Then, I got to the next room...and I had to stop.

LEGRASSE READ ON, FASCINATED. Claro has stopped for he had found his home filled with vast lengths of roping flesh, something like the tentacles of a squid, but longer, thinner, and possessed of individual skills no cephalopod imaginable had ever displayed. He stood frozen, terror gripping his every muscle, as he watched the roaming tendrils poke and pull and slither in the moonlight. Then, the one werewolves and winged lizardmen, cast the abomination known as Lilith back into the pit and thwarted the rapious desires of more than one inter-dimensional traveller.

"Ah, you see..." answered Goward with hesitation, "The reason I know about Mr. Walters' gem is...it was sent to me for study. I didn't know what it was when I first began to examine it. But, after I looked into it under a microscope, and saw that terrible face leering back at me across the endless tracts of history..."

The professor paused to remove his glasses, wiping away imaginary grime as he said, "Anyway, according to the best information available, the hound should arrive here somewhere in between four and five days from now. At which time, I imagine, it will destroy my physical being and then return to Tindalos with my soul which it will keep, and torment, throughout eternity."

Seen it all, I asked myself. We hadn't seen anything yet. But we were about to. And it wasn't going to be pretty.

WE PUT THE NEXT few days to good use. Knowing that a sphere would keep the professor safe, our first priority was to come up with a safe house. Pa'sha solved that problem for us by taking us out to the Brooklyn docks. New York's shipping industry used to be one of the greatest in the world. Times change, though, and over the years more and more of the city's harbor area had been allowed to drift into disrepair.

What Pa'sha knew about was a foundry that at one time had worked in die casting wrecking balls. The firm had sold all its molds to the Japanese just before World War II. When hostilities broke out, the massive casting blocks had been stored rather than shipped out to the enemy. Too bulky to move, they'd simply been warehoused, then forgotten. The die stood some fifteen feet in height. When Cat noted that the sphere inside was rather cramped, Paul quipped that it was a lot more roomy than a coffin. Goward agreed. That closed that deal.

Our plan was simple. As the final moments arrived, Goward would enter the spherical interior of the mold through the pour hole in the top. After that, we would wait for the arrival of the hound. As soon as we got a fix on it, a second mold would be lowered on top of the other to eliminate the entrance and keep the Tind'losi at bay. The only things we stocked the sphere with were water and scuba gear. There wasn't any use in wasting space on food or a chemical toilet or most of the other things that got suggested. Oxygen tanks are fairly bulky for the amount of breathable atmosphere they can hold. The professor was going to run out of air long before he got very hungry.

After the defense was set, it was time to work on the offense. This was where Cat and Pa'sha came in. Cat, of course, worked on our sensors, setting up a relay system that would drop the second mold atop the first as soon as we had confirmation that the hound had arrived. She also worked out a few other tricks to help give us an edge.

We were stymied for a while on how to aim our weapons, but Goward himself gave us the answer to that one. Not knowing from which angle in the warehouse the creature would appear, he suggested we simply eliminate all but one of them and then concentrate our fire power there. We did. The entire warehouse was lined with chicken wire and then sprayed with plaster foam. As the foam set, we carved the corners into pockets. None of them were perfect, but that didn't matter. As long as we didn't leave any angles steeper than forty-five degrees, the Tind'losi would be denied entrance. Only one corner, the one furthest from the mold in which we would hide Goward, was left untouched. In that space we concentrated our bombs and nets and everything else we had to throw against the monster.

We didn't, however, expect any of this to stop it. We would happily accept a miracle, obviously, but if Goward's research was accurate we pretty much knew nothing we were doing there in the warehouse was actually going to stop the beast. Bullets, electricity—petty annoyances like these were only going to enrage the thing. Madden it beyond reason. Which, of course, was our plan.

THE LAST NIGHT BEFORE the Tind'losi was supposed to arrive, I sat up with my fiancé, Lisa Hutchinson. I couldn't sleep and neither could she. Lisa is a partner in my agency. We met when I saved her from an experience that didn't do either of our mental states much good. I spent a long time in the hospital after it was over. Lisa was there every day at my bedside, refusing to let me just slide into the madness that beckoned so comfortably from the edges of my mind. Since then she's done her best to keep me sane. I try not to let on what a crummy job I think she's doing.

"What're you thinking about?" she asked me. I told her.

"Tomorrow, mostly. How I'm going to...um, handle this whole mess."

"Translation...'how you're going to live through it'...was that more what you meant to say?"

"Well, something on that order, I guess." I stared into Lisa's eyes, drinking in the shining blue of them, concentrating on their color, letting blinding nuisances like thought and reality fall aside into disrepair.

"You want to talk?" she asked, knowing I didn't, but that I had to. I'm the kind of person who thinks well on their feet, but I'm not much of a planner.

"Like to," I admitted, "but there isn't much to say. Sometime tomorrow this thing is going to show up. We'll seal Zach in the mold and then we'll try to get rid of whatever it is that wants to get him."

"And if you can't?" Her voice was tense. Not tearful or threatening, she covered herself well. But there was no getting around that she was worried. Then again, why shouldn't she be? I was worried, too. "What then?"

"Then," I told her, "I guess people are going to die."

Her fingers tightened around mine, her body falling in closer to me, pushing us deeper into the couch cushions. She didn't start crying, or asking foolish questions like why was I the one who had to face this thing. She knew why. For some reason when Lisa had been in trouble a few years back, fate had shoved her in my direction, made me her protector whether I wanted to be or not. A lot of people didn't live through the experience. I did, though—barely. I survived with the knowledge that these things are powerful and fearsome and evil. Some will try to tell you that these creatures are so cosmically almighty that they're beyond good and evil, but that's a crock.

Everybody acts with intent. Everything has motivation. Nothing is random, and that means the actions of gods, monsters and heroes are no exception. Surviving that first attack moved me up a square, made me more visible. After that, stuff just kept finding its way to my doorstep—faster and faster. For me to turn away from any of it would be to surrender. Not facing this Tind'losi, whatever it turned out to be, would be a death sentence for the professor. If I didn't try to stop it, I might as well just put a gun to Zach's head and pull the trigger myself. Certainly it would be more merciful than leaving him to it.

Lisa knew all that, though. She knew I had to play the hand I'd been dealt, like we all do. I could have turned my back on her when we'd met. If I had, of course, she would have died and shortly thereafter the entire world would have been nothing much more than a cosmic cinder. But I didn't. I faced what was after her and managed to stop it. I ended up with four broken ribs, a shattered leg, pneumonia and scores of gashes and burns. I also went somewhat insane. But I was rewarded with Lisa's love, a pure and guiding comfort that in the end seemed worth a thousand such conflicts. Feeling her next to me on the couch, the pattern of her breathing, the rhythm of her heartbeat, the anxiety that had been digging its ragged nails under my skin began to dissolve—dissipated by the care of a loving woman's heart.

I was counting down the minutes to when I would be forced to face a creature that was—for all intents and purposes—quite literally straight out of Hell. In a matter of hours I would pit my few score pounds of flesh and brain against a monster every source available to us considered unkillable—unstoppable by any means. Looking into Lisa's eyes once more, however, I simply couldn't find it within myself to worry any further. I had no illusions about my chances.

Most likely, a voice from the back of my brain told me, *there is no way we can survive.*

Nodding in unconscious agreement, I smiled at my beautiful Lisa and then bent toward her. Our lips touched and the next day was forgotten. Eventually one of us turned out the lights, but for the life of me I can't tell you who it was.

"So," CALLED OUT PAUL, grinning as he stood in the center of the foundry, hands on his hips, "are we all ready to kick a little monster ass?"

"Oh, ho," answered Pa'sha, "And tell me, my friend, what is it that leads you to believe this approaching monster has a small buttocks?"

"Dis guy," complained Paul, grinning as he did so, "he's so stupid he's makin' me look smart."

"Now, now, Morcey-mon," answered Pa'sha with feigned indifference, "you know full well there's none in all this wide world quite that stupid."

The two laughed, coming together for their ritual drink. Pa'sha's been known to toss down more than his share of alcohol, true enough, but Paul isn't that much of a drinker. The pair of them always get together before things get started, though, to knock back a couple of shots together. Pulling his usual silver and glass flask from inside his jacket, Pa'sha handed it to Paul, telling him warmly;

"A coconut rum from my father's own hometown. Fiery and dangerous, but a true flash of lightning, you shall see."

Paul unscrewed the cap and took a whiff.

"Whooo—" he exclaimed. "Some strong stuff here. Kind that puts hair on your chest."

As he hoisted the flask in a momentary salute, then moved it to his mouth to take a drink, Pa'sha answered him, saying, "This one does not put hair on the chest, Morcey-mon...it burns it off."

The two laughed and drank, Pa'sha waving various members of his crew over to join them. His "Murder Dogs," as he calls them, were happy to oblige. The heat in the foundry was punishing and after the grueling preparations we'd readied during the previous few days, there weren't any of us who weren't primed to take a break. All of Pa'sha's troops set aside their weapons, crowding forward to partake in their boss's bounty.

While they did, I turned away for a moment, needing to complete a ritual of my own. Opening my bag, I began the process of slipping into my shoulder holster. I already had my ankle sheath in place, my stiletto, Veronica, secure inside. With a shrug and a twist I had my holster on, my .38 Betty snug under my arm.

Don't ask me why I named my weapons after the girls from the Archie comics. For some reason, a very long time ago, I thought it was funny. Don't ask me what I thought either one of them was going to accomplish in a battle with a Tind'losi, either. I knew neither weapon would be of much use considering what I was going up against, but there're things we do that make us feel prepared, relaxed—more confident. It was a morning for such rituals. Those who didn't have any were advised to start making some up.

Professor Goward was smoking his pipe—maybe not a ritual, but certainly a relaxant. All things considered the Doc looked to be holding up pretty well. Sure, he was worried, being the one directly in the line of fire—who wouldn't be? But still, he was calm enough on the outside to help keep the tension level down, which is always a good thing. Wiping a handful of sweat from my brow, I crossed the room to check on him. I made sure all the rebreathers that'd been loaded into the die with him were full, then I reviewed how to use one properly with him. He reached out while I spoke, catching hold of my shoulder. Grasping it firmly, he said in a low voice.

"You know, I never really have thanked you for taking all this on."

"Don't thank me yet, Zach," I answered him honestly. "We've got a long way to go before we see who lives through this."

"True enough, Theodore," he told me. "But you know what they say about 'thoughts and deeds' and the such. I just didn't want to appear ungrateful—especially considering the fact that I might not get a chance to say it later on at all."

"Jeez," I answered, only half in jest, "and they call me a cynic."

The professor extended his hand toward me. Although the angle was difficult due to how high off the ground he was situated, I reached out to take his hand when suddenly a burning, acrid scent pushed its way into and throughout the room. It was an unbelievably pungent odor, one so nauseous that for a split-second everyone's attention was frozen. We sprang into action, however, as Cat's voice bellowed through the speakers we'd strung throughout the foundry.

"Incoming!"

I snapped my hand back as the top half of the spherical mold began to lower into place. The professor flipped his pipe outside the die and then began fumbling into his breather. Above, the second mold followed the top half of the first weighing the first down and sealing it shut. Racing across the room, Paul threw himself upward forcibly, climbing the ladder to the control room where Cat was waiting two rungs at a time. Pa'sha and his men scattered as well, each man heading for his prearranged station. Gas masks and earplugs were hurriedly slipped into place. The muffled sounds of footfalls and weapons being cocked filled the large room, echoing off the cold concrete walls and floor and ceiling.

All eyes stared at the entry point. The one remaining corner in all the building gushed with a thick, purplish billow. Tendrils of it lurched awkwardly upward and outward, looking more like one liquid forcing its way into another than smoke filling the air. The impenetrable haze grew heavier, crimson sparks flashing randomly within its spreading body. Then, suddenly, something solid emerged from the depths of the cloud.

"It's here!"

An awkward, almost crab-like paw stepped down out of the putrid swirl of gases and scratched along the concrete floor. A bulbous snout followed, red and hard, masking a jaw possessed of multiple layers of needling teeth and fangs. What we could see so far indicated a being roughly the size of a large cow, or perhaps a rhinoceros. Bluish pus dripped from the creature's sides, splattering the floor, burning into the poured stone wherever it landed. Another paw followed the first, striding forward, pulling more of the loathsome body into view. It was long, like a hound, but the comparison was strained—like describing a hand grenade by saying it was oval-shaped, like an egg.

The thing's mouth opened, and a black and yellow mix of gases shrieked out into the room. As hand's cocked weapons, I stepped back further away from the stacked molds, my eyes firm on the creature's advance. Then, once I was certain its entire mass had exited onto our plane, I dropped my hand. In the control room Cat flipped a massive connecting toggle, electrifying the steel mesh net we had spread across the floor.

The beast howled as current filled it. Hundreds of thousands of volts filled the thing's massive body. Its screams were ghastly, bright gray things, darts of sound that shattered glass throughout the building. At the same time, Paul threw a second toggle. This dropped a reinforced mesh net from the ceiling, one layered with thick, but sharp, metal hooks, each of them covered with scores of wicked barbs. The Tind'losi, bucking and straining against The current, only succeeded in snarling itself totally in the two nets, a score of the hammer-sized hooks tearing into its body. In addition, the barbs were coated with every available poison—hemlock, arsenic, strychnine, everything we could find. The hounds of Tindalos might be power incarnate within their own realm, but to walk amongst men they had to take on flesh of one form or another, and in that one tiny weakness we'd put our hopes. For a moment, it seemed as if our hopes might not be vain ones.

The horror in the nets screeched and bellowed, sizzling pus and bile flying from its body as it writhed in electrical pain. In the control room, Cat targeted the creature with a ringed battery of white sound cannons, blasting the demon with high frequency noise. As she guided both attacks, she also watched over the power meters, making certain we stayed at maximum output without going into overload. While she did, Paul started setting things into motion for the second part of our plan. We'd selected the Tind'losi's entrance point carefully, making certain it brought the beast directly beneath the foundry's pour bucket. As the nets below began to smoke and spark, Paul prepared to drop the load of molten metal we had waiting.

"The power's topping out," shouted Cat. "We've got to slice it or we're going to burn down the neighborhood."

Paul nodded, his hands gliding through the routine he had practiced a thousand times over the last few days. As the power to the nets was cut, we all prayed the poison had had a chance to have some kind of effect as the pour bucket released its contents. Ironically, the Tind'losi looked up just as the molten metal dropped down onto it.

New razor-bellowed screams lashed through the building, the force of them etching scattered cracks in the walls and ceiling. The smell of burning bone and organs filled the room. Combining with the smell of the creature's arrival, the stench grew almost overpowering, easily reaching us through our gas masks. As the pour bucket emptied, the entire room hued over in reflected oranges and reds. A torrent of molten splash was flung everywhere, hot metal burning the floor, melting the nets, searing the alien flesh of the Tindalos hound. Not ready to leave anything to chance, however, I gave Pa'sha the high sign from my hiding place. He cued his men. Explosions filled the air.

The Murder Dogs targeted the glowing, thrashing figure in the center of the room, pumping hundreds of bullets a second into the monstrous thing. A two man team fired anti-tank missiles into the burning form, blowing out successively larger chunks of the creature with each fearsome strike. Shotguns and flamethrowers were added to the mix, our redundant efforts hoping to enrage and confuse as much as to weaken. It was amazing how little good any of it seemed to do.

With a hissing whisper the Tind'losi stood erect once more. Poison gas canisters were released by Pa'sha and his men, as well as chemical burners and flash bombs. More miniature missiles were launched. Grenades followed. Even though every man fought from behind a steel-reinforced lead shield of considerable thickness, three of the Murder Dogs were already out of the action, one felled by an unfortunate ricochette, two hit by molten slag thrown off by the screaming monster in the center of the foundry.

And then, suddenly it seemed like we were getting somewhere. For a moment it'd appeared the creature was rallying, but then the moment passed and the Tind'losi sank to its knees, crippled beyond repair. Pa'sha and his Murder Dogs kept firing, throwing everything they had left into their attack. Thousands of rounds were launched, enough fire power slamming into the burning thing on the floor to pierce the side of a battleship. And still, somehow the terrible form threw itself up off the floor, it's forward legs pawing the air violently.

But then came another massive howl, an almost sonic blast of hate and fear, erupting from the creature. Lashing through the room, the horrid screech shook the entire building, piercing our ear plugs, rocking the floor, even moving the five ton mold we'd used to seal in Goward by several inches.

The thing fell to the ground completely then. Its burning head slammed into the concrete, cracking it open to the depth of eighteen inches. Its massive legs kicked brutally against the air, sending more molten slag and super-heated bits of netting flying through the air. But, as each second passed its thrashing grew less and less violent. And then, suddenly, the unstoppable beast simply ceased moving.

In the control room, Cat switched on the massive roof fans. We hadn't dared run any power equipment while trying to electrocute the beast, but the moment for caution seemed to have passed.

"We did it!" shouted Paul. Dancing a victory shuffle in the control room, he pulled Cat from her chair, laughing as he twirled her around the room. "We killed it! Ding, dong—the humpin' bastard is *dead!*"

A part of my brain was amazed at how easy it had all been. Another voice from within my mind snickered at my naivete. We had gone through enough power to keep Time Square lit up for several months. We had fired some fifteen thousand projectiles into the thing—followed by several hundred compressed pounds of various gases and chemical poisons. All tolled, we had spent nearly a million and a half dollars of the company's money. The rest of my brain told the single dissenter to shut up, though. Yes, we had thrown everything we had against the creature. If it had lived another few minutes we'd have been reduced to hurling rocks at it. But it hadn't. We'd beaten it. The battle was over. The professor was safe.

Or...so we thought.

"Hey," called out one of the Murder Dogs, "what dey hell be dot, mon?"

From the initial entry point, once more there came a gushing, thick, purplish billow. Once more tendrils of it lurched awkwardly into our dimension, the same heavy, crimson sparks flashing through the mounting haze, the same vague solid stirring moving forward from deep within the depths of the cloud.

"Sweet bride of the night!" shouted Paul. "There's *two* of them!"

Again, an awkward, almost crab-like paw stepped down out of the newly forming swirls of smoke and gas stretching through the foundry. But, unlike the first attack, this time there was a substantial difference. This time, there was more than one of the creatures. As everyone around the room simply stared in amazement, a second bulbous snout moved out of the haze, followed by another, and then another. Behind them, receding down the corridors of time, stretching off through some unbelievable chain of right-angled space, waited an infinite number of the pus dripping creatures, all of them straining to pass through into this world.

My eyes darted throughout the room, time splitting into microseconds as I checked on everyone. Cat had fallen back into her chair, stunned into immobility. Even through her gas mask her eyes showed wide and unblinking. One of her hands was raised to her face, her forefinger upheld, the entire hand trembling.

Paul was still standing, his shoulders stiff and tight. He had already pulled his Auto-Mag from his shoulder holster and was headed for the control room door. The same held for Pa'sha and his men. None of them had more than a few rounds of ammunition available to them. Most had nothing left, but they were ready to fight nonetheless. If only one more of the creatures had arrived it might have been different. One more might have inspired terror within us—or a sense of futility. But, there were so many coming toward us that fear became useless.

So was throwing away lives, however. Knowing there was no sense in everyone dying, I stepped forward into the room, drawing as close to the volcanic heat of its still molten center as I dared. Hoping the fans had already completed their job, I tore off my gas mask and addressed the Tind'losi in the lead.

"And just what the fuck do you want?"

The creature was taken aback for a moment. It sniffed the air between us, its cautious movements halting its massed fellows. The thing stared at me with interest, like a child wondering exactly what kind of bug it was that stood on its hind legs and dared bark so. There was no fear in the thing—its curiosity was borne more of an awesome delight, the joy in finding an unexpected treat. Some of the Tind'losi behind it began to snarl and jabber, bucking to push their way forward into the foundry. The leader silenced them with a tearing hiss that blew bloody steam from its nostrils. Then, returning its attention to me, it spoke.

"To step into the world once more, and to find man so utterly unchanged." Its voice was a harsh, yet elegant sound—the clattering growl of a cultured cement mixer. "As if a hundred billion revolutions round the center were but a yawning brief pause."

The creature smiled, horrible rows of devilish teeth grinding against one another in its terrible jaw. Taking another step into the foundry, the thing reared upward, then sat down on the floor, its body towering over us all. Looking down at me, it announced;

"You may call me, Belial. It means…"

"It means," I cut the thing off, "'Without a master.'"

"Why—what a clever puny you are." Turning to its fellows, Belial snarled contemptuously, "You see—I told you. There will be more sport here than simply slaughtering them all."

"You're not going to slaughter anyone."

A great angry barking arose through the crowding horde. Their master silenced them with another steaming shriek. It turned languidly, its torso twisting unnaturally, and then struck the two closest Tind'losi devastating blows with its forepaws. As it did, I bent my head slightly, trying to corral my runaway nerves. I knew what I had to do next.

You do, do you? A voice from the back of my consciousness, some ancestor from the early recesses of my racial memory, shouted at me, *This isn't what you expected—is it? No—things have gone far beyond anything you imagined, haven't they?*

We still have a plan.

You had a plan for dealing with one of these things—ONE! screamed another, albeit less stable, one of my forefathers. *This is more than ONE!*

SILENCE, I thought darkly, flooding the single word throughout my consciousness. Several other dissident voices were trying to speak up, but the creature had turned back toward me and I had to be ready for it. The struggle for power between us was about to commence and it wouldn't do if I was too busy comforting myself to play its game.

"So, my little puny, you are the one called 'the Destroyer'—yes?"

"There are some who call me that," I admitted.

"Well then, tell us, Destroyer, how is it that we are not going to do that which we have come to do—that which we have dreamed of since a trillion centuries before you had form?"

"Because you're all going to turn around—right now—and go back to where you come from. And then you're going to stay there."

Clearing my mind, pushing panic and all her sisters away from me, crushing terror and fear, I sent my senses out beyond my body, feeling my way into the city beyond. On any given day there are at the very least well over five million people in New York City. Gently, from each one of them, from their pets and all the trees and plants of every shape and size—from every living thing in every direction I began the siphoning of tiny bits of power.

"And why would we do this, my puny?"

"Because I'll destroy you all if you don't."

Globs of mucused spittle spat from a thousand throats, yellow-brown fangs clattering in raucous glee. I got the feeling the Tind'losi didn't believe me. Not that I cared. The longer they allowed me to stall, the better my chances got. Unfortunately, they didn't give me all that long.

"Anduscias," snapped the creature. "Attend to my puny."

As the thing to Belial's left moved forward, I continued stealing what power I could—the energy to run up a flight of stairs, a week's life here and there, the power to mix a pan of batter, a toss of a bowling ball, five minutes walking, et cetera—storing it all in an ever-tightening clutch as I casually asked;

"This Anduscias, not a close friend, is he?"

The second Tind'losi stared at me, taking my measure for a split-second. The right side of its maw curling in a wicked sneer, it dug a claw into the foundry's floor, flicking brick-sized chunks of concrete this way and that.

"Why do you ask?"

Anduscias sprang, his motion a blur. My hand shot up of its own volition, releasing a huge blast of the energy I had stolen. The Tind'losi was torn in two, its organs splattering across the floor, a length of its spine splashing up through its back, shattering against the ceiling, various bits of it clattering back to the foundry floor. My nerves tingled throughout my body from the release, burning flashes tearing at my flesh, unraveling my tendons, grinding my bones one against the other. I kept my face calm, somehow, and answered Belial.

"I just hate to break up happy couples." I gave the words a second to penetrate, then tried my bluff again. "Be that as it may, that's all the time we have. I want to thank you for playing with us. Be sure to pick up a copy of our home game on your way out. You know where the exit is. Don't let the door smack you while you're leaving."

"I do not believe you understand the situation, my puny." Leaning forward, Belial bent its massive head downward until it was within a few feet of my own. "We were locked away from this world for not bowing. We chose to be the lords of Tindalos rather than to bend our knees to others—to be told we were not the equal of what was to come. Of you."

"My heart's bleeding, pal. Tell it to someone who cares. Now are you going calm, or do we have to have trouble?"

"Thrown from this world," snarled Belial, "we were refused entry to it, unless called by human voice. Only a handful of times have you punies reached out so far as to touch us. We have always come. But when puny blood has cooled our throats, back always have we been flung. Until now."

I followed the creature's eyes as it looked at its fallen comrades. Knowing where it was going next, I prepared myself for the inevitable.

"No anchor would we have in this world. One puny found allowed one of us to escape, but contact was always fatal, and fatality always sent us back. But, you, Destroyer—you have ended that. You have spilled Tind'losi blood. You have given us our anchor here. Now, this world is ours. We shall scatter across the face of it, and everything shall be consumed. Beginning with *you*."

I threw myself back just as Belial came forward, its wicked fangs snapping the air where my head had been. Instantly those others behind the monster pushed their way into the foundry. As they turned their attention this way and that, their master commanded—

"No! None other than the Destroyer! He dies—then we live!"

I threw a mental challenge out to all the Tind'losi, driving it straight into their brains, daring them to come after me. Then I turned tail and ran, heading for the outside. I didn't bother to waste time looking over my shoulder. The sound of walls being smashed, of the ground itself being ripped asunder as the monsters tore through everything in their path, let me know I had no worries about being followed. Diving into my waiting car, I punched the ignition and headed for the gate.

My rearview mirror was filled with the sight of scores of slavering monstrosities galloping down the road after me. Even over the roar of the car's engine I could hear the screams of those people who spotted the horde tearing through the streets. Did any of the monsters stop, changing targets, gobbling down those innocents who just happened by? They did. I couldn't see them, but I could feel each strike—each stopped heart and silenced brain—all of them cutting through me like thrusts from wide, dull knives.

I couldn't worry about that, though. We'd miscalculated—badly. Seeking only to save our friend we had unleashed a Hell throng upon the Earth, one that would wipe out every last living soul if they weren't turned or stopped. Luckily, we had a plan that might just do the trick. It had been our last ditch reserve, a dodge we'd cooked up in case our more conventional weapons failed. It had seemed a foolproof fail safe—for taking care of the single hound we'd expected. As for hundreds of thousands...that I didn't know. What I did know, however, was that the trap we'd come up with was the only chance we had, and that I'd better concentrate on springing it.

With a lurch I threw my car into a hard right, sending it flying down a broken side street. The Tind'losi piled up on each other, clawing and biting their own, giving me a chance to get a few blocks ahead of the pack. I gunned the motor, ignoring red lights, laying on the horn, chasing cars out of my way, using any lane I needed to, or even the sidewalk, to keep moving forward. Behind me the monsters charged headlong, crashing into buildings, tearing storefronts away with glancing blows of their bodies.

People staggered in the street, reeling with disbelief at what they were seeing. Fangs and claws tore them apart without compunction—practically without notice. A bus ground its brakes, screeching to a halt as the wave of Tind'losi filled the street behind me. I swerved around it, crashing against the mini-van behind. Caroming off the damaged vehicle, I reached out with my mind toward the souls in the bus, even as I fought with the steering wheel to straighten out my car. As I found each pulse on the bus I extinguished it, seconds before the Tind'losi could tear the fragile steel and iron to shreds.

"After him!" came the great, growling shriek. "Kill the Destroyer—kill him! Only him!"

I'd led the attack that destroyed one of their own. I'd killed another right before their eyes. Now, whenever they tried to take the souls of the humans that crossed their paths, I reached out and stole those first, as well. I was hoping this tactic would outrage the monsters. From what I could see in my rearview mirror—it was working. Praying that it was working well enough, I floored the gas and threw my car onto the ramp exit leading down to the Battery Tunnel. Breaking through the toll barrier, I shot down into the descending opening. Behind me, Tind'losi tore great gashes in each other trying to be the first to enter the tunnel after me.

Reaching a point beyond the monster's line of sight, I slammed on the brakes and stopped the car. Leaping out as fast as I could, I concentrated deeply, working to open a doorway to the dream plane. I knew where I wanted to go, I knew when I wanted to arrive. I just had to make certain my timing was perfect. Sensing the approaching Tind'losi, I closed my eyes and stepped forward, disappearing into the dimensional rift I had opened. Behind me, I could hear the creatures running forward, screeching over what I'd done. They had seen me, had figured out what I was doing and were following me through the gateway.

Excellent, I thought. *Now if I could just get them all there on time.*

I USED NEARLY HALF the energy I'd gathered from the dying to cut a swath across the dream plane. I needed to take the Tind'losi to another location on Earth. Opening the doorway there in the tunnel in Brooklyn, I opened another into a tunnel in Switzerland—in Geneva to be exact. The Cern Facility is built in a tunnel some three hundred feet underneath Geneva. It is a circular burrow some twenty-seven kilometers in length. I didn't open the gateway exit into that tunnel, however, but rather into the metal pipe suspended in the center of that tunnel. The Cern Facility is the world's largest particle accelerator, a massive, city-sized machine scientists use to split atoms and create new elements. It is a perfect cylinder, designed so to keep radioactive particles—which can only travel in straight lines—from escaping its confines.

"Good God," exclaimed one of the control technicians. "There's some massive build-up in the core pipe."

"Yeah," I snapped. Stepping into the control room, from out of thin air for all the scientists there knew, I ordered, "start it up, now."

"You're mad—there are hundreds of thousands of alien particles in the cyclotron chamber. They're simply appearing from nowhere. The vacuum isn't..."

"Don't even talk to him," interrupted an older man. Snapping his fingers at another, he ordered, "Call security. Get someone in here right away."

They were all speaking French, of course. I was talking to them by thought, putting words directly into their brains which they translated themselves. Not having time to argue, I started putting orders in instead of suggestions.

"You've got plutonium tests scheduled all day today. I know the rail gun is loaded and waiting. Fire it—*now!*"

The man's hands moved to obey my orders even as his conscious brain protested. It didn't matter. I had influenced the day's schedule when we'd first decided on this plan. By leading the Tind'losi into the tunnel, I'd hoped to trick them into not noticing they were being moved from one type of tunnel into a vastly different one. I wanted them to think I was trying to escape them so they would rush in after me. Once in the gateway, our relative size would become unmeasurable. There would be no way for them to notice they were being shrunk by the exit portal to sub-atomic size. Sidedooring on them, I had led them into the particle accelerator while I dropped into the control room.

The rail gun was primed to fire an atom of plutonium into the accelerator. We had assumed if this was done with the Tind'losi that was coming after the professor inside, that the thing would be atomized—split asunder in a nuclear reaction that would create a new element with a half life of a millisecond. That was one Tindalos hound, of course. What would happen with hundreds of thousands was anyone's guess. But, it was the only chance the world had. If the Tind'losi escaped, billions would die. Casting aside the seductive pleasure of doubt, I pushed my anger into the operator's brain and squeezed his soul until his hands did my bidding. The single atom of plutonium was fired into the accelerator tube. And then, their world ended.

As the technicians screamed, the entire control room began to vibrate. One by one the monitors covering the accelerator tunnel glowed then exploded. The curving atom's merging with the angles of the Tind'losi set off a chain reaction which shattered the central tube, incredible explosions ripping along the miles of subterranean passages. In seconds vast sections of Geneva began tumbling into the ground. Gas lines erupted, flames shooting hundreds of feet into the air. Buildings crashed against each other, falling into the vast, mile wide cracks opening everywhere throughout the city.

In my head, I could feel thousands dying all around me. Those in the control room had gone first. I'd plucked the energy of their wills to power my escape, feeling them curse me with their dying moments. Fine by me, I thought. They weren't the first.

Sliding into the dream plane, I gathered what force I could from the legions of the dying below. Staring down into the city from the safety of my ethereal vantage point, I steeled myself against the wail of sorrow I could feel drenching my soul. Thousands dead. Crushed, ripped apart by shrapnel, burned, asphyxiated, atomized in nuclear-force blasts. I was as staggered by the enormity of what I'd done as that of why I'd done it.

An accident had brought a friend under the sights of a thing from Hell which meant to wear his soul for lunch. Determined to save him, I had put together a group that stood up to the beyond thing and annihilated it. Which, it turned out, was exactly what the horrors had wanted us to do. Simply trying to save a friend's life had resulted in a staggering loss of life—blood spilled and souls consumed on both sides of the world—thousands sacrificed so that billions could live.

Was it worth it?

The question came from the back of my brain—not one of the sneering voices I so often have to argue with, but one of my calmer ancestors, one given to asking direct questions without any ulterior motives. I looked at the horrible welter of black clouds rising up out of the billowing rage of fire consuming Geneva, and I wondered—was it?

Should I have let the Tind'losi consume the Earth rather than risk having the tragedy below on my conscience? Should I have simply told Goward he'd sealed his own fate and allowed him to be taken away?

No, I thought, it had to be done. Whatever they were, whatever force had sealed them away in the dark origins of the Earth, the denizens of Tindalos had waited eons to attack mankind. If they hadn't been stopped now, they would have had to have been dealt with later. Coldly, I looked out at the horror spreading across the face of Geneva and decided that, monstrous a measure as it had been, it had been worth doing if it stopped the Tind'losi.

The only problem was, they hadn't been stopped.

As I watched in blank and numbing horror, scores of the nightmare beasts began to pull themselves up out of the burning wreckage of the city. Many of them were gone—most of them. But still, thousands had survived. Thousands of immortal Hell beasts. Thousands of supremely powerful agents of chaos. Thousands of...

"Destroyer!" Belial's voice growled clear and harsh across the dark madness of the blazing havoc. "There will be now a reckoning!"

I hadn't stopped them. Some of them—yes. Their forces were crippled—certainly. But, stopped? No. Were they still a force to be reckoned with? Could they still end all life on the planet? Had Armageddon finally arrived? Before I could decide on an answer, I turned and ran instead.

I didn't return to Geneva, but stayed on the dream plane. Not that it mattered. I had led the Tind'losi to that separate dimension beyond man's normal consciousness and now given the monsters free reign within it. It wouldn't take them long to realize its many uses. Indeed, with access to the powers it gave its users over the dreamers of Earth, there was no telling what insanity they might visit on the planet. Running straight across the vast open plane before me, I taunted the Tind'losi madly, doing everything I could to keep them concentrating on me.

"There is no escape this time, Destroyer."

"You might be right," I agreed truthfully. Playing off the honesty Belial could sense in my voice, I added, "But then again, maybe I'm just toying with you."

"I have read you now, my puny," the thing answered, its galloping strides dragging it quickly across the dream plane. Red dust splashing up around its great legs, Belial growled, "That was your master plan. You have nothing left now. You are finished. And we are coming for you."

"You come right along, pal," I shouted back. Something was stirring within my memory, one last place I might be able to take the remaining Tind'losi. I'd learned to twist space on the dream plane, to make it do my bidding, to open doorways to here and there at the slightest whim. It took power, of course, life force stolen from the world about me, so it wasn't a skill I utilized often. Still, if I could mold space...why not its cousin?

What was that date, I whispered to myself, begging my brain for the answer. When? When do I want to be?

"We are coming for you, Destroyer!"

I reached the base of a staggering orange and purple mountain range. Throwing myself upward, I clawed at the brilliant rocks, my hands tearing on the glass-sharp facets. I ignored the pain, though, ignored the blood, ignored the baying of the creatures behind me and the mindless screams of the thousands of dead Swiss still howling in my brain. I ignored everything, demanding of my memory one simple thing. A date and a time.

April 26, 1986, came a whisper. *1:23*

A smile crossed my lips. I had them now. With the horrors clawing their way up the mountain after me, I knew they would now follow me anywhere. To anytime. So I took them where I wanted. To the Soviet Union, and the nuclear reactor at Chernobyl.

My memory had given me the exact time of the accident that had shocked the world. I would open a doorway into the reactor core at the top of the mountain. It would take the Tind'losi and myself directly to that moment and place when the world was presented with its first nuclear meltdown.

Giddy with anticipation, I threw myself up and over the top of the summit's edge. As I did so, I found myself in the doomed Soviet plant's main generator room. All around me people stood staring. People with clipboards. People who did not look as if they were in the middle of the most terrible man-made disaster of all time. Not knowing how many seconds I had before the Tind'losi crossed the threshold into the same reality, I grabbed the nearest person I could. Shaking him, I screamed a thought into his brain.

"What're you doing? Don't you know the reactor is melting down?!"

The technician looked at me as if I were a lunatic. Mostly, he was correct. I was dirty and bleeding, my clothing in tatters, my hair soaked with sweat and blood, my eyes wild and stained with tears. Others approached to free their friend, but I knocked them away with a sonic blast of energy. The man I had seized was stammering, confused by my presence, frightened by my urgency. I probed his brain with a thought, forcing him to answer me. Suddenly coherent, he said;

"There is no meltdown. We are only carrying out tests today. We need to prove that the coasting turbine can provide sufficient power to pump coolant through the reactor core while waiting for electricity from the diesel generators. The circulation of coolant, you see, will be sufficient to give the reactor an adequate safety margin while we wait for..."

Because I had ordered him to explain, he continued to speak even after I no longer needed him. Looking around myself, I began to laugh. Suddenly, everything had been made clear to me.

"Destroyer—now you will learn what it means to dare the wrath of Tindalos."

I turned and stared at Belial. The thing was burned and scarred, but hardly injured. Scores of Tind'losi were already in the massive generator room. Hundreds more were cramming in behind them.

My laughter had now turned into a wild cackling. Belial and his fellows stopped their forward progress for a moment, staring in wonder at my antics.

All of the workers from the generator station had fled the area. Searching my mind, I remembered that the only thing the investigating authorities could agree upon about the Chernobyl disaster was that there had been an unexpected fall in power. Knowing what had to come next, I reached into my shoulder holster and pulled out Betty. Aiming her at the reactor's main control panel I fired, squeezing off round after round. A warning siren sounded as suddenly the control rods began sliding back into their slots. This set into operation additional pumps which began removing heat from the core causing the spontaneous generation of steam. Almost instantly, the reactor's power rose to more than one hundred times its design value. Inside, fuel pellets started shattering, fuel channels ruptured, and while monsters howled, the explosions began.

As ALWAYS, I LIVED. How many died, I don't know. Think what you want, but at this point, I don't even care. Somehow I managed to slide back through the dream plane to New York, right back to the foundry. The others bundled me up and took me home. It was only a week before I was coherent again.

The professor, of course, is very grateful. He says it was something that had to be done. Knowing what we know now, it's certain the Tind'losi would have found a way to invade the Earth sooner or later. They'd been waiting a long time. They'd have found a way. Everyone else agrees. Hell, maybe they're right.

But then again, they didn't sink a score of square miles of Geneva under the mantle of the Earth. They didn't decide it was all right to set off mankind's only nuclear disaster and let a bunch nobody particularly liked take the rap for it. And they don't have to live with the screaming in their ears of the souls they harvested, using their life energy like a marathon runner does pasta—pounding them down without a second thought, all sacrificed for some overwhelming goal.

Of course, we don't even know if the Tind'losi are gone for good. Yes, as best I can tell they sank into the ground, trapped in the molten core of the Chernobyl reactor. But, what are we supposed to do, gaze into the professor's goddamned gem once more and pray we don't see anything? Not bloody likely.

And that's the other problem with investigating this stuff. You never really kill any of these things off. Maybe you disperse one, stall it for a while, shut a door in its face. But end one of these things for good? Not really.

The only things that ever die permanently are human beings. I should know, I've killed plenty of them. All in the name of protecting humanity.

Oh yeah, the hounds of Tindalos—gruesome things—unstoppable monsters—all legs and claws and molten muscle that fangs down on a man like water cascading across pavement. Everywhere at once, relentless—unkillable, unturnable, unavoidable. Inevitable as tomorrow, final as judgment. That's what they whisper, anyway, about the Tind'losi.

I wonder what it is they whisper about me?

In many ways, fiction overlaps reality, taking a bit of the "real" world and turning it into a metaphor or character or plot. Sometimes, this is how we see where the monsters really dwell, and who are the villains and heroes in our world.

In "Degrees of Fear," this literary trick is executed superbly. Sometimes to understand something, we need to look at it through different eyes.

DEGREES OF FEAR

"You are not required to complete the task, yet you are not free to withdraw from it."
–Anonymous Rabbi in Mishnah

He couldn't believe it.

For a frightened moment, he actually could not. But it had been true. The old man had caved. Seemingly on a whim, he had simply turned around and given him everything he wanted. Everything. The wards would be his, control of all treatment, all group strategies–everything.

Everything.

As of that very day, a breezing, lazy, scotch-warmed, golden leaves kind of a day, the honorable Dr. Morgan Hall was stepping down as director of Derringol Asylum for the Hopeless. It was not shocking. He was, after all, a wizened and broken sixty-seven years old. He talked slowly now, moved slowly, and his eyes focused only after noticeable effort. He was tired and enfeebled long before his time, in the service of the dregs of humanity.

Hall was the disappointment of disappointments. The medical world had been stunned when he, the brilliant son of the world's most honored medical couple, had opted to take the position at Derringol. At first, it had been hoped he would merely use the monstrous position as a stepping stone. At first it had seemed so.

But not for long.

Something, all those decades ago, had moved the man. Something about the monsters preserved within the asylum's protection had tied him to them—kept him working them day and night, forsaking his career. Forsaking, some said, all human decency in his attempts to find ways to force interaction between the various demented lunatics and savages, the pinheads, mongrels and rabid flesh weasels that made up the clientele of the still festering pile of gray rock known politely as Derringol Asylum for the Hopeless, civilization's dumping ground for the absolute dregs of the world's nightmares, those which—for one insane, but legal reason or another—we were forced to keep and shelter among us.

Finally, the old man was walking away. Retiring. Giving up. At long, horrible last. The damned old man was finally giving him his chance.

"Absolutely. Ron," he had said, somehow finding the energy to smile, "I've had it. The whole place will be yours to deal with as you like by Monday."

Matter-of-factly, that was how he'd said it. He had let the words fall from his mouth in the way of table manners, simple as asking for the butter. The emphasis was on the "asking," however. There had been a hint in his tone that part of that asking was a shield, one positioned there to keep Ron from hearing exactly what the old man was asking for, that in his mind his request was for something rich and wonderful.

Ron Thompson was clever. The back of his mind read people perfectly—caught all the signals. He interpreted the tone as Hall hoping to surrender with dignity. That was the way he chose to hear it, for it encompassed all that mattered to him. It announced to him that he had won.

"As a matter of fact," the older doctor suddenly added, the weight of the idea hitting him evident in the shake of his frail shoulders, "why don't you just pop into my office tonight…oh, say 7:00, 7:30…is that good? We could go over a few things, and as far as I'm concerned—you could take over tomorrow."

He had won big time.

Of course, Thompson had agreed. Sign everything over, one quick motion? Of course he did. And yes, he had had his flicker, wondered if there was some sort of scandal, some reason for Hall to not want to be legally culpable for something. The idea had been dismissed instantly by a sturdy knowledge of medicine and the laws that bind it. Indeed, all he had to do was show up at Hall's office that night, and legally, it was all over. He would be in charge.

And, he thought, I'll use it the way he should have. Pathetic, the way Hall has embarrassed the profession in this hell sty. Not one patient ever released. Not one cured. Christ above, with his methods, you'd think he *wanted* them to all stay here forever. Well, no more. I'll be the doctor who has the courage to admit this mad palace should be fumigated, and either get its mongrel inmates released or put mercifully to sleep.

Thompson had no pity for the inmates of Derringol. Multiple rapists, cannibals, serial killers—practitioners of matricide, patricide, genocide, suicide—Thornton, endless picking at his skin, tearing it away a sliver at a time, Goldfarb, spinning in endless circles, teeth constantly chattering, or Bezzle and his endless screaming, Howdilk and his stamping, stamping, stamping—all of them, *all of them*—simply an endless stream of shattered egos and wounded nerve endings that had slaughtered everything in their path, including themselves, now caged and wounded and slobbering for the world to put them to death. Begging for it.

Beg no more, thought Thompson as he stepped through the doorway into Dr. Hall's office, eyeing it, wondering how it would feel, day after day, thinking of it as his office, his name in bronze—for all the time the horrid haven for the damned would survive under his mastership.

Beg no more.

"Ron," called out Hall, his rasping whisper of a voice filled with a delight the younger man could not remember ever hearing before, "oh, wonderful. Come here, lad."

Thompson took a seat across the desk from the older man. Hall indicated a bottle of well-aged bourbon on his desk, two snifters to the side. Another smile indicated perfectly to Thompson that he was to pour. The younger doctor eyed the vintage, feeling as triumphant as a gladiator who had just won his freedom in the Coliseum, and now was being served Caesar's wine as further reward. He filled the blunt but serviceable snifters, handed one to Hall while hoisting his own. They touched glasses in silence. Old to new. And then they drank.

Talk continued for several hours, a rapid transfer of duties from the old regime to the new. Each bit of needed lore passed on was accompanied by another toast. One bottle became a second. Hall drank as a dying man, come crawling from the desert—in short, but plentiful sips.

Thompson drank deeply, often, laughing as he did so, moving his hands in quite animated fashion as he talked. He pulled at his beard, losing his fingers in its curly strands, feeling remarkably light and invincible. He beamed with happiness and sweat from the pounding warmth of the fast-flowing amber that somehow swirled to the top of his glass every time the younger doctor looked away.

For a moment, he thought Hall was trying to get him drunk. Then he had brayed with mirth. What would the old boy be up to? Was it Edgar Allan Poe time? Could Hall be getting ready to brick him into the wall? Thompson snorted. Hall was lucky he could pick up the bottle.

Tired old fool, thought Thompson with contempt. In his youth Hall had been a powerful man, handsome, athletic. Now, after his decades of living within the confines of Derringol with its herd of demented charges, he had become diminished. He was less than adult, now, less than a boy, really. Hall had become fragile, a wisp of a man, the merest dust that could still hold blood and breath and thought together. He was worn thin by the life he had chosen, a ragged towel of a man.

"Come with me to the ward, Ron," said Hall of a sudden, hopping out of his chair with a speed and ease that practically shocked the younger man. Hall had actually slid with one smooth motion and arose—something a man of sixty or seventy might still do easily, but a Homeric rally for him, the type of motion which Thompson had thought the old man long incapable.

Thompson staggered quickly along in the older doctor's wake, knowing the ward he meant was the infamous Ward 17. He noticed Hall was lugging a third bottle with him, as well as a set of paper cups.

You can try alcohol poisoning, old man, Thompson thought. Hell, you can try shooting me, I don't care. Just as long as I'm in charge of this place tomorrow.

The two men entered one of Hall's most controversial dormitories. Motioning to an old couch against a far wall, Hall indicated that his colleague should park himself there. Thompson fell into the chair heavily, his legs leaden from the amount of liquor he had consumed. The short walk had left him dizzy, unfocused. The younger doctor suddenly realized, like any heavy drinker who has finally arisen, that the sense of control he had felt while still seated was a fleeting thing.

"Just one more thing to show you, Ron," whispered Hall, leaning heavily against the overstuffed arm of the couch opposite the one Thompson was half hanging over. "Then, all of this is yours."

The old man slid carefully down into his corner, cradling his bottle and the fragile cups into which he meant to empty it. Pouring carefully, he handed a stiff six fingers of bourbon to Thompson. The younger man stared at the cup as Hall filled one for himself.

"I don't..." Thompson sputtered, worked his eyes and mouth for a moment, searching for control of their various muscles. Then he inhaled deeply and tried once more to speak. "I mean, ohhhh, I'm sorry, but...I think I've had, had...had enough."

"Nonsense," answered Hall, kindly but dismissively. "You'll need at least one more of those, maybe two, before you'll be able to see them."

"See...who?" asked Thompson in a voice more puzzled than curious.

"The hydras."

Hall took a deep pull from his paper cup. As Thompson stared at him absently, only steps away from tumbling over the edge of consciousness into the land of Nod, Hall told him, "Oh, you'll want to know all about the hydras. They were, after all, my *real* reason for chaining myself to this dreadful place."

Something sparked awake within Thompson. Old rumors filtered upward through his brain, stories of Hall, locking himself in that very ward for days at a time, muttering nonsense about "having to change the hydras' diet." The staff had buzzed for decades, hinting that Hall had brought all manner of things to that ward in particular, giving the inmates liquor, sometimes drugs, bringing in prostitutes both male and female. Animals had disappeared into the ward. Raucous parties had been held, week-long binges from which the staff had been barred.

And, any time Hall had been questioned, he had always waved his questioner off, mumbling something about having to take care of "the hydras."

Was the old man actually offering him the answer to all the whispered questions? The long wondered-about truth of truths? Adrenaline pumped into his system, what was left of his conscious mind screaming at him to fight his way clear of the descending veils of fog all about him. With a Herculean effort, Thompson slid himself several inches forward.

"Ah, yes—I thought that might catch your interest. Is that a story you would actually like to hear, young Ronald?" When Thompson nodded his head as vigorously as he could manage, Hall smiled. He had known things would work as he had planned. Taking another long sip from his cup, he waited until his colleague did the same, and then he started.

"When I first came here, my aims were simple. I would examine the freaks and jugheads of Derringol, write up a recommendation that they all be sterilized, make the points I needed with the proper people in power, and then move on to the next step in my well-planned career. But, something happened. Indeed, it much happened the way it is about to happen to you."

Thompson stared. He had no other response within him. Hall smiled, reaching over to tilt the younger man's cup to his lips. As Thompson drained his drink, the old man filled it again as he continued.

"The night before I planned to submit my report, I came here to drink to the inmates. It was a cruel action, but I was a cruel man. I wanted to get drunk, to show them my human side, to stagger about, just out of their vengeful reach, and laugh at their upcoming doom.

"I sat on this couch—yes, this very one—I sat here and I drank. And I drank. And I cursed the foul shapes before me, hating them beyond reason. I drank more, and muttered, and swore, and when I had run out of liquor I cursed something terrible, then leapt to my feet to go and fetch more. And that, that was when it happened."

"What?" asked Thompson, honestly curious, drinking from his cup unconsciously.

"Can't tell you," whispered the older man. Reaching across the couch, he tipped his bottle into Thompson's cup, sloshing it full to the rim. "Have to show you."

The younger doctor blinked repeatedly, trying to focus on his cup. Hall had filled it yet again. But why? What was his game? What was it all about? He had watched the old man closely. They had drunk equal amounts. They both had to be close to alcohol poisoning at this point. His previous joke now turning to ashes in his memory, he choked out a question.

"What's going on, Morgan? What is this?"

The old man took another drink from his own cup, mindful of where the thin construct was growing structurally unsound as it absorbed more and more liquor. Exhaling with force, panting after the effort of forcing more bourbon down his throat, he answered;

"I'm making to tell you my secret, Ron. Haven't you wondered why I've run these wards the way I do? Why I've juggled the personalities here as I have, mixing homicidal practical jokers with complete withdrawns, bullies with cowards, atheists with born agains, sadists with...oh, you know what I've done. You've written report after report, criticizing my methods, dropping hints about me drinking in the wards...here in 17, especially. Well, I tell you now, I don't blame you in the least."

Thompson blinked. What was happening? What was the damned old man getting at? Without thinking, the younger doctor sipped at his drink once more as Hall continued, his ancient voice a far away rasp in Thompson's ears.

"When I leapt to my feet, my system told me how drunk I was. It hurled me back into the couch. Crammed me in there, laughed at me. I tried to pull myself up, but my hands were no longer responding to my commands. I was drunk right up to the line of passing out. And that...that...*that* is when I saw them."

"Who?" asked Thompson. "The hydras?"

"Yes," agreed Hall, his eyes aflame, his spindly frame shaking with anticipation. "And now, you must learn to see them as well."

Thompson snorted. So the old man was simply mad. Amazing. Remarkable that he had been able to hide it from everyone so completely. Again the younger man lifted his cup and drained it. As he let the sogging paper slip from his fingers, he noticed Hall staring at him as intently as he could through his own alcoholic haze.

"You, you don't see anything yet, do you?" Thompson shook his head, a sudden deep and numbing yawn overtaking him. Once it passed, he murmured in a lazy, almost giddy voice.

"No hydras, doctor," the younger man snorted, a wad of snot blowing free of his left nostril, smearing across his jacket. "No hydras at all."

Thompson laughed, his head flopping back, banging against the worn padding of the old couch, just missing connecting with the far more substantial cement block wall behind. His voice cracked and sputtered, his gasping cackles loaded with derision.

"Is this the whole show then," he tittered. "You had me expecting so much more."

With a monumental push of effort, Thompson thrust himself erect, staggering to catch his balance. By now, his harsh noise had woken several of the inmates, dragging forth a mixture of bitter and confused noises from their cells. The young doctor laughed at them, dancing awkwardly there in front of Hall.

"Shut up, you miserable savages, you excrement, shut up, shut up—*shut up!* I've got to find the damn *hydras*."

And then, Thompson spun around and grabbed the bottle from Hall's hand. Unscrewing its plastic top, he lifted it to his mouth and poured a great quantity down his throat.

"So, the hydras only come out for drunks, do they, Hall?" The younger man growled threateningly. "Well, mustn't disappoint the fucking hydras, must we?!"

Again Thompson tilted the bottle, splashing the remaining liquor against his face. Much of it missed his mouth, but more than enough made it to its target. The young doctor staggered. The massive influx of bourbon hit him hard, draining his anger, sending him back to the couch in a helpless crab-stepping motion. He collapsed into the worn piece of tattered furniture, his head spinning, eyes itching.

Shutting them, he hid in the darkness for a long moment. His stomach was protesting, his arms twitching, his head beginning to throb. He groaned as vile eruptions within his guts began to pain him. With concentration, however, he forced his body to hold the line. He would not throw up, he commanded. He would not soil himself. He would not do anything but get himself under control once more and take his leave. With a powerful effort, Thompson steadied his nerves and reined himself in. Satisfied he had compensated for the damage done to his system sufficiently that he could leave without embarrassing himself, he struggled his frame upright on the sofa, took a deep breath, and then finally opened his eyes.

And then, he saw them.

The hydras.

They were not really hydras, of course. They were not actually animals at all, not animals in the normal sense, not what we think of as animals. Thompson stared in wonderment, not actually capable of identifying what he was seeing.

Translucent they were, floating in the air, crawling on the walls, purple veins pumping beneath their scarlet skin. The things had no eyes that Thompson could discern, no ears, either, or sex organs. They were long, covered with ridges of tri-jointed legs running the lengths of their cylindrical bodies. A horrid slit ran their length as well, exactly where a fourth set of legs should have been if symmetry was what their designer had intended.

"You see them now, don't you?"

Thompson nodded weakly, all his effort, all his energy focused on staring forward at the impossible horrors floating all about Ward 17.

Hall's hydras moved through the walls and doors, through the floor and ceiling, with little effort. When crawling along a physical surface, their legs sent them gliding with a remarkable efficiency. They seemed to only barely understand the boundaries of human constructs as solid, and would gleefully use them as such until some urge would catch hold of them and they would either glide through the object, or float off away from it, using the beating of their hundreds of legs for locomotion.

Indeed, the entire room seemed different now, as if the doorway to some other place had been superimposed over the ward. Odd, fractured angles boiled across the familiar surfaces, sharp geometric motions shimmered indignantly, deep cobalt ellipses crackling within moving pockets of emerald and scarlet. He soon became aware of other levels of existence, all of them superimposed over the one reality he understood, limitless abysses of inexplicably colored twilight and strange disordered sound and animation that shrieked an oppressive, polyphonic whining that drilled into him, clawing at his mind.

Thompson felt his heart racing. He blinked, then blinked again, forcing his eyes to concentrate on the level of beyond he had first noted, the layer containing the hydras. The young man knew with an absolute certainty that he was not imagining the horrid beasts. He could feel them through the air, could feel the moving currents as they drifted through the room. But, he wondered, what *were* they? Why were they here at Derringol? What was their purpose, what did they want—and moreover—what did Hall want with them?

And, his mind questioned, why does he want me to know about them?

More thoughts battered conflictingly within Thompson's mind, but the distraction of them was hurled from his mind as he suddenly looked upward. Somehow, his vision slipped past the boundaries of his own world, folding outward into the realm of the things floating all about him. As he stared through the ceiling above his head, and the various other ceilings above it, he realized there were hundreds, and thousands, millions of the raw, cylindrical creatures, swirling in a vast galactic tornado of electrically charged flesh, all of them gnawing the air, searching for a meal more substantial than random molecules.

Suddenly, one found what it was looking for.

Gray and wrinkled, one large specimen broke off from the others, circling downward toward the mere men below it. The thing had a look of age to it. Thin wavering spikes of jellied flesh hung from its ends, drops of a rotting green ichor dribbling from their tips. The slit running the length of its body opened and closed slowly, laboriously. And then, Thompson noted something which told him what the slit was. Hundreds of curled and broken fangs lay semi-hidden beneath the thing's glowing, transparent skin. Thompson shuddered at the sight, true fear crackling along his spine at the sight.

"I caution you not to panic," whispered Hall, edging away from the younger man.

"Look at it," hissed Thompson, his eyes bulging, drool dripping from his lower lip. "My God, *look at it!*"

As the young doctor screamed, the slit on the hovering thing jerked open, forcing the creature's body to assume a more oval than cylindrical shape. The teeth sprung outward, glistening. Thompson screamed again, staggering upward from the couch. The beast dropped from its near ceiling-high position, tumbling in its languid fashion toward Thompson's head. The howling man managed to make some four steps toward the door before the thing snapped its jaws shut, and drank deeply.

"Feeling any better," asked Hall with compassion.

Thompson came fully awake at the words, his legs kicking, mouth screaming. The older man waited patiently, allowing the disturbance to pass in its own fashion. The younger doctor clawed at the air, bubbling spit foaming over his lower lip, the spheres bursting and reforming as he gasped for air. Hall touched the young man's shoulder gently.

"It's all right," he said with assurance, "you're safe, now."

Thompson shuddered. Safe. What a ridiculous word. What a meaningless phantom of a suggestion. Safe. No one was safe. Everyone was doomed. Everything...

Thompson shook his head harshly, chasing the depressing voice from his mind.

No, he told himself. No, no. No...

"It's all right to be frightened. It's natural," Hall assured the younger man. "I know."

"I'm...I'm not hurt—am I?" Thompson's left hand ran over his scalp. His fingers searched for the ragged gouges that should have been there, deep, multitudinous...

"You're all right."

Thompson closed his mind to memory, forcing himself to flounder forth into the present. Chilling images—the fanged mouth closing over his face, teeth shattering his eyes, puncturing his ears, blood gushing in all directions, it had all seemed so, so...*real*.

"I am all right," he agreed. His hand had discovered the slightest line of depressions which he realized with a shudder must align with the monstrous teeth that had snapped at him across dimensions the night before. But, his humor improved greatly from the simple realization they had not even broken the skin. Stirring himself, sliding his body into a more comfortable position, he accepted the cup of coffee the old man was handing him and started to assess his situation. They were in Hall's office. He could tell it was early morning from the position of the sunlight coming through his windows.

"How did we get here?"

"You passed out when the hydras started nibbling on your aura. Understandable, of course. I had Lafferty put you in a wheelchair, bring you in here. You slept until now. I've been waiting for you to wake up. You managed to recover more quickly than I did."

"What?" Thompson meant to say more, but his mind would not work. He had no explanations, no ideas that would even allow him to begin to form questions. With pity, Hall sat down and began to talk softly.

"I told you that I had gone into Ward 17 when I first came to Derringol, drank myself into a stupor in that very room. That was how I discovered the hydras. The sane can not see the overlap in realities which exists here, at least, not without the help of far too much libation. Tell me now, do you remember anything after the beast made contact with you?"

Thompson thought for a long moment. His first response was to deny any memories, but after a few moments a terrible chill settled into his spine. It ran from vertebrae to vertebrae, branching out into the connecting muscles, sending pain throughout his back and shoulders. Twisting his body, screwing it into the couch, he closed his eyes as he answered.

"It talked to me, didn't it?"

"What do you remember?" asked Hall.

"It... it questioned me, probing, curious. It felt as if my ears were flowing with burning honey, not fiery, not hot, but spicy, as if my ears could *taste* the thing's words."

"It's what they do," Hall agreed. Sipping from his own mug, coffee steam fogging his glasses, he said, "Don't think for the moment. Just listen. Let me tell you what I know."

The older doctor closed his eyes for a moment, lowering his

head. He filled his lungs once, then again, bracing himself, steeling himself as if he were about to enter a boxing ring, or clamber up out of a trench into full blown combat.

"Our world touches upon other worlds, other realities. These extra dimensions share the same space as ours, but they are out of sync, out of phase with our world. There are, however, as you found last night, moments where inhabitants of these various planes of existence can see one another.

"We drank last night to where we were close to alcohol poisoning. This brutal abuse separated our minds from the pulpy tethers of our brains, allowing our consciousness to expand outward. The hydras are what we stumbled across."

Hall shuddered, partly from the pain of his hangover. Partly from having made yet another round trip to Hell and back.

"It's possible extreme religious fervor can bring about a like state. Perhaps those who see angels and the such are merely... only making contact with some form of elder thing more benign than... than others. None of this would matter, however, if it weren't for the fact there is another pathway to these other realities...

"Madness."

Hall paused, sipping his coffee, steeling his nerves. He watched the younger doctor closely, waiting to see how long it would take for the connections to seize within his mind. The old man smiled with satisfaction. He could tell from the way Thompson's mouth had begun to hang open that it had not taken long at all.

"You understand."

"You mean..."

"Yes, when the insane complain of creatures, crawling on them, flying about them, entering their bodies, their minds, some of them are not hallucinating. Some of them are being flown around, crawled upon, chewed upon—worse."

Hall lowered his head for a moment. It took so much of his strength to think of the hydras during the day, when the sun was bright and the idea of them seemed so foolish. After all his many years, he was so very tired. All he wanted, so very dearly, was to simply rest for whatever time he had left to him.

But, he told himself, not yet. You still have work to do here.

Sighing, the old doctor pulled himself together once more and continued his story.

"The befuddled, the confused, the pitiful, they do not attract attention from beyond. I have studied the insane around the world now for more than half a century, and, without the benefit of inebriation, it is only the vibrations of the criminally deranged, the truly evil, which attracts our friends of last night."

Thompson nodded weakly, understanding. He shuddered at the impact. His hands shaking, he tried to drink more of his coffee.

"They swarm here, drawn by the smell of madness. They feed on it, relish it, drink it with abandon. Over the years I have come to learn that despair, hopelessness, these are their special treats. It is why I have done what I have here, the way I have done it."

Hall stopped again. The air wheezed out of him as he sat back in his chair. He knew he need not say more for the moment, however. Already the truth was beginning to show in Thompson's face.

"That's why you haven't calmed the inmates on the ward, why you've paired them combatively—you…"

"Yes," Hall agreed in a whisper. Waving a stick-thin arm feebly at the piles of binders heaped upon the shelves behind him, he said, "it's all in my notes. How to keep them insane, keep them at each other's throats. Tricks for pumping up their egos, lighting the fires of arrogance within them…"

"B-But, doctor," stammered Thompson. "Wait. I, I…why do you keep them here, keep them at each other? Shouldn't—"

Hall held up a hand. The look in his eyes told the younger man there was far more to the story he was learning.

"The hydras have no name of their own. Terrible as they seem, they are but a scavenger force, a servitor race created by creatures of cold power and long reach. The hydras are…advance scouts, as it were. Countless trillions of them thrown out through multiple realities, all searching for feeding grounds."

"But, but," Thompson struggled to his feet. His head was throbbing, nerve endings misfiring, inflaming his skull, beating against him, but within his mind, he saw vast armies of the nightmares he had witnessed, covering the Earth, tracking down humanity, bleeding it, absorbing…"Then, we…we have to seal this place, *destroy* it. Derringol is what—a flare? A menu?"

"Doctor, Derringol is humanity's last hope!"

Thompson lowered himself back onto the couch. His brain did not hurt—it suffered. A great part of him was already willing to retreat into madness, to refuse to take in any more of the fantasy nonsense he was being fed, to instead simply embrace the fact he must be insane, and to ignore the horrible duty he saw forming before him.

"Ron, the hydras are attracted to Derringol because of its overwhelming mixture of exactly what they want. If the place were to cease to be, they would simply move off to other points around the globe sending out the same vibrations. There is no end to the third world prisons alone that might distract them. But, to pierce the veil of beyond, they have to concentrate their efforts. That's why they swarm *here*."

"And that is why they must be *kept* here."

Hall stood with effort, then came around his desk to stand before Thompson. Taking the man's hand in his own, he whispered;

"When I force one of our catatonics to rebel, it blunts their curiosity about us. They diffuse, look elsewhere for a while. Their attention wanders. But, they will never leave our world. Humanity stinks of the fear they seek. And, the day they are certain of it, the moment we finally become attractive to them, they will throw themselves against the walls of reality until they are breached. If it kills them all, they will do it without question so their masters," Hall shuddered, air leaking from his mouth to make a pitiful noise, "their terrible, terrible masters, can come forth to devour humanity."

Thompson heard the words, but he could not accept them. His fright turned him aside, convinced him there was too much to take in, too much to believe. And then, a notion frosted with the aroma of hope caught the younger man's attention. Staring at Hall, he almost chuckled as he asked;

"How could you know all this? How can you make these fantastic assumptions? Elder races? Servitors hunting through all of existence? These are guesses, theories, but they aren't facts. You don't know any of this for sure."

Hall looked sadly at the younger man, his head shaking to and fro unconsciously. Loosening the knot of his tie, the older doctor said softly, "Do you remember what you said before, about speaking to the thing which attached itself to you last night?"

Thompson nodded. Even though the contact between the two of them had been slight, still he had heard its thoughts, knew its memories, its intentions. He knew...

"No," the young man croaked pitifully. Hoping, the fear in him pleading with the God he had learned about in grade school to deliver him from the monstrous truth he saw descending toward him, filling the room around him, he closed his eyes. "It can't be."

Thompson sat in the darkness behind his eyelids, rocking gently back and forth on the couch. As he did, Hall's voice invaded his terrified retreat.

"You knew what impressions you received from the creature were real, were true things, despite the minor, almost intangible nature of the connection between the two of you—didn't you?"

Thompson's mind flashed to the barely perceptible bumps on his scalp and neck, his eyes watering, nose running. He made gasping noises in his throat, his fingers curling into impotent fists, weak clubs with no target.

"I have talked with them, too," said Hall. "Over the years. Armed with bourbon, I have called them to me, luring them with alcohol-fueled despair, only to baffle them with the layers of undigestible logic I kept hidden beneath."

Thompson heard Hall pull his tie free. Heard his fingers fumbling with the buttons of his shirt.

"I have talked to them and played their game, and protected this world as long as I can. And now, now it is your turn."

Thompson opened his eyes, his head moving up to stare at Hall as the old man pulled his shirt from his body. As he did so, the young doctor saw all the proof he needed. Striping Hall's body, down his back, across his chest, circling around and around his shoulders, ran row after row of uniform gouges, hundreds upon hundreds of savage bite marks, festering sores drilled with hideous patience over far too many years.

"Oh God," whispered Thompson, his body shaking, bowels shriveling, "*Oh my God!*"

Hall said nothing more. The older man simply fumbled his way back into his shirt, buttoning it, replacing his tie. He shrugged his vest on then, following it with his jacket. Dressed, he opened his desk drawer to retrieve his wallet and keys. Nothing else did he wish to take with him. No reminder of Derringol did he need past those etched into his tired brain and his failing flesh.

He stood for a moment, staring sadly at the young man who, less than twenty-four hours earlier was laughing at the thought that he would soon have everything Hall had. Awash with pity, he touched the young doctor on the shoulder.

"You can do this," he said.

"I can't," responded Thompson. "I'll fail. I'm, I'm…I'm not brave enough for this."

Tightening his grasp, surrendering all the energy he had to spare, the old man told his protege;

"Remember the words of Wainwright, 'there is no such thing as bravery; only degrees of fear.'" Releasing his grasp, Hall made his way slowly to the door, adding, "Find a degree you can live with, and carry on."

Thompson wiped his eyes with his palm, cleaned his nose on his sleeve. If Hall was right in all he said, then he had just left Thompson as humanity's only defender. Horatio at the bridge. If he was right.

Well, the young doctor thought, as any researcher knows, there's only one way to find things out.

Pushing himself to his feet, Thompson grabbed the fifth of bourbon Hall had left on the desk and then staggered off to Ward 17.

"Repeat the experiment," he said softly. Lifting the bottle to his lips, he took the first of many deep drinks.

AFTERWORD
by Joe Mauceri

Given the scope of these tales, you feel like you might expect the doors to swing open as you exit the ride you've just experienced. However, as your psyche begins to digest and assimilate them into your subconscious you might very well experience an awakening. Not necessarily the earth-shattering equivalent of a supersonic jet as it breaks the sound barrier, but the awakening of a small voice it your head that possibly prevents you from accepting the world before your eyes at face value. A voice that seductively bids you to return to the shores of legendary epic realms where monsters, madness, and heroes reside.

C.J. Henderson is a contemporary Sherpa that leads readers up the precarious bookshelf ridges to the breathtaking vistas of the ancient literary peaks of fantastic fiction. In this single tome he not only guides readers to foreign and exotic places, but he takes them on a journey into the realms of the dark fantastic first explored by the likes of H.P. Lovecraft, Robert E. Howard, Lin Carter, Lars Anderson, Lee Falk, Henry "Harry" Steeger, Lester Dent and Carl Kolchak. Henderson relentlessly strives to instill new life into these landscapes so that modern readers will continue to seek their own adventures, deeper into the ancestral tales of yore.

As Henderson's explorations have left us guideposts to follow into literary antiquity, he has also used this knowledge and experience to blaze new trails into his own literary landscapes. His vast collections of short stories have ventured beyond space and time, and touch the stellar fabric of the universe. He has exposed the raw beauty and terror of the universe, and exposed the raw nerve of the human condition.

Like Arthur Conan Doyle, Henderson tries to facilitate our grasp of these things outside our daily consciousness by introducing us to his private detectives, Teddy London and Jack Hagee, men best described as "dark knights, noble men that are guns for hire." Although Hagee may not cross the borders into the fantastic, London and his associates constantly find themselves in unknown destinations where there be monsters. Some have chronicled their own tales as they embark on their sole journeys, emerging with some scars of their own, warning us to take heed.

Along the way Henderson has been accompanied by fellow explorers who share his own macabre curiosity and have captured those nightmares with pen and ink. Several haunted these very pages. These terrifying images will eternally damage your dreams. For myself, I have found some relief by purchasing these images so they adorn my walls and act as a talisman to appease these night specters.

Henderson is a lone gunman, a tireless traveler of the roadways in his efforts to ever expand the Henderson universe. He will wear the guise of an author, speaker, guest of honor, and bookseller. To me, he operates like a sinister bible salesman; he draws you in with the warmth of his greeting and that twinkle in his eye. He will size you up, make you a deal, and once you've cracked that first volume, you are his. You will forever be haunted and compelled to seek him out in those dark places where fandom dwells. For those brave enough to seek his advice, he is forthright and brutally honest. If you go away feeling challenged and duty-bound to pursue your own voyages into mystery and imagination, then he has achieved his ultimate goal, transcending simple entertainment.

However, for all the things dwelling in the shadows of his table where he displays his wares, there are few who actually perceive the goodness of what he achieves. For the majority of his books, like the one you are holding in your hand, are story collections. Those who come seeking Henderson will find the exploits of other accomplished wordsmiths who believe in the darkness. Some join him in sustaining our beliefs in the ancient things that dwell beyond the veil of our sanity, others on his quest to find humanity in space and beyond. And so we are left pondering how we can rearrange our own personal space to accommodate another bookcase for the new literary journeys we have yet to take.

It is obviously too late to warn you of the consequences of exploring Henderson's mysterious territory. The only judicious resolution I can offer you is that you place this book into the hands of another lost reader before you head out into cyberspace, where you will find author C.J. Henderson waiting to continue the danse macabre begun here.

–Joseph B. Mauceri (a.k.a. J.B. Macabre)
Executive Editor, FEARSmag.com

ABOUT THE AUTHOR

C.J. Henderson is the creator of the Teddy London supernatural detective series, as well as the author of fifty some other books, containing titles as diverse as *The Encyclopedia of Science Fiction Movies* to *Baby's First Mythos*. An award-winning author published in over a dozen countries, he is one of the most consistently enjoyable writers working today. He lives in Brooklyn with his wife, fashion designer Grace Lo, and welcomes visitors to come to his website *www.cjhenderson.com* to read the stories posted there and to leave what comments they may.

ABOUT THE ARTIST

Illustrator Ben Fogletto began his career as a political cartoonist at the age of 15 working for a chain of weekly newspapers in the Southern New Jersey area. While attending college at Glassboro, he continued political cartooning, while also illustrating children's literature and teaching aids for Scholastic as well as contributing cartoons to men's magazines under a pen name. After college, Ben turned down an art position at Marvel Comics to go full time as a staffer for newspapers. Ben's duties included cartooning, illustration, layout, design and photography.

Today, Ben is a staff photographer at The Press of Atlantic City, a daily newspaper covering the Southern New Jersey area. Since the early '90s he has worked in the comics field as well, contributing cover and inside illustrations for comics and graphic novels, as well as for numerous paperbacks for various publishing houses. Ben lives in Egg Harbor Township, close to Atlantic City New Jersey with his wife, Cynthia, and two sons, Connor and Chase.